PERFECT
BONES

BOOKS BY ELLERY KANE

Watch Her Vanish

HER PERFECT BONES

ELLERY KANE

bookouture

Published by Bookouture in 2021

An imprint of Storyfire Ltd.
Carmelite House
50 Victoria Embankment
London EC4Y 0DZ

www.bookouture.com

ISBN: 978-1-83888-862-6
eBook ISBN: 978-1-83888-861-9

For Gar
My partner in crime

A photograph is a secret about a secret. The more it tells you, the less you know.

—Diane Arbus

PROLOGUE
September 1985

Life as she knew it had ended. That was an absolute fact. The irrefutable evidence could be neatly catalogued, the same way Mr. Humphrey classified species of reptiles in her sophomore biology class. To start with, the interior of the Greyhound bus had the odor of Kris's football cleats the day after a game. No matter how many times their mother doused them with bleach, they reeked of wet dog and cheese. Strange, but she already missed her big brother, even if he did stink to high heaven. Everything she owned now fit into the oversized blue duffel bag she'd swiped from his closet. That included her Def Leppard T-shirt, a worn copy of *Pride and Prejudice,* the ragdoll she'd kept on her bed since kindergarten, and twenty-two dollars that she'd gutted from her own piggybank. Thankfully, her ticket had been paid for and delivered to her after school in a crisp white envelope.

Then, there was the sickness. Twice, she'd thrown up into the bus's metal toilet. Once, while riding waves of nausea like a wayward boat in a storm, and then again, as she stared into the toilet's disgusting throat. The remains of the peanut butter and jelly sandwich she'd packed floating like icebergs in blue liquid below.

But worst of all, the bus had been lurching down the freeway for over thirteen hours now, slumping its way toward Fog Harbor like a dying beast. Every time it stopped, the doors opened with a death rattle sigh, and she wondered if the old thing would make it there at all. Even the batteries in her Walkman had finally given out. Her mixtape grinding to a sudden stop, the final nail hammered into her proverbial coffin.

Without Journey and Air Supply, she'd resorted to playing the alphabet game with road signs. But after the signs dwindled, the road winding its way deeper into the forest, she had nothing left to do but stare at the towering redwoods and wonder if she'd ever see the pale blue sky again. Everything in her old life faded from view, getting smaller and smaller out the bus's rear window.

The moment the bus finally arrived at the Fog Harbor station, she felt an unexpected burst of energy. A need to suck up the salt air and feel the sand between her toes. To see the cabin in the woods, the river behind it that led to the ocean. It all sounded like a dream. She hurried then, cursing under her breath while she struggled with the duffel and up the narrow aisle.

But after she clunked down the two steps and dropped the bag on the pavement, the whole journey and what it meant finally caught up with her. Exhausted, she rested on the curb, waiting, while the other passengers filed past her to destinations unknown. Her hand wandered to her face, pressing against the days-old bruise on her cheek. It had faded to an ugly yellow, easily hidden beneath her Cover Girl foundation, but it still ached.

When the car arrived for her, she felt a sickening flutter in her stomach that she blamed on nervous butterflies, beating their demented little wings inside her, stirring up a strange mixture of anticipation and dread. She walked toward it anyway, stepping over the still-warm corpse of her old life and into the new one that lay out before her like a highway to all the places she'd never been.

CHAPTER ONE

Detective Will Decker recognized the smell of death. He knew it the same way he knew the brine of the ocean, the tang of the Hickory Pit, the vanilla aroma of Olivia's hair.

He closed the pruning shears and dropped them at his feet, wiping the sweat from his forehead. Above him, a buzzard circled in the cloudless sky, confirming what he already suspected.

With a gloved hand, Will pushed back the weeds he'd been whacking and searched for the source of the foul odor. The flies led him right to it, swarming the bits of fur and gristle with frenzied delight.

He grimaced as he tossed the remains of a gray squirrel into a trash bag.

"Cy! Not again, dude."

The prime suspect in the homicide—Will's one-eyed cat, Cyclops—stretched in the sun, gloating like a true psychopath. At least he hadn't deposited his victim on Will's tailgate this time.

Not even an animal carcass could ruin the first warm day of March. Will had left the station early, intent on finally tackling the weeds behind the cabin that had grown knee-high in the wet winter. He'd finished unpacking the last of his boxes a few weeks ago, unofficially declaring himself a permanent resident of Fog Harbor, seven months and several brutal murders after his arrival.

Will checked his watch: 4:30 p.m. Hopefully Olivia would know soon, if she didn't already. These things are unpredictable, she'd told him. Sometimes, they go on for hours. Sometimes, they're over before they even start. Either way, she'd promised to call right after, but he chided himself for expecting it. She owed him nothing. They were friends. Just friends. Try telling that to his stubborn heart that wouldn't stop jumping like an eager puppy whenever she came around.

Will grabbed the pruning shears with newfound purpose and turned back to the weeds, taking out his frustration by beheading a few stalks of thistle. He trampled their purple heads underfoot as he made his way around the side of the cabin.

The fine hairs on his neck raised when he heard the sound behind him. He looked to Cy first, thinking the cat had yowled. But Cy, sensing danger, had already taken off for the sanctuary of the garage, disappearing inside the hole in the door Will had yet to fix.

The sound came again, closer this time. The frantic cry of a terrified man.

Up the road, Will saw him coming closer in a dead sprint. *Sam…* He searched his memory for the man's last name and came up empty.

Over the weekend, Will had spotted an unfamiliar face clearing out the old cabin next door—the one that had been vacant for so long he'd been certain it was abandoned—and the detective in him had insisted on going over to flash his badge and take a look around.

Fog Harbor was no San Francisco, so Will had almost hoped to catch the guy robbing the place, just to get his blood pumping again. But Sam had introduced himself and assured Will that his grandfather, Jack, had owned the worse-for-wear cabin for twenty years until his pack-a-day habit caught up with him. Apparently, Grandpa Jack hadn't lasted long once they'd moved him to Sundown Nursing Home.

Weatherby. That was it. *Sam Weatherby.*

"Are you okay?"

As Sam drew closer, Will realized the utter stupidity of his question. The man's face had paled beneath the sheen of a cold sweat. His breath came in shallow gasps. He pulled up short and doubled over, wheezing as he spoke.

"The barrel."

For a full minute, those two words were the only ones Sam Weatherby could say.

"I'm not going back down there." Sam planted himself on the top step of the basement stairs, his hands shaking, his breath ragged. Will didn't argue with him, the steps creaking with his weight as he padded down alone into the nearly empty basement. According to Sam, all of his grandfather's possessions had been donated, trashed, or sold for pennies on the dollar at the estate sale last weekend. All except for a large barrel too heavy to lift.

In the light from the single bare bulb, Will took in the barrel's rusted bottom. Its black paint peeled back like burnt skin. Corrosion freckled its belly. At the bottom, faded white letters spelled out HAZARDOUS.

A crowbar rested at Will's feet, discarded in a panic. The lid too, thrown aside on the dirt basement floor. A few feet away was a puddle of what Will assumed to be Sam's vomit.

Will's body filling with dread, he approached the steel drum with his nose and mouth covered by his shirtsleeve, and looked into the throat of the barrel to confirm what Sam had described.

The skin of the hand extended toward him had turned an unnatural brown. Will didn't touch it, of course, but the fingertips were likely stiff as stakes, unyielding as cheap leather. They reached upward, in a permanent grasp toward freedom. The rest of the body was coiled like the shell of a snail and packed into the barrel with sand, which explained why it had been too heavy to move.

"You said your grandfather didn't know where the barrel came from?"

Will didn't buy that for one second, but he felt bad for poor Sam. Saying what he really thought would only add insult to injury. How could a man have a body in his basement and not have a clue?

"He told me the thing was down here when he moved in. Since it had those markings on it, hazardous and all, he figured it was better to leave it alone. When I was a kid, we joked about it whenever we'd come down to the basement together. Imagining what might be inside. Pirate's chest, time capsule, alien pod. It was like a game between us. But I never…"

Sam trailed off as Will backed away from the barrel and pointed up the stairs. "Let's head outside. We can talk while we wait for my partner."

Judging by JB's curt—*this better be good*—followed by radio silence, Will expected Detective Jimmy Benson to arrive in his usual mood. Since JB had given up nicotine and sugar cold turkey a few weeks ago at his ex-wife's request, he'd been all black cloud rainbows and arsenic lollipops. At least Fog Harbor's medical examiner, Chet Clancy, had picked up on the first ring. The doc had a way of smoothing everyone's rough edges.

Sam plodded through the empty kitchen and onto the front porch, where he leaned against the railing while Will sucked up the fresh air, questions sprouting like thistle weeds in his mind.

"Why'd your grandfather move out to Fog Harbor anyway? It's a big change from San Francisco."

And didn't Will know it. He still had a hard time sleeping. It sounded crazy. But a place could be too quiet.

"Well, I was a kid, maybe eight or nine, when he bought the cabin, so I can't say for sure. But after my grandma died, I think he wanted a change of pace. He retired early and moved up here. My mom always said he needed a place where his ghosts couldn't find him."

Good luck with that. Will knew better than most that you can't outrun the past. All of his own ghosts had located him easily enough. Like someone had gone and given them his goddamned GPS coordinates.

Sam frowned. "You don't think Grandpa Jack had something to do with it, do you?"

"To do with what, exactly?" Will felt like a prick for saying it, but that was the job sometimes. One minute you had your knee in a guy's back, the next you were rescuing kittens.

Sam opened his mouth, closed it again. It stayed that way until JB's blue Camaro made a sharp turn, kicking up dust in the drive.

"Is that your partner?"

Will nodded, though he hardly recognized JB as he emerged from the car in a crisp white polo, white shorts, and a pair of blindingly white sneakers. Only his beer belly gave him away. The scowl too, after he removed a matching visor from his head and flung it onto the passenger seat.

Moments later, Chet's old truck rumbled up the drive, grumbling as it came to a rest next to JB's Camaro. JB headed for the porch, shaking his head, and motioned Will over.

"C'mon, Deck. What happened to taking the afternoon off?"

"Duty calls, man. I didn't realize you and Federer were going five sets at Wimbledon. You pick that outfit yourself?"

"You're a real joker, aren't you? I'll let you have the pleasure of explaining to Tammy why I had to leave our first doubles tennis lesson before she got to show me her backside."

"You mean 'backhand'?"

JB winked. "If you say so."

Will huffed out a quiet laugh, still amazed JB had convinced ex-wife number four to give it one more go. Though he supposed JB had a certain charm. If you could look past the dumpster fire of his personality. His reunion with Tammy benefitted both of them, since she'd worked for years as a technician at Del Norte County crime lab.

Chet sidled up between them, giving JB a once-over. "So, what do we have, gentlemen?"

"I'm still waitin' on City Boy to enlighten me."

Will rolled his eyes at JB's ridiculous nickname for him. He had no doubt his partner would be calling him City Boy no matter how long he'd lived in sleepy Fog Harbor. "You've got to see it to believe it."

Will glanced in Sam's direction. The color had returned to his face, but his eyes looked haunted. A look Will understood well; death was a hard thing to shake.

"He found a body in his basement."

Chet made a few slow circles around the barrel, studying the contents with a small flashlight, the wrinkles in his forehead deepening. His voice came out muffled from behind a disposable face mask.

"It's a body, alright."

"Anything else you can tell us?" Will couldn't look away from the barrel, no matter how much he wanted to. He'd seen his share of dead bodies, but this one horrified him in a way none ever had. While Sam Weatherby had grown from a boy to a man, the body had been here, cold and alone in its dark tomb; frozen in time, reaching for a rescue that never came.

"I'd speculate it's a woman. There's a ring with a stone around the fourth metacarpal. And she's been here a hell of a long time. With no air in the barrel, the body mummified. That's a lucky break. We need to get this whole thing to the medical examiner's office where I can inspect it properly."

Tearing himself away, Will followed JB past the barrel and further into the bowels of the basement, where the light from the single bulb didn't reach. Before the darkness swallowed them whole, JB clicked on his own penlight, sweeping it across the brick walls and bare dirt floor. In the corners, the spiderwebs hung heavy with dust.

"This place is like something out of a bad horror movie." JB ran his hand along the bricks, inspecting the mortar.

"Got something?"

"Maybe." He directed his light at the back wall. "Take a look."

Will stepped closer, scanning the rows until he'd found what drew JB's attention. A large U-shaped bracket was affixed to the wall, its surface rusted with age. Near it, two perfect holes punched in the clay. "What do you make of it?"

"Looks like there might have been another bracket hanging there. Could've been a shelf or…"

"Grandpa Jack told me a story about that bracket." Sam appeared on the top step. Backlit by the sun, he loomed over them in a way that made Will uneasy. Even if his voice still wavered when he spoke. "You're right. There used to be another one."

With JB behind him, Will made his way back past the barrel and across the dimly lit floor so he could look Sam in the eyes. "A story?"

JB snuffed his penlight, leaving the lone bulb to spotlight Sam. "Let's hear it. I love a good yarn."

Will conjured his own childhood bedroom, huddled with his brothers Ben and Petey under a blanket fort, Ben spinning the classic tale of an escaped serial killer with a hook for a hand to distract them from their parents going nine rounds in the kitchen. The thought of Ben grabbing Petey from behind after he delivered the final line, of them collapsing into giggles, caused a familiar ache behind Will's breastbone.

"But I don't know if there's any truth to it."

"That's the best kind of story." JB gave Will a look that said he'd gone into full Good Cop mode now, complete with the gracious smile and the trite reassurances. Already Sam seemed more relaxed.

"Well, Grandpa Jack said the man who owned the cabin before him had these two wolfdogs, Zeus and Hera. Scariest dogs you ever saw, with teeth sharp as razors. One day, the dogs got out of the yard and killed a bunch of chickens at the cabin next door. You know, a real bloodbath. The cops told him he had to keep Zeus and Hera chained up down here. But then, the strangest thing happened. The chickens kept disappearing. Other animals too. The neighbor—fella's name was Crawley—decided to keep watch on the cabin. He hunkered down in the redwoods with his Winchester and waited."

JB rubbed his arms. "Anybody else gettin' goosebumps?"

"Under the light of a full moon, old Crawley caught the man red-handed, sneaking into his chicken coop. As you can imagine, Crawley didn't take kindly to it. No one ever saw that man again."

"I feel like you're settin' me up," JB said. "But, I've gotta ask. What happened to the man? Did Crawley shoot him?"

"Nope. According to my granddad, Crawley shackled him up down here and raised Zeus and Hera as his own. Turns out those wolfdogs got along with the chickens just fine." Sam half-smiled, reeling them in. "As long as he kept them well fed."

"Jeez." JB's eyes widened. "Your grandpa could spin one hell of a story."

"See for yourself."

When Sam gestured back toward the belly of the basement, where the shadows melded into a pool of darkness, Will felt like a boy again, imagining that hook hand scraping down his back. To be a cop, you had to welcome fear. To claim it as your friend.

He snatched the penlight from JB and directed it at the courses of bricks below the brackets. Down, down, down. Until, sure enough, several long, thin scratches marred the clay.

"Grandpa Jack always said he tried to claw his way out."

CHAPTER TWO

It took three men and a heavy-duty dolly to haul the barrel up the stairs and out of the cabin, into the last rays of sunlight. Now it stood empty in the corner of Chet's examination room. Under a thick layer of dust near the base, Will uncovered a stamp, bearing the name RILEY CORP. A quick Google search turned up thousands of results but nothing of interest in Fog Harbor.

The body inside it had been laid on the metal autopsy table. As Chet inspected the victim with gloved hands, Will surveyed the rest of the contents of the barrel, which had been tipped out onto a plastic sheet once the body had been removed.

Sand. A helluva lot of it. They'd all agreed it looked too clean to have come from the beach. More than likely, it had been purchased at a hardware store. But they would send it to the lab for further analysis to be certain.

Buried in the sand, they'd uncovered a Nikon FA camera with a cracked lens and an undeveloped roll of film that Will couldn't wait to get his hands on once it had been dusted for prints.

And from the left hand of the mummified corpse, Chet had removed the ring with a cheap red stone and placed it next to the camera.

According to Chet's initial assessment, the yet unidentified Jane Doe was a young Caucasian adult female with a medium build. Her skin, rubbery. Her blonde hair, matted. As Chet had predicted, as soon as the corpse had been exposed to the air, decomposition had begun. Will had never seen anything like it in his life, and hoped he never would again. Reduced to a shell of skin and bone, he wondered what dreams and hopes had once fluttered inside her head. What possibilities had died with her in that barrel.

Chet motioned them over. "Take a look at this, guys."

The red cotton on the girl's T-shirt had darkened to a dingy brown, but the logo on the front remained legible: *1984 Summer Olympics.*

JB staggered back. "Do you really think she was in that barrel for over three decades?"

Chet nodded. "It's certainly possible. Her clothing looks to be from that era. The stonewashed jeans. The high-top sneakers. Even that camera is a fossil."

"Hey, easy there," JB said. "I prefer the term 'relic', myself."

Will shook his head at his partner. But he'd done the math too. Back then, Will would've been fifteen years old with peach fuzz and braces. JB, somewhere between wives one and two. In other words, a lifetime ago. "Do we know how she died?"

Chet cupped the girl's head gently in his gloved hand. "See that?"

Will forced his eyes downward to a tear in the sickly yellow skin.

"A two-inch-long laceration to the back of the head. And there's another here. And here." Chet pointed to two more nasty gashes. "Blunt force trauma, likely caused by a heavy object, possibly with a sharp edge. We've got multiple skull fractures, and the bloodstaining indicates she was alive when these occurred."

Chet directed the overhead light onto the girl's extended arm. "I see splotching on both wrists, too. Could be bruising. And what looks to be a cutting-type wound on her abdomen. I want to run the body through an x-ray before I draw any conclusions. But, given the circumstances, I'd classify these wounds as highly suspicious."

"Damn right, it's suspicious." JB guffawed. "You can't very well stuff yourself into a barrel."

*

As Chet prepared the body for the x-ray machine, Will fled the autopsy room in search of fresh air. He shed his gloves and pushed through the double doors into the brisk March evening. The parking lot had emptied, but the lights of downtown Fog Harbor twinkled like fireflies in the distance. It rankled—always had—the way death, however brutal, changed nothing. While Jane Doe had been entombed in the basement, the world marched on. Even now that she'd been discovered, the world kept right on marching. Her killer included. It took a special kind of sicko to stuff a dead girl in a barrel and walk the other way.

Desperate for a distraction, Will checked his phone. Still nothing from Olivia. Which must've meant it hadn't gone well. He thought about calling. But if he called, he'd have to hear her voice. If he heard her voice, he'd make an ass of himself trying to make her feel better and she'd laugh out of pity. If she laughed, he'd just end up liking her more.

"Anything from Olivia?" JB asked, craning over his shoulder.

"No." Will tucked his phone inside his pocket. "Why?"

"Because you started getting all googly-eyed like usual."

"Can we just do our jobs, please? Dead girl. Barrel. Remember?"

JB shrugged. "Suit yourself. I figured we'd wait for Chet to finish up, then head over to the station and see if we can track down the prior homeowners. We should get the prints back from the lab tomorrow, along with that film from the camera."

Will nodded. "Why don't you head home? Spend a little time with Tammy. I can start making calls."

"Are you kidding?"

"I thought you'd be happy."

"And let you handle the investigation? You'll muck it by morning, City Boy."

Chet burst out the door, still wearing his gloves and white coat, but without his usual calm demeanor. His eyes were wide. His jaw tensed.

"What the hell?" Will heard the shock in JB's voice as Chet doubled over and vomited.

Wiping his mouth on his coat sleeve, Chet didn't look up, delivering the news to the freshly mowed grass. "She suffered several skull fractures. One of the blows was so severe, it caused an intracranial hematoma. There's a laceration, probably a knife wound, to the upper abdomen. The right wrist is broken. The left is sprained. Makes me wonder if Weatherby's story had some truth to it. She might've actually been locked up down there."

JB let out a low whistle. "Cause of death, homicide?"

Chet nodded, drew in a ragged breath, and met their eyes.

"There's something else. It's the reason I'm out here puking my guts up. Hasn't happened since my first day on the job. I couldn't help but think of my own daughter."

Will braced himself, waited for the worst.

"Upon x-ray, I located a fetus. A close to full-term baby boy."

"Come again?" JB's mouth hung open.

"That poor girl was going to be a mother."

CHAPTER THREE

Olivia Rockwell had never seen her father cry. Not when he crashed his Harley and had to wear a neck brace for six months. Not when her mother slapped his face so hard it left a palm print on his cheek. Not when the cops hauled him away to prison for murder. Not even the first time he held her little sister, Emily, in the miserable prison visiting room. No wonder Olivia had always kept her own tears securely dammed; stoicism was in her DNA.

But now, the tears streaking Martin Reilly's face couldn't be denied.

The parole board could do that to a man. Make him wait twenty-seven years. Plus another two hours when the hearing before his ran late. Then reduce him to a puddle in a moment, with a single question. The tattoo on his forearm—a distorted clock face with no hands—made perfect sense now.

"What happened on the afternoon of May 3, 1992?"

Olivia's father wiped at his face, his sniffling broadcast through the pin-drop quiet boardroom by the microphone on the table. Olivia wished she hadn't called in a favor with the District Attorney. That she hadn't made the five-hour drive from Fog Harbor to Valley View State Prison in San Francisco, where her father had been transferred ten years ago. That she'd waited out in the hallway with her sister, Emily. But that very question had chased her like her own shadow. To finally be rid of it, she needed the answer.

Her father reached clumsily for the microphone. It screeched back at him when he cleared his throat into it, and Olivia winced.

It struck her how small he looked. How insignificant. Prison could do that to a man too.

When his eyes found hers in the corner of the room, she smiled at him. She could give him that much at least.

"I—I'm sorry. Up until my psych eval a couple months back, I'd never talked about any of this stuff. As you can tell, I'm not too good at public speaking, but I'll give it my best shot." He paused. "Back in '92, they called me Mad Dog. I belonged to a—"

Commissioner Portee raised his finger, stopping her father mid-sentence. Olivia pitied her dad then, knowing broad-shouldered, good ole boy Portee and his partner, Deputy Commissioner Alleva, held the proverbial keys to his freedom on their nondescript black leather belts.

"Why 'Mad Dog'? That's quite a nickname."

"Well, I was quite an asshole."

Commissioner Portee chuckled, surprising her. Maybe her dad would be better at impressing The Man than she thought.

"I never backed down from a fight. In fact, I welcomed it. I'd swing until the other guy hit the ground and keep on going. I wanted everyone in the Double Rock Projects to fear me. And for the most part, they did. There was no line I wouldn't cross."

"You were in a gang, is that correct?"

"Yes, sir. The Oaktown Boys, just like my daddy. *God rest his soul.* My father-in-law too. To me, the gang was like family. I'd have taken a bullet for any of them. A few weeks before, Chris Desoto—we called him Baby Face—got hooked up for a murder at the Double Rock. Word got out that Tina had seen the whole thing go down. That she'd ratted him out and was planning to testify against him."

"Did you know Tina Solomon?"

"We all did. Her mom had her working the streets before she turned eighteen. Tina's mom had a coke problem. Eventually, so did Tina. She needed money and there were only so many ways to make a living in the Double Rock. I sold drugs. Tina sold her body. She was a hooker. I mean, *prostitute.*"

"Had you ever used her services?"

Her father took a gulp from a bottle of water on the desk. His eyes cut to Olivia and back again. She held her breath, watching his throat constrict and expand before he spoke. She recognized this moment. The one where the rubber met the road.

"It's hard for me to admit, but yes. I had a drug problem myself back then. Alcohol too. Hell, I had all sorts of problems. But the biggest one was me. I can't make any excuses. I lived up to my nickname. Running around on my wife. Behaving recklessly. Hurting people. Shirking my responsibilities as a father."

Olivia felt a sharp ache in her chest.

"What happened next, Mr. Reilly? After you heard Tina had seen the murder?"

"A few of us got together and decided I'd put the squeeze on her. Slap her around a little, so she'd shut her trap. That's all it was supposed to be."

Stiff in their suits, the commissioners nodded at him as if they understood. But Carmen Sanchez, her dad's attorney, had warned Olivia that both men had a background in law enforcement, and Olivia could see it in their faces. The blatant skepticism. The thinly veiled judgment.

"That day, I drove around the neighborhood looking for her, but I couldn't find her at the usual spots. So, I headed back to the Double Rock, thinking she might be there. But no such luck. After a while, I just gave up."

"You went back to your apartment?"

Her father nodded. "I knew something was wrong right off the bat. Tina was lying on the floor of my living room, bleeding out. I ran over, not thinking. Grabbed the knife, left my fingerprints all over it. It was bad. Real bad. And my little girl, Olivia—well, she's not a little girl anymore—she walked in and witnessed the aftermath. She was only eight years old. I take full responsibility for my actions. The decisions I made caused Tina's death. But I want to be clear today. I was set up. It wasn't me who cut her throat."

The memory flickered across Olivia's mind's eye like a photo in a viewfinder. Her father gripping the bloody knife. The teenaged boy they called Termite at his side. All of it, come and gone in a blink.

Commissioner Portee raised one bushy eyebrow. "Who was it then, Mr. Reilly?"

"I can't say."

"Can't, or won't?"

"Both. I want to be honest with you. I really do. But I can't put my life at risk. Or my daughters' lives. I've already put my family through enough."

"Sounds like you're still making excuses, Mad Dog. Either you're lying to us today or you're protecting a murderer. Neither one makes you fit for life on the streets, now does it?"

Her father slumped, defeated. His heavy sigh, the sound of hope leaving his body. Olivia dug the points of her heels into the floor and forced herself to stay seated. She wondered why anyone had ever deemed her worthy of a Ph.D. in psychology—chief psychologist at Crescent Bay State Prison, no less—when she couldn't even find the right words to say how she felt. Only that she desperately wanted to run from this room with its savagery disguised as decorum. From the two stuffy barbarians at the helm. From her spineless father, too.

Commissioner Portee paid no mind to her father's drooped head or his trembling shoulder, as he addressed the room with the same voice he'd used to order a chicken sandwich during the lunch break.

"We'll take a brief recess before we render our decision."

*

Once the decision was made, they took her father out first. Two officers led him through a side door and into the hallway, where he'd be locked inside a holding cell until he returned to his bunk in the dormitory with a hundred other men just like him. Olivia watched him shuffle past her, both relieved and disheartened she couldn't speak to him. Emily would've waved or reached for his hand, but Olivia kept both of hers clasped in her lap.

Her former patient, Drake Devere, had once told her that to survive a life sentence you only had to learn to wait. The thought of Drake somewhere out there, biding his time before he found her again, made her skin crawl. But, as her father returned to the belly of Valley View State Prison, Olivia figured Drake had it right. Commissioner Portee had issued the board's verdict in that same *hold the mayo* tone.

Parole denied for five years.

Waiting was the only thing left to do.

Olivia forced a smile as she picked herself up and followed Attorney Sanchez into the hallway. She wished she could call Deck, text him at least. But cell phones weren't allowed inside the prison.

"Well?" Emily's wide eyes met hers, as expectant as a child's. The same way she'd looked every time Dad had made his *I'll be home soon* promises in the prison visiting room. Conceived during a family visit, Emily had only known their father behind iron bars.

Olivia shook her head.

"How long?"

"Five years."

"*Five years?* In five years, I'll be thirty."

"I told you not to get your hopes up. Nobody gets out on their first try."

Attorney Sanchez patted Emily on the shoulder. "Your sister's right. Assuming your father keeps up the good work, we'll petition for an advancement in two years."

Emily disappeared inside the nearest bathroom. When the lock clicked into place, Olivia silenced her inner big sister, the pestering nag who wanted to chase after her, pound on the door, and tell her she shouldn't waste any more tears on Dad.

Em had been through enough. Her move from Fog Harbor to San Francisco in January to attend art school, the least of it. But Olivia had gotten better at letting go, so she pressed her ear to the door instead. She wasn't ready to relinquish the big sister mantle just yet.

"Is she okay?" A brief frown wrinkled Attorney Sanchez's forehead, but she didn't wait for Olivia's answer. She glanced over her shoulder down the empty hallway and back again before handing Olivia an envelope.

"Don't open it here."

"What—"

The prison alarm blared, jolting Olivia bone-deep. Like a foghorn waking her from a nightmare. She heard yelling from the direction of the boardroom, from the other side of the door where they'd escorted her father fifteen minutes ago. She shoved the envelope in her purse.

"Stay with my sister." Then Olivia ran toward the sound, her blood crashing loud as the ocean in her ears.

Olivia emerged in a long corridor of holding cells, amid a frantic crowd of correctional officers who swarmed the middle cell, its door wide open.

No one stopped her.

No one told her to turn back.

No one even noticed her.

"Cut him down!" someone yelled. "Hurry!"

When she reached the cell, it took a moment to make sense of what she saw. A moment that stretched like an eternity but vanished in a heartbeat. Inside, she saw a man's boots swinging a foot off the ground.

Though she went no further, saw no more, she knew. Those boots belonged to her father. He'd hanged himself.

CHAPTER FOUR

Olivia felt the weight of Emily's hand on hers. The cold metal of the bench beneath her legs. Her body was seated outside Warden Sandra Ochoa's office in Valley View State Prison, but her mind, untethered, traveled elsewhere.

Twenty-seven years ago at the Double Rock, her father had scooped her up with his blood-red hands and carried her to Miss Pearl's apartment. He'd taken her into the bathroom, locked the door, crouched down to her level and held both her hands so she'd stop wiping at the bloodstains on her dress.

Listen to me. You can't tell anyone who you saw in there. It was just me, okay? Just me. I did this.

She'd opened her little mouth but her voice stayed hidden deep inside her.

Let's practice. Tell me who you saw.

C'mon, Liv, he'd urged her.

Finally, the word came out, betraying them both.

"Olivia." Em nudged her shoulder. "The medical examiner wants to speak with us."

Warden Ochoa led them down the hallway to the infirmary, where they were greeted by David Plunkett, Chief Medical Examiner. He shook Olivia's hand, his own limp and sweaty, and she pulled hers back sooner than was polite. He gave her a pitying look.

"I'm sorry about your father. I know you must be in a state of shock. But I'll need you both to make a decision about the autopsy.

My preliminary examination of the body showed no evidence that this was anything other than a suicide."

A sob escaped Emily's throat.

"We can have your father transported down to the morgue and do a full autopsy, or we can release the body to you for burial. It's your call."

Emily wiped her face with a crumpled tissue. "I don't like the idea of them cutting on Dad."

Olivia glanced at the envelope she'd tucked in her purse, still sealed. "Before we make any decisions, I want to see his body."

"Liv, are you sure you want to remember him like that?"

Dr. Plunkett's frown deepened. "Your sister is right to be concerned. You've already been through a lot today."

He had no idea what she'd been through. How she'd stood there unnoticed while Officer Boon cut her father down from an exposed pipe, where he'd hung from a strip of bedsheet.

Resolute, Olivia stood up and steeled herself. "I need to do this, Em. You can wait outside." Little sisters had that luxury.

Dr. Plunkett pulled back the sheet, then retreated to the corner while Olivia studied the contours of her father's face, half expecting him to sit bolt upright from the examination table. *Gotcha*, he'd say, laughing.

His skin hadn't yet begun to gray, but she couldn't bring herself to touch him. Then, there would be no denying it. It seemed impossible that only a few hours ago he'd been spilling his guts and contemplating his freedom. That she'd been sitting a few feet away as he'd walked past. That she hadn't reached for him.

"What are those scratches?" Olivia looked closer at the frantic red marks on her father's neck.

"It seems at some point he must've changed his mind." Dr. Plunkett made an awful *tsk*-ing noise. "Most do, you know."

"And this swelling on his head?"

He joined her at the table, slipping on a pair of gloves. The aggressive snap of the latex against his wrists seemed directed at her. Lifting her father's shaggy gray hair, he studied the raised bump on his temple.

"Hard to say. Could've been there already."

"I didn't notice it during the hearing." Olivia focused on the bluish lump, suspicions spinning through her mind, making her dizzy. She leaned against the counter to steady herself. "I don't understand why the officers put him in that holding cell anyway. The only one with exposed pipe. There were plenty of others available."

Dr. Plunkett released a long breath.

"And how did my father reach the pipe? Did you check the distance? Was it even possible for him to reach on his own?"

He wrestled off his gloves and chucked them in the trash can.

"I don't work for the prison."

"That's right. You don't. I hope you remember that when you autopsy my father."

Olivia stood on the small balcony outside her sister's studio apartment, the lights of downtown San Francisco shimmering in the distance. The beauty and bustle of the city twisted a knife inside her, and she turned her face from it, peering through the sliding glass doors that separated her and Emily.

She'd promised herself she'd stop protecting Em. She'd stop keeping secrets. But it had been hard enough letting Em traipse off to San Francisco for art school. Letting down all the walls around her heart had proven impossible.

Olivia took the envelope from inside her jacket, slipped her finger beneath the seal and removed the single folded page. Suddenly terrified, she contemplated dropping it and letting the wind carry it to parts unknown. She didn't fear what her father had written, but rather what he hadn't. That these few words were all she had left of him:

> *Box 19 has your answers.*
> *Miss Pearl has the key.*
> *Talk before you leave tomorrow? Visiting hours start at 7:45 a.m.*
> *P.S. Always keep the rubber side down and the shiny side up.*

Overcome, she collapsed into the plastic chair behind her. Her father had been making plans, thinking about tomorrow, dishing out his special brand of motorcycle slang in his postscript. She read the note again, turned it over. Looked inside the empty envelope. As if she'd find him in there.

A single tear tracked its way down her face before she remembered she was angry and wiped it away.

When Olivia's phone buzzed, she stared at the name on the screen. She wanted to talk, needed to. But she couldn't imagine saying the words. *My dad is dead.* Especially not to him. He'd probably blame himself, and that she couldn't bear.

Still, her finger hovered over the answer icon, swiped.

"Deck?"

He'd already hung up.

CHAPTER FIVE

Will slipped his phone back into his pocket, disappointed. He told himself he'd only been hoping to pick Olivia's brain about the girl in the barrel. A pathetic excuse.

He poured two cups of watered-down coffee from the office machine, loading his with cream and sugar to make it palatable, and returned to his cubicle, where he found JB scrolling through the cabin's property records and talking to a celery stick.

"You are a chocolate bar. Delicious and creamy and filled with peanut butter." He closed his eyes and nibbled on the end.

"How's that working for you?" Will laughed as he rolled his chair over to JB's desk.

"About as well as it looks." JB chewed, grimaced, and swallowed, chasing the bite of celery with a swig of coffee, then pointed to the computer screen. "Jackson Weatherby, aka Grandpa Jack, owned that cabin since '98. Before that, it was a guy named Frank Schmidt. I found a contact number for him, if you want to give it a go?"

Will eyed the digits JB had scrawled on a pad of paper. "Why can't you do it?"

"Remember the story Sam told us? He's probably the one who had the wolfdogs. I'm not gettin' on that guy's radar. No, siree."

With a roll of his eyes, Will punched in the number on the desk phone and waited.

"Hello?" Frank Schmidt sounded a few beers short of a twelve pack, punctuating his greeting with a belch.

"Detective Will Decker. Fog Harbor Homicide. I apologize for the late call, but I was hoping you could help me with some information on a case I'm working."

"Depends. I ain't done nothin' wrong, have I?"

"Not that I know of." Will pictured that bracket on the wall, the scratches beneath it. "I'm wondering if you could tell me about the cabin you owned a while back on Wolver Hollow Road."

The silence stretched, and Will wondered if Frank had hung up the phone. "What about it? I didn't own the place for that long. Sold it years ago. Moved up the coast to Mendocino. "

"Did you ever come across a barrel in the basement?"

Will hit the speakerphone, and Frank's baritone voice filled the empty station. "A barrel, huh? Come to think of it, that thing was there when I moved in. Along with a bunch of other useless crap I tossed out. Couldn't budge that barrel an inch, though. I figured it was left over from the prior owner. The movie guy."

"The movie guy?"

JB gestured to the screen. To the entry below Schmidt, Frank.

"Does the movie guy have a name?"

"Can't say I recall it. Real eccentric fella. But his studio went belly-up. That's how I got the place for a steal in the early nineties."

"Anything else you remember that might help us track down the owner of that barrel?"

"Are you talking about the rumors? You know, everybody's got their nose in your business in Fog Harbor."

"Rumors?" Will hoped he didn't sound too eager.

His laugh was loud and pickled in alcohol. "I heard that Movie Guy kept somebody chained up down there."

"Did you believe it?"

"Sure as shit. I found the chains."

*

As Will pounded out combinations on the heavy bag in his garage, Cy watched him with a judgmental eye. Like he wondered when Will would finally give it a rest and admit defeat. No matter how many jab-cross-hooks he landed, he couldn't shake the unsettled feeling in his stomach. He had to keep punching hard and fast. His opponent, the monsters in his head.

It turned out Frank Schmidt had discarded part of a rusted chain he'd found coiled in the corner of the basement when he'd taken possession of the cabin. With the injuries to the victim's wrists, Will suspected she'd been held prisoner down there.

First thing in the morning, he and JB planned to locate Maxwell Grimaldi, former owner of the now-defunct Obscura Studios. Property records showed Grimaldi purchased the cabin back in 1983, selling it ten years later, after the studio closed its doors. Will and JB had a much-needed laugh perusing the studios' catalog of B horror movies. Classics like *Cheerleader Massacre* and *The Zombie in my Bedroom*.

Will planned to finish his boxing round with a flurry of uppercuts to the body—something to tire him out—but the buzz of his cell phone stopped him short, its sound as jarring as the ring of a boxing bell.

He didn't recognize the number but the voice on the other end was as familiar as his own. Even if it had been over two years since he'd last seen his brother, Ben, when they'd carted him away in handcuffs to Valley View State Prison to serve six years for voluntary manslaughter in an officer-involved shooting.

"Hey, little bro."

"Ben?" Will didn't know if he should be relieved or panicked. "Are you alright? How are you calling me right now?"

Ben's groan meant he didn't want a lecture, so Will left it alone. He could guess the answer anyway. An illegal, ill-gotten cell phone.

"I can't talk long. Petey told me it's you who's been sending the money. I didn't believe him at first, but then I remembered that between his gambling and the overhead on the nightclub, Petey's flat broke."

"I know you think I hate you, but—"

"Now's not the time for a heart-to-heart, man. You've gotta get me out of here. I'm a dead man walking."

Will stumbled back, steadying himself against the tailgate. He flashed to that night in the Tenderloin, when he'd watched Ben—Officer Decker, then—shoot an unarmed woman. To the courtroom, where he'd said the words that put his brother away. To the agonizing moment the jury foreman had read the verdict. *Guilty.*

"They got to him. I don't know how. But he's dead. If I don't transfer out of here, I'm next."

"Slow down. Got to *who*? Who's dead?"

"The Oaktown guy who's had my back for the last couple months."

Will couldn't speak. He felt tied to the tracks with a train rushing toward him at breakneck speed. As Ben barreled on, he braced for impact.

"Martin Reilly. They called him Mad Dog."

Script: *Good Morning, San Francisco*

Cue Heather

Good morning, San Francisco. I'm Heather Hoffman. It's 5 a.m. on Friday, March sixth. Time to rise and shine.

Roll intro music

Today's show promises to be one of our most exciting yet, starting with our groundbreaking new crime segment, *Murder in the Bay,* where we take our viewers behind the scenes of local homicide investigations.

Roll segment intro

Our first case takes us to Fog Harbor, California, a town close to my heart. Last winter, Drake Devere disappeared from Crescent Bay State Prison located in the small town, following a bungled police rescue, an incident which was caught by my cameraman and debuted exclusively on this show.

Roll video excerpt of Devere escape

Here at *Good Morning, San Francisco,* we pride ourselves on being the first to the story, and we are indeed the first to report that tragedy has returned to this quaint seaside community. Yesterday afternoon, a man made a gruesome discovery in his grandfather's basement. The body of an unidentified woman was found mummified in a barrel that had sat untouched for over thirty years. Though the story is still developing, our sources in law enforcement have confirmed that the young victim was pregnant at the time of her death.

Stay with *Good Morning,* San Francisco for the latest in this haunting mystery. Next up, Fitness Trainer Chrissy Quan shows us how to turn fat to fit and whip our assets into shape.

Cut to commercial

CHAPTER SIX

The sky still dark, Olivia slipped from beneath the blanket and padded across her sister's living room. She dressed in the pitch-blackness, tugged her hair into a ponytail, and snagged a banana from the kitchen counter, dropping it in her purse with the caution of a cat burglar.

Before she made her way to the door, Olivia jotted a note on the board that hung above the table, scribbling her message next to Em's impressive chalk drawing of the Golden Gate Bridge. She wiped the white dust on her jeans, carefully unlocked the door, and turned the knob.

The soft *click* of the light switch behind her froze her in her tracks.

"Where are you going?"

"I just need some air, Em. I can't sleep."

"Me either. I'll come with you."

Emily grabbed her jacket from the closet and stuffed her feet into her fuzzy pink slippers. In the soft glow of the bathroom light, her little sister looked every bit the part; curls askew, a pillow crease on her cheek, she could've been sixteen, not twenty-five. Not living on her own in the big city.

"You can't."

Emily walked over and erased her note from the chalkboard in one adamant swipe. The look in her eye reminded Olivia of their mother, Louise. How willful she'd been, refusing to go to the doctor even when her skin turned a sickly yellow and her abdomen swelled like a blister.

"When are you going to stop lying to me? I know you were there that day at the Double Rock. Dad told me everything."

Olivia sucked in a breath. "When? What did he say?"

"I visited him a few weeks ago. Right after you helped me with the move down here. He said there were a few things he needed to get off his chest. Things he was planning on telling the parole board. Is it true? You saw Tina dead?"

Olivia nodded. Though dead seemed too nice a word for the garish wound across Tina's throat. The bright red blood seeping from her neck. If Olivia shut her eyes, she could still smell the sharp metal of it.

"Why didn't you tell me? All these years, you've been keeping that inside. That's messed-up, Liv. Especially for a shrink."

"I know, I know. But Dad made me promise not to tell anyone what I saw. And by the time you were born and old enough, it felt safer not to." She searched Emily's face, wondering how much she really knew. "Did he say anything more? About that day, I mean?"

"Someone else was there. He said you'd tell me at the right time. That I shouldn't push you. That I'd know when." Em shuffled toward her and took a seat at the kitchen table. Olivia sat down too, grateful for the near darkness. "So?"

Olivia knew the power of that word. A prod, gentle but too pointed to ignore. She'd used it enough times on her patients. She swallowed hard. "So…"

Olivia had hoped never to come back here. To the squalor of the Double Rock Projects. And especially not with Emily, who had never laid eyes on this place. By the time Em had been born, they'd already relocated to Fog Harbor to be close to their father at Crescent Bay State Prison. Except for the bright green spray paint that declared this Oaktown Boys' territory, the jaundiced color of the long two-story buildings still matched the dying grass.

Cigarette butts and food wrappers dotted what was left of the lawn like wildflowers. Even the air seemed different here, heavy as concrete on her chest.

Still, she felt lighter, unburdened, having finally told Em the truth.

Why would Dad lie about something like that? her sister had asked when she'd spit it all out. *For so long.*

Olivia couldn't answer. Could only see her father's prison-issued boots swinging above the ground.

As they crossed to the sidewalk, Olivia pointed to the twin hulking rocks in the courtyard. No one knew where they'd come from or why, but they'd always been treated with reverence, unlike the rest of the Double Rock. No graffiti, no climbing, no public urination.

"This is it."

"Wow." Emily ran her hand along the top of the first stone. "I didn't expect it to be so… literal."

Olivia stared up at the second floor. A set of concrete stairs led to Apartment E, the blue door she'd called home for the first eight years of her life. The same blue door she'd seen in her nightmares ever since. "That's our unit. *Was* our unit. A woman called Miss Pearl lived two doors down. She took care of me sometimes. Dad carried me to her apartment after the murder."

Olivia remembered Miss Pearl's face turning white at the sight of them, but she hadn't sent them away. Her father had washed Tina's blood from his hands in her kitchen sink.

"Do you really think she's still there?"

Olivia shrugged and started up the steps, with Emily following behind her. When she passed the door marked E, she didn't slow down. Didn't even look. She felt a heat from within, though. Like the past was still alive in there and burning.

Apartment G was a few doors down at the end of the hallway. Olivia recalled it being farther away; in her memory, her father had carried her for miles, her heart thumping like a rabbit's foot in her chest.

"Ready?" She directed her question to Em, but she meant it for herself.

Olivia had already knocked by the time Emily nodded. The sharp sound echoed in the early-morning quiet. As she raised her fist to the door again, it flew open, and she gasped.

Termite Colvin.

"What the hell time is it, lady? Are you a cop?"

She blinked at him a few times before she realized the skinny, pimple-faced kid in front of her with his lanky arms blocking the doorway couldn't be Termite. Termite had grown into a tattooed beast of a man, like his father. She'd seen him herself months ago at Rocky's Salvage Yard, the Oaktown Boys hangout spot in Fog Harbor.

"I—I'm sorry. I must have the wrong—"

"Settle down, Scotty. Is that little Olivia Reilly?" A sun-spotted face appeared beneath the boy's arm. "Not so little anymore, I see."

Miss Pearl smiled at her, and the years fell away. Olivia saw herself at five, six, and seven years old, eating chocolate chip cookies at Pearl's cracked Formica table, while her parents screamed bloody murder at each other two doors down.

"How long has it been, dear?"

Olivia knew it to the day. "Twenty-seven years, give or take. This is my sister, Emily."

"And who are you again?" Scott narrowed his eyes at them both, his mouth a grim line.

"Scott Michael Colvin, show our guests some manners." The old woman nudged him, and his spine straightened. "You remember Xavier? Termite, they called him Termite back then. Scotty is his boy. He's staying with me for a while."

At the mention of his father's name, Scott's face softened, turned boyish again. No wonder Olivia mistook him for Termite. The same Colvin blood ran through his veins.

"You know my dad?" he asked.

"Knew him. A little. It was a long time ago. He gave me some shoes once." Olivia left out the other parts. That Termite had stolen those shoes, and everything else he'd ever given her. That he'd been there the day of Tina's murder, her blood pooling around him.

Miss Pearl ushered them inside, and Olivia found herself running her finger down a familiar crack in the table, noticing how much smaller everything looked. The cookie jar. The brown armchair. The dolls Miss Pearl sewed—Olivia had one growing up—two yellow buttons for the eyes. Even Miss Pearl.

"You two look just like your mama. I was real sorry to hear she passed away a few years back."

Emily's eyes welled, and Olivia found her hand beneath the table. "We have some bad news."

Miss Pearl waved Scott down the hallway, shooing him into another room. When she returned, her blue eyes went glassy. "I already heard about your dad. Word gets around fast at the Rock. You know that."

"What did you hear exactly?"

"He got denied parole and couldn't go on living in that hellhole." She leaned in, drawing Olivia and Emily toward her. "Between us girls, I know that ain't what happened. Your daddy was a complicated man. But he loved two things more than himself. His family and the Oaktown Boys. It took him too long to figure out there ain't no good solution to that equation."

"By any chance, did he leave something with you?"

Miss Pearl reached into her housecoat and withdrew a plastic key chain decorated with a single faux pearl. She pointed to the longest key in the batch, the number 19 engraved on its small brass head.

Emily took it from her, worked the key off the ring and placed it on the table.

Olivia touched it with reverence. "I don't understand. Did he mail this to you?"

"Oh, honey." Miss Pearl patted her arm. "I've had it since May third, 1992. The day your daddy burst through that door, carrying you, both of you looking like you'd seen a ghost. His hands dripping red all over my linoleum. He pressed the key into my palm and told me exactly what to do. And Lord knows, I did it."

She lowered her head, her tears falling freely now. "Sometimes, I thought about getting rid of it. Couldn't stand the sight of it. But I kept it for you. When I look at that key, all I see is the blood it left on my hands."

CHAPTER SEVEN

Will had hoped to never come back here. To the barbed wire and concrete walls of Crescent Bay State Prison. Every time he drove past the sprawling gray structure on Pine Grove Road on his way to the station, he averted his eyes. Because the last time he'd set foot inside it, its most dangerous inmate, Drake Devere, had escaped on his watch.

But he had no choice now. His brother Ben needed his help. Carrying his guilt like a stone on his shoulders, he plodded down the hallway toward the administrative offices to find Warden Lester Blevins.

After pressing the button at the door, Blevins' secretary, Leeza, ushered him inside, and he followed her clicking heels to the end of corridor. "He's waiting for you."

"Detective Decker, to what do I owe this pleasure?" The warden leaned back in his desk chair and regarded Will through wire-rimmed glasses, his lip curling as if he smelled something unpleasant.

Without asking, Will took the chair across from him and tried to hide his own scowl. He had a laundry list of reasons to dislike Blevins and an even longer list to justify his mistrust. "Nice plaque."

"I don't recall seeing you at the ceremony."

Will read the words that had been immortalized on cheap mahogany after Blevins' supposed heroics during Drake Devere's escape. *Fog Harbor Police Department Bravery Award. For outstanding heroism by a citizen.* "Something came up."

"No doubt. I'm sure you've been busy hunting the Vulture. It must sting, knowing he got the better of you."

In the silence, Will choked on his pride. It stuck in his throat like a shard of bone, but he swallowed it anyway. Along with that damn nickname—the Vulture—that reminded him of the way Drake had disappeared completely. Like he'd up and flown away. "Listen, I'm not here on a social call. I need a favor. It's for an inmate at Valley View."

"An inmate?"

"Not just an inmate. My brother, Ben Decker."

The warden's brows raised. "Ah, I see."

"So, you know about the case?" Will waited for the look. Pity, revulsion, or curiosity. But Blevins' face was unreadable.

"Doesn't everyone? It was quite a media spectacle. I imagine it was hard for you to show your face around San Francisco after that." Revulsion, then. "Of course, I fully support your decision to testify against him. Sometimes, you have to do the right thing, even if it leaves you all alone."

Will nodded, feeling those words like a punch to the gut. "Ben's been having a hard time with the Oaktown Boys at Valley View. He's in danger. I was wondering if you could help him."

"I'm not sure what you have in mind."

"A transfer. Here. To Crescent Bay. As soon as possible. Where I can keep an eye on him. *You* can keep an eye on him. Just get me an audience with the warden down there, and put in a good word. That's all I need."

"That's a big ask, Detective. Warden Ochoa doesn't like people getting in her business any more than I do."

Will set his eyes on Blevins. "Having a former cop in Crescent Bay might have its advantages. Unless you've got something to hide?"

Blevins paused. "I'll see what I can do."

*

Will sat in his truck in the prison parking lot, staring at his phone. He still couldn't dial Olivia's number. She probably hated him right now, and rightfully so. He'd been the one to ask her to call her father back in December, to tell him to look out for Ben in Valley View. And look what it got him. Another body piled on his conscience.

He tossed his phone on the seat and sped back to the station, grateful JB had been too stunned by the news about Olivia's father to ask any questions when Will told him he'd be late. As he floored it down Pine Grove Road, Will felt hunted by the ghosts of his past. He could almost see them in his rearview mirror, snapping at his heels, refusing to let him go.

Will parked the truck and hurried inside to find Officer Jessie Milner occupying JB's seat. Her smile faltered when she saw him approach. Will wondered if he looked that bad, as Jessie usually saved her frowns for her numbskull partner—Olivia's ex, Graham Bauer. After their help on the Seaside Strangler case, Graham and Jessie had been given permanent promotions to Minor Crimes, which sat fine with Will as it gave him more time for the real detective work of homicides.

"Where's JB?"

"Chief Flack's office. She wanted a full debrief on the Jane Doe case. In the meantime, Detective Benson asked me to make a few calls about that guy who once owned the cabin—Grimaldi."

"Any luck finding him?"

"Turns out he's still alive and kicking at the Knotted Pines Retirement Home in Brookings. About fifteen miles from here. The head nurse said he doesn't get many visitors."

"I guess that means he'll be happy to see us."

Will made an effort, but the corners of his mouth couldn't quite reach a smile.

"You alright?" Jessie asked.

"Peachy."

"Well, this might cheer you up." She handed him a printout of Grimaldi's criminal record. Only one entry, but it was a doozy. Kidnapping, forcible confinement, and assault and battery. "I pulled the police report too. There wasn't much to it. I guess they had trouble tracking down the victim. But I'll give you one guess where it happened."

"The cabin?"

Jessie nodded.

"Good work." Will tucked the sheet into the file folder on his desk, a twinge of excitement piercing the numbing fog of the morning. "Is Graham here today?"

"Called in sick."

"That's a shame. What do you think? Hung-over? Bad hair day?"

Jessie's mouth twisted. Like she couldn't decide whether to spill it or let the truth burn her tongue. "I'm guessing you didn't catch *Good Morning, San Francisco*?"

"The TV show?"

"Yeah. His new girlfriend, Heather Hoffman, is the host."

"Girlfriend?"

Jessie shrugged. "That's what I heard. But it's just Hickory Pit gossip. Take it with a grain of salt."

Will shook his head, already fearing the worst. Hoffman had gotten her start at the Fog Harbor *Gazette* and catapulted to journalistic infamy after she'd released video of Drake Devere's escape. It wouldn't be the first time Bauer had tipped her off, and now she must have decided to put him on the payroll. No other reason she'd be interested in that buffoon.

Jessie searched her phone for the footage, finally displaying the screen to Will. A regal Heather Hoffman sat behind a news desk, her perfectly straight blonde hair catching the light. A garish headline scrolled behind her. *Mummified pregnant girl found in barrel.*

"My guess is Graham leaked her the story, and he's playing hooky to avoid the chief's wrath."

*

Chief Sheila Flack didn't say a word to Will when he poked his head into her office. She simply gestured to the empty chair beside JB with a sympathetic nod. Which could only mean JB had gone rogue and told her something resembling the truth.

"Fill me in, gentlemen."

After they'd recounted the whole sordid tale, from finding the barrel and its contents, to the bracket on the wall and Chet's gruesome discovery, Chief Flack shook her head and sighed. "Sounds like Grimaldi's got some explaining to do. I assume you two will head up to Knotted Pines before lunch and give him the old Decker and Benson shakedown."

Will chuckled. "With all due respect, the man is eighty years old. Too much shaking and he might break a hip. We'll be lucky if he can remember back that far."

"Any other leads? What about the sand? Those fingerprints on the camera?"

JB leaned forward, excited. "Just like we thought, the sand is man-made. The kind that's produced from hard granite stone by crushing, probably purchased at a hardware store. But that's not the good part." He rubbed his hands together, flashing Will a devilish grin. "We got a match on the prints. An ex-con named Chuck Winters. What d'ya say, Chief? That's worthy of Detective of the Year, isn't it?"

"Do we know his whereabouts?"

Will matched JB's smile and looked right at him as he spoke, waiting for his jaw to drop. "Second Chance Halfway House in downtown San Francisco. He's a third striker, who just got out on parole."

"What?" JB looked as incredulous as Will had hoped. "How could you possibly know that? You said you needed the morning off. You weren't even here when Lieutenant Wheeler dropped off the report."

Will shrugged. "The real Detective of the Year doesn't take vacation. I'm always working. I called the lab on the drive over. Tammy was more than happy to fill me in."

"That devil woman."

Chief Flack played referee. "Don't get ahead of yourselves. Either one of you. We've got a dead girl in a barrel. The media vultures love this stuff. Hoffman's already circling. Let's wrap this one up quick. We can't afford any more bad press."

"You hear that, City Boy? She's talking to you."

"We should take a trip down to San Francisco," Will said. "Pay Chuck Winters a visit."

Chief Flack nodded. "*You* should take a trip, since you're familiar with the city. Head down this afternoon. JB will stay close to home and canvass the area. Maybe one of the locals remembers a young pregnant girl from way back when."

Will side-eyed his partner. "You're okay with that?"

"The chief has spoken. Besides, I can't miss another tennis lesson or Tammy will be swinging at my balls."

"Alright. What do we do about SFPD?" As soon as Will uttered those four letters, shame flooded his body, taking him right back to the moment he'd turned in his badge at the police headquarters in downtown San Francisco. It had been months since he'd been run out of town by his old department. He couldn't imagine going back. "Should we call ahead? I don't want to step on any toes."

"Already done," JB told him. "I talked to one of the detectives this morning. She said she'd relay the message to Winters' parole agent."

With a droll smile, Chief Flack smacked the table. The signal to get their asses in gear. "Okay, gentlemen. Don't let me down. I want an ID on our victim ASAP."

In the hallway, Will caught up to JB, who'd bolted from the room faster than the time Chief Flack had brought a plateful of her leftover Christmas cookies for the break room.

"You told her, didn't you? About Olivia's dad. Did she already know about Winters, too?"

JB held up his hands in surrender.

"That's why I'm going to San Francisco."

"Listen, City Boy, you should be thanking me. This is how you get out of the friend zone with Olivia. You show up and be the hero."

"You're kidding, right? Olivia just lost her dad and I'm supposed to put the moves on her? Real gentlemanly, JB."

JB parked himself in his desk chair, wiggled his eyebrows. "Hey, I never claimed to be a gentleman. Love is guerrilla warfare. And I fight dirty. Ask Tammy."

"I'll take your word for it." Will grabbed the keys to the Crown Vic, ready to hit the road to Knotted Pines, so they could speak with Grimaldi face to face. "Did you happen to get the name of that homicide inspector from SFPD? In case I need a point of contact."

"*Homicide inspector,* huh? You San Francisco folks are real fancy." When Will gave him an impatient look, he added, "I left it on your desk."

He followed JB's finger to the scrap of paper tucked partway beneath his mouse pad and his stomach dropped.

Amy Bishop.

"Shit."

"Funny. That's the same reaction she had." JB grinned at him. "You never told me your ex-fiancée was a cop."

CHAPTER EIGHT

Squeezing her father's safety deposit box key in her hand, Olivia paced outside the double doors of Golden State Bank and Trust while Emily sat on the hood of the rental car, biting her fingernails. Five more minutes till opening.

Olivia pressed her nose to the glass. Every strike of the second hand on the oversized clock inside the lobby stung like a lash to her skin.

"I can't imagine Dad coming here." Olivia kept talking, trying to distract herself.

"To downtown San Francisco? It's only a few minutes from the Double Rock."

"To a *bank*. The only money he saved went straight into a boot box under the bed."

Olivia had never actually seen her father put cash inside the box, but she'd snooped inside it once or twice when he was out. Until the time she'd found a gun buried at the bottom, alongside several plastic baggies of white powder.

When the clock in the lobby read 9 a.m., Olivia released a breath, then gulped it right back up when a woman appeared in the doorway, dressed in a navy skirt suit as tight as her pinched smile. "Good morning. Can I help you, ma'am?"

"We need to look in a safety deposit box."

"Right this way."

Olivia followed the woman into the expansive lobby, Emily trailing behind. Olivia pictured her father traipsing across the cold marble in his hulking black motorcycle boots. His tattooed arms resting on one of the fancy wing armchairs. A total fish out of water.

At the counter, the woman examined Olivia's driver's license. After confirming Olivia had been authorized to access the box—along with Louise, her mother—she jotted down the details in neat script, and Olivia signed where directed.

"Could I take a look at that entry log?"

"Not much to see, I'm afraid."

As Olivia examined the entries for Box 19, she heard Emily gasp over her shoulder.

Martin Reilly had been here only once. May 2, 1992. The day before he'd been arrested for murder.

The woman placed Box 19 on the table and left them alone.

"What do you think is in there?" Emily pushed the metal box toward Olivia, designating this as a big sister job.

"Whatever it is, we handle it together." But already she cursed herself for bringing Em here, for getting her involved. Her hands trembled as she inserted the key, lifted the metal cover and peered inside. Her initial reaction was disappointment – expecting a photo, a letter, something sentimental – then she remembered that Mad Dog had packed this box, not Martin Reilly. Her father had changed over the years, even if she'd been too hardheaded to admit it.

Olivia removed a stack of receipts, each one identical, stamped at the top with the SFPD logo, and paid to Confidential Informant 983 in the amount of $200.

Emily flipped through the stack, her mouth twisting. "These are all signed by Dad."

"I know."

Olivia had already recognized her father's messy scrawl, penned on the RECEIVED BY line. Her eyes drawn to the other signature, the name printed beneath in neat block letters. She placed her finger on it before she said it out loud, her voice cracking. "Detective Henry Decker. That's Deck's father."

CHAPTER NINE

Knotted Pines Retirement Home rose up on the cliffside, nestled in a grove of redwoods just across the Oregon border. Will took his time up the cobblestone path to the entrance, inhaling the crisp sea air.

"A man could get used to this view." With a relaxed sigh, JB dropped into a rocking chair on the porch before a nurse came out to greet them. Behind him, a picture window provided a view of the spacious lobby. "It ain't a bad place to wait on the Grim Reaper."

"Hello there, I'm Nurse Thornton. Are you checking in, sir? Or just here for a tour?" The nurse placed a slick brochure in JB's hand. When he stared at it blank-faced, she gestured to Will. "Is this your son?"

JB sprang to his feet, quick to flash his badge, and Will bit the inside of his cheek to keep from laughing.

"Ma'am, I'll have you know I'm still on the good side of sixty. I don't even qualify for the senior discount at the Hickory Pit. And believe me, I plan to take full advantage of that ten percent when the time comes."

"Please accept my apology. I just assumed—well, we don't get too many detectives around here. One of our residents is convinced he's a Russian spy, though. Doesn't speak a lick of Russian, but he sure is good at hiding his roommate's dentures."

"Sounds like an interesting fellow," JB said. "By any chance, is his name Max Grimaldi?"

"Grimmy, you mean?"

"If you say so."

"No. Grimmy doesn't have a roommate. He didn't get along so well with the last one. Let's just say there was an unfortunate incident in the dining hall involving a walker and some mashed potatoes. Since then, Grimmy eats all his meals alone. He hasn't had any visitors either. Not after his daughter, Caroline, moved to the East Coast."

"How long ago was that?" Will asked.

"Ten years, give or take. Unlike a lot of our patients, Grimmy's got a sharp mind. But sometimes forgetting can be merciful." *Amen to that,* Will thought, wishing he could take a blowtorch to some of his own memories.

"So, it sounds like he's a credible witness?"

"Credible but not exactly cooperative. He can be a real handful." Though they were completely alone, Nurse Thornton lowered her voice. "Just between you and me, don't sit too close. When he gets mad, he's been known to bite."

As they followed her inside, Will smacked JB on the shoulder and fought off a smirk. "Sounds just like you, *Dad.*"

Max Grimaldi's bright pink gripper socks poked out the bottom end of his bedsheet, his wiggling feet the only part of him that didn't look unhappy. His hands were clenched at his sides and the crepe paper skin draped over his arm bones resembled the surface of a distant planet. He had grunted and grumbled through most of Nurse Thornton's introductions. But, after she'd wished them luck and left them alone, he turned to them with his rheumy blue eyes, and waited, curious enough not to send them away.

JB took the plush sofa by the window, leaving Will the folding chair nearest the bed. He slid it out of Grimaldi's reach before sitting down. Better safe than sorry. "Mr. Grimaldi—"

"Everybody here calls me Grimmy."

"Grimmy it is then. We need to ask you some questions about the cabin you owned a while back in Fog Harbor. Do you remember it?"

Grimaldi scrunched his face in confusion and scratched the top of his head where only a wisp of white hair remained. "Fog Harbor? Where's that?"

Will suppressed a groan. "Uh…"

"*Gotcha.* Of course I remember. This old noggin is a steel trap. But I'm not sure how I can help ya. I sold that place a while ago."

"According to property records, it was 1993."

"Sounds about right. I had to dump the place when my production company, Obscura, went bankrupt. We just couldn't compete against those blockbusters with their big name actors and silly plot lines. Who wants to see a snarky brat fend for himself at Christmas?"

JB chuckled. "Apparently, a lot of people. They made a sequel."

"Sure did. It came out the year before Obscura went under."

"You ever think maybe *Obscura* wasn't the best choice for a studio name?"

Will cut his eyes at JB. They needed to keep Grimaldi happy to get him talking. "It's named after the Camera Obscura, right? Over by Ocean Beach in San Francisco?"

"That's right. I grew up near there. Always loved that place. There's something a little creepy about it. You know, I made my first horror flick there. Shot it on a Kodak Instamatic." Grimaldi looked off toward the curtained window, his gaze frozen for a moment, caught in the amber of the past. "But, you got me curious now. Why would you two come all the way up here to ask me about a place I haven't owned since Bill Clinton took office?"

"Did you ever let anyone stay at the cabin? A girl, maybe?"

"Is this about those trumped-up charges that no-good hussy Brenda filed against me? Those never stuck. The judge knew she was lying when she didn't show up to court."

"You mean, the forcible confinement charges?" Kidnapping and assault and battery too. But Will knew that if he said too much, it would shut Grimaldi up tighter than a clam shell.

"Kidnapping, my ass. Hell, is it a crime to pick up a lady of the night? Take her somewhere special? I give her an opportunity like that, and how does she repay me? She owed me a thanks for getting her off the streets and giving her a decent meal. Most guys are just wham, bam, thank you, ma'am. Am I right?"

Will spoke fast, before JB could open his mouth and put his foot in it, as usual. "So, you brought this lady of the night to the cabin?"

"She agreed to it."

"To *all* of it?"

"Every last bit. I'd even say enjoyed it. Right up until I refused to pay her double. That's extortion, if you ask me. She should've been the one spending the night in jail. Anyway, when it came time for court, the cops couldn't locate her. Typical broad. She'd told a whopper, and she had to save face."

Will nodded, as if he agreed. Sometimes you had to trade your soul for answers. "Did you use the cabin often?"

"I rarely went there myself. Mostly used it for storage. My ex-wife didn't like me keeping my props in the garage. Fake blood, monster masks, replica chainsaws. I can't say I blame her."

"Why Fog Harbor? It's a pretty long drive from San Francisco."

"One word, Detective. *Atmosphere.* I'd been hoping to use the place as a movie set. Plus, the real estate was dirt cheap. The San Francisco views without the jacked-up prices. That's why I retired here in Brookings."

Will produced the photographs of Jane Doe's makeshift coffin. "Do you recognize this?"

Grimaldi fumbled for his glasses on the nightstand, positioned them atop his hook nose. He shuffled through the photos, shaking his head in astonishment. "Well, I'll be damned. *Chained.* This must be about that hooker then. *Brenda.* Did she get herself killed and stuffed in a barrel or something?"

"Excuse me?" Will swallowed hard, tempering the urge to cuff the old guy right then and there. "Did you say *chained?*"

"That was the name of the only flick we ever filmed up at the cabin. Real gritty stuff. I wrote the script myself. Employed a couple of wannabe actors, Brenda included, and shot the whole thing in one day."

"Funny. We didn't run across that one in your catalog. Did we, partner?"

JB shook his head. "I was partial to *Cheerleader Massacre* myself."

"That's because we never released it. After Brenda made a big stink, my attorney told me it would be best if I destroyed the copies."

"When did you shoot the film?" Will asked.

Grimaldi tapped the side of his head, pondering it. "Summer of '85. July, I believe."

"Summer of '85." Will repeated Grimaldi's words, giving JB a pointed look. "And what was the premise?"

"Husband has affair with secretary. Wife finds out and chains her in the basement." Grimaldi grinned, revealing a fence of broken teeth. "I've got the only copy marinating in a box in my closet if you boys want to crack her open and take a look."

Will inserted the unmarked tape and powered up the ancient VCR Nurse Thornton had lugged in from the day room. He drew the curtains and shut the lights, plunging the room into darkness. Behind him, Grimaldi's eyes widened, his limbs stiffened with excitement.

"Haven't watched this one in about twenty years. Not to sound like a braggart, but it was my best work. It was raw and unfiltered. Before I got too busy trying to pander to the masses."

As the title credits rolled in bold, red letters, JB leaned in Will's direction. "I'm getting a craving for popcorn. Extra butter."

Grimaldi shushed him, pointing his bony finger at the screen. "It's starting."

CHAINED

Produced by Obscura Studios, 1985

Starring:

Victoria Ratcliffe as … the Vengeful Wife

Brenda Samson as … the Tortured Lover

Donald Eggerton as … the Unfaithful Husband

The cabin's dirt basement came into view. The barrel pushed against the wall of the room, barely visible behind a stack of wooden crates.

Will pressed pause. "When you sold the place, what happened to your props? To the barrel?"

Grimaldi gave a beleaguered sigh. "I told the movers to pack up anything of value, things I could resell to offset my losses. The rest they could trash or take for themselves. It wasn't worth the time or effort to ship it back. I assume it got tossed or left behind."

"As far as you can remember, was the barrel empty?"

"I can't say I ever looked. But I moved it in myself. Now, can you let a man enjoy his own genius?"

When Will pressed play, the camera began a slow and steady creep, homing in on a shadowy back corner where a girl struggled against the chains on her wrists, straining the wall brackets. Her torn clothing hung loose from her thin frame. Her brown hair framed a face contorted in terror. The dissonant chords of the soundtrack ratcheted to a high-pitched screech that turned Will's blood cold.

"That's Brenda," Grimaldi whispered, and then, as another female entered the shot and lorded over Brenda with a look of sheer delight, "and Victoria Ratcliffe. Ain't she a natural?"

From behind her back, Victoria raised a leather whip and brought it down hard against Brenda's shoulders. Brenda collapsed to the dirt and turned her watery green eyes to the camera, pleading, but the woman struck her again. A few more lashes, and a red stain seeped through Brenda's shirt.

"What the—" JB muttered. "Is that real?"

"It looks real, doesn't it?" Grimaldi beamed with pride. "Fake blood packets. All part of the illusion."

Will pressed pause, freezing Victoria mid-strike. "Mr. Grimaldi, would you mind if we had a closer look at this back at the station? We'll return it to you as soon as we're able."

Grimaldi narrowed his eyes. "I'd rather you didn't. We haven't even gotten to the good part."

"Can't wait to see that," JB deadpanned.

"Are you insulting my work?" snarled Grimaldi.

"Not at all." Will intervened before JB earned himself a tetanus shot. "We're working a case. We need your help. This video could be important evidence."

"Then it'll cost you."

"We can get a warrant."

Grimaldi shrugged. "Suit yourself. But I'm a forgetful old man. Always misplacing things. The tape might come up missing by the time you get back here."

"How much?" JB asked.

"Three bags of Swedish fish from the gift shop in the lobby."

JB nudged Will. "What are you waitin' for, City Boy? Pay the man."

CHAPTER TEN

A short while later, Will waved to JB from the tiny window of the old twin-engine Cessna—Fog Harbor PD's fanciest toy—as the plane took flight for San Francisco, where Will hoped he'd get some answers from Chuck Winters. He fought off a smile as his partner flashed his middle finger, then blew him a kiss, then gradually diminished until he was just an ant on the runway.

Will turned from the window, the rippled blue canvas of the ocean beneath him, and retrieved the case folder from his bag. He went straight to the photos, tucked inside the evidence envelope. He'd all but memorized them since this morning, when the lab had processed the Nikon, developed the film roll, and delivered it to his desk. Still, when he tore into it, his heart sank again, as he flipped through the mostly blank images.

The victim had only taken six photographs. He laid them out in order on the empty seat next to him, studying each one and letting them speak to him, as clear and urgent as her voice from the grave.

The first, a bedroom Will recognized as similar to his own. The Weatherby cabin resembled all the others on Wolver Hollow Road, with its high ceilings and exposed redwood beams. The subject of the photograph, a handful of wildflowers stuck inside a pickle jar on the windowsill.

The next, a man. A bad man. Even if the second set of prints on the camera hadn't revealed him to be Chuck Winters, career criminal, Will would've seen it in the sharp glint of his blue eyes, in the knife's blade of his broad smile as he leered at the girl behind the lens from the cabin's front porch step, his meaty hand gripping the banister.

He skimmed over the other photos and set them aside; useless snapshots, dark and oddly angled, of storm clouds gathering in a bruised sky; a bee perched on a windowsill; a chest of drawers squatting in the corner of the bedroom with a few items—a paperback novel, a tube of lipstick, and a homemade doll with strange button eyes—scattered haphazard on top.

Last, a blurred image. Indiscernible, but it chilled him just the same. With its violent motion, its vibrant colors. Will could make out a hand reaching toward the camera. A flat palm, terrifying in its whiteness, the fingers stretched, long and talon-like, by a trick of the camera. The arm covered by the sleeve of a dark jacket. A patch of color on the shoulder, distorted. Another burst of color on the wall behind.

Earlier, JB had taken one look at the photos and the fingerprints on the camera and pronounced the case solved. Chuck Winters, guilty. Another notch on his imaginary Detective of the Year belt.

Unconvinced, Will sorted through the rest of the folder, including Winters' mug shot, taken in 1980, just before he'd served half of an eight-year sentence for rape. Then, he reshuffled the photographs, losing Winters and his shit-eating grin somewhere in the middle. JB had a point, but Will's cop clairvoyance—that wicked sixth sense he'd inherited from his father, Henry—had never let him down.

On top of the stack, he placed the last photograph Jane Doe had taken. He traced the fingers, thin and bony as twigs, certain of one thing: that hand did not belong to Chuck Winters.

As Will tossed his overnight bag in the trunk of the rental car, his cell buzzed in his pocket. He groaned at the number on the screen. Mainly because it didn't belong to Olivia. He'd missed a call from her in the air, and she hadn't left a message.

"Hey, JB. What's up?"

"Clearly not you. Looks like you beat the odds for a safe landing."

"Sorry to disappoint." Will opened the door and positioned himself behind the wheel, already feeling out of kilter; back here in San Francisco, his personal ground zero, having to answer to his ex, Amy Bishop. Homicide Inspector Amy Bishop, no less. "Any news? Got an ID on our victim yet?"

"Not yet. But I have been doing some first-class detective work. Prepare to have your mind blown, City Boy."

Will shook his head, catching his own tired eyes in the rearview mirror.

"I canvassed your neighborhood. As you'd expect some thirty years later, nobody knows a goddamned thing. And I watched the rest of Grimaldi's little home movie. That guy is one sick puppy. I tell ya, I could barely keep down my kale chips. Do you really think that blood was fake?"

Remembering the way Brenda had cried out in pain, he certainly hoped so. "The police report didn't mention any serious injuries related to the kidnapping, but we need to find out. Either way, Grimaldi's a suspect."

"I still like Winters for it though."

"Really? Don't you think Brenda could be our Jane Doe?" Even as he said it, Will wasn't convinced. He'd pegged Grimaldi as a narcissist, but not a dummy. If the old man had killed Brenda, he would've left that tape buried in a box until they put him six feet under.

"I could see how a lesser detective might think that. But, I did a deep dive in Winters' file. It takes a sharp eye, an *experienced* eye to spot—"

"Just spit it out already."

JB whistled through his teeth. "Alright, alright. Guess you haven't talked to Oliv—"

"No, I haven't." Will suppressed a growl.

"Sheesh, somebody's in a mood. Just check your email, City Boy. And turn that frown upside down. Research says you look smarter when you smile."

Grumbling, Will hung up the phone.

Smarter when you smile, my ass.

He pressed a few keys on his cell and opened JB's message, clicking on the attached arrest report.

FOG HARBOR POLICE DEPARTMENT
ARREST REPORT

NAME: Charles "Chuck" Winters
ADDRESS: Unknown
DOB: 2/3/60   AGE: 26   SEX: M   RACE: CAUCASIAN
ARRESTING OFFICER: JOHN McWATERS
INCIDENT TYPE: TRESPASSING; BURGLARY

NARRATIVE:

AT 10:30 A.M. ON MARCH 13, 1986, CHARLES "CHUCK" WINTERS WAS PLACED UNDER ARREST AT 246 WOLVER HOLLOW ROAD ON SUSPICION OF TRESPASSING AND BURGLARY.

ON THE ABOVE TIME AND DATE, I WAS ON UNIFORMED DUTY IN A MARKED PATROL CAR, ASSIGNED TO WEST FOG HARBOR. AT THAT TIME, I RECEIVED AN ECC BROADCAST FOR A POSSIBLE BURGLARY IN PROGRESS AT A CABIN ON WOLVER HOLLOW ROAD.

THE CALLER, MARGARET ROLLINS, MET ME AT THE FRONT ENTRANCE OF THE RESIDENCE. SHE REPORTED THAT SHE RETURNED TO HER VACATION PROPERTY AFTER OBSERVING UNUSUAL ACTIVITY ON HER ELECTRIC BILL. UPON ARRIVAL, SHE DISCOVERED WINTERS NAPPING IN HER BED.

I ENTERED THE PREMISES AND FOUND THE SUSPECT SLEEP-ING, AS ROLLINS HAD DESCRIBED. I PLACED HIM UNDER ARREST WITHOUT INCIDENT. WINTERS WAS A PAROLEE-AT-LARGE AT THE TIME OF THE OFFENSE.

SEVERAL ITEMS WERE LATER DETERMINED TO BE MISSING FROM THE HOME, INCLUDING THREE BOTTLES OF WINE, SEVERAL ITEMS OF WOMEN'S CLOTHING, A FAUX RUBY RING, A MAGNAVOX VCR, A NIKON CAMERA, AND CAMERA ACCESSORIES. THE ITEMS WERE VALUED AT $2000.

CHAPTER ELEVEN

After leaving the bank, Olivia and Emily had parted ways, with Em rushing off to her afternoon class and Olivia returning to Valley View to collect the remaining artifacts of her father's life. The gray walls of the prison entrance closed in around her, and her lungs pinched shut as she examined the contents of the prison-issued plastic bag. A single tattered photograph of her, Emily, and their mother, taken years ago, before her father had transferred from Crescent Bay State Prison. Her father's wedding ring, the simple gold band he'd worn even after Mom had died two years back. His Narcotics Anonymous booklet, highlighted and dog-eared. And a sketchbook, nearly full with lifelike pencil drawings that she couldn't wait to show Em, though a part of her also dreaded it.

Olivia cradled the bag against her chest like a shield of armor and plowed through the exit door, straight into Warden Ochoa. Her grip loosened, and the bag dropped to her feet.

As she collected it, the stunned warden blinked at her. "Doctor Rockwell, are you alright?"

"Fine. Just a little queasy."

"I can imagine. This place will do that to you. Even on a good day. Again, please accept my sympathies for your loss." Warden Ochoa brushed past her, straightening her suit jacket as she walked.

"Wait. I was hoping to get a word with you."

"I'm sorry. I'm running late for a meeting. Get in touch with my secretary. She'll pencil you in."

Olivia's fists tightened at her sides, squeezing the bag in a stranglehold. "I want to read the incident report."

Warden Ochoa turned to her. "I'm afraid that's not possible. Not until we finish our inquiry."

"Then, I'd like to see the video. Surely there are cameras on that hallway. At least, let me visit the holding cell where it happened. Or talk with the guards who were on duty. How about Officer Boon? He was the one who cut him down."

"Also not possible. Working at a prison yourself, I'm sure you understand protocol."

"Protocol?" Olivia reeled back as if she'd been slapped. "You mean, like checking a cell for safety hazards before locking an inmate inside? Or not leaving an inmate unsupervised?"

"I understand your concern, and I assure you we are looking into those issues." Warden Ochoa reached for the entry door, already signaling to the guard to buzz her through.

Olivia told herself to let it go. But her father's eyes, smiling at her from that old photograph, wouldn't let her. "You're right. I do work at a prison. I know how to recognize bureaucratic BS. And I can certainly tell when I'm getting the runaround. Which makes me wonder if you had anything to do with—"

"I think what Doctor Rockwell means to say is that she understands what a difficult job you have and would be grateful to be kept up to date on the investigation."

The familiar know-it-all voice came from behind her. As Olivia turned to meet its source, she didn't know whether to knee him in the groin or collapse into his arms.

CHAPTER TWELVE

"And who are you, exactly?" Warden Ochoa's voice didn't ask. It demanded. She bore little resemblance to her employee picture on the prison website—her frown lines deeper, her eyes less forgiving—but Will supposed working in a place with iron bars could do that to a person; harden them from the inside out. He wondered if his brother still looked the same, living behind these stone walls for the last two years.

"Detective Will Decker, Fog Harbor Homicide. I believe Warden Blevins told you I'd be stopping by."

When the warden's scowl softened at his smile, Will made a mental note to thank JB.

"Oh, yes. Detective Decker. Funny, I pictured you differently. Not quite so…"

"Pushy?" Olivia hissed.

Warden Ochoa seemed not to hear her, remaining oblivious to Olivia's side-eye as she leaned in conspiratorially. "It's just that most cops who pass through here are not *nearly* as friendly."

Will directed his smirk at Olivia as he answered the warden. "You catch more flies with honey, I've heard."

Olivia groaned, stalking away from them toward the parking lot. When he realized what she carried, he excused himself from the warden for a moment and took off after her, wishing she would've just kicked him below the belt instead.

"Hey, hold up."

She spun around, her knuckles whitening as she gripped the bag. He thought of reaching for her hand but her clipped tone cut him off at the knees. "What are you doing here?"

"I've been trying to get ahold of you. We found a body in a barrel in the cabin next door to mine. I'm hoping to talk to the guy who left his prints behind."

"And he's in Valley View?"

"No, he's at a halfway house downtown. I'm here about my brother." Will hung his head, spoke to the pavement. When he peeked up, she glared at him like he'd committed a crime. "Did I do something wrong?"

"Aside from you waltzing in here with your *friendliness* and butting into my private conversation with the warden?"

"It looked like you needed a little help. Charming wardens is obviously not your forte."

"Well, I didn't ask for your assistance." In the silence, he caught a glimpse of sadness behind the walls she'd put up around herself.

"Ben called me. He told me about your dad. I'm really sorry." His brother's revelation—*They got to him. I don't know how. But he's dead*—bit at the back of his brain, derailing his focus. "We should probably go somewhere private to talk."

She paused briefly, before she rolled her eyes, dismissing him. Then, she turned tail, losing no time covering the expansive parking lot and leaving him trailing behind.

"Am I missing something here?"

The click of her heels against the pavement gave him his answer. A definitive *yes* that stopped him cold.

"Are you coming?" she called to him, hand on hip.

"I didn't realize I was invited."

As Will jogged toward her car, Olivia retrieved something inside it. She thrust an envelope at him, smacking it against his chest. "Go on. Open it."

"Is something in there gonna bite me?"

She cocked her head at him.

"Just checking."

Will slid his hand into the envelope, his thoughts spinning as he withdrew a stack of SFPD Confidential Informant expense vouchers. He'd rarely used them himself. He kept most of his CIs off the books and paid them in whatever currency they valued most—cash from his own pocket, food, a hot shower, or a clean bed.

"What are these?"

"It turns out my dad was an informant for SFPD. But look who signed off on the payments."

Will scanned the first receipt, until he located the signature line. He gaped at it, as if it really had bitten him. Two poisonous fangs straight through the heart.

CHAPTER THIRTEEN

Deck's mouth hung open, much the way Olivia's had, and she felt stupid for assuming he'd already known about his father's connection to hers. Stupid for not trusting him. For acting so childish. She should've just phoned him that morning, the moment they'd left the bank, and let him talk some sense into her.

"So you didn't know about it then?" she asked.

"No. Of course not. I haven't talked to my dad since Ben's trial. And anyway, he never would've told me something like this. Besides, these are old. Really old."

Olivia leaned against the car, feeling lightheaded again. "I just figured you knew. That maybe you'd asked me to have my dad look after Ben because of it."

She could still picture Deck fighting his tears when he'd come to her back in December. First, to tell her the Oaktown Boys had threatened him. And then, to ask her for a favor. To tell her father to protect his brother from the gang.

"I promise you, I had no idea. I'm the detective with a dead body in the basement of the house next door to his, remember?"

"True." She attempted a laugh. "You are pretty clueless. It sounds like we're getting to the real reason you came to San Francisco. Go ahead. Admit it. You want me to look at the case file."

Truth, she wished she could snatch the file from him right there, open it up and get lost in someone else's pain for a while. Every last grisly bit of it. Sometimes it felt selfish, being a forensic psychologist, because lately, losing herself in the misery of others had become as necessary as breathing.

Deck held up his hands in mock surrender. "You got me. I do want your help. But I need to talk to the warden about Ben. I came to Valley View to get him the hell out of here."

Olivia hunkered down in the driver's seat of her idling rental car and studied the case file Deck had left with her. She'd opened it carefully, sifting through the evidence and leads Deck and JB had collected so far from the scene at 248 Wolver Hollow Road. More than once, she'd paused to study the photographs taken on the camera found with the body. The last one transfixed her. Especially when she closed her eyes and imagined it from that poor young girl's perspective. The final picture she'd snapped, a blur. Still, that palm reaching out to block the camera made an emphatic statement about her subject. Whoever had been there, pinned by her gaze and the lens of the Nikon, had been desperate to remain unseen.

As riveting as she found the photographs, Olivia's eyes kept drifting to the prison entrance where Deck had disappeared at least fifteen minutes ago. After he'd told her about Ben's panicked call, she'd insisted he track down Warden Ochoa immediately. Partly, she'd needed time to think, to let the truth settle into her bones: her father hadn't killed himself. Warden Ochoa's evasiveness had convinced her of that. And it ached in a way she'd never expected. Like a hole in the center of her chest, punched clean through.

She sorted the photos again, this time with a different focus. The girl behind the camera, rather than the subjects she'd captured with it. Jane Doe had appreciated the wonder and beauty of simple things; a bouquet of poppies and yellow violets in a makeshift vase, a cluster of clouds just before the rain. Even the photograph of hardened ex-con, Chuck Winters, cast him in a lovely light. Somehow the girl had coaxed a genuine smile from him, the kind that reached his eyes, which more than unnerved Olivia. But what struck her most about Jane Doe's photos was an unusual absence. Most teenage girls, no matter the generation, preferred people as the subjects of their snapshots. Jane Doe had photographed no one but Chuck. By chance or by choice, she'd been completely alone in Fog Harbor until—Olivia glimpsed the last photo once more, suppressing a chill. That slender hand didn't belong to Chuck.

"Who are you, Jane Doe?" A flash of the girl's mummified face, her hollow eyes in pictures of a different kind—Chet's autopsy photographs. "How did you end up dead?"

CHAPTER FOURTEEN

Will waited until he cleared the prison control booth to curse. If he'd had a rock, he would've hurled it back at the bullseye center of the Valley View entrance door, just to watch it crack.

He hurried across the parking lot, flung open the passenger door of Olivia's car and dumped himself inside.

"I'm guessing you're not as good at charming wardens as you thought, Detective."

Will forced a grin, knowing Olivia was just trying to make him feel better. "Warden Ochoa said she couldn't help me. That I'd have to go through the official channels like everyone else. File a hardship request and hope for the best with the classification committee."

"Are you serious?"

His shoulders lifted in a sad shrug.

"Well, that settles it. I don't trust her. She's just as corrupt as Warden Blevins."

"You're probably right. You know, Blevins told me they worked together at San Quentin." Will smacked the glove box half-heartedly, the last remnants of his anger turning to guilt. "If anything happens to Ben…"

"It's not your fault."

"I wish I could believe that. But he's sitting in that prison cell because of me."

Olivia shifted in her seat, tucking one knee beneath her and facing him head on. He wondered what she saw in his face that made her own eyes go glassy. "Don't make me go full therapist on you."

"I might be in need of a session."

She looked at him sternly, placing both of her hands on the forearm he'd rested on the console. He didn't dare move. "Ben is in that cell because of the decisions *he* made. You can't take that on. If you're at fault, then so am I. I never told anyone about Termite being at the scene of the murder that put my dad away. I let the cops believe my dad's story."

Olivia hadn't even confided in Will until recently, after one too many beers at the Hickory Pit. "Yeah. But you were eight."

"And you are an officer of the law. You swore an oath to do the right thing."

"The *right* thing. I thought I knew what that was. But how could the right thing end up so wrong?"

Olivia squeezed his arm. She drew him to her with those green eyes, the soft curve of her lips; pulled him straight into her gravitational field again, where he lost all common sense. No use fighting it, he leaned toward her.

She cleared her throat and returned her hands to the folder on her lap, sending him crashing back to earth. "I looked through the case file. I agree that those photos are the key."

Still reeling, he managed to nod, while she produced the first snapshot and pointed to the pickle jar vase. "Poppies bloom in Northern California in early spring. Same for the yellow violets."

"Hmph." He hadn't thought of that, but he didn't want to give her the satisfaction of admitting it. Not after he'd just embarrassed himself. "Any ideas about that last photo?"

"It's so out of place with the others. These are all understated. Like she's a quiet observer." She flipped through the stack to the end, her voice darkening. "But this one. It's jarring. It's loud. It's angry."

He didn't disagree. "So, what next? Let me guess, you want to go visit my father in Bernal Heights, to ask about those Confidential Informant receipts."

Olivia passed the folder to Will and buckled her seatbelt, its definitive click the only answer he needed. "If you're okay with it…"

He wouldn't back out now, even if he wanted to. "It's long overdue. But we should take your car, so I can't chicken out."

With a sympathetic smile, she steered them toward the tower, where he'd deposited his service weapon. "What about your case?" she asked.

"It can wait. I'll see Winters after. Besides, I'm counting on you to break it wide open."

"Should we have called first?" Olivia sounded as uncertain as Will felt. But he already had one foot out of the car door.

"It's like ripping off a Band-Aid. Best to get it over with."

She tucked the envelope full of receipts under her arm and followed him up a set of stairs which led from the sidewalk to the tiny patch of weeds that passed for a yard in San Francisco. A lawn chair took up most of the real estate, its thatched bottom sagging with age. Beneath it, a few beer bottles had been turned upside down and stuck into the earth. They leaned sideways like the markers in an old graveyard.

Will's eyes lingered there but he didn't slow down. They'd come here to ask her questions, but there were answers he needed as well.

He raised his fist to the door and summoned his past with three loud knocks.

CHAPTER FIFTEEN

The last time Will had stood on this porch there'd been a welcome mat. There'd been ferns in the planters and a fresh coat of yellow paint on the stucco. Grass, not beer bottles, growing in the front yard where his dog was buried.

"What the hell are you doing here?" Henry Decker glared at them from behind the screen door, the butt of a gun protruding from the waistband of his plaid pajama bottoms. Will wished he could hide, the way he and Petey had always ducked behind Ben.

"Nice to see you too, Dad."

"I thought I made it clear you aren't welcome here." He opened the door anyway, just wide enough for Will to take in the sour smell of him. To spot the towering stack of newspapers by the recliner. To hear the drone of a police scanner, dispassionately delivering the bad news his father could never get enough of.

"Actually, what you said was, 'You're a disgrace to the badge, son. You're not a Decker anymore.'" Will pointed to the shiny detective badge he'd clipped onto his waistband. It glinted in the sunlight. "Funny, I still have this. And you're still pickled drunk."

His father scoffed, his eyes darting to the watch on Will's wrist. The one his dad had given him the day Will had taken his oath. "That badge is nothin' more than a participation trophy. Like that watch I gave you. Just because you have it don't mean you deserve it. I heard you let that serial killer, Devere, escape. You ever get wind of me letting any bad guys get away?"

"Congratulations. You were all about the job, and you lost your family in the process. Now look at you."

"Is that why you came then? To judge me? You wait. Give it another thirty years. You'll turn out just like your old man."

Will burned from the inside out, his blood forged like steel and weighting him to the spot. He wanted to run, but he couldn't. Just stood there like a tin man, daring himself to say something he'd really regret.

Olivia stepped up from behind him, pushing him aside. "I need to talk to you about Martin Reilly."

"And just who do you think you—"

She silenced him, pointing to his signature on the expense voucher in her hand. "I'm Olivia Rockwell, Martin Reilly's daughter. Judging by these receipts, he worked for you as a CI for at least two years. I think you owe me a conversation."

"Do I now?" Age had only improved his father's poker face. "I'm sixty-two years old. Forty years on the force, I had my fair share of informants. My memory ain't what it used to be. And I don't owe nobody a goddamned thing."

"He was a member of the Oaktown Boys. They called him Mad Dog."

"Mad Dog, huh? Wasn't he the one who got busted up at the Double Rock for slicin' up that hooker?"

Olivia nodded, impressing Will with a poker face of her own. Probably something they'd taught her in shrink school.

"And you say he worked as my informant, huh? Surprised he's lasted this long in the joint."

Will decided right then he'd sooner eat his gun than turn out like his dad. The brown eyes he had passed on to all three of his boys had gone cold as marbles. His chest, empty as a steel drum. Will imagined his father's heart shriveled inside it like a raisin. He regretted bringing Olivia here, but she barreled on, determined as ever.

"Could you tell me what sort of information my father might have given you? Was it about the gang?"

"They call 'em CIs for a reason, honey. It's confidential. You get it? Even if I could remember, I wouldn't tell you. And I certainly wouldn't tell that rat fink. What's this all about, anyway?"

Will recoiled, absorbing his father's blow like a jab to the face. *Rat fink.* At least he knew where he stood. Beneath the steel toe of his father's boot, same as ever.

"My dad kept these receipts in a safety deposit box for twenty-seven years, hidden from me and my mom and my sister. There must be some reason for that."

"Well, here's an idea. Why don't you just ask him?"

Olivia lowered her head, released a shaky breath. "I wish I could. He died yesterday in prison, serving time for a murder he didn't commit. They said it was a suicide."

"Let me guess. You don't believe it."

"I don't know what to believe. That's why I'm here. I'm sure you can understand wanting justice for someone you love. Even if that someone disappointed you."

Grumbling, Will's father waved them inside the door with strict instructions to *not go snoopin' around,* while he disappeared into the back. Will didn't move, a part of him still fearing the belt that had hung on a brass hook inside his parents' bedroom. But Olivia stepped into the hallway, surveying the wall Will's mother had hung floor-to-ceiling with family photographs, but was now peppered with faded, blank spaces. All evidence of Will's existence, gone. Same as Petey's. Only a few pictures of Ben remained.

Olivia looked back at Will with questioning eyes.

He's an asshole, Will mouthed. *I'm sorry.*

She kept his gaze, even as she called out to his father. "Is this you in your dress blues, Mr. Decker?"

His father surprised him, rounding the corner with a binder in his hand and a sheepish grin on his face. "That's the day we got married. My Virginia was always a sucker for a man in uniform. Now, have a look at this, will ya."

A pile of unopened mail tumbled to the hardwood as his father swept his hand across the console table to clear a space. "SFPD started a gang task force back in 1990. They put me in charge. I reckon that's why I recruited Mad Dog. If I recall, he was a heavy hitter back in those days."

"I can't imagine my dad breathing a word to the cops. He never met a law he didn't break. Or a cop he didn't run from."

His dad's hearty chuckle came as another surprise. "Everybody has a price. Back then, Oaktown was just makin' a name for themselves. There were a lot of power plays at the top. I still remember the day we arrested Chris Desoto. They called him Baby Face, on account of those cheeks he had, chubby as a newborn's. A numbskull name for a gangster, if you ask me."

As Will's father bent his balding head, busying himself turning the sheet protectors inside the binder, Will craned his neck to see into the living room. His dad still hadn't gotten rid of the patterned sofa they'd climbed on as kids. They'd used the cushions for fort-building and whacking each other senseless. They'd burned a hole in the arm, lighting up the cigars they'd snuck from their father's nightstand. And once, they'd left their mother there, sleeping, to play baseball at the park down the street, and come back to find her gone without a trace, their dog Max whining at the door.

Will shook his head, scattering the memories, sending them back down the hole where he'd banished them. He focused on the soothing, flat tone of the police scanner in the background. When he located the source of the sound—a laptop computer balanced on the sofa's giant arm—he took several surreptitious steps toward it, gaping in disbelief.

First, that a stubborn dinosaur like his father had learned to use the Internet. But mostly, at the screen itself, and the large block print, which read: **Now Playing: Fog Harbor Police**. Beside the computer on an index card, his father had printed a list of frequencies from several major cities in Northern California as well as tiny Fog Harbor.

"Found it!" His dad smacked the page with his palm, cracking the air like a starter pistol. Will's heart beat even faster. "You might be interested in this one."

San Francisco Post

"Oaktown Boys Gang Member Arrested in Brutal Slaying"

by Bobby Long

San Francisco police arrested Christopher "Baby Face" Desoto in the gang-related shooting of Jorge Pedron, who was gunned down outside his home in the Mission District. Desoto was known to police as the leader of the Oaktown Boys street gang, whose members have been linked to an increase in violent crime and drug trafficking in the Double Rock Projects in downtown San Francisco. Pedron was identified as a high-ranking member of the rival Los Diabolitos street gang.

Pedron's murder had remained unsolved for several months until detectives received a tip from a confidential informant identifying an eyewitness in the investigation, as well as the location of the murder weapon, a Smith and Wesson .38 Special Revolver, found in the air-conditioning vent of an abandoned building in the Tenderloin District.

The motive for the shooting remains under investigation but San Francisco Police Detective Henry Decker, who arrested Desoto early this morning, called the crime gang-related. "Since Desoto took over the Oaktown Boys, they've terrorized the Double Rock and started an all-out war with Los Diabolitos. We're lucky an informant came forward to help us get this monster off the streets before he hurt someone else."

CHAPTER SIXTEEN

Olivia snapped a photo of the *San Francisco Post* article with her cell phone. She kept her focus there, preferring it to the steely brown eyes of Henry Decker. "Was my father the informant?"

"Can't say I recall for certain." He tapped his head with his finger. "I told you this old thing doesn't work like it used to. But if he ratted out Desoto trying to claw his way to the top, he would've had a target on his back. Snitches get stitches, you know."

She winced at the sudden image of her father on the autopsy table. "If you think of anything…"

"I don't do much thinking these days. But if something pops up, I'll let you know."

Olivia saw the tension tightening Deck's shoulders as she followed him to the door. With his hand on the knob, he spun suddenly, glaring at his dad. "Why are you spying on me?"

"What the hell are you talkin' about?"

Deck pointed back toward the living room. "You don't want anything to do with me, but you've got Fog Harbor on your police scanner. Sounds like somebody can't get his story straight."

"Just waitin' for your next screw-up. I heard about that body you found in the barrel up there. Helluva thing. You ID the vic yet?"

Deck's jaw tensed. It seemed his father knew exactly where to aim and exactly when *not* to stop.

"That's what I thought. You know what I taught you. If you know the victim, you know the killer. You gotta figure out what a young pregnant girl was doing up there in the middle of nowhere. I'd start with the guy that knocked her up, if you can find him. Husbands, boyfriends, lovers. That's always a sure bet. But then, what do I know? You never did listen to me. Probably why you didn't last in the big city. Did ya hear Amy Bishop's got your job now? How's that feel?"

With a guttural groan, Deck pushed through the door, slamming it behind him so hard the pictures rattled on the wall.

"It's probably not my place to say this—" Olivia mustered the courage to turn around and face Henry Decker.

"Then don't." Two words spoken in a voice hard as nails. But a familiar pain softened his eyes.

She wouldn't look away again. "The only thing anger will get you is a lifetime of regret. Take it from someone who knows."

Olivia kept quiet as she drove away from the Decker house in Bernal Heights, taking her directions from the monotone voice of the GPS. At least it made the silence less awkward. Kept her attention on the road ahead of her, not lost in her thoughts, branching like paths in a maze. At the elusive center, Martin Reilly: Father, gang member, police informant.

Deck's eyes hadn't moved from the folder in his lap. He'd been reviewing the same police report for the last ten minutes, occasionally huffing out a frustrated breath.

Olivia risked a glance in his direction. "Do you want to talk about it?"

"About which part? Me storming out? The beer bottle garden? Him calling me a rat? Or the laptop police scanner tuned to Fog Harbor?"

"Isn't that a good thing? The scanner, I mean."

He cocked his head at her, unsmiling, as she made the final turn down the crowded Embarcadero, nearing Second Chance Halfway House, a high-rise building across the street from Pier 25. *Your destination will be on the right.*

"I mean it. He's checking up on you, giving you advice. Your dad still cares even if he doesn't show it."

"Didn't you hear him? He's just waiting for me to fail so he can rub it in. Did you forget his parting shot?"

The fire in Henry Decker's voice was impossible to forget. "Who's Amy?"

Another drawn-out sigh.

"That bad, huh?"

"The day after I testified, she chucked her engagement ring out the window. It fell into a storm drain, and I had to bribe a city worker to fish it out. So, you tell me."

"Ouch." Olivia smirked. "How many carats?"

"One and a half."

"She must've really hated you."

"Thanks," he deadpanned. "You sure do know how to make a guy feel better."

"I wasn't finished." She gazed at her own ringless finger, remembering the two-carat monstrosity her ex-husband, Erik, had bought her with his father's money. Too bad the vows he'd said after he'd slipped it on her finger had been worth less than cubic zirconia. "Amy is obviously not that smart. Or she would've kept the ring and pawned it like I did."

He raised his eyebrows, the clouds lifting from his face. "You're saying it could've been worse then?"

"At least you didn't catch her in a broom closet with a brides-maid." It was out of her mouth before she could stop it. The memory, too, untethered; Erik's mouth lingering near the neck of her bridesmaid. *Just helping pack up the gifts,* he'd said. As if that explained the lipstick on his collar, his zipper undone.

"True." Deck paused for a beat. "Though some lesser men might be into that."

Chuckling, Olivia pointed up ahead at the sign for Second Chance. Pulling into an open parking spot near the door, she felt a tiny spark of life inside her weary heart. At least she could help Deck find this poor girl's killer. "Ready to have a go at Winters?"

"I think you should wait in the car."

"Chief Flack made me a part of the team, remember?" Olivia's quick thinking in the Seaside Strangler case had earned her the chief's respect, along with a permanent spot as Fog Harbor PD's resident forensic psychologist.

"As a profiler. Not a cop. You'll have to leave Chuck Winters to me. I do the interviewing."

Olivia kept pace with Deck as he hurried toward the building on the corner. Second Chance Halfway House, halfway between prison and the free world. She couldn't argue with him. But she couldn't stay in the car either, alone with her thoughts. "Who said anything about interviewing?"

"Just reminding you, I'm the detective."

"Pretty hard to forget with that badge clipped to your belt. But it's the chip on your shoulder that really gives you away. Is that standard issue?"

He waited until they reached the door to level her with those brown eyes. "I thought you liked a man in uniform."

"What gave you that idea?" Technically, she'd never witnessed Deck in his dress blues, but that didn't mean she and her friend, Leah, hadn't scavenged the Internet after a few glasses of wine. They'd hit the jackpot with a photo from an SFPD fundraising gala a few years back. And now, Olivia had a name for the pretty brunette she'd seen on his arm: Amy.

"Two words: Graham Bauer."

Olivia groaned. But she suddenly realized she felt better. Human again.

With his hand on the door, Deck paused. "Seriously, though. Are you sure you're okay? I know it's been a rough couple of days."

"This helps."

"Distracting yourself with a case, huh? Maybe you are a cop, after all."

She didn't correct him. Didn't tell him *this* meant *him.*

Olivia took a seat in the empty lobby, which looked more like a run-down living room, watching as Deck disappeared inside the program office. She surveyed the selection of reading material on the water-stained coffee table and picked up a Narcotics Anonymous Booklet, just like the one her dad had kept in his cell. Flipping through the pages, she still felt shaken by the thought he'd been working for the cops.

A voice broke through her unease. "What is this about, anyway? I just saw my PO yesterday."

Chuck Winters looked like a shell of the man in his mug shot. His shoulders slumped, his head hung low and the prison tattoos that decorated most of his body were covered with long sleeves. But mostly, it was the way his eyes shifted warily, like he expected to be strip-searched, shoved against the wall and cuffed and carted back to the big house at any moment.

Mr. Guthrie, the house manager who'd greeted them at the door, offered him no comfort. "A detective wants to talk to you."

Chuck grimaced but went along anyway, trudging through the door and into the lion's den.

Olivia allowed thirty seconds to tick off her watch, just in case Chuck grew a backbone. Decided to flip a table and storm out, demanding to speak with an attorney. But she knew better. She'd counseled enough lifers to suspect Chuck would sit there and take whatever punishment Deck dished out. Just like her father had in front of the parole board. Twenty-seven years with a boot on his neck, and he'd finally fallen in line. Look where it got him.

Heavy-hearted, she got up and slipped down the hallway, leaving Chuck at Deck's mercy.

CHAPTER SEVENTEEN

"So, how long have you been out on parole?" Will lobbed an easy one over the plate, taking the time to study the man seated in front of him.

Chuck Winters couldn't fool him. He still had the worn look of a career criminal. With the warpaint he couldn't quite hide beneath his shirt. The chiseled frame he'd earned behind bars doing burpees and push-ups in his cell. Mostly, the way his eyes darted, guiltily, looking everywhere and nowhere, and certainly not at Will.

"Two months. But I still feel like the odd man out."

"You working?"

"Trying to. It's hard to find a job with a record like mine. When the boss finds out you're a convicted sex offender, your skills don't matter. You might as well call it a day. I swear, I'd have more luck if I was a straight-up serial killer."

Will didn't blink.

"It's no different out here than in prison, Detective. I'm the lowest man on the totem pole. The one nobody wants. I practically begged my way into Second Chance. And still, you saw how Mr. Guthrie looks at me. Like I'm a piece of dirt on his shoe."

Will had read Winters' file, and he couldn't say he disagreed. But that would get him absolutely nowhere. "Mr. Winters, I need your help on a case I'm working. I'd like to show you some photographs."

He laid out five of the six photos taken by the girl in the barrel, holding one back in the folder as his ace in the hole.

"Anything look familiar here?"

Winters briefly glanced at the photographs, but he didn't touch them. His hands stayed hidden beneath the table. "Should it?"

"You tell me. Look closer."

He took the pictures one by one into his meaty paws, holding them gingerly. As if Will had dipped them in cyanide.

"It's a house. Can't say I've ever seen it before."

Will nodded. Like he believed the guy. "You got arrested in 1986 for burglary, right? Your third felony strike."

"That's right. Three strikes and you're out. It's a helluva way to end up doing life in prison."

"Can you tell me about the burglary?"

"Not much to tell, really. I got released from Valley View on that rape charge a month prior. Went right back to my old ways, using coke and doing crime to support myself. After one dirty drug test, I got the hell out of San Francisco. Hitchhiked to Fog Harbor and scoped out this little cabin in the redwoods. A real peaceful spot. I figured nobody lived there. I watched the place for a few days and moved in. But then, I got cocky. I started using the electricity. Before you know it, I woke up staring down the barrel of a Glock, surrounded by the entire Fog Harbor police force."

"That must've been a shock. Did you associate with anyone in Fog Harbor? Any friends? Relatives?"

Winters scoffed. "Nah. I'm a lone wolf. Always have been."

"What about women?"

"Are you askin' if I reoffended? Because the answer is no. That case was a one-off. Like a crime of opportunity, you know? I broke into a house, high as a kite. I didn't know there was a woman at home. I don't even remember what happened, to tell you the truth."

"So, you didn't go to any bars in Fog Harbor? Pick up any women? A good-looking guy like you, I'm sure you had some offers."

"No. I already told you." Winters eyed the door, shifting restlessly in his seat.

"What if I said I think you're hiding something?"

"It wouldn't be the first time a cop didn't believe me. This is starting to feel a lot like an interrogation. Am I a suspect in some kind of crime?"

"Sounds to me like you've got a guilty conscience." Will reached inside his folder and played his ace. He set the last photo on the table and pushed it toward Winters. "Recognize this guy?"

Will had to give Winters some credit. The guy could keep a straight face. Emotionless, he stared at the picture of his younger self for so long Will wondered if he'd claim him. But finally, he spoke. "That's me. A lifetime ago. Where did you get that?"

"I'll ask the questions, alright? Who took the photo?"

Winters picked it up, a slight tremor in his hands. "Do I need a lawyer?"

"Why would you?"

"Because you're a homicide detective."

"How do you know that?"

Winters sighed, laying the photo on the table face down like he couldn't bear to look himself in the eyes either. "Ain't no other kind of detective who'd make the trek from Fog Harbor. Plus, I saw the story about the barrel on *Good Morning, San Francisco.* I figured it might be her."

Will waited, but Winters said no more, retreating inside himself. That was alright. Will would peel back the truth layer by layer. Right down to the rotten core. He'd stay here all day if he had to. "'Her'? So there was someone?"

"A girl staying at the cabin next door. A pregnant girl. She took that photo of me. But I didn't hurt her. I know how it looks, but I swear it. I barely knew her. Then, she up and disappeared a week or so before I got arrested. I just figured she went back home where she belonged. Maybe changed her mind about giving up the baby."

"This girl, do you remember her name?"

"She never would tell me. I thought she might be hiding out from someone. Her family or her good-for-nothing boyfriend. I got the impression she didn't want to be found."

"What *can* you tell me about her?"

"Like I said, I didn't know her that well. I was only there for two months or so. Blonde hair, average height. Probably seventeen or eighteen."

"Pretty?"

Winters groaned. "I know what you're gettin' at."

"Well?"

"Yeah. She was pretty. Pretty knocked up."

"You weren't attracted to her, then?"

The sweat beading on Winters' forehead, the flush creeping on his neck, spoke for him.

"Look, I was a twenty-three-year-old horndog, so yeah, I thought she was cute. But she had a boyfriend. She told me he didn't want the kid, but she wasn't sure what to do. She'd come up to Fog Harbor to figure it out."

"You sure do remember a lot about someone you didn't know that well." Will revealed another photograph. The faux ruby ring Chet had removed from the victim's finger.

"Recognize this?"

Winters shrugged.

"It belonged to Margaret Rollins. She reported it missing from the cabin where you were squatting. Guess where we found it?"

A hard swallow told Will that Winters understood he meant business. That this was his show. That he had the winning hand.

"On the ring finger of a dead girl," Will said.

CHAPTER EIGHTEEN

Chuck Winters' room resembled a prison cell. Small and sparse. Olivia had found it easily enough. A board hung on the wall in the hallway with the residents' last names and room numbers. Little magnetic circles to mark themselves in or out. Room 5 belonged to Chuck. He'd tried to make it his own with a stack of Jack Reacher crime thrillers and a gray bedspread. Who's the detective now, Deck?

Feeling smug, she rifled through the nightstand drawer, flipping through a bundle of pens and a stack of handwritten job applications. A dead giveaway for a man who'd been locked in a box for the better part of the twenty-first century, he'd left the same question blank on each one: *Have you ever been convicted of a felony?*

Closing the drawer, she turned her attention to a bag of toiletries at the foot of the bed but it revealed nothing out of the ordinary. The closet, too, gave no clues. The lone dress shirt with a missing button only made her sad. Somehow, it reminded her of her father. How she'd never given him credit for starting over. How hard it must've been. How lonely.

Those thoughts slowed her down, so she pushed them from her mind and pondered what she knew of Chuck. The profile she'd gleaned from his file. With the exception of the rape conviction in 1980, most of his arrests were property crimes—burglary, theft, shoplifting—and it seemed unlikely he would've stuck around if he'd killed someone in the cabin next door. Still, there was no denying he'd been on the victim's film roll. Even if thirty-five years had passed, the vestiges of twenty-three-year-old Chuck still lived in the sixty-year-old man who'd dragged his feet into the program office to meet Deck like he'd been anticipating the guillotine.

Olivia tried to imagine where Chuck might hide the traces of his real self. The self he'd learned to keep well-hidden. The definitive evidence of the kind of evil that would lead a man to stuff a girl in a barrel. A pregnant girl, at that.

She slipped her hand beneath the mattress, searched the light fixtures and the trash can. Even tugged on the threadbare carpet that didn't budge. All she had to show for it was a tattered *Hustler* magazine that had been folded and tucked along the bed frame.

Olivia sat on the bed, defeat weighing on her chest. She didn't want to give up, didn't want to leave empty-handed. It felt critical to get this one thing right. But she'd already been here too long.

Last resort, she opened the drawer again and plucked out the applications. She read through them again one by one—fast food, construction, janitorial—thinking again of her father. She'd never have the opportunity to see for herself if he'd really changed. To watch him have his own second chance outside of the prison gates. The unfairness of it cut deep.

Setting the papers aside, she searched the drawer for a false bottom. Instead, a purple marker shoved in the back caught her eye. Its vibrant, happy color seemed out of place among the cheap ballpoint pens. She plucked off the cap. Shocked, she pulled the contents from the otherwise empty tube. Unrolled it and gasped.

She'd found their Jane Doe.

Olivia ran down the hallway like a woman possessed, knocked once but didn't wait for an answer. Just burst into the program office, breathless.

Both men gawked at her, Deck's surprise quickly turning to exasperation. "What're you doing?"

"I need to talk to you."

"Right now?" he asked, through gritted teeth. "I'm in the middle of something."

"It's important."

Chuck's eyes volleyed between them and settled on Olivia's hands, widening at what she held there. What she'd found.

"Just let me finish up here. I need five minutes." When she didn't move, he raised his eyebrows, jerked his head toward the door. "Five. Minutes."

Olivia felt an inexplicable panic rise up in her throat. She smacked the table with the photograph she'd found, leaving it there, its edges curling in.

"You may want to ask him about this."

Pulling the door shut behind her, she collapsed against it. All she'd been through in the last two days swelling like the waves at Little Gull lighthouse, taking her feet from under her. When she reached the safety of the hallway bathroom and locked the door behind her, she finally, *finally* let herself cry.

CHAPTER NINETEEN

Will sat there for a moment, reeling. Olivia had really outdone herself this time. Barged right into the middle of his interrogation—when he'd explicitly asked her not to—and detonated a bomb. He didn't even want to imagine how she'd gotten the photograph. What laws she'd broken. What lines she'd crossed. The worst part, she'd seemed a little unhinged. Like grief had finally caught up with her, sunk its claws in, and shredded all her common sense.

"Care to explain this?" Will unrolled the bent photo paper. No matter how reckless she'd been, he looked at it with awe.

"Did that woman search my room? Is she even a cop?"

"That's the least of your worries." He pointed to the young girl, posing on the front steps of the same cabin where she'd been found dead. Her shy eyes avoided the camera, her hands resting on her very pregnant belly. "Right now, from where I'm sitting, you're looking like the prime suspect in my case. If I were you, I'd start talking. The truth this time."

"I told you the truth. I didn't know her that well."

"But you held onto her photograph for how long? *Thirty-something years?* I don't buy it. And neither will your PO." No quicker way to get to the real story than to remind a man on parole how easy it would be to send him back to the joint. Will might as well have pressed a knife to his jugular.

"Okay, okay. When I transferred to state prison, they shipped what little stuff I had on me to my cousin. I didn't even remember

I'd kept the photo until I got out. The truth is, she's the only gal who ever treated me like a person. I wanted to find her to say thanks. To see how she turned out. If she had the kid. And yeah, maybe ask her out, if she was single and the timing felt right. She told me she was from San Francisco, so I was gonna show her picture around. See if anybody recognized her."

"Do you have any other pictures of her?"

"I wish. She gave me that film roll the last time I saw her. I had it developed at the drug store after she went missing. It was mostly pictures of me and the house. She liked taking pictures of random shit. Typical girl, you know. That's the only one I saved."

"And this photo?" Will pulled out the last shot from the film they'd found in the Nikon, the blurred hand reaching to block the camera. "What do you make of it?"

Winters studied the image, inspecting it from all angles. "It ain't me. Looks like somebody who didn't want to be photographed. And…" He squinted, held the picture up in the light.

"And what?"

"Well, she never invited me inside the house. She said it didn't belong to her. That we could get in trouble. But, one time, I peeked through the front window and saw this painting above the fireplace. A bunch of nothin' willy-nilly on a canvas. I think they call it abstract art. These bright colors here, in the photo, remind me of that. 'Course, you can't really make anything out. It's all fuzzy."

Will made a mental note to have JB ask Grimaldi if he'd hung any artwork in the cabin.

"What about the camera? You stole that too, huh?"

Winters hung his head. But Will couldn't let himself feel sorry. Not now. Not when he had him on the ropes.

"So, you stole the ring and the camera. Both of which we exhumed from the barrel. Your photo is one of the last ones she took. And you admit you had a thing for her. That you looked in through the window. Maybe she caught you. Maybe you came on a little too strong. She told you to back off. You got angry, and you lost control. You didn't mean to do it. But you couldn't very well call the police. Not when you'd absconded from parole. Is that pretty much the way it happened?"

Will only half believed the story he'd just spouted. A guy on the run like Chuck Winters probably wouldn't have stuck around the neighborhood if he'd offed a pregnant girl. Will only had to convince the man of one thing: that he had the power to cuff him up right now and take away his hard-earned freedom.

"You can answer me here or back at the station."

"I didn't do anything."

"Let's go then. Get up."

Winters anchored himself to the chair, even as Will stood and lorded over him.

"I was a bonehead back then. A total idiot. The old me made a lot of stupid mistakes. Like taking the stuff from the cabin to impress her."

Will grabbed Winters by the arm, forced him to his feet. Reminded him what it felt like to be this close to a badge. "Give me one reason I shouldn't arrest you for her murder."

"I would never hurt Shelby!"

They regarded each other, as the name—now spoken aloud—drifted between them like a ghost.

CHAPTER TWENTY

Deck glowered as he exited Second Chance and stalked toward the car. Before he reached the passenger door, Olivia glanced up into the rearview mirror, certain the day's wreckage would be apparent on her face. Thankfully, she'd beaten her tears back into submission, even if her green eyes had dulled.

Deck dropped into the seat. Spoke to the glove box, his voice one-note. "Anything you want to say to me?"

Olivia knew exactly what he wanted. What he deserved. But she hadn't been all wrong. "You're welcome?"

"I'm sure I don't need to tell you that you crossed a line. You jeopardized a homicide investigation. Not to mention, snooping through an ex-con's room? It's dangerous. Those guys are on parole for a reason."

She offered him an olive branch. The best contrite smile she could manage. "I'm sorry."

He buckled his seatbelt with a sigh. "And thank you. He eventually gave up her first name. *Shelby.* And said she ran away from San Francisco. He claims that's all she told him."

"But you don't think he did it?"

"Do *you?*"

"Not likely. A guy like that, young and impulsive, he wouldn't have put so much effort into hiding the body. He would've dumped her and been out of there."

"Maybe. But where could he go? Besides, he knew she was a runaway. He probably figured no one was looking for her. That the body would never be found."

Olivia didn't have the strength to argue. "What now?"

"We need to get a firm ID on Shelby. I'll give JB a call, have him get a jump on searching our missing database before I head back tomorrow."

Olivia started the car, the rumble of the engine turning her stomach. They drove for a while in silence. Back up the Embarcadero, the road mostly deserted now in the twilight. "What do you think will happen to Chuck?"

"Winters? I can't arrest him, if that's what you mean."

"I know that. I just wondered, do you think he'll end up back in prison?" She saw her father's sky-blue eyes as she spoke.

Deck didn't answer right away. She liked that about him. That he took his time, even with her silly questions. "There are two kinds of people I encounter in this job. A few are monsters, like Drake Devere. The rest are just men who've made big mistakes. Winters didn't seem like a monster to me."

"That's pretty enlightened for a cop. Are you sure I'm not rubbing off on you?" She joked but his words soothed her soul. Still, she had to ask one more. "What about my dad? What kind of person was he?"

She'd never said it out loud before, but the words had weighed on her for years, heavy as stones. She'd seen her father in every patient she'd sat across from. Every murderer, every criminal, every gang member. And now, knowing he'd been an informant for the police, she understood him even less than she had before.

Deck lifted his hand to reach for hers. Stopped short. Returned his hand to his thigh. It disappointed her but she knew better than to do anything about it. This was how she wanted it. How she needed it. *Simple.* No strings and no complications.

"I could tell you what I think. But I'm pretty sure that's one of those questions you have to answer for yourself."

*

Twenty minutes later, Olivia parked alongside Deck's rental car outside Valley View State Prison. Still feeling melancholy, she suddenly wished she didn't have to leave him here in the dark lot. "So, any plans for tonight?"

"Drowning this day in ginger ale at Aces High nightclub."

"Aces High? Why does that sound familiar?" When his face darkened, she cursed herself for asking, remembering that the nightclub had been the site of the officer-involved shooting that had sent his brother, Ben, to prison. "Sorry, I—"

"It's okay. My other brother, Petey, still runs the place. It's a local cop hangout." Which probably was Deck's way of saying shrinks were not welcome. She could take a hint.

"So, we'll catch up tomorrow then."

After he'd exited the vehicle, he tossed the case folder on her seat. "Some light reading in case you can't sleep."

Olivia drove from the prison in a fog, replaying the day in her head. From Henry Decker to Chuck Winters and back again, she felt the weight of them pulling her under, fraying her nerves until she sped down the highway toward the San Francisco Art Institute, imagining all the dreadful things that happened in the world. All the dreadful things that could happen to little sisters in the big city.

When Olivia spotted Emily waving to her from a bench outside the entrance of the art institute, she felt relieved. She pulled over at the curb and waited for Em to toss her supplies and portfolio in the back seat next to the case folder Deck had insisted she keep.

"How was class?"

Emily crossed her arms over her chest, shook her head. "Spill, Liv. Why did you need to pick me up? I thought we were past this overprotective big sister thing."

Olivia shrugged, pointing to the glove box. "I picked up Dad's stuff this afternoon at the prison."

Em went straight for it, forgetting about her big sister shake-down—at least for now—and opened the plastic bag. "Is this a sketchbook?"

She flipped through the first few pages, beaming. But the tears came quick behind.

"I think we finally figured out where you got your artistic talent."

Emily sniffled, then smiled. "Remember that time Mom tried to paint a unicorn on my wall?"

"You mean, the rhinoceros?"

"The ugliest thing I ever saw."

They both laughed, Em wiping at her eyes, as she reached the final page in the sketchbook. "Look at this one. It's so elaborate."

Olivia leaned over, caught her breath. Her father had titled the drawing *In the Old Days* and signed his name in the right corner.

"That's the Double Rock, isn't it?" Emily pointed to the pencil-shaded building in the background. In the foreground, he'd drawn the faces of his past. Olivia recognized her mother, herself, Miss Pearl. Even Termite. Around the border, he'd added the intricate details, the pop of color that surprised her. A motorcycle, its tank painted green. A door in a haunting shade of blue. One of Miss Pearl's dolls, unmistakable with its yellow button eyes. Her father had captured it all, like a dream.

"Hand me that folder." Olivia reached over her shoulder to the back seat, her heart thwacking away at her rib cage.

"What's wrong?"

She didn't answer. Couldn't. Not yet. She opened the case file and removed the envelope with the photos, hurrying to find the right one. She spotted it, then. Just as she'd remembered.

Opened the magnifying app on her phone. Zoomed in.

A shiver zipped up her spine. As if a gust of wind had blown straight through the yawning hole in her rib cage.

She and Shelby shared something in common. They'd both grown up in the Double Rock.

CHAPTER TWENTY-ONE

The gaudy lights leading to the Aces High nightclub stained the sidewalk red, and Will cursed his stupid brain for not understanding the difference between then and now. He hadn't expected to feel this way; like no time had passed at all. Like he might blink and be right back there, watching himself stumble out of those doors with Ben behind him. Both of them drunk and looking for trouble when they'd spotted Rochelle Townes loitering in the shadows. He couldn't have known then where that night would lead. His brother, in prison. Him, living with the memories. He thanked God he hadn't invited Olivia here, as much as he'd wanted to spend more time with her. He didn't want her to see this part of him. Not ever.

As Will left his rental car and approached the entrance, his legs grew heavy, and he nearly turned back. But a familiar voice pushed him forward, head first into the past.

"No way. Is that Will Decker? Or am I seeing ghosts?"

"Hey, Rudy. It's me. In the flesh." Though Will couldn't deny the place felt haunted. Or that standing here again, in the glow of the neon, leeched the life from him, left him half-dead inside. "Long time, no see."

Rudy shook Will's hand, then pulled him in for a bear hug. At least someone around here still had his back.

"Too long, man. Way too long."

Rudy had been there too, the night it happened, looking much the same. With his ponytail and his black cowboy boots and the

ACES HIGH SECURITY T-shirt stretching across his broad chest. Will knew Rudy had blamed himself. He'd told Will as much outside the courtroom.

"Rumor has it the boys in blue ran you clear out of town."

"You know what they say about rumors."

"Where there's smoke, there's fire?"

"Whoever yells smoke probably started the fire." Will chuckled, but the truth of it all hurt. "Is Petey working tonight?"

"Petey's always working. He's inside." Rudy swung open the door, and the scent of booze and cigarettes grabbed Will by the throat. He could hardly breathe through the thick of the past. "Hey, Deck. Friday is cops drink for free. Unofficially, of course. Be careful in there."

"I'll let you know if I need you to crack any skulls."

As Will pushed through the door into the darkness, he thrust his shoulders back and forced a grin, even as the memories flooded in around him, threatening to drag him under.

"Ginger ale on the rocks."

"You sure you don't want somethin' a little stronger?" Petey wiggled his eyebrows and reached for a bottle from the stocked shelf behind him. More red lights behind the bar cast an eerie glow on his brother's pale face. "What about a splash of caramel vodka?"

Will shook his head. More than two years sober, he could still feel the heat of Grey Goose spike the roof of his mouth, burn his throat, incinerating every bad feeling on the way down. The only problem with torching his sorrows was that somehow his were fireproof.

"Man, it's good to have you back here. I didn't think I'd ever see you sittin' on one of my barstools again. Gimme a little spin for old times' sake."

Will frowned at his brother and kept both feet on the ground. Though he had more than a few fuzzy memories of drunken whooping as he spun, the room blurring around him, he didn't know that guy anymore. And with a few off-duty cops sharing pitchers in the corner, he wasn't about to draw attention to himself.

"Don't get used to it. I came here to find out what the hell's going on with Ben and the Oaktown Boys. I thought they were supposed to lay off him. We've been making the payments."

Since Petey had shown up in Will's garage a month ago, telling him Ben had to pay to stay alive at Valley View, Will had been mailing $150 a week to Aces High. Petey had promised to take care of the rest.

But the moment Petey shrugged his bony shoulders, Will wanted to pummel him.

"You have been sending them the money, right?"

Petey sidled over to Will's corner of the bar, his hands raised in surrender. "All but last week, bro. I had to settle up with Vinnie for bailing me out."

"You're unbelievable. Everything that happened with Ben, and you haven't changed a bit. Thirty-eight years old and still stealing money from the collection plate." Even Will's best efforts hadn't stopped their father from snatching the belt off the brass hook and taking it to Petey's backside after he'd caught him swiping money from the church's donation basket as they'd passed it pew to pew. "From your own brother, no less."

"You sound like Dad." Petey always knew exactly where to aim his arrows. "Always callin' me a loser. I never was good enough for him."

But then, so did Will. "Turns out Dad was right about some things."

"Yeah, I guess he was."

"What is that supposed to mean?"

Petey had already turned his back to Will, skulking off to shake a martini for a redhead in a slinky black top. Will stared after him, unsatisfied. It wasn't like Petey to give up mid-fight.

"I think it means you're still an asshole." The woman's voice came from behind him, straight from his old life.

Before he saw her, Will felt her hand squeeze his shoulder, smelled the intoxicating lilac of her perfume. Now, he understood. Petey hadn't given up. Petey had left him alone with Amy Bishop—*Homicide Inspector* Amy Bishop, *ex-fiancée* Amy Bishop. No doubt about it, Petey had won.

"At least I'm consistent."

Amy's head tipped back as she laughed, revealing the ivory hollow of her throat. Will could still remember the places she'd liked to be kissed.

"How are you, Deck?" She sipped from her glass. *Irish whiskey, neat.* Will remembered that, too.

"Great. Actually, better than great. Fantastic." He noticed her hand on the bar, her bare ring finger.

"Well, you look good," she said. "I guess the simple life suits you."

He had no intention of telling her how she looked. Perfect, as usual. With her brown hair coiled at the nape of her neck. Her fingernails, slick with red polish.

Amy slid onto the barstool next to him. "I heard you might be in town working a case. I figured you'd show up here."

"Couldn't let that chance pass you by, huh?" Will took a swig of his ginger ale, rethinking his sobriety. "So, is that what this is? One more kick to the dead horse?"

"Actually, I wanted to apologize. I handled our break-up poorly."

Will had waited a long time for her to say those words. But now, hearing them, he wondered why he'd cared so much. "Don't sweat it."

"Seriously, though. I shouldn't have—"

"Thrown your engagement ring out the window?"

"That too." She laughed again, a little too hard. Leaned in, invading his space. "But, I was going to say, I shouldn't have left you when you needed me most."

"It's water under the bridge. Two cops together would've never lasted."

"Hey, Bishop!" A voice bellowed from the back of the bar, looking for trouble. From the same table where Ben had once toasted to Will and Amy's future. Where Will's brothers in blue had raised their glasses to him. "You're starting to smell like a rat."

"Pipe down, Mussman. You're an idiot."

"You should go," Will told Amy. "I'm on my way out anyway."

She nodded, gave him a Mona Lisa smile. "You're different."

He shrugged. Not sure how she meant it but knowing she was right.

"In a good way." She pressed her lips to his ear, whispered. "Wanna get out of here?"

After Amy retreated to the table in the corner, Will knocked back the last of his ginger ale and waved Petey over. "We're not done talking about what you did. But you need to make it right. Now."

"I will. I promise. Just as soon as I—"

Will slipped him three hundred dollars. More cash sacrificed to the Oaktown fire. "Tonight."

"Tonight. I swear." Petey gestured to the back table, where Amy had found a seat between Mussman and another drunk loon out of uniform. She commanded the attention of every man within a five-mile radius. Always had, even as a rookie cop. "Are you sweet on somebody new, Deck?"

"None of your business. Why?"

Petey chuckled. The mischievous snicker he'd had as a boy. "'Cause I've never seen you tell Amy no."

Will said his goodbyes to Petey and pushed through the door in a hurry, anxious to get back to the hotel and take a long, hot shower. To wash off the stink of cheap booze and cigarettes. To cleanse himself of the memories, too—Amy and Ben and SFPD. To watch all of it swirl around the drain. If only it worked like that.

In an instant, it hit him. The past could do that. Blindside you like a ton of bricks. Will raised his eyes to the parking lot, half expecting to see Rochelle Townes up to no good. She and her boyfriend, Mac, peddled drugs in the Tenderloin. But that night, they'd been peering into the window of Ben's brand-new Dodge Charger. One word from him and they'd taken off running, Will and Ben in drunken pursuit.

"Leaving already?" Rudy's voice startled him.

"Not my scene anymore, I guess."

"Not mine either, Detective. But somebody's gotta pay the bills."

Will gave Rudy a friendly pat on the shoulder. "Take care of Petey for me, will ya?"

"Don't worry about Petey. That man is like a cat. He's got nine damn lives and he always lands on his feet. You just look after yourself."

As Will headed down the sidewalk back to his rental car, he checked his phone. One missed call from Olivia. One unread text message.

Spotted something in the photos. Might be important.

Will stumbled over the concrete wheel stop, catching himself before he bit the asphalt, just as a camera flashed at him from the parking lot. He righted himself, held up a hand to block his face.

"Detective Will Decker, stumbling drunk out of Aces High nightclub. Just like the night his brother shot that poor woman. That's quite a teaser for the morning news, don't you think?"

"Who the hell are you?" He'd recognized her right away. But he wouldn't give her the satisfaction of knowing that.

She pursed her lips, irritated. "Heather Hoffman. Journalist for *Good Morning, San Francisco.*"

"Journalist? I assume you're using that term loosely."

"My reporting on the Drake Devere case was nominated for several national awards. You must remember I was there the day you let him escape."

"I'm sure you're next in line for the Pulitzer." Will pushed past her, hoping she'd go away. But she matched him stride for stride.

"So you don't mind, then? If I run this photo on the air tomorrow. The viewing public will be riveted by my tale of the do-gooder Decker gone wrong."

"I didn't drink a drop, and you know it. Are you seriously trying to blackmail me? You've already got a cop on your payroll. What more could you possibly want?"

"I thought you'd never ask." She grinned broadly, revealing her unnaturally white teeth. "The scoop on your cold case. A pregnant girl bludgeoned to death and mummified in a barrel. People go crazy for that kind of thing."

Cold case. Will bit his tongue at her misuse of the term. The victim's body had long gone cold, of course, but the case had just been uncovered. "No comment."

"Suit yourself, Detective. You know, some might say drunk looks good on you. How 'bout one last photo op? We'll call this one 'Intoxicated Cop Armed with Service Weapon'. Come to think of it, that should sound familiar."

She raised her fancy lens and aimed it at Will. Never mind that he'd left his Glock back at the hotel, locked in the safe, for that exact reason. Guns and alcohol didn't mix. He'd learned that lesson the hard way.

Just then, Amy walked up on them, recording the exchange on her phone. "You know what people would *definitely* go crazy for? A sleazy wannabe reporter manufacturing stories."

Heather stared blankly, her cheeks reddening, before she turned tail.

"Wait." Amy winked at Will before she approached Heather, her hand outstretched. "I'm going to need that camera."

After Heather had sped off in her red Corvette, Will turned to Amy, uncertain. "What are you doing out here?"

"I needed some air. Testosterone overload, you know. Typical job hazard."

"Well, thanks. For having my back."

"No problem." Amy shrugged at him. Like it meant nothing. But Will sensed the irony, felt the heat boiling beneath her cool exterior. He'd told her no and now he had to suffer the consequences. "Besides, her morning show is one step up from Jerry Springer."

Will's laugh clunked out as he waited for the other shoe to drop. "So, I'll keep you posted on the barrel case."

"That's it?"

"What more do you want from me? It's been two years. You called off the engagement. You left me hanging. Now, you expect me… to *what?* Roll over and play nice just because you suddenly decided I might be worth keeping around for the night. That's all this was, right? A ploy to get what you want."

"You're wrong." When she laid a tender hand on his bare forearm, he swallowed hard. He couldn't remember the last time she'd touched him like that. Couldn't deny it still felt good. "Wanna know why I stepped in and defended you? It's called the thin blue line, Decker. We cops have to stick together. You forgot that once. Don't let it happen again."

VALLEY VIEW STATE PRISON DEATH INVESTIGATION REPORT

NAME: MARTIN REILLY
INMATE NUMBER: 22CMY2
DOB: 11/5/63   AGE: 56   SEX: M   RACE: CAUCASIAN
DEATH DATE: 3/4

AT 5:20 P.M., ON WEDNESDAY, MARCH 4th , INMATE MARTIN REILLY WAS DISCOVERED BY OFFICER MARCUS "MAC" BOON DURING A ROUTINE CHECK OF THE PAROLE BOARD HOLDING CELLS. REILLY WAS OBSERVED HANGING FROM AN EXPOSED PIPE IN THE CEILING. OFFICER BOON ACTIVATED HIS PERSONAL ALARM, CUT REILLY DOWN, AND ADMINISTERED CPR. REILLY WAS PRONOUNCED DEAD BY SAN FRANCISCO COUNTY EMERGENCY PERSONNEL AT 5:45 P.M. NO SUICIDE NOTE WAS PRESENT AT THE SCENE OR IN A SEARCH OF REILLY'S CELL.

OFFICER BOON REPORTED PLACING REILLY IN A HOLDING CELL #3 AT 5 P.M. FOLLOWING THE CONCLUSION OF HIS HEARING. HE STATED HE WAS UNAWARE OF THE PLANNED REPAIRS TO THE LEAKING PIPE WHICH HAD NOT BEEN LOGGED PER PROCEDURE. ADJACENT SINGLE CELLS WERE OCCUPIED BY OTHER INMATES WHO HAD BEEN KEPT APART FROM REILLY DUE TO THEIR ASSOCIATION WITH HIS FORMER GANG, FROM WHICH HE HAD DEBRIEFED.

DAVID PLUNKETT, CHIEF MEDICAL EXAMINER FOR THE COUNTY OF SAN FRANCISCO, CONDUCTED AN AUTOPSY AND DEATH INVESTIGATION PER THE REQUEST OF THE DECEDENT'S FAMILY ON BEHALF OF VALLEY VIEW STATE PRISON.

THE INQUIRY AND INVESTIGATION REVEALED THAT THE DECE-
DENT DIED AS FOLLOWS:

MANNER OF DEATH: SUICIDE

CAUSE OF DEATH: ASPHYXIATION BY LIGATURE

**MOTIVE: DEPRESSION SECONDARY TO LONG TERM INCAR-
CERATION**

BASED ON AN ANALYSIS OF THE SCENE, THE LIGATURE WAS
FASHIONED FROM THE CUT PORTION OF A PRISON ISSUED BED-
SHEET. THE LIGATURE MEASURED 2 X 8.5 FEET AND MATCHED
AN EXTRA SHEET FOUND IN REILLY'S CELL. PRISON LAUNDRY
CONFIRMED REILLY HAD BEEN ISSUED AN ADDITIONAL BEDSHEET
TWO DAYS PRIOR.

DECEDENT APPEARS TO HAVE ACCESSED THE PIPE BY STAND-
ING ON THE EDGE OF THE TOILET. DECEDENT LOOPED THE FREE
END OVER THE PIPE, THEN SECURED THE LIGATURE AROUND HIS
NECK WITH A SLIP KNOT. ONCE THE APPARATUS WAS IN PLACE,
DEATH LIKELY OCCURRED WITHIN THREE TO FIVE MINUTES.

SCRATCHES ON THE DECEDENT'S NECK WERE JUDGED TO BE
SELF-INFLICTED. AN ABRASION ON THE DECEDENT'S FOREHEAD
WAS CONSISTENT WITH BUMPING THE HEAD AGAINST A HARD
OBJECT SUCH AS THE EXPOSED METAL PIPE IN THE HOLDING CELL.

DECEDENT'S BODY TO BE TRANSFERRED TO REDWOOD MEMO-
RIAL FUNERAL HOME PER FAMILY'S REQUEST.

CHAPTER TWENTY-TWO

Olivia slammed her phone against the sofa, disgusted. She squeezed her eyes shut, wishing she'd stayed half-asleep. Red-eyed tossing and turning on her sister's futon seemed preferable to the abomination of a death investigation report that had greeted her the moment she'd opened her inbox.

The email had come addressed from Warden Ochoa herself, along with the three little words that sounded a lot like a death knell. *Per your request.*

With all that Olivia had witnessed working at Crescent Bay under the watchful eye of Warden Blevins, she should have known Valley View would be no different. Most days, it was hard to tell the good guys from the bad.

"You okay out here?" Emily poked her head out of the bathroom, her wet hair twisted in a towel on her head.

"Plunkett ruled it a suicide."

Emily's face fell. Her feet still damp from the shower, she left prints on the hardwood as she joined Olivia on the sofa. "Well, maybe he's right. I know you don't want to hear that, but—"

"No, Em. He's *not* right." Olivia retrieved her phone and stabbed at the screen, holding it out for her sister to see. "A bump on his head from hitting the pipe? That makes no sense."

"I'm just saying, this part seems accurate." Em pointed to the motive. "He felt so ashamed about how his life turned out. That parole denial was probably devastating for him."

"But he didn't know how the hearing would turn out. Why would he rip up his bedsheet and take the chance of being caught with it? For all he knew, he could've gotten a parole date."

Emily raised her eyebrows, disbelieving. "How many times have you told me, nobody gets out on their first try?"

"Fine. But Plunkett is either incompetent or corrupt, and I'm going to prove it. The Oaktown Boys are behind this. The report even said that Oaktown members were in the adjacent cells."

"You always do this, you know? When Mom died, you threw yourself into work at the prison. I barely saw you. Now you're getting caught up in this conspiracy theory rather than focusing on what's really important."

"And what's that? What could be more important than figuring out what happened to Dad?"

"Dealing with your feelings, for one. You are a shrink, aren't you?"

Olivia sighed in frustration. "You weren't there that day at the Double Rock. You didn't see what I saw. The Oaktown Boys killed our father a long time ago. On the day he agreed to take the rap for a murder he didn't commit. I've had twenty-seven years to deal with my feelings, because all that time he's been dying. This so-called suicide was just the last nail in his coffin."

Em stood up and padded back to the bathroom, stopping when she reached the door. "I'm driving back to Fog Harbor tonight. With or without you. I want to be there when Dad's body arrives. He deserves that much."

Olivia nodded. "I'll be ready." Sometimes big sisters had to go along to get along, but she had no intention of giving up.

She dressed in a hurry, pulled her hair into a ponytail and brushed her teeth in the kitchen sink. No time for breakfast, so a few bites of the leftover pizza she scavenged from Em's fridge would have to do for now. Before she headed out the door, she texted Deck to meet up with her about the clue she'd spotted in one of Shelby's photos.

Be at the Double Rock in thirty minutes.

CHAPTER TWENTY-THREE

Will floated down the stairs into the gossamer dark. He knew exactly what it looked like down there, in the belly of the basement, even though he couldn't see his own hands in front of him. On the shelf to his right, he felt the worn leather of his childhood baseball glove. The tail of an old kite tickled his face. His knee bumped against the solid antique trunk stuffed full with his mother's clothing that his father never had thrown out.

Will didn't know how he'd come to be there or why, only that he had to keep moving toward the center of the room. Toward the string that dangled down like a fishing line into the abyss. Pulling it felt essential. If he pulled it, he would see. He would know.

Paralyzed by a sickening dread, Will stopped when he reached the string. He forced himself to reach into the pitch-blackness above him, feeling for the cord. He gave it a solid tug.

The light popped on, then off again, like a camera flash, briefly revealing the horror around him, before plunging him back into darkness. Not a trunk, but a barrel. Not a kite tail, but a long strand of dark hair. Not a baseball glove resting atop the shelf, but the mummified head of a woman.

Not just any woman. *Shelby.*

He pulled the cord, looked again. *Amy.*

Again. *His mother.*

Terrified, he jerked the cord once more, a scream bursting from his throat as Olivia's dead eyes looked back at him.

*

Will sat bolt upright, his T-shirt drenched in sweat. A sliver of daylight shone through the cheap motel curtains, but he fumbled for the light switch anyway. Then for his phone, its shrill ring doing nothing to stop his heart racing.

Before he answered JB's call, he spotted Olivia's text.

"Hey, partner. What's up?"

Will needed some good news. Between the cheap motel sheets, the pancake-flat pillow, and the couple arguing and making up in the room next door, he'd barely slept. And after he'd finally dozed off, his warped brain still couldn't give it a rest. Olivia would probably tell him it all meant something. That his twisted dream was a pit stop on the road to his subconscious. Which meant his subconscious was royally screwed up.

"You sound half-asleep, City Boy. Have you solved our case yet?"

Will croaked out a groggy laugh, swinging his feet out of the bed and onto the carpet.

"I'll take that as a no."

Bleary-eyed, he gazed into the dresser mirror as JB droned on.

"Tammy and I had plans to stay at a little B&B last night. Take Princess for a walk on the beach, get some sand between my toes. Hell, maybe even channel my inner Burt Lancaster. You ever seen that old movie, *From Here to Eternity?*"

Will grimaced, imagining JB dropping to his knees on a beach towel with the iconic bombshell Deborah Kerr.

"But guess where I spent my evening? At the station. Alone. Mining the missing persons' database for our girl, Shelby. You know what I found? Zero. Zilch. Nada. There wasn't a single Shelby matching our description and time frame."

"Olivia might have a lead. She spotted a clue in one of the photos. I'm supposed to meet her in…" Will checked the motel clock, glanced down at the message on his screen. "Shit. Fifteen minutes."

"Olivia? As in your schoolboy crush, Olivia? Make sure you smell good."

Groaning, Will tucked the phone against his cheek and tugged on his jeans. "Gotta run, man. I'll call you as soon as I've got something. Why don't you get some sun like you planned?"

"Now you're talkin'. Tammy bought herself a slinky halter top swimsuit just like—"

Will shoved his silenced phone in his pocket. Changed his shirt. Ran a careless hand through his hair.

Securing his Glock in his waistband, he paused at the door— *damn JB*—and took a whiff of his armpit.

A quick birdbath and two swipes of deodorant, he headed out, smelling like a rose. Or, according to the manufacturer, *leather and sandalwood with earthy undertones.*

CHAPTER TWENTY-FOUR

Miss Pearl poured three steaming cups of coffee. Her hands trembled as she set the mugs carefully on her kitchen table. Olivia sipped hers a little too fast, desperate for a caffeine buzz. Judging by Deck's bed hair and the dark circles under his eyes, he needed it just as badly. Although—she leaned in—he smelled like he'd had time for a shower.

"Can I interest either one of you in a chocolate chip cookie?"

Deck raised his hand unapologetically.

Olivia laughed and shook her head at him. "It's seven thirty in the morning."

"And?"

"It's never too early for chocolate." Miss Pearl deposited two cookies on a small plate and placed it in front of him.

"Fair warning." Olivia lowered her voice. Mostly to bring Deck closer. "Those things are seriously habit-forming."

He broke off the edge and popped it in his mouth, grinning. "What can I say? I live on the edge."

Miss Pearl joined them at the table, lowering herself to the seat slowly, effortfully. Her old bones practically creaked as she arranged them beneath her. She hadn't seemed surprised to see Olivia at her door, welcoming them both inside as if they belonged at the Double Rock. As if Olivia had never left.

"Is Scott here?" Olivia cut her eyes down the hallway. The closed door at the end left her unsettled.

"That boy hasn't dragged himself out of bed before noon since Termite dropped him off here. Teenagers these days. If it doesn't have a screen and an on switch, they've got no use for it."

"How long has he lived with you?" Olivia asked.

"Off and on for his whole life." Miss Pearl shook her head, whispered. "His mom took off when he was a baby. We haven't seen her since. Now he's stuck with Termite for a daddy."

"Must be tough." Olivia could relate. But for all her parents' flaws, they'd never abandoned her. No wonder Scott had a bad attitude.

Deck devoured the last bite of his cookie and produced a single photograph from the folder on the table. "Pearl, I'd like you to take a look at this for me. It's related to a case I'm working. See if there's anything you recognize."

Miss Pearl squinted at the mundane subject of the photo—a large chest of drawers in the cabin's bedroom. The angle of the photo made Olivia suspect Shelby had been lying on the bed when she'd taken it. On the smooth redwood surface, a tube of lipstick stood guard over a beat-up paperback book, the pages fat and parched from the sun. The only other item visible, a homemade doll with yellow button eyes.

"Olivia, dear, would you mind fetching my magnifying glass? It's on the coffee table, right next to the newspaper. Lately, I can't even read the obituaries without it. I suppose I should be thankful for that. Most everybody dying is younger than me."

Miss Pearl's eyes widened once she studied the photo under the lens. "That sure does look like one of my Mary Jane dolls. Olivia had one. I made them for a lot of little girls in the building."

"Starting when?" Deck asked.

"Oh my goodness. When *did* I start?" Miss Pearl tapped her head, as if she could shake loose the rusty memories. Then, her eyes got shiny, and she wiped at them with a napkin. "Well, I started sewing just after the accident. The one that took my Melvin and our daughter, Mary. She was only five years old. That was back in '75. I made those dolls in her honor, called them all Mary Jane. I used the yellow buttons because that was her favorite color."

Olivia rubbed Miss Pearl's knobby shoulder. It felt as fragile as an eggshell beneath her fingers. "You never told me that story."

"It took me a long time before I could talk about it. But sewing those dolls saved my life. It gave me a purpose to see all you girls so happy."

"Do you remember a girl named Shelby?" Deck asked, pointing back to the photo. "She might've lived here in the early eighties. I think it's her doll in the picture."

"Shelby. Shelby. *Shelby.*" Miss Pearl said the name aloud a few times, before she clapped her hands together. "Shelby Mayfield. She and her mama lived here. Her brother too. Apartment K, if I remember correctly. They moved out when Shelby was yay-high. Never heard from them again."

"What did Shelby look like?"

"Cute little thing. Blonde hair, big brown eyes. Puppy dog eyes, I used to call 'em."

Deck nodded as he jotted notes on a pad.

"Did Shelby get herself mixed up in some kind of trouble?"

"I'm not sure yet," he said. "But you've been a big help. Do you have an extra Mary Jane doll we could take with us?"

Miss Pearl lit up at Deck's question, sprang out of her seat. She started down the hallway. "Come with me. I'll let you pick the one you want. But we may have to wake the sleeping dragon."

Olivia tiptoed inside the cave of the bedroom. With its sunshine-yellow walls, she suspected it had once belonged to Mary. Now, Scott had claimed it as his own, sullying it with the debris of his life—dirty clothing, sneakers, cigarette butts.

Scott lay, unmoving, in the center of the bed, a frilly pink comforter tangled around his legs. A brand-new Oaktown tattoo flamed, red and raised, on his bicep. Same as his father's. Looking at it, Olivia felt inexplicably sad for him.

Miss Pearl raised a finger to her lips and pointed to the white bookcase, lined end to end with Mary Jane dolls. Beneath their yarn hair, their yellow button eyes seemed to stare in judgment.

Your choice, Miss Pearl mouthed.

Olivia stepped over a T-shirt and a dingy black sock, Deck close behind her. She reached the shelf, where the dolls gathered dust, waiting for someone to love them threadbare. But a framed picture on the nightstand called to her instead.

She picked it up, brought it close to her. Her breath caught in her chest as she realized.

"Is that your dad?" Deck asked, over her shoulder.

Scott's eyes popped open. His nostrils flaring, he lurched up and snatched the frame from her hands. "Gimme that."

"Sorry, I just—"

"What the hell are you doin' in my bedroom? Where's Pearl?"

"I'm right here, Scotty." Miss Pearl stepped in from the doorway, motioned with her hands to soothe him. "Cool your jets. Calm down and count to five, just like your counselor taught you."

His voice shaky as a tripwire, Scott began to count. His knuckles whitened as he squeezed the frame.

Olivia turned to Miss Pearl. "Why does he have a photo of my dad?"

"What the hell are you talkin' about, lady?" So much for his anger management.

Olivia grabbed the picture back from him, ripped it right out of his hands. She jabbed at the image of her father, clad in a blue jumpsuit, posing in front of a prison mural, the words "Valley View" stenciled in black paint beneath it. A younger Scott on one side of him, Termite on the other. Her father had wrapped the both of them beneath his burly arms.

"This man, Martin Reilly, was my father." As Olivia spoke the words to him—practically shouted them—a sickening shame coursed through her; it had taken her this long to truly claim him.

She looked into Scott's eyes, the glinting blue both strange and familiar. Watched his fire dampen, his anger turn to confusion. "Mad Dog, ya mean? He's my grandpa."

Olivia stood open-mouthed and staring at Scott—her *nephew?* Still rumpled from sleep, he seemed genuinely confused by her indignation. She couldn't stand to look at him any longer. Spinning around, she directed a question to Miss Pearl. "Is it true?"

Miss Pearl nodded and hung her head as she released a world-weary sigh. She motioned for Olivia to follow her from the bedroom, padding back down the hallway to the kitchen. Both of them shell-shocked, they sat at the table, avoiding each other's eyes.

"How long have you known?"

"It wasn't my secret to tell, dear. Your father was a complicated man."

"*How long?*" she asked again.

"Since Termite was a baby. His mama, Ruby, came to me, told me the truth. That Three Fingers wasn't Termite's daddy. That she and Mad Dog had a fling. This was right before your father met your mother. Ruby asked me for my advice on what to do."

"And you told her to *lie?*"

"Three Fingers Colvin wasn't nobody to mess with. You know that. He would've beat her to a pulp if he'd known she was steppin' out on him. Especially with his long-time buddy. I thought maybe a baby would settle him down."

Scott had slunk down the hallway to listen in. She couldn't fault him for being exactly like her. Desperate for the scraps of her own history. "So if you didn't tell anyone, how did *he* find out? How did Termite?"

While she spoke, Miss Pearl motioned Scott to the table, pulled out a chair for him. "Your dad contacted Termite a year ago, after Three Fingers had that heart attack. I guess he figured it was about time to come clean."

"To everyone but me, apparently."

From behind her, Deck placed his hand on her shoulder. The solid warmth of it grounded her, even as she felt herself breaking into pieces, scattering. He handed her the Mary Jane doll he'd rescued from Scott's room, and her fingers busied themselves in the reddish-brown yarn covering its head. "What about the safety deposit box? Did you know what was inside? That he was an informant for the cops?"

Miss Pearl clutched her chest. "Well, I'll be darned. I had no idea. Honestly, I'd always imagined he'd left you a letter, telling you Termite was your brother."

"*Half*-brother." The word stuck in Olivia's throat. Bad enough her father had been a shot caller for the Oaktown Boys. Her half-brother was too. Turns out she'd been related to a murderer after all. Termite had surely slit Tina Solomon's throat. And as the shot caller for the Oaktown Boys, she felt certain he'd had a hand in her father's death.

Olivia gripped the doll in her hands, squeezing the life from poor Mary Jane. She turned to Scott, unsure how she felt about him. "That photo… your dad looked happy." Until it all came out, the storm inside her building to a crescendo. "Why did he have my—*our*—father killed?"

Scott considered her, puffed his chest and sized her up like a wannabe tough guy. His stare, hard as nails. He looked exactly like his father. But seconds later, the mask slipped. A teenage boy after all, he just shrugged.

CHAPTER TWENTY-FIVE

Will followed Olivia to her car, neither of them speaking. He marveled at the strangeness of it all. At how she'd been completely right about the doll on the dresser. At how she'd held it together in there, taken the blow to the gut like a prize fighter and stayed standing. But mostly, at how their fathers had been so much the same, burying their secrets deep. Unearthing them now felt fated somehow. It scared him too, the razor-thin difference between the two men. One man who'd called himself Detective, the other Mad Dog.

Olivia stopped short suddenly, as if she'd been thinking the same. "That went well." She held up the Mary Jane doll, looked it in its button eyes, and laughed as she placed it in his hand.

Hysterical but contagious, her laugh bubbled over, and he couldn't stop himself from joining in. And so it went, until they'd both doubled over.

Will wound down first, wiping his eyes while Olivia's shoulders shook. When she looked up, her eyes were wet too. From laughing or crying, he couldn't tell which, but the sadness there made him reach for her. Drawing her to him, he held her against his chest. As her hands clutched at the sides of his shirt, he hated himself for liking it.

Finally, she let go, lifted her face to glance up at him. "Emily's right. I'm the worst psychologist ever. I can't even manage my own…" She gestured to the whole of herself. "Whatever this is."

"You just found out you have a brother. Called *Termite.* I think that warrants at least a minor downward spiral."

She shook her head, seemingly still disbelieving. "It was bad enough when I thought he was behind the murder of *my* dad. Now, I find out he killed his own dad, too. What am I supposed to do?"

Will hardly felt qualified to give advice, especially to a psychologist. But he wanted her to keep looking at him like that. Like she needed him. "Just put one foot in front of the other. Get back to Fog Harbor and bury your dad. We'll figure out the rest."

"I really blew it." She lowered her eyes again, spoke to the sidewalk. "I should've forgiven my dad a long time ago. I just want him to have some justice. Even if he didn't always deserve it."

"He will. I promise you." Will knew the danger in making promises. He'd learned that lesson as a rookie detective, when his first murder case—a homeless woman found stabbed in a dumpster in the Tenderloin—had gone unsolved. His badge was made of brass; he was no superhero.

"You should see Ben before you leave."

"He doesn't want to see me. He made that clear last time."

"That was what, two years ago? He called you for help, didn't he? Don't be like me. Full of regrets."

"Trust me. He still blames me for everything." But he had to admit, Olivia had a point. "I'm probably not even on his visitors' list."

"Just try." The way she squeezed his hand, her fiery green eyes imploring, he would've done anything. Even if it meant swallowing the bitter pill of his pride. "For me."

After they parted ways—Olivia driving north to join up with Emily and head back to Fog Harbor, Will south to Valley View—Will dialed JB's number, expecting to reach his voicemail. Instead, his partner picked up, heaving a sigh into the phone the size of a gale force wind.

"Didn't you tell me to take the day off?"

"Then why'd you answer the phone?"

"I figured you missed me, City Boy. It's okay to admit it."

"About as much as I miss hell week in the academy." Will chuckled at his own joke. "Big news, buddy. I got a last name. Mayfield. Shelby Mayfield."

"Sounds like Doctor Rockwell's solving your cases again."

Even now, with the Mary Jane doll riding shotgun, Will could hardly believe it. "I'll be back in Fog Harbor by tonight. We can start looking for next of kin first thing in the morning."

JB made a noise of half-hearted agreement. In the quiet that followed, Will swore he heard Chief Flack's commanding voice.

"Are you at the station? What happened to Tammy at the beach in her halter top?"

Another gust of wind from hurricane JB. "Started drizzling as soon as we got there. Forecast said sunny. Tammy headed to the nail salon for her weekly session instead."

"Well, you could've joined her."

"Trust me, City Boy, when a woman gets her nails done, she doesn't want male company. It's meditative. Like spending an hour at the shooting range, putting holes in paper targets. Or going fishing in the bay. Fishing is *never* about catching fish."

"Not the way you do it." Will swallowed his laugh, as the sign for Valley View loomed up ahead. The hunkering beast of the prison just beyond it. Its gray walls and barbed wire an eyesore in the otherwise picturesque landscape. On a clear day like this one, you could see the Golden Gate Bridge in the distance.

"Hey, remember that reporter, Heather Hoffman?" JB asked.

Will stifled a groan. Like he could forget the scornful look on her face when she'd handed over her camera to Amy. Beneath her humiliation, she'd seethed, more than likely plotting his demise.

"She's been poking around our case. She called my cell last night, asking if we'd ruled out old man Grimaldi as a suspect."

"How'd she know about Grimaldi?" Will asked.

"I tell ya, that woman's got more moles than Cindy Crawford."

"*What?*" As usual, JB spoke his own language. "Cindy Crawford had one well-placed mole, if I remember correctly."

"Exactly. Just like Hoffman. One well-placed mole. And we both know who it is."

"Graham Bauer." Will had no doubt.

"Bingo."

"So, what did you tell her?"

"Not a damn thing." JB cackled, and Will braced himself for another humdinger. "I shared my suspicions with Chief Flack. And she had a little powwow with Bauer. Let's just say, Cindy finally got that thing removed."

"If I can't see my brother, can I at least speak with Warden Ochoa?" Will directed the question to the CO at the entrance of Valley View, who was too busy shooting the shit with his cronies to pay him any mind. Luckily, he'd also been too distracted to notice Will peering over his shoulder at the computer screen.

As Will suspected, his name did not appear on Ben's approved visitor list, which bore only one entry: Their father, Henry Decker. Petey's criminal record had surely disqualified him right off the bat. And Ben's buddies from the department had long since dwindled. Say what you want about the thin blue line, nothing will sort your real friends faster than a prison term for voluntary manslaughter.

"Thought you were just visiting," the CO said finally, after Will repeated the question. Twice. And loud enough for the lieutenant to hear. He emerged from his office, and the CO's spine immediately straightened.

"You have an appointment?" the lieutenant asked.

"Official police business." Will flashed his badge to legitimize his little white lie.

With the lieutenant's solemn nod of approval, the CO buzzed Will through a chain-link gate and into the courtyard. The final stop before the cold, concrete corridors of the prison where real life ended and purgatory began. A man with a jagged neck scar and a double teardrop tattoo stopped his work sweeping the sidewalk to politely inform Will that the door to the warden's office was just inside the administrative building. But Will never made it that far.

"Hey, mister!" The CO called him back. "About your brother…"

"What about him?" Will's stomach curdled, as the dread from last night's nightmare returned.

"The lieutenant just chewed my ass. He said I overlooked a flag in the system. Apparently, Ben Decker shipped out of here this afternoon. He's on a bus headed north right now."

On a prison bus. Not dead then. Not strung up like a fish. But Will's relief quickly turned to confusion. "Where to?"

The CO grimaced. "The boonies, if you ask me. Crescent Bay State Prison in Fog Harbor."

Script: *Good Morning, San Francisco*

Cue Heather

Good morning, San Francisco. I'm Heather Hoffman. It's 5 a.m. on Monday, March ninth. Time to rise and shine.

Roll intro music

We have a thrilling show for you today, starting with our crime segment, *Murder in the Bay*.

Roll segment intro

We begin with the story we've been following closely in the small town of Fog Harbor, where a few days ago, a man discovered the mummified remains of a still-unidentified pregnant young woman. According to the latest information from our sources in law enforcement, at least two persons of interest have been identified in the case.

Good Morning, San Francisco has also learned that the secluded cabin was the scene of a sordid movie produced by Obscura Films, which may have been shot in the months, weeks, or even days surrounding the victim's death. The short clip we obtained depicts violence toward women. Due to the graphic nature of the film, viewer discretion is advised.

Roll *Chained* excerpt

Our sources at Fog Harbor PD tell us that convicted sex offender and recently paroled third striker, Chuck Winters, has been interviewed at a local halfway house regarding the murder. He has not yet been charged with any crime.

Please stay tuned to *Good Morning, San Francisco* this week. Starting tomorrow, we will be on location in Fog Harbor to keep abreast of the developments in this case, and will bring them to you the moment they occur.

Next up, celebrity dating coach Orlando Gray shares his insider tips on how to make that spring fling last until summer.

Cut to commercial

CHAPTER TWENTY-SIX

Will knew he'd come to the right place. He felt it even before his GPS confirmed he'd arrived at 221 County Road 37, the last known address of Shelby Mayfield they'd dug up yesterday in Vital Records. Even before he'd spotted JB's Camaro parked in the ditch nearby, or the dilapidated mailbox that read **MA IE D** in faded black paint. Set back in the redwood grove, a rusted travel trailer had rooted itself to the earth. Vines of ivy rose up from the underbrush. Like long fingers, they'd crept across the aluminum siding, staking their claim. Growing so thick they'd nearly concealed its rotten tires. Given enough time, ivy could strangle even the largest redwood. Block its light, restrict its growth. Insidious as grief, it wore down its opponent. Grief had grown unchecked here for a long time.

Will tucked a DNA swab kit into his breast pocket, along with Miss Pearl's Mary Jane doll. He hoped to find out if Shelby had still owned hers when she'd gone missing. By the end of the day, he felt certain they'd have a probable ID on their victim and Shelby's mother would have the answers she'd been seeking for the last thirty-five years. It all felt bittersweet.

JB leaned against the hood of his car, chewing on a blade of grass and looking like a man in desperate need of a cigarette. He pointed into the woods, the sunlight dappling through the canopy. "You sure she still lives here?"

"That's what she said on the phone yesterday. She moved out here about a year after Shelby ran away."

"Alright. But if this is an ambush, don't say I didn't warn you."

Will plodded into the forest, JB behind him, careful to stay on the narrow path. More worried about snakes and spiders and sprained ankles than sixty-eight-year-old Trish Mayfield. Still, he'd holstered his Glock just in case.

Movement in the underbrush caught Will's eye. A squirrel launched itself atop a rusted VW that had also fallen victim to the ivy, then scurried inside it, where the vines protruded like entrails, and disappeared.

When they reached the front door of the trailer, Will found the lock broken, the latch closed with wire looping from the outside in. A butterfly perched on the knob took flight when he knocked. "Ms. Mayfield?"

Footsteps approached from within. A clouded eye appeared in the crack above a sun-spotted nose. "Who is it?"

"Detectives Decker and Benson. We spoke on the phone."

The woman slowly unwound the wire, and the door creaked open. A mangy cat shot out from between her slippered feet—JB yelped—and disappeared into the thicket. Judging by the odor that wafted from within, the cats outnumbered Trish ten to one.

"Did you find her? Did you find my Shelby?"

Will peered over her shoulder into the dimly lit trailer. The sink, stacked with dishes. The window shades drawn. Suddenly, he thought of his father. The inside of a home said a lot about the inside of a person.

"That's what we're trying to figure out. Do you mind if we come in and chat?"

She shuffled aside, allowing them entry. JB first, then Will. He left the door open behind him, hoping the spring breeze would help air out the place.

JB shooed two calicos from Trish's recliner and guided her to her seat. "You like cats, huh?"

"It sure beats being alone. I used to have a parakeet too. *Pippen.* I taught him to say a few things like, *Pretty bird* and

Here, kitty, kitty. But he flew off a while back, when I left the window open."

"Flew off?" JB grimaced at the claw marks on the pullout sofa, which had already been claimed by several of Trish's feline companions. Then muttered, just loud enough for Will to hear, "You sure he didn't meet a bad end?"

Will cut his eyes at JB as he made his way across the linoleum, almost invisible beneath the newspapers and discarded food wrappers.

"Always been a dog man myself. But Detective Decker has an old tabby with one eye, believe it or not."

"Oh, I believe it. Cats always land on their feet and keep right on truckin'. Wish I could say the same."

Will understood exactly what she meant. Life could be as ruthless as a prize fighter. Dealing out blow after blow. He detested this part of the job. Delivering a knockout to someone who didn't deserve it. To someone who'd already been backed against the ropes.

"Tell me about the day Shelby ran away." Will plucked out his notepad, his pen at the ready. Since he'd been the one to phone Trish, he'd take the lead here.

"It was Monday, September sixteenth, 1985. Shelby was sixteen years old." Trish closed her eyes as she spoke. Like she'd travelled right back there. "I worked as a janitor at SF General Hospital in the mornings. Three days a week, I cleaned houses in Pacific Heights. Sometimes Shelby went with me. We'd get the work done faster, and she got a kick out of seeing inside those fancy homes. Plus, she could stash a little money in her piggybank. She was saving up for a new Walkman."

"But she didn't go with you that day?"

Trish's eyes filled with pain but no tears fell. "She told me she had to stay after school to take pictures at soccer practice for the Yearbook Club. But I think she just wanted to meet her boyfriend, Brandon. That kid was no good and way too old for her. I tried to tell her. Tried to make her listen, but Shelby was hardheaded. She kept sneaking around to see him. Like any teenager, I suppose. Even me. Way back when, I did the same. My mom warned me the kids' dad was a deadbeat. I thought I knew better. Now, I've got no one, so I guess the joke's on me."

"What about your son?" Will had found no online presence for Kristopher Mayfield, only an entry in Vital Records designating him Shelby's older brother, born one year before her.

Trish fell silent, and Will waited, dreading her answer. "He was a real good football player until he blew out his knee horseplaying with his buddies. Then, he got mixed up with drugs. Drove head on into a tree and turned himself into a vegetable. I couldn't afford to take care of him myself, so I had to put him in a home. Both my babies, gone in the space of two years."

"I'm sorry." Will wondered how the woman had managed to stay upright. "What time did you arrive home the night Shelby ran away?"

"Probably around nine o'clock. To get from Pacific Heights back to Bayview usually took about forty-five minutes by bus. When I came in, I knew something was wrong. Kris had already found the note."

Will and JB exchanged a hopeful glance. "Do you remember what it said?"

Trish laughed softly. "As long as I live, I'll never forget it. 'I'm sorry. Please don't worry about me. You've been a great mom but I need to be on my own for a while. I'll call when I can.'"

"And did she? Call?"

"Not once."

"Did she take anything with her?"

Trish nodded. "There were a few of her things missing. Clothes. Her Walkman. Kris's sports bag. A doll she kept on her bed."

Will withdrew the Mary Jane doll, held it up to Trish's wide eyes. "Like this one?"

She took it, clutched it to her. "Is it Shelby's?"

"No. I'm afraid not." Will wished he had the heart to lie.

"She was still a little girl, you know. She thought she was grown up, but…" The tears came now, freely tracking down her cheeks. Filling the well-worn grooves. "She slept with that doll in her bed every night."

"Any idea where she went? Or why?"

A sleek black cat joined Trish on the recliner, pawing at her leg, while she rubbed its head and sniffled. "Detective Decker, I've racked my brain, wondering what I did wrong. Was I too hard on her, trying to be mom and dad? Did I work too much? What signs did I miss? Whatever happened to her, it's my fault."

"I'm sure that's not true." Will knew the danger in blaming yourself. Guilt seeped into your heart like poison, souring everything it touched. "What else can you tell us about her boyfriend, Brandon…?"

"Simpkins." She wiped her eyes on a handkerchief, pulled herself together. "As far as I remember, he never had a job. Unless you count selling weed on the corner. But he had a car and a chip on his shoulder, so naturally Shelby fell head over heels in love. Not too long after, her grades dropped, and she started acting a fool. She gave up her college ambitions and was hanging out over at the Double Rock Projects, where Brandon lived. We lived there too for a while."

"Did Brandon ever get violent with her?"

"I wouldn't put it past him. A week or so before she ran away, they had a big fight. She didn't tell me, of course. I was always the last to know. But I heard her on the phone with her so-called best friend, Drea. That same week, Shelby turned up after school with a shiner. Told me she got hit with a softball. She didn't even *play* softball."

"So you didn't believe her?"

"Hell no. If you took one look at that punk, Brandon, you'd understand why." Trish pointed to a yellowed album on the arm of the sofa. "I dug up an old picture of him, if you're interested. Shelby had to beg him to take her to that school dance."

Will snagged the photo atop the binder, studying it. A too-cool-for-school Mohawked teen peered up at him from the photopaper. The kind of guy who would've chased him and his brothers home from school, threatening to beat their asses for being a cop's kids. All talk and no follow-through, he would've played it off as a joke when the Decker boys had turned to him. Said, *Let's go then. Three on one.*

But Will felt himself drawn to Shelby. To her infectious smile that in no way foreshadowed her future. Whoever had snuffed out the light in her eyes deserved the same.

"Any idea where Brandon is now?"

"Last I heard, prison."

A fat tabby studied JB with suspicion while he paged through Trish's photo album.

Will had already plowed ahead through the hard parts, looking Trish right in the eye when he'd delivered the news blow by blow. He'd owed her that much.

We found a body in Fog Harbor.

A female, Shelby's age.

Pregnant.

We have reason to believe it's her. But we need confirmation.

The dreadful part over, out came the swab. Trish dutifully opened her mouth, and he collected the cheek cells. Then he popped them in the sterile tube and nodded at her. Done.

"How long will it take?" she asked.

Will pondered that long wait, her question heavy on his chest. "We've got an in at the lab, so a few days at most. We'll rush it. I'll call as soon as I hear something."

"Would it help if you had her dental records?"

JB froze, Will too. "Do you have them?"

Trish nodded, grim. "A year or so after she left, a friend suggested I ask the dentist for a copy. Just in case. I didn't want to do it, but… well, I never even opened that big manila envelope. I couldn't bear it. Couldn't stand to think that's what it would come to. My girl, identified by her teeth. When you told me you were coming, I dug it out of the box where I buried it."

She reached beside her chair, producing a large envelope. "It's her. I have a feeling. As soon as you called, told me who you were… a mother always knows. That shirt you asked about—1984 Summer Olympics—I bought it for her at the secondhand store. She and Drea were obsessed with Mary Lou Retton."

"Do you have any photos of Drea in here?" JB raised his eyes from the album. "It seems like she was a big part of Shelby's life."

Trish let out a scornful laugh. "Look in the pocket in the back. I'd have burned every photo of that backstabbing snake if it weren't for the fact that my Shelby is in them."

Drea was a foil for Shelby in every way. Raven-haired and pale-faced, she sported a pink skull tattoo on her forearm and stuck her tongue out at the camera, more subversive than playful. "What happened?" Will asked, returning the photo to JB.

"Not two weeks after Shelby left, Kris spotted Drea making out with Brandon under the bleachers after the football game. Like either of those two had any interest in football. Or school. Drea had all but flunked out."

"Any idea why Shelby would run to Fog Harbor? Did you ever take a trip up the coast? Or have family in the area?"

"Heck, I'd never even heard of the place until my friend's boy got sent to prison up there after Shelby disappeared. I'm as shocked as could be that's where you found her. But if she was knocked up, that would explain why she ran. I always told her if she got herself pregnant like I did, she'd be in big trouble. 'Course, I was just talkin'. We would've figured it out."

"Did you file a missing person's report?"

Trish hung her head, no doubt blaming herself again. "The cops told me there was no need. They didn't even bother to talk to Brandon or Drea. They said they considered her a runaway since she left of her own accord."

"But she was only sixteen."

"That's what I told them. Back then, things were different. Nobody paid too much attention to us poor folks. Come to think of it, I guess it's not so different now. After I got the letter, I gave up trying. Figured maybe they were right. She didn't want to be found. But it never really made sense to me that she misspelled her brother's name. Plus, Shelby never learned to type."

JB perked up, shutting the album with a thwack. The cat darted down the hallway and into the shadows, as they both spoke at once.

"Letter?"

Trish stood up and moved toward the back of the trailer, motioning them to follow. As they followed her through the refuse and the clutter, JB nudged Will with a sharp elbow and a pointed gaze at a few green feathers and a tiny rib cage half-hidden beneath a paper bag. Will poked at the bones with his dress shoe, concealing them entirely. Though he couldn't change the past, that much he *could* do for her.

Oblivious, Trish led them to a cabinet near the bathroom, where she kept a small safe.

Will watched her fingers make slow work of the knob. When it clicked open, his heart thumped faster. She handed him another envelope, the paper soft and yellowed with age.

He read the postmark. *May 7 Pistol River, CA.* And now he understood.

"That's why you moved here. Why you've stayed here all this time."

Her eyes gone faraway, she nodded.

Dear Mother,

I am finally happy. I met a nice boy with a rich family to take care of me. We've been traveling the country together, and I've had the opportunity to see all the places I dreamed of. Please don't try to find me. I want to be left alone. Tell Chris goodbye for me.

Your loving daughter,
Shelby

Trish insisted on walking them to the corner. When Will protested, she told him she needed to check the mail anyway. His legs felt leaden on the walk out, his heart heavier. But he smiled at Trish when she shook his hand and thanked him for coming.

"Shelby deserves justice. And so do you. I promise we'll find the bastard who did this and make him pay."

Trish's eyes welled. She watched them for a moment before she turned and disappeared into the redwood grove. The mail, completely forgotten.

Will checked his watch and took a soul-cleansing breath. He needed a hard reset if he was going to make it through Martin Reilly's funeral. There's a limit to how much death one man can take.

"I say we divide and conquer." JB leaned out the window of his Camaro. While Will talked to Trish, he'd retreated there, hiding his own somber eyes behind his sunglasses. Maybe he had a soft side after all. "I'll take the letter down to the lab. Let them get started on the prints. After the funeral, you can meet the crime scene tech at the cabin. We'll regroup at the station afterward."

"You just want to see Tammy, don't you?" Will tried to cheer himself up.

"If I happen to run into her and we happen to bump lips, so be it." JB puckered up, checked himself in the rearview. "It just might be her lucky day."

"Do you ever stop?"

"I'll assume that was rhetorical." JB lowered his shades, peering up over them with concern. "But it looked like you needed a laugh."

Will gave a weary nod. "What about Simpkins? We need to find out where he's locked up."

JB grinned. "One step ahead of you, City Boy. While you were talking to Trish, I phoned the station and got the intel from Lieutenant Wheeler."

"And?"

"I'll give you three guesses, and the first two don't count."

CHAPTER TWENTY-SEVEN

The black dress from Neiman's still fit. It had been so long since Olivia had worn it—over two years now—it felt like a costume for a different person. Uncomfortable, she pulled at the hem as she took her seat in the white folding chair beside Emily. The sun as cruel and bright as the day they buried their mother. The whole scene, like a dream. A strange déjà vu.

Two days had passed in a blur since she and Em had made the five-hour drive back to Fog Harbor and agreed on a small graveside service for their father at the cemetery behind Grateful Heart Chapel. Afterward, he would be lowered into a hole in the ground and covered with a mound of dirt. His date of death would be chiseled into a gravestone next to their mother's. The mound would grow smaller over time; the grass would return. The earth would settle back into itself. Dust to dust.

Adjacent to her father's casket, a small crowd of Olivia's friends and colleagues had gathered. Her best friend, Leah, and her husband, Jake, with their newborn baby, Liam. The interns she supervised at the prison. Even Warden Blevins had come.

Thankful as she was that she and Em didn't have to go it alone today, it made Olivia impossibly sad that no one here had ever even met their father. But she knew it wouldn't have come as a surprise to Martin Reilly. Most of his old friends were doing time in prison or six feet under themselves. *Gang members have a short shelf-life,* her mother had told her more than once. Her dad had lasted longer than most.

Olivia waved to Leah, who smiled at her after she kissed Liam's tiny head. He'd been born with a full head of his daddy's dark hair. Already a heartbreaker. Light-years had passed since last Wednesday when they'd met for a walk during his naptime. Leah had always managed to lift her spirits, and since she'd gone on maternity leave, the whole world seemed a little darker. Olivia tried to take solace in a single daisy blooming near her feet when a pair of polished dress shoes appeared on the grass beside them. Emily nudged her with an elbow.

Olivia lifted her gaze and traced Deck's long, lean silhouette. The pressed gray slacks, the navy tie. The freshly shaven face. The usually disheveled chestnut hair that had, regrettably, been tamed. And finally, those eyes.

"You made it." She smiled, stupidly, feeling a sudden surge of relief.

"Of course. I wanted to be here. To pay my respects."

Another elbow from Em brought Olivia to her feet and into Deck's waiting arms. A perfunctory hug, she told herself. Perfectly safe. But with the hard muscle of his heart beating against her ear, it didn't feel that way. Every time she got this close to him, it felt dangerous.

Still, she wished he wouldn't let her go.

Deck turned to Emily, clasped her hands. "I'm sorry about your dad. "

"What about your meeting with Shelby's mother?" Olivia asked.

"Already done. JB and I stopped by first thing this morning."

"How'd she react?"

His dreary expression told the story. "About as well as you'd expect. It's hard to say what's worse. The knowing, or the not knowing."

Olivia spotted Father Frank approaching from the chapel's rectory, gliding across the lawn in his white robe. Behind him, a lone figure who made Olivia's stomach clench on sight.

"I had plans to grab dinner at the Pit later. Maybe go a few rounds on the heavy bag. If you feel up to it, you're welcome to—"

Olivia silenced Deck, pushing past him as she stomped up the grassy hill, the heels of her shoes spiking the soft ground, until she stood Manolo to motorcycle boot with Termite. He'd already stripped off his helmet revealing his wiry red beard, with a shock of hair to match. His blue eyes, cold as ice water, aimed straight at Olivia.

"What the hell are you doing here?" She glared at the Oaktown tattoo, visible on his bicep, beneath his leather cut. "You're not welcome."

"Oh, c'mon. Is this how you treat family? Scott told me the cat's out of the bag. I just assumed Mad Dog had told you years ago."

"He didn't want to claim you. And can you blame him? You've got no right to show your face. Not after what you did."

Termite moved in closer until she could smell the tobacco on his breath, the sweat that had beaded in his hair underneath the helmet he'd left hanging on the mirror of his Harley. "The way I see it, I've got as much right as you do. I'm fifty percent Reilly. No different than you or your sister."

"You had your own father killed. That's unforgivable."

Termite snapped his head back. Like he'd been slapped. Under the thick cover of his beard, his lip curled in disgust. "Is that what you think? That I killed him? After all he'd done for me? You're wrong. Dead wrong."

"We both know he'd kept your secret for too long." Olivia glanced back down the hill. At her sister, mortified. At the warden, curious. At Fr. Frank, who'd stopped midway on the grassy knoll, perplexed. At Deck, walking determinedly toward her. "You thought he was going to expose you. That he'd tell the parole board what you'd done."

Termite guffawed. "Then why would I wait until after the hearing? Huh?"

"Get out of here, man." Deck stepped into the slim space between her and Termite, forcing Olivia to take a step back.

"Careful, Detective. I heard Benny Boy ain't doin' so well in the joint. It's a real depressing place. I'd hate to see him end up hanging from a bedsheet."

When Fr. Frank appeared, his eyes wide, and cleared his throat, Deck retreated. Even Termite's fists unclenched. The priest gestured down the hill to the casket. To the grave yawning beneath it. "Ready, my dear?" he asked Olivia.

Olivia took a breath and nodded at Fr. Frank. As if she could ever be ready for this.

"I can't believe Dad had so many secrets. I wish I could've known him better." Emily dropped a white lily onto the top of the redwood casket, while Olivia looked on. Everyone else had left, including Termite. After the service, he'd tromped back up the hill without a word, revving his engine as he'd ridden away.

"He liked ketchup on his pickles. He took me to Rollerama for my seventh birthday and taught me how to skate backward. He knew all the words to 'Billie Jean'. And he literally jumped up on the visiting room table when Mom told him she was pregnant with you. The COs took him out in handcuffs." They both laughed, Emily wiping at her eyes. "For all his flaws, he did some things right."

Emily leaned her head against Olivia's shoulder. Textbook little sister move, tugging at Olivia's heart. "Want to walk down to the river?" Em asked.

Olivia heard the burbling of the water nearby. It beckoned, soothing as a lullaby. But the ding of her phone alerted her to a new email from Marcus Boon, the officer who'd escorted her father to that ill-fated holding cell, who'd been the one to cut him down. "I'll meet you there."

Before she plucked her phone from her purse, she laid her own white lily down, said softly, "Love you, Dad."

She hoped, wherever he'd gone now, he could still hear her above the roar of his mighty Harley.

To: Olivia Rockwell <olivia.rockwell@cbsp.gov>
From: Marcus Boon <marcus.boon@vvsp.gov>
Date: March 9 11:15 AM PST
Subject: Re: Death Investigation

I'm sorry about the loss of your father, but I'm not sure what more I can tell you about that day. As I explained to Dr. Plunkett, following the conclusion of the hearing, I placed your father in a secure holding cell. I had assumed that, per our standard procedure, one of the other officers escorted him back to the Sensitive Needs Yard a short time later. We had a number of gang-affiliated general population inmates in the other holding cells. Though I can't provide you their names, for obvious reasons, the Oaktown Boys were represented.

As to whether I knew your father or thought he might be depressed, I can only tell you what I've learned in my twenty-five years working as an officer at Valley View and a lifetime spent in law enforcement. A man can live forever with no hope. But give him a glimmer of hope and take it away… you may as well put the bullet in his head yourself.

CHAPTER TWENTY-EIGHT

Olivia hated proving her sister right about always distracting herself with work. But after the funeral, she did just that. Driving straight to the prison, leaving Em alone at the house. The same way she had the day they'd buried their mother. She'd been running away back then. Now, it felt purposeful. Necessary even.

With her head down, Olivia fast-walked toward her office in the Mental Health Unit at the end of the long hallway. A few inmates called out to her. But she couldn't afford any distractions before her three o'clock appointment. She had to be on her game.

She unlocked the door to the MHU, grateful that the place seemed quiet. That Leah still had eight weeks left on her maternity leave. If anyone could see through her, Leah would.

Sergeant Shanice Weber poked her head up from the computer at the officers' station. "Hey, Doc. Didn't think you were comin' in today."

It had been three months now since Sergeant Weber had transferred from the control booth, and Olivia still hadn't grown used to seeing her there, with her tight braids and cheerful grin.

"I've got a new patient who I didn't want to reschedule."

"That him?" Sergeant Weber nodded her head at a figure wearing out the floor at the back of the MHU lobby. Even with his back to her, she could read him. Reminiscent of a caged animal, the tightness in his shoulders scared her. His muscles loaded, ready to strike. "When the CO escorted him down here, the first thing he told me was he didn't ask to meet with a psych doctor. And he doesn't need any help."

Olivia selected a push-button alarm from the box and clipped it to her waistband. "That's what they all say."

Sergeant Weber gave a solemn nod. "Let me know if you need me."

She approached the patient with caution. She'd lied to get him here, scheduled him herself. But her father—the man who relied on no one—had trusted him. That gave her hope. As she drew nearer, he spun around. The eyes, she recognized.

Still, she asked anyway. "Benjamin Decker?"

Ben didn't sit in the chair reserved for her patients. Instead, he glared at it as if it had spat in his face. "Why am I here?"

From her seat across the desk, Olivia studied this darker version of Deck, clad in a white SNY jumpsuit that branded him a target. His hair, buzzed short. His body, leaner. His face, all angles. Like prison had sharpened him to a point.

"Officially, or unofficially?"

The way he cocked his head and frowned, impatient, felt familiar though. Best to meet it head on, with an honest answer.

"Officially, I ducated you for an appointment with a psychologist. That's me. Doctor Olivia Rockwell. Unofficially, I need to know who killed my father, Martin Reilly."

"This is some crazy shit. I'm leaving." But he didn't move. Just stood there staring down at her, waiting for her next move. Still every bit a cop.

"My dad was looking out for you."

"I've got no clue what you're talking about, lady."

"I *asked* him to look out for you."

Ben's jaw clenched.

"Your brother, Will, *told* me to ask him to look out for you."

She had his attention. His lips turned up in an incredulous smile. He barked out a laugh—a single discordant note.

"Now I know you're messing with me. My brother has never had my back."

"*Never?* He asked Warden Blevins for your transfer. He sent his hard-earned money somewhere so the Oaktown Boys wouldn't stick a shank in your neck. So…"

Deck would certainly not approve of her speaking any of that out loud. Much less using it against his brother. But, desperate times.

"Are you trying to get me killed?" Ben's eyes darted over his shoulder to the empty MHU. "I don't have to listen to this."

She continued anyway. "My father once worked as an informant for yours. Did he tell you that?"

His hand reached for the door, leaving her no choice but to beg.

"Please. I know he didn't kill himself. The Oaktown Boys did it. I just need proof."

"I can't help you." He paused and turned to her, and she froze under the weight of his gaze. She thought of Rochelle Townes, the woman he'd shot, pinned by those same eyes before she'd taken a bullet. "You go looking for that kind of proof, you end up one of two ways. Empty-handed or dead."

CHAPTER TWENTY-NINE

After the funeral, Will headed to meet the CSI techs at the cabin on Wolver Hollow Road where Shelby's body had been discovered. While he drove, he downed the last dregs of the coffee he'd bought at the Stop-and-Shop, hoping to clear the cobwebs. He felt like a dog chasing a rabbit—one lead to the next—only to discover he'd been after his own tail.

Even with Trish's revelations about Shelby's loser boyfriend, Will still liked Winters for the murder. But DAs wanted more than a body. A murder weapon and a motive at least. Thirty-five years later, it would be tough to prove a case with just a few photographs and a hunch. The same way he couldn't prove Blevins had orchestrated Ben's sudden transfer, waiting for the opportunity to call in his favor, to cash in on his quid pro quo. Will feared he'd made a deal with the devil. But at least Ben was safe for now.

Will frowned at the Fog Harbor PD cruiser beside the crime tech van. He threw his truck into park, grabbed a pair of latex gloves, and made quick work of the front porch steps. Ducking under the yellow tape, he groaned the moment he set foot inside the cabin. Two techs Will recognized as Li and Munroe busied themselves with the set-up, arranging the camera on a tripod and preparing the bottle of Bluestar, a reagent that Will hoped would shed literal light on his crime scene.

Graham Bauer greeted him with a smirk, gloveless hand on hip. As usual, his hair had been gelled to within an inch of its life. "'Bout time you showed up. We already did the basement."

"What are you doing here, Graham? Nobody invited you."

"Steve-o did. Didn't ya, buddy?"

In the semi-darkness, Steve Li peered from behind the camera. "Detective Decker, I was told you were running quite late and might not make it after all. Graham suggested he could fill in for you."

"I got here just in time then." Will cocked his head at Graham. "Go find yourself a bicycle theft to investigate. I don't need you traipsing on my scene, contaminating it with your fingerprints, and blabbing about it all to Heather Hoffman."

"I have no idea what you're talking about."

"Sure you don't. Now that the chief's on to you and your reporter girlfriend." Will conjured the mental image of Chief Flack, scalpel in hand, removing Graham like a cancer. "Hoffman's just using you, you know. JB told me she once sliced a woman's tires to steal a story. Better watch your back."

"Whatever, man. This voodoo spray isn't gonna work anyway. It's been thirty-five years. Get a grip."

No surprise that Graham had a lame comeback. Or that he didn't know his ass from his elbow. He'd obviously slept through Evidence Collection 101. Blood evidence had been detected in hundred-year-old crime scenes. "We'll see."

"Yeah. We'll see... *nothing.*"

Graham finally got the message when Steve cleared his throat and directed a question to his partner, Kelly Munroe. "Ready?"

Atomizer in hand, Kelly hunched over the hardwood in front of the fireplace, coating a small section of the floor and the stones with Luminol. She worked carefully and methodically while Steve snapped the pictures.

Will's heart thrummed in his ears as the past seemed to come alive in front of them. A blue glow on the hardwood formed a light-puddle in front of the fireplace and in between the floorboards. Just below the location where Winters had described the abstract painting in Shelby's last photo. On the phone yesterday, Grimaldi had confirmed he'd hung a picture there that his daughter had painted in her fifth grade art class.

Someone had spilled blood beneath that painting. A lot of blood.

Will examined the owl-shaped andiron to the right of the fireplace. The first time he'd noticed the set of two on the hearth, the eyes—made of reflective green glass—had chilled him. Now, he felt a full body shiver as the entire head of the owl lit up with luminescence.

Graham harrumphed. "Probably a false positive. I heard that stuff can react to just about anything."

Will celebrated his victory in silence. Certain he'd found the murder weapon, he wouldn't dare let Helmet Hair rain on his parade.

"Detective, check it out." Steve drew his attention to the paneling just beside the hearth. Blue dots spattered the wall like paint.

"Could be anything," Graham insisted, pressing his hand to the wall before Will could stop him. Though Will knew better, he half expected Graham's hand to come back smeared with blood.

"Actually…" Steve approached the blood spatter. "These look like cast-off stains. The kind that occur when an assailant swings a bloody object back before he inflicts another blow. I see at least two arcs here."

"That seems consistent with Doc Clancy's findings. There were three major head wounds."

Muttering under his breath about junk science, Graham retreated toward the kitchen, pouting like a schoolboy in the corner, while Kelly took swabs from the floor, the hearth, and the far wall. The andiron was loaded into the back of the van for further testing.

After Steve and Kelly finished up inside, Graham followed them out without a word. Relishing the quiet, Will peeled off his gloves and wandered through the cabin once more, revisiting the rooms he'd seen in Shelby's photographs.

He gazed at the hearth that gave away none of its dark secrets, his father's voice bending his ear. *If you know the victim, you know the killer.*

Now that he'd met Shelby's mother and wallowed in her pain awhile, he felt he understood Shelby better. She'd been a typical teenage girl, always skirting the edge between promise and disaster. Between rebellion and conformity. If her life hadn't been cut short, he felt certain she'd have come out on the other side.

Will shut the door behind him, leaving Shelby's ghost alone again, and joined Steve and Kelly at the van.

"What'd you find down there? In the basement."

Kelly scrolled through a few of the long-exposure photos on the digital camera. Just a few specks of blue light on the stairs. "Given the conditions—the dirt floor, the length of time that's passed, the multiple owners moving in and out—it's not ideal for reagent use. In fact, even if we had seen a strong reaction, I'd be concerned about false positives. Fecal material in the soil, that sort of thing. There were some large droplets on the steps, though, and a few more in the kitchen. The kind of passive stains that result from the effects of gravity on a wounded victim. I took samples of those as well. Nothing on the walls."

Will nodded. "So, here's my working theory. The guy kills her in the living room. Hits her over the head with the andiron owl. Then, he transports her body—maybe on a sheet or a tarp—through the kitchen and down into the basement, which explains why we don't see much blood there. He loads her in the barrel. Fills it with sand and seals it up. Maybe he intended to move her but never got around to it. Fast forward thirty-five years."

"Assuming what we found today is the victim's blood, that certainly fits the evidence."

"Right." Will sighed, still feeling lost. "That only leaves two little problems."

They waited politely for his answer.

"The who and the why."

When Will returned to the station, he found JB hunched over the computer, scrolling through photographs of a lavish Mediterranean-style villa.

"House hunting?"

JB guffawed. "I wish. Remember our Vengeful Wife from Grimaldi's film, Victoria Ratcliffe? These are her digs. Her and her husband, Reid, have themselves a ten-thousand-square-foot monstrosity in Sea Cliff. And I dropped the letter Shelby wrote to her mother off at the lab. Tammy said she'd put a rush on it, as long as I toe the line."

Will nodded, dully, slumping into his desk chair. At least JB's reconciliation with Tammy had given them a leg-up at the crime lab.

"You okay?" The way JB looked at him, there was no hiding it. "How was the funeral?"

Will shrugged, intending to avoid the subject entirely. It pained him to picture Olivia, sitting beside her father's casket. No dimple in her cheek. The light in her eyes, doused. "One of the Oaktown Boys showed up."

"Hopefully you sent him packing."

"Tried. But Fr. Francis had other plans." Will half-smiled. "It's hard to argue with a priest."

"That's exactly why I never got married in a church."

"Vegas? All four times?"

"Double down and let it ride, City Boy." Grinning, JB pointed back to the computer screen. "I did some research on the *Chained* cast. Turns out Brenda Samson is MIA. Hasn't shown up in a police database since the spring of '86. Her last known address is now a strip mall."

"Any relatives?"

"A brother. Earl Samson in Pomona. Didn't pick up the phone."

"What about Eggerton?"

"The Unfaithful Husband? He got arrested a couple times for possession of cocaine. Otherwise, he's been off the radar and living in LA for the last twenty years with his wife and kids. He owns an adult bookstore called the Hollywood Vixen. But that sounds like the most exciting thing about him. I hope you found something better at the cabin."

"Other than Graham violating police procedure, you mean?"

JB let out an exasperated breath. "Again? Why am I not surprised?"

"There was one little thing." Will slipped his cell out of his pocket and smugly displayed the photo he'd taken of the andiron. "The murder weapon."

CHAPTER THIRTY

Olivia needed a beer. Or two.

And a number five.

With an extra-large side of mac and cheese.

She'd come to the Hickory Pit straight after work. Do not pass go. Because sometimes, even shrinks required a healthy dose of unhealthy coping. As soon as Jane, the bartender, slid a frosty mug her way, Olivia headed back to the booth she thought of as theirs now. Hers and Deck's. Thoughts like that were risky, she knew. But the way Deck grinned at her from the vinyl bench seat, they couldn't be helped.

"Fancy seeing you here." He polished off the last bite of a spare rib, discarding it in the paper tray. She raised her brows at the carnage.

"So, you too?"

"A number five, side of mac and cheese, kind of day apparently."

"*Extra-large* mac and cheese." She returned his smile as she slid into the booth opposite him. "Believe it or not, the outlaw half-brother I never knew existed turning up at Dad's funeral was the least of it."

"Oof. Sounds brutal. What happened?"

Olivia had prepared for this. Still, looking Deck in the face, she found it hard to lie. Even by omission. But she needed a little more time to work on his brother before she told Deck what she'd been up to, certain he'd put the kibosh on her one-woman investigation if she pushed too hard.

Instead, she took a drink, chasing her guilt with a slosh of cold beer. Then, she plucked the folded sheet of paper from her pocket, the email from Marcus Boon that had greeted her that morning. She'd printed it at work, mostly so she could hold it in her hand while she seethed with rage. She pushed it across the table toward him.

This she could give him. This felt safe.

"Take a look."

CHAPTER THIRTY-ONE

Will envied Olivia that beer. He needed something with bite to quiet the fluttering in his stomach. Not butterflies but bats, with sharp little teeth, gnashing on his insides. He stared at the printout of the email, pretending to be a slow reader, until Olivia got up to collect her order. With her out of sight for the moment, he took a deep breath and tried to stop his thoughts from spinning.

He'd been surprised to see her here. Surprised that she'd walked right over to him, like this was their booth, with a smile that soothed his tired soul. After he and JB had spent the rest of the afternoon researching the *Chained* trio, as they'd started calling them, the lab had called with the bad news. Not a single print on Shelby's letter. The DNA on the seal, if there was any, would take a while.

But all of it—the trailer in the woods, the parakeet bones, Trish's tears and regret—paled next to this single sheet of copy paper with a few lines of black ink. Because that asshole, Boon, had deflated Olivia's heart. Had made her wonder if her dad had given up on life. Given up on her and her sister.

"It's a total sham, right?" Olivia returned with her haul, carefully balancing the steaming-hot container of mac and cheese alongside her number five.

Will nodded. "Your dad just happened to end up in the holding cell with the pipe. Just happened to get an extra bedsheet. Detectives don't believe in coincidences."

"Neither do psychologists."

"What can you do?"

"I'm working on it." She took a delicate bite from a spare rib. "What about Shelby? Any new leads?"

"CSI found a lot of blood in the cabin. The place lit up like a Christmas tree. We'll have to wait on the lab to confirm that it's Shelby's. But I'm fairly convinced this is the murder weapon."

For the second time that day, he displayed the photo he'd taken of the owl andiron set in its usual position on the hearth.

"Creepy." Olivia grimaced, wiping a little sauce from her lip. "It certainly speaks to the planning, or lack thereof. The killer made a split-second decision. Used whatever was available to him. Same with the barrel, you know?"

Will's suspicions turned to Winters again, but he kept it to himself for now. He slid the case file across the table and pulled up the photo he'd taken on his phone of Trish's letter. "Shelby's mother got this in May of 1986, supposedly from Shelby, saying she'd met a nice rich boy and taken off to travel the country. She misspelled her own brother's name."

"That sounds fishy." Olivia enlarged the image of the yellowed paper, its creases well worn. "The language is oddly formal for a rebellious teenager, don't you think?"

"Exactly what her mom said. She gave us some photos of Shelby's loser boyfriend and her best friend, Drea, if you want to take a look. Apparently, those two hooked up not long after Shelby disappeared."

As Olivia flipped through the photographs, Will kept talking, full steam ahead, to distract her from that awful email. He couldn't fix it for her but he'd damned sure try.

CHAPTER THIRTY-TWO

Thankful for Deck's nervous chatter, Olivia worked her way through the photographs and JB's notes on the *Chained* trio. Lead actress, Victoria Ratcliffe, lived with her husband, Reid Vance, in Sea Cliff, an upscale neighborhood in San Francisco. There was no trace of Brenda Samson, the prostitute Grimaldi had been accused of kidnapping, and her next of kin hadn't returned JB's call. Donald Eggerton and his wife, Lucinda, owned an adult bookstore in Hollywood. He'd been arrested a few times as a young man but had no known history of violence.

Closing the folder, Olivia raised her head to look at Deck. "Do you really think any of these folks were involved in Shelby's murder?"

Deck shrugged. "Well, I figure whoever killed her had to have known about the cabin, that Grimaldi wasn't around a lot. They filmed a movie called *Chained*. And from the injuries Chet identified on her wrists, it seems like Shelby was chained up down there, so…"

"What's the story then? The *why?*"

"Hell if I know." He flashed a mischievous smile but it didn't quite reach his eyes. "That's what I keep you around for."

"Sometimes the *why* leads you to the *who.*" Olivia tried to push away the thought of her father and the Oaktown Boys and *why* they'd wanted him dead. It clung at the back of her brain, refusing to release its tenterhooks.

"I'm listening."

"No prints on the letter and the misspelled name must mean it's a farce, meant to stop anyone from looking for her. You've got to assume she was dead by then, which tells me she was already pregnant—likely with Brandon Simpkins' baby—when she ran away." Olivia finished the last of her beer and sat back, thinking. She liked the way Deck listened to her. The way he noticed every word, even when she was just spitballing. Even when he disagreed. "We also know that Chuck Winters last saw her a few weeks before he was arrested in March."

"If you believe a word out of his mouth."

"I do."

"You do?"

Olivia laughed at Deck's incredulity. "You're the one who tossed his room."

"I didn't say he was pure as the driven snow. I just don't think he killed Shelby. Does he seem like the type to concoct a letter like that? And why would he go out of his way to get that picture back? I'll bet he wanted to find her, just like he said. Besides, he was more of a career criminal than a sex offender."

"Maybe he broke into the cabin, hoping to rob the place, and Shelby caught him by surprise. He didn't want to go back to prison, so he panics, hits her with the andiron, and stuffs her in the barrel."

Olivia squinted at him skeptically.

"He's the best suspect I've got."

"Well, you're going to have to do better, Detective. Shelby didn't come to that cabin by accident. Think about it. Crescent Bay State Prison wasn't built until 1989. In the mid-eighties, Fog Harbor would've been a ghost town, especially in the fall. Even Winters said he came out here to disappear. How'd she end up at that cabin of all places? On a dirt road you'd need a map to find?"

Will wished he'd ordered dessert. Surely one of the Pit's giant chocolate chip cookies would ease the sting of Olivia and her pointed questions. Which were all infuriatingly legitimate. "You gonna answer that question for me?"

"I can tell you my best guess. Whatever the *why,* the baby is what brought her here. She was scared out of her mind to be pregnant. According to your notes, her mom said she still kept that Mary Jane doll on her bed. She was still a child at heart, not ready to be a mother."

Will tried to catch Jane's eye at the bar. "What about this guy, Simpkins? Do you know him from Crescent Bay?"

Olivia shrugged. "I think he's in the domestic violence group Leah facilitated before she went on maternity leave. One of the interns leads it now."

"Figures."

"What's he in for?" she asked.

Will had finally got Jane's attention. He held up the laminated dessert menu stanchioned between the ketchup and the salt and pepper. Picked his poison. As Olivia laughed, Will wondered when JB's soul had invaded his body, taken over his mouth too. "I'll give you three guesses and the first two don't count."

CHAPTER THIRTY-THREE

Deck cut the chocolate chip cookie right down the middle, a perfect dissection. "That's your half."

Olivia grinned as she broke off the crispy edge and popped it in her mouth. "I'm surprised you didn't use a ruler."

"When you have three brothers, you learn the art of precision. If you took less than your third, you'd be out of luck. And if you took more, you'd end up with a wedgie."

"No mercy, huh?"

"Not for the middle brother. I got it from both sides. Either taking up for Petey or taking licks from Ben."

"Typical middle child. The peacekeeper."

His mouth full, Deck rolled his eyes at her, and she chuckled.

"Researchers determined the birth order thing is mostly a myth. But did you know, astronauts and serial killers are usually firstborns?" Olivia asked him, taking another bite, savoring his flirty smirk.

"Hmph." Deck matched her with a bite of his own, both their halves dwindling.

"So, what was Ben like, growing up?" She felt guilty for fishing but it didn't stop her. The better she understood Deck's big brother and what made him tick, the better chance she had of convincing him to help her.

"Dad's favorite. Bossy. Stubborn. Kind of a know-it-all." Deck ticked the words off one by one on his fingers before he shrugged. "Typical firstborn."

Olivia snagged the last bite of Deck's half of the cookie.

"Hey—"

"That's what you get." She disappeared the morsel in her mouth. "You forgot *ruthless.*"

Deck stopped mid-laugh, his eyes widening. "Don't look now, but—"

She glanced over her shoulder anyway, following his gaze to the bar, where Jane was slinging drinks for the off-duty cops. "Is that Heather Hoffman?"

"Mm-hmm."

Olivia watched as the reporter rested her delicate hand on a beefy shoulder. A shoulder where she'd once laid her head, regrettably. "With Graham?"

"Not jealous, are you?"

A comeback on the tip of her tongue, Olivia's phone buzzed on the seat next to her. An unknown number with a San Francisco area code. She held up her finger to Deck. Mouthed, *one minute,* and left the table. Skirting past Graham and his arm candy—or was it the other way around?—she found a semi-quiet spot in the hallway near the bathroom.

"Hello?"

"Is this Olivia Rockwell?" She recognized the gravelly voice but couldn't place it. "You alone?"

"Yes. To both."

"This is Henry Decker. We need to talk about your father."

Olivia leaned into the wall at the Hickory Pit, keeping herself grounded by running her fingers over the couples' initials carved in the redwood. "Okay."

"I talked with a couple of my old buddies from the police force who work down at Valley View. Apparently, Mac Boon was on duty that day working the parole hearings. I knew Mac back when he worked for SFPD. Between you and me, I trust the guy about as far as I can spit."

A rush of air escaped her lungs, but no words came.

"Now, this part you can't go repeating. But word up at the prison is your daddy was still working as a CI. If Oaktown had gotten wind of that, he'd be a goner."

Olivia turned back toward the crowded restaurant, where she spotted Deck looking at her, his forehead creased with concern. She shook the shock off her face and forced a smile.

"A CI for SFPD?" Her voice didn't sound like her own, but the little girl she'd been before they'd left the Double Rock. Fearing her father as fiercely as she'd loved him.

"I can't say."

She couldn't tell if he meant can't or won't.

"But there's one more thing. You ever hear mention of the General being involved, you best drop it. Whoever or whatever he is, he's got eyes and ears everywhere. Foot soldiers, too." Olivia didn't tell him she'd already heard plenty about the General. He'd been at the rotten center of a contraband-smuggling operation at Crescent Bay State Prison.

"Why are you telling me this?" she asked, wondering if her words about holding onto anger had thawed him somehow.

"After you left, I remembered something else about ole Mad Dog. I always vet my CIs. Find out what makes 'em tick. Your daddy told me he started informing because of you…"

A lump formed in Olivia's throat, as she listened to Henry Decker break her heart.

"So one day you could be proud of him."

Lost in the fog of her thoughts, Olivia stared out at the ocean, listening to the numbing push and pull of the waves through the open window of the station wagon she'd inherited from her mother. After leaving the Hickory Pit, she'd come straight to her thinking place. The bluff overlooking Little Gull lighthouse.

The gleaming beacon shone down on the bright pink ice plants that had started to bloom on the hillside and creep up through the rocks. But the place still felt haunted by the long, wet winter. By the ghosts that roamed the shoreline, tortured and lonely like Little Gull, the Yurok woman who'd thrown herself from the bluff in the name of ill-fated love. Never at peace. Perhaps poor Shelby walked among them now.

Olivia rubbed the goosebumps on her arms. Her mind roiled and churned like the black water near the cliffside. She thought of her father and how she'd misunderstood the most essential piece of him. Of pregnant Shelby, arriving in Fog Harbor, scared and confused. Of the way they'd both ended up victims of their own foolish choices and the cruelest twists of fate. And of Deck, and the curious way he'd studied her when she'd returned to their table pretending she'd fielded a call from work and not his estranged father.

A knock on the passenger window, and Olivia yelped. She'd been so far gone, she hadn't noticed the car parked alongside her. "Em? What are you doing?"

"Looking for you, obvs." She made a face as she climbed in. "I figured I'd find you here. And this monstrosity is easy to spot. I can't believe you didn't try to salvage the Bimmer."

After her BMW had been wrecked that winter, Olivia put the insurance money toward refurbishing her mother's Buick station wagon instead. Clunker that it was, when she'd needed it most, it had still gotten her where she'd needed to go. She owed it one.

Emily ran her hand across the new leather seats. "But Mom would've loved this."

They sat side by side for who knows how long, listening for the cries of the gulls, and watching the unwavering bright light from Little Gull illuminate the deep, black water.

CHAPTER THIRTY-FOUR

Will found Cy dead asleep in a musty box in the corner of the garage. Apparently, slightly moldy cardboard made a more comfortable bed than the plush money pit Will had procured at the pet store in San Francisco before he'd returned. But he'd figured he owed it to Cy for sticking him with self-proclaimed *dog man* JB for two days.

After topping off Cy's food and water, Will took a seat on the tailgate to think. Though he hated to admit it, Olivia had a point about Winters. The ex-con didn't seem shrewd or sophisticated enough to create a ruse like that letter Shelby's mother had received. According to Olivia, Shelby's baby had brought her here, to a cabin in tiny Fog Harbor, where it would've been easy to disappear. But was she running from her mother? Or someone else?

A sharp sound started Will's heart firing like a piston. Cy had heard it too. Ears on high alert, his body stayed still as a stone.

Will tucked his gun in his side holster and slipped out the half-open garage door. He peered into the dark woods that separated his cabin from 248 Wolver Hollow Road and waited, holding his breath. Then, through the tangled bodies of the redwoods, a light flickered.

Will jogged up the dirt path that led from his house, skirting into the ditch when he reached the main road. The grass had already grown thick. Its blades calf-high and tugging at his jeans. Like sinister fingers meant to hold him, to sink him into the earth.

He ran without looking down. When he reached the turnoff for the neighboring cabin, he stopped. Listened again for the sound, for *any* sound, besides his own labored breathing. Hearing nothing but the soft call of the katydids, he crept forward across the lawn toward the cabin's cavernous eyes and the light, seeping through the slit in the curtains.

Someone was inside.

Will put one foot on the porch steps, wincing at the creak of the old wood. The yellow crime scene tape shivered in the wind.

"Put your hands where I can see 'em." The familiar voice came from behind him.

Will froze, momentarily confused, until he spotted a car parked on the lawn alongside the house, with the unmistakable front end of a Corvette.

"Are you trying to get yourself shot? I said, put your hands up."

Will could think of nothing he'd rather do less than to be held at gunpoint by a cowboy cop like Graham Bauer. But he complied, raising his hands to the sky.

"It's Will Decker, Fog Harbor PD." The gun in Graham's shaky hand kept him from adding, *moron.* "I live next door, remember?"

"Well, what the hell are you doing sneaking around out here?"

"Shouldn't I be asking you that?" Will pointed to the unoccupied vehicle. "And what's *she* doing here? Did you let her in?"

Looking surprisingly sheepish, Graham lowered his weapon, then his voice. "Look, man. I really like her, and she's into the badge. You know the type. She wanted to see the crime scene. Off the record, of course. Can't you just mosey on home and pretend you didn't see us? I'll return the key to the office in the morning."

"Nothing Heather Hoffman does is off the record. If I were you, I'd check your bedroom for a listening device." Will bounded up the last two steps, leaving Graham slack-jawed.

"At least there's something to *listen* to. Your bedroom is nothing but crickets." Graham laughed softly. "Guess she's just not that into you, Decker."

Will didn't need to ask who he meant. He flung open the door, just as Heather flicked the light off and strode out of the dark living room, ducking beneath the yellow tape. With a smirk, she dropped the key into Will's outstretched hand.

"No need to go to blows, gentlemen. I'm all done."

"Done with what, exactly?"

Heather shrugged and flipped her hair over her shoulder, descending the steps in her three-inch heels. "I needed a look at the crime scene. That's all. No biggie."

"'*No biggie*'?" Will groaned. "You're trespassing. Not to mention, it's dangerous. We don't know who killed Shelby Mayfield. Or why."

"That's why I brought an officer of the law."

Graham followed after her like a puppy desperate for a belly rub.

"Some of my viewers are real crime buffs, Detective. You never know, I may help you solve this case."

"I think we've got it covered." Will watched her toddle through the damp grass toward her car. "If I catch you out here again, you're leaving in handcuffs. And I don't want to see any photos of this place on your show tomorrow."

"You watch my show?"

He sighed when she looked at him, doe-eyed.

"I'd never," she insisted. "Besides, it's the darnedest thing. Someone stole my camera."

Script: *Good Morning, San Francisco*

Cue Heather

Good morning, San Francisco. It's 5 a.m. on Tuesday, March tenth. Time to rise and shine.

Roll intro music

Today we bring you our *Murder in the Bay* segment on location from the quaint seaside town of Fog Harbor, where I cut my journalistic teeth, so to speak, as a reporter for the local newspaper, the Fog Harbor *Gazette*.

Roll segment intro

Just behind me, you'll see the police station, where detectives are heads down, working the brutal murder of the young pregnant woman whose body was discovered here last week. Though police are awaiting DNA confirmation, sources close to the investigation have identified the victim as Shelby Mayfield, a sixteen-year-old runaway, who fled her home in San Francisco. Why did she run to Fog Harbor? What evil did she meet here? And how did she end up bludgeoned to death, with a barrel for her resting place?

Cue Shelby Mayfield yearbook photo

Good Morning, San Francisco obtained exclusive video of the cabin's living room, believed to be the crime scene, parts of which reportedly tested positive for blood evidence.

Roll video of cabin

When we return from commercial, we'll be joined via satellite by Donald Eggerton, owner of the Hollywood Vixen bookstore in Los Angeles. In an interview exclusive to *Good Morning, San Francisco*, Mr. Eggerton will share his experiences working with person-of-interest Maxwell Grimaldi, as an actor in *Chained*, a never-released film which by Mr. Eggerton's account could only be described as garish. Can he shed light on Shelby's killer? Stay tuned to find out.

Cut to commercial

CHAPTER THIRTY-FIVE

Will sat on the edge of his bed, half-dressed, with his cell pressed to his ear. He clicked off the television, grateful to be rid of Heather Hoffman's lying face. Though he figured she'd insist she hadn't been untruthful. Still, a video wasn't what he'd had in mind when he told her *no photos.*

"Good morning, Detective. This is Victoria Ratcliffe. You tried to reach me in reference to a homicide in Fog Harbor?"

She sounded way too put together for five thirty in the morning. Hell, Will never sounded that put together. The voice, though, had the same clipped timbre of the Vengeful Wife—*You will be punished for what you've done, you little hussy!*—barking at poor Brenda before she'd brought down a whip.

"Yes, ma'am. We're investigating a homicide that took place here, likely sometime in the spring of 1986."

"I saw it on the news. *Good Morning, San Francisco* too. It chilled me to the bone to think I'd been there. In that cabin. You don't think Max Grimaldi was involved, do you?"

"We're following all leads. That's as much as I can tell you. So, you were in the film called *Chained,* correct?"

Will took advantage of the long pause to tug on one arm of his shirt. "Goodness. How embarrassing. I had hoped that thing would never see the light of day. Then, I turn on my favorite morning show, and it's right there. In all its grainy horror. Back then, I had stars in my eyes. Obscura Studios was in need of a young actress. I applied, and Grimmy hired me on the spot."

Of course he had. Grimaldi had compared Victoria to a young Rita Hayworth. *If Rita had starred in* Sharknado, JB had quipped. "You only did the one film?"

"Have you seen it?"

Will chuckled, caught off guard by her unexpected humor. He shimmied into the other arm, practically pulling a muscle to do up the first button without dropping the phone.

"I'll take that as a *yes.* The whole experience was a little trauma-tizing, to be honest. But I went along. Thank God my husband was there. Though I'm sure he'd deny it."

"Why is that?" Will knew exactly why. He'd heard the name even before he'd googled them, trolled them both on Facebook. In her profile pic, Will saw the face her family's money had bought her. Unnaturally smooth, like stretched leather.

"My husband is Reid Vance. City councilman. My family owns Ratcliffe Chemicals. Surely you've heard of it."

"Sounds vaguely familiar." Only one of the wealthiest families in San Francisco. Which explained why she hadn't taken Reid's last name. "Your husband wasn't listed in the credits."

"Reid fancied himself a director. He preferred to work behind the scenes. He had helped Max on a few other projects. I guess you might say we both had silly Hollywood ambitions until our Jacqueline came along, and we started thinking about the kind of legacy we wanted to leave. Kids will make you grow up fast."

Will made a noise of polite agreement. Gave up on his buttons and leaned against the dresser. He needed to focus now. "Did you know Brenda Samson was a prostitute? That Grimaldi allegedly kidnapped her?"

Victoria sucked in a breath. Will pictured her behind a cher-rywood desk, her perfectly manicured fingers clutched to her chest. "Heavens no. He told all of us she'd auditioned for the part. But it doesn't shock me. Grimmy used to spend a lot of time in North Beach. He liked trashy women."

"*Young* and trashy?"

Victoria's laugh cut right through him, sharp as a blade. "What man doesn't? But never underage. Not that I knew of anyway. Reid and I wouldn't have stood for that. But Grimmy is a good man underneath all the bravado. I can't imagine him mixed up in something as untoward as kidnapping."

"So, you'd never heard of Shelby Mayfield?"

"Not until yesterday when my assistant fielded a call from that reporter. Naturally, she politely declined an interview on my behalf and directed her to Ratcliffe Chemicals' PR division. But all I could think of is that girl's poor mother. The loss of a child, a grandchild too. That's something you never get over. If I ever had to bury my Jacqueline, they'd have to dig two graves."

Will thought of Trish, holed up in her trailer in the woods. Give it some years, the vines would swallow it whole, sink it like a casket into the ground. It takes a long time to die of a broken heart.

CHAPTER THIRTY-SIX

Fifteen minutes late for their first post-baby breakfast at Myrtle's Café, Leah flumped into the booth opposite Olivia, looking bone-tired. As she directed her red-rimmed eyes at the menu, she rolled the stroller back and forth alongside the table with Liam napping inside.

Myrtle leaned in, cooing at him. "Does your mommy need a cup of coffee?"

"Mommy needs a caffeine drip."

After Myrtle had taken their orders, Leah sat back and shook her head. "Girl, this baby is doing a real number on me. I got two hours of sleep last night. My eyes feel like sandpaper. And my brain is mush." She held up a blue plastic rattle. "I tried to put this in the ignition."

Olivia laughed.

"It's not funny. If he wasn't so damned adorable, I'd have no choice but to give him back. This morning, he smiled, and I swear I started crying."

"He is pretty cute."

Just then, Liam started to fuss. Leah shook the rattle, and his eyes widened. "Cute and ruthless."

"Thanks for coming to the funeral yesterday. It meant a lot to me and Em." Olivia's chest ached when she thought of her sister leaving that morning under the cover of darkness and piloting her rental car back to San Francisco. It never got easier letting her go.

"Of course. I still can't believe you never told me about your dad being in prison. I would've understood."

"I know you would've. I just got so used to hiding it that it was easier to keep it a secret. Especially working at the prison."

"Speaking of, I assume the whole place has fallen apart in my absence?"

"Absolute shambles." They both chuckled. Though the Mental Health Unit had been a lot less sunny without Leah's smile. "Hey, don't you have a guy named Brandon Simpkins in your domestic violence group?"

"Yes…" She drew out the word, narrowed her eyes. "Is he giving the intern trouble?"

Olivia shrugged, noncommittal. "What's your take on him?"

"The usual domestic violence perp, I'd say. A repeat offender with about as much insight as a rock. He tries, though, for what it's worth."

When the bell on the front door jingled, Olivia glanced over, then to Leah, and back again for confirmation. The ball cap and sunglasses wouldn't work in a town this small. "That woman is everywhere."

"Who?"

"Heather Hoffman."

"The reporter?"

Olivia nodded, watching as Heather found a seat at a table in the back corner already occupied by an unfamiliar middle-aged woman. "Deck and I saw her at the Pit last night, too."

Leah wiggled her eyebrows.

"Don't say a word."

She held up her hands in mock surrender. "*Never.* What could I possibly have to say about your totally platonic friendship with a very attractive male detective?"

Looking past Leah, Olivia frowned at the envelope Heather slid across the table. Showing no restraint, the woman snatched it up and opened it, counting out the crisp bills before she slipped it into the purse at her feet. The way she moved, desperate and unashamed, set her apart among the usual morning crowd at Myrtle's, a mix of white-haired busybodies and professional folks on their way to work downtown.

Olivia willed herself to stay seated. But her muscles tensed with an urgent need to know. Without thinking, her hand gripped the stroller.

"Can I borrow your baby?"

Olivia kept her focus on Liam's cherub cheeks and his sky-blue eyes, that shock of brown hair—*damned adorable,* Leah had been right about that—as she pushed the stroller down the aisle toward the bathrooms. With a baby in tow, she hoped Heather wouldn't recognize her. But she needn't have worried. Still hiding behind her sunglasses, Heather didn't glance up from the handheld recorder placed in the center of the table.

It seemed impossible, but the strange woman in front of her—witch-black hair and haunted eyes and a smattering of ink on every inch of visible skin—had Heather enraptured. Their voices, too low to make out.

After Olivia passed the corner booth, she dropped Liam's rattle. It skittered farther than she'd intended, knocking up against the woman's cheap flip-flops. While Olivia panicked, a pair of slender legs slid out from beneath the table. A hand, with chipped black polish, reached for the toy. An arm extended toward her.

Olivia barely looked up. Just snatched the rattle and muttered *thanks,* while she studied the available evidence. The woman's forearm marked with a faded pink skull tattoo. Her red purse set atop the linoleum, the envelope of cash protruding from its insides. On it, Heather had written a name: *Drea.*

A pot of coffee, two scones, and Leah's amused expression awaited Olivia when she returned to the booth with Liam.

He'd fallen asleep again, snug in the stroller beneath his teddy bear blanket.

"Well?"

Olivia shrugged. "It could be nothing. But I think she just paid a source related to the barrel case Deck's investigating."

"Isn't that frowned upon?"

"Who says Heather Hoffman does anything by the book?"

Leah checked on the baby, her face softening as she watched his eyelashes flutter. "How'd my boy do?"

"A flawless performance in his first undercover operation. You should be proud."

CHAPTER THIRTY-SEVEN

Will followed JB into the bowels of Crescent Bay State Prison, already on edge. For one thing, a call from the lab had caught him halfway to the station, confirming that the ancient blood they'd swabbed in the cabin did indeed belong to Shelby. Not that he'd doubted it, but the thought of her bleeding out in the cabin next door brought him no comfort. Two, he hated feeling like he owed someone. Especially a phony like Warden Blevins. But he'd brought it upon himself, asked for it even by begging the warden for a favor with Ben. Now, he had to live with that nagging shadow, with the smug look on Blevins' face, when he greeted them outside the administrative office on their way to interview Brandon Simpkins.

"Another murder suspect here on my turf? It seems we can't keep you two detectives away from our fine establishment." Blevins shook both their hands, taking his time to look Will right in the eyes. "Though it's always a pleasure to see you both."

After Blevins had swiped his access key card and gone in ahead of them, JB dipped his head to Will, muttering under his breath. "A murder suspect in a prison. Who would've thunk it?"

"He's not a suspect," Will called to Blevins, fast-walking to catch up. "We just want to talk to him."

"No skin off my back either way, Detective." He came to a stop in front of a closed door, where a CO waited outside. "But let's try to keep the inmate inside the prison this time, shall we?"

*

As Will expected Shelby's ex-boyfriend, Simpkins, had a permanent scowl on his face. He'd lost the Mohawk, his bald head gleaming under the fluorescent lights, and put on twenty pounds of belly fat. Prison food will do that to you. But the attitude still belonged to the nineteen-year-old boy Will had seen in Trish's photo. As far as criminals go, he figured to be about as cooperative as Cy had been on his way to the vet a few weeks back; legs splayed and claws unsheathed, howling bloody murder, Will had battled for twenty minutes to force the tabby into his newly acquired pet carrier.

This was certain to be twice as long and half as fun. All the more reason he and JB had agreed to tag-team the interrogation. To wear Simpkins down with their good cop–bad cop routine.

Will stood by the door, watching. He'd let JB have the first crack at him, get him warmed up.

"Good morning, Mr. Simpkins. We appreciate you agreeing to speak with us." JB smiled, effusive as a game-show host.

A grunt and a nod from Simpkins. "I gotta be at work at nine."

"A working man. Impressive. My partner and I don't want to waste your valuable time, but we sure could use your help."

Simpkins leaned back, resting his palms on his thighs. His knobby knuckles a far cry from the blade-like fingers in Shelby's last photograph. "I watch the news. I know exactly what this is about, and I'll save you the trouble. It ain't me you're looking for."

"Who are we looking for then?"

"Hell if I know. That broad went and got herself killed. It's not my fucking problem." Once he'd spit the vile words out and had a chance to consider them, his sour face softened. "Pisses me off, though, about our kid."

"I'll bet. So, you knew about the baby? It was yours?"

"*He,* right? I heard that reporter say it was a boy. *He* was mine. As far as I know. That's what Shelby told me."

JB nodded. "And you wanted a kid?"

"Thought I did." Simpkins shrugged. "Figured I could at least do it better than my deadbeat dad."

"What did Shelby want?" Will spoke up, finally. As he said her name, he studied Simpkins' eyes. No flinch. No regret. Nothing.

"She wanted to get rid of the baby."

Will frowned, ready to poke the bear. "Really? I heard she was pretty hung up on you."

"Shelby thought she was too good for me. That she was going places." Simpkins laughed, all breath and irony. "Guess she did go someplace. Just not the place she thought."

"If she wanted to have an abortion, how'd she end up nine months pregnant?" *And dead.* Will left that last part unspoken for now. He'd take Simpkins down one rung at a time. "Why'd she tell somebody else she was giving the baby up for adoption?"

"All I know, she made an appointment at one of those clinics. We had a fight, and I refused to go with her. But Drea told me she didn't go through with it. She disappeared a couple days later. I never saw her again. Until the photo on that morning show took me right back."

JB gave Will a look before he laid it on thick. "I'd have been mad as an old wet hen if my woman had ever threatened to get rid of my baby. Nobody touches my girl. Ain't no tellin' what I would've done. How did you get through that, man?"

Simpkins was unmoved. "I'm sure you've already talked to Shelby's mom. And I figure she fed you all kinds of lies about me. That woman never liked me."

"Can you blame her?" Will asked. "Her sixteen-year-old daughter dating *you?* By that time, you'd already been locked up in youth authority for slinging dope. Then, her daughter shows up with a bruise on her face and an unconvincing story. Not exactly the future she had in mind for her little girl."

"I never hit a female without a good reason. Like this case I caught. You slap me in my face. You act like a man. I'm gonna treat you like one."

"The case with Drea, you mean." Will had been saving that one, and it felt damn good to use it. "Shelby's best friend. Your common-law wife. The probation officer's report said you two lovebirds have been on and off for a good thirty-five years. I'm no mathematician, but—"

"So what? Am I the first guy to mess around? Go ahead, indict me for cheating."

Will felt his own past rising up in him. Like a dead thing he'd buried. The nights his dad didn't come home, chasing leads until the sun rose over the Golden Gate. The nights he did, Will's mother cleaning crime scene blood from his boots. No wonder she'd gone off the deep end. "Maybe you got tired of Shelby. Maybe that baby was a complication. Or maybe you're just the kind of asshole who can't pick on someone their own size."

"I'm done talking. I told you what I know. Anything else, you can ask my lawyer."

Simpkins shot daggers at Will as the guard escorted him out. But Will paid him no mind. These DV guys were all the same. At the first sign of a challenge, he'd lawyered up. The playground equivalent of getting a bigger bully to fight your battles.

Will smacked his hand against the wall. "Sorry. Guess I pushed too hard."

"Nah. We got what we needed for now. Besides, I kinda like seeing you hot under the collar. Not so buttoned-up and by-the-numbers."

Will rolled his eyes. "Hey, since when do you have a kid? I thought you said you—"

"I did. Right after my first divorce. *Snip, snip.*"

"Then who were you talking about?" But as soon as Will said it, he knew. An entire wall of JB's cubicle bore the photographic evidence.

"My dachshund, Princess. Anybody lays a hand on her, it's lights out, brother."

*

Warden Blevins waited for them outside the door. "A fruitful conversation, I trust."

Will preferred Blevins stay out of it, so he let JB answer. The surest way to keep the warden in the dark. "About as fruitful as a peach tree in the desert."

Blevins puzzled for a moment. "I see."

"We'll let you know if anything comes up."

"Please do. As warden, I like to have my finger on the pulse of this place. Every one of these inmates is my responsibility. I take that seriously."

Will started to feel uneasy again. That nagging shadow darkening his mood. When the warden asked him for a word in private, he suspected his day was about to take a turn for the worse.

"Forgive me if I'm overstepping here, but I've been keeping an eye on your brother's safety, as you asked, and I thought it peculiar that he'd been ducated two days in a row for an appointment in the MHU. In fact, he's there as we speak. Were you aware that he's being treated by Doctor Rockwell?"

CHAPTER THIRTY-EIGHT

Seated in her office in the MHU, Olivia returned Ben's hard stare. She waited for him to break the stalemate and blink first. Apparently hardheadedness came standard issue in the Decker family.

"Look, I know you don't want to be here, but I'll call you back every day if I have to." He'd learn she could be just as stubborn. "I heard my father might've still been informing, possibly for SFPD or…"

"I told you, I can't help you." Today, he'd reluctantly sat in the chair reserved for her patients but only because Sergeant Weber had made her rounds. Frowning and pointing at it until he'd lowered himself onto the seat as if it had been rigged for explosion.

"You're not at all like your brother, are you?" If he expected a bomb, she'd give him a dirty one. "He always does the right thing. Even when it's hard."

"Fuck you, lady. What do you know about it?" *Boom.*

"I know he didn't have to spend his money to keep you safe. Or get you transferred here."

Ben's laugh had a sharp-toothed bite. "Yeah. He did some good. But he's the main reason I'm in this shithole."

"So it's Deck's fault you shot and killed someone? In my profession, we call that externalization of blame."

His smile set her on edge. But she'd keep pushing through the bravado. She hadn't given up on him.

"Deck was there. And he's not as innocent as he seems. It could've just as easily been him that pulled the trigger. Problem was, he didn't have the balls to do it. But he didn't think twice about selling me down the river."

"That's one way to look at it. It probably helps you sleep at night."

"Go ahead then. Tell me the right way to look at it, Doctor."

"You both made bad decisions, drinking too much and bringing your guns with you. You both violated police procedure. But you're the one who shot Rochelle Townes. Deck just had the guts to admit it." She paused, took a breath. Sent up a silent prayer that Ben still had at least one soft spot left in him somewhere. "And now you're the only one who can tell me what my dad was up to. The only one who can set this right."

She listened to the seconds on the office clock tick by until she couldn't bear it any longer. "Too bad you're too much of a coward. Deck is braver than you. And you'll always resent him for that, won't you?"

Ben leaned forward, studied her with those familiar brown eyes. His lacked light, though. Snuffed out by this place or never there to begin with, she couldn't tell which. "Damn. It sounds like you're into my brother."

Olivia opened her mouth to mount a half-hearted protest. But the door banged open instead. Deck charged in first, chastising her with his glare. Then his mouth.

"What do you think you're doing talking to my brother behind my back?"

JB lingered back at the lobby desk, grimacing, but Sergeant Weber had followed right behind.

"I tried to stop him," she said, helpless.

Only Ben seemed amused. He stood up, smirked at Olivia. Nodded at Deck. The history between them palpable. As if the past had taken shape, forming a visible wedge. "Guess we're done here."

Deck blocked the doorway, glaring at them both, until Ben forced him to move. He headed straight for Deck, took a cheap shot with his shoulder on the way out. But he stopped then, looked back. "Don't pull a Radovsky, man."

CHAPTER THIRTY-NINE

A Radovsky. Will blinked, temporarily stunned by the name he hadn't heard since high school. Pretty boy Phil Radovsky had been the definition of clueless, always insisting the girls who swarmed his locker and left him notes with red lipstick just thought of him as a friend. Or worse, a kid brother. He'd maintained the party line right up until he'd been voted Most Handsome by Ben's senior class. *A miscount,* he'd argued.

Olivia's eyes shot daggers straight at his heart. "Is there a reason you're in my office, Detective?"

The desk sergeant who'd chased after him cleared her throat in obvious triumph. Behind her, JB approached the door.

"Will, let's go. Doctor Rockwell's got work to do." Not a trace of sarcasm. Not one bad joke. Didn't even call him by his nickname. Now Will knew he'd messed up big.

Still, he couldn't let it go. His mind flashed to the Hickory Pit, to Olivia's pointed questions about Ben. To that white-hot sting of betrayal he could trace right back to Amy Bishop, and even further. To his mother and her leaving. "We'll talk about this later."

When Will spun around, he spotted his brother waiting for his officer escort at the locked outer door. A part of him ached for the big brother who'd always been faster, stronger, smarter. But this man was someone new. A stranger who knew everything about him. And maybe that's what bothered him most about seeing him in Olivia's patient chair.

JB tried to hold him back, but Will shrugged him off and stalked toward Ben, feeling both curious and mad as hell.

"A Radovsky, huh?"

One corner of Ben's mouth turned up. Then the other. That smartass smile one of the few holdovers from the old Ben. "Don't worry. I didn't tell her you wet the bed at sleepaway camp."

When the officer unlocked the door, Ben stepped forward, his eyes cutting to the badge clipped to Will's belt. He walked away without another word, and Will watched him go. His broad shoulders, his purposeful swagger.

"Escort!" the CO called out. The inmates stepped toward the wall, giving them a wide berth.

Will stayed there, rooted to the concrete, until Ben had disappeared from sight. When JB patted him on the shoulder, he realized how lonely he felt. How stupid he'd been to storm in here, taking Warden Blevins at his word. But mostly, how much it unnerved him that his convict brother still moved like a cop.

When they reached the Crown Vic in the prison parking lot, JB held out his hand. "Keys."

"I'm driving."

"Like hell you are. Blevins got you all wound up. What'd the guy say to you anyway?"

Will eyed JB over the hood as he opened the driver's door. The mention of the warden reignited the fire in his blood. "I'm over it."

"Well, I'm glad to hear it. But you made an ass of yourself in there. Good luck getting Olivia to speak to you again."

"Thanks for your support." He'd be lucky if she even looked his way. "But for your information, she didn't tell me she was talking to Ben. She was probably pressing him for information about her dad."

"And how do you know that?"

"Because I know her. And I know Ben. He'd never go within fifty feet of a therapist, even if he did need help. And she'd never do therapy with him. That would be unethical, given our… friendship."

Will didn't say that Warden Blevins had shown him the ducats for a mental health assessment originating from Olivia's computer. Had wondered aloud if Olivia had crossed the line. *She's been through a lot with her father. Perhaps it's impacting her professional judgment. I wouldn't want the other inmates to get the idea he's a narc. But don't worry, I'll look out for him.*

"Friendship. Right. And yet, you took Blevins' word over hers. That's messed-up, City Boy."

Will sighed; he hated when JB was right. He slid the keys across the hood and slunk around the back of the car toward the passenger side. "Just drive."

CHAPTER FORTY

Shaken, Olivia stared across the quiet lobby of the MHU at Leah's office. The closed door, the darkened window. She needed a friend right now. She couldn't stop seeing Deck's face, his outrage. Couldn't stop wondering how he'd known. But the worst part, he'd been right to be angry with her.

"Doc?" Sergeant Weber waved to her from the desk. "Come over here a sec."

Olivia dragged herself over, hopeful the sergeant wouldn't try to apologize. She'd done nothing wrong. A few of the inmate patients followed her with their eyes, and she found herself hoping they hadn't seen the outburst in her office. Nothing like a little drama to spark the Crescent Bay rumor mill.

"I found this on the desk after Inmate Decker signed out. Should I document it?"

She slid a small scrap of paper toward Olivia. Ben had torn the corner from the treatment sign-in log and scrawled a message in pencil.

"No need." Coming alive again, she balled it in her fist. "I'll handle it."

Olivia returned to her office, shut the door. She opened her palm and read the message. *Check 115s for Wyatt Anderson.*

Half-smiling again, she turned to her computer. Maybe Ben had a little of his brother in him after all.

RULES VIOLATION REPORT

INMATE NUMBER: 36RHU3   INMATE'S NAME: <u>WYATT ANDERSON</u>
FACILITY: VVSP   VIOLATION DATE: <u>2/17</u>
VIOLATION LOCATION: <u>SENSITIVE NEEDS YARD (SNY), UNIT Z</u>

SPECIFIC ACT: <u>POSSESSION OF INMATE MANUFACTURED WEAPON</u>

CIRCUMSTANCES OF VIOLATION:
On February 17th , Valley View State Prison (VVSP) officials received information from a confidential source indicating that Oaktown Boys dropout Wyatt Anderson was in possession of an inmate-manufactured weapon, endangering the safety and security of inmates and staff within the Sensitive Needs Yard (SNY). According to the confidential source, the weapon was intended for use in an attack on SNY inmate Benjamin Decker (Inmate Number 57YVI9).

Correctional Officer Reynaldo Ortiz searched cell 3L in Unit Z, belonging to Anderson. Hidden in the spine of a book, Officer Ortiz located an inmate-manufactured weapon measuring five inches long. The weapon was made from round metal stock and measured approximately six inches in length and one quarter inch in diameter. It had been sharpened to a point on one end, with masking tape around the other to form a handle. The weapon was marked and secured in the Captain's safe.

INMATE STATEMENT:
"No comment."

FINDINGS: GUILTY, SHU TERM 6 MONTHS

CHAPTER FORTY-ONE

Lieutenant Wheeler met Will and JB at the station door, trailing them back to their cubicles. "Chief's in a mood. You two best mind your p's and q's."

"Yes, sir." JB grinned as he gave a stiff-armed salute. "I take it she saw the morning show."

"Oh, she saw it alright. She's been on the phone with the execs at SFTV for the past hour, trying to convince them to pull the plug on that crazy reporter."

"Fat chance of that." JB dropped into his chair, started rummaging through his snack drawer, which had been reduced to a gluten-free shell of its former self. "Blonde hair, blue eyes, not a shred of journalistic integrity. She's a ratings boon."

Lieutenant Wheeler nodded gravely. "Any idea how she got into the cabin?"

"No telling with her." JB opened a bag of unsalted pretzels and popped one in his mouth. "That chick would sell her grandmother for a story."

"Easy there." Graham poked his head over the wall that separated their cubicles. "She's just doing her job."

"I'd keep that thought to myself if I were you," Will told him. "Unless you want to explain to Chief Flack—"

Wide-eyed, JB coughed, alerting Will to the looming shadow over his shoulder. The chief's scowling face was reflected in his computer screen.

"Well, somebody damn well better explain it to me."

Lieutenant Wheeler backpedaled toward his office—"p's and q's, gentlemen"—and disappeared inside. Will felt the heat of Graham's eyes on him, relieved he'd thought to return the key to the small envelope in the case file first thing that morning before Chief Flack arrived.

She made her way to the other side of the cubicles, stopping just short of Graham's desk.

"Got anything to say for yourself, Bauer?" A flush crept up Graham's neck. He swallowed hard. Opened his mouth, shut it again. "Think carefully. Because you're one morning broadcast away from the unemployment line. If it weren't for your uncle, I would've canned you already."

"I—I don't—"

Will looked right at Graham, momentarily savoring the grim pallor of his face. Word around the station was that his uncle Marvin had donated a shitload of money to the mayor's re-election campaign, which explained a lot. Like why Graham still carried a badge. "I have a pretty good idea what happened, Chief."

"I'm listening."

He took his time, while Graham squirmed. "Me and the lab techs were the last at the cabin. Somehow we must've forgotten to lock up." It pained Will to say it, but he figured she'd buy it. Back at SFPD, some detectives had been notorious for neglecting to secure their crime scenes. "That, or Hoffman broke in. It wouldn't surprise me if she knew how to pick a lock."

JB chuckled. "Probably keeps a burglar kit in her handbag."

The chief expelled an exasperated breath, glaring at them all before she walked away. When she reached her door, she cast a final disapproving look over her shoulder. "Whoever was responsible, don't let it happen again. Next time, I'll involve Officer Schmidt with Internal Affairs, and he won't be so forgiving."

"Damn. Officer Schmuck." JB crunched another pretzel. "Chief's not messin' around. "

"No, she's not." Will stared at Graham until he lifted his eyes. "The key will stay in my pocket from now on."

Will studied the stack of old police reports he'd printed. They spanned the course of thirty years but each read the same as the one before it. *Officers were contacted by female complainant Drea Marsh who alleged*—[insert despicable violent act here]—*by cohabitant Brandon Simpkins.*

The photos told the story. Each picture screamed a thousand awful words. The blue-black eyes, the jagged split of the lip, the defensive bruises on her arms, the bald spot where Simpkins yanked a handful of hair. Somewhere along the way, the spunky Drea who'd posed with Shelby had died. Her spark doused, so you couldn't see the light in her eyes anymore. In her place, a gray imposter. And with every photograph, it seemed Drea too had marked her body until even her delicate neck bore a spiderweb tattoo.

"Looks like we caught a break. Shelby's friend, Drea, moved up to Fog Harbor last October, after they transferred Simpkins to Crescent Bay." Will tossed half the pile on JB's desk. "They're not exactly a match made in heaven. If she knows something, maybe she'll finally be willing to talk."

JB winced after he'd scanned the first report, then the second and the third. The end results also identical. *Complainant refused to cooperate with investigation.* The cops had gotten lucky the last time, when Brandon hauled off and clocked Drea in the crowded parking lot of a Raiders game after she'd smiled too long at a fellow tailgater. When she'd slapped him back, he'd rammed her head into the side of a pick-up truck in front of a dozen witnesses, leaving her with a missing tooth and a concussion.

"My money says she's not talking." JB gestured to the sheaf of papers. "That's what you call graveyard love."

"Graveyard love?"

"Till *death* do you part."

Will let that settle into his bones. Cold and hard, it felt like the truth. Even so, he jotted down Drea's most recent known address.

"Did you see this one?" JB asked, sliding a 2013 arrest report back to Will's desk. "Second paragraph. Remind you of anything?"

Victim reported being secured with zip ties by suspect before he assaulted her. Reporting officer observed bruises on victim's wrists consistent with her statement. Will grimaced, recalling the splotchy marks Chet had observed on Shelby's wrists during the examination.

Lieutenant Wheeler poked his head from his office. "Good to see you boys still standing. Just got a call from one of your *Chained* trio, Donald Eggerton, in reference to the barrel case."

"Put him through." Will raised his eyebrows at JB, pushed a notepad in his direction. He wondered what Eggerton would have to say for himself, spilling his guts on a television show. "You're on speaker, Mr. Eggerton."

"Alright." The voice faltered, not nearly as confident as the one Will had heard answering Heather Hoffman's questions that morning.

Do you think Max Grimaldi is a killer? she'd asked.

That voice hadn't wavered. *With what I know, it's certainly possible.*

"We saw your interview on *Good Morning, San Francisco.* Any reason you went to SFTV with your story first?"

"Well, I'll be honest, Detectives. The adult bookstore business is not what it used to be."

JB scrawled a note. With a smirk, he pushed the pad to Will. *Does this guy know porn is free on the Internet?*

"I've got one kid in college and another in grad school. This old belt can't get much tighter. When that reporter called and offered me cash for an exclusive, it was pretty hard to resist. Especially after she told me she'd mention the bookstore on air. You can't beat that kind of publicity these days."

Will stifled a groan. "You do understand we're not running a TV station here? We don't work for a competing network. We're investigating a brutal murder. A young girl, an unborn baby. If you had information that could help solve this case, why wouldn't you call the police?"

"I get it, I get it." Eggerton sighed. "That's why I'm calling now. I do want to help."

Will paused to read JB's scribble—*Only if we agree to a bulk purchase of edible panties*—and chuckled under his breath.

"Okay. So, let's start with what you told the reporter. Apparently, you knew Brenda was on the film set against her will. That Max Grimaldi had kidnapped her. Is that right?"

"Not at first. But I figured it out pretty quick. He kept her chained up between takes, and she had no scripted dialogue. Honestly, she seemed really out of it. Like she might've been on something."

"Did you confront Grimaldi about it?"

"Heck, no. I was young, and I looked up to him. I took a couple of his film classes at San Francisco Art College. Anyway, Max kept saying he wanted the film to feel authentic. He told us Brenda was just method-acting."

Yikes. JB punctuated his note with a grimace.

"A few of the scenes in the film are quite realistic. Whips, blood, screaming. Was Brenda harmed on set?"

"Not that I recall. Aside from being chained to the wall, of course. Max was his own prop master and makeup artist. He had everything the big studios did. It's all fake blood packets and camera angles. For one scene, Max put a sponge on her back, filled it with red colored water. Instant blood spray."

Will conjured it in a flash. With a fearsome yell, Victoria had brought down the whip, sending a red mist into the dank air of the basement.

"What about the other actress, Victoria Ratcliffe? Did she know Brenda had been kidnapped?"

"She must've." Eggerton paused. "Her husband—Reid, if I recall correctly—was the one who helped Max find her."

CHAPTER FORTY-TWO

The shingled house at the end of Alder Street belonged to Drea Marsh now. It sat on a small fenced lot at the edge of town. Behind the bare wood planks, a dirt path led down to the Earl River, the burble of the water audible in the late-afternoon quiet. Standing there, inside Drea's screened porch, Will closed his eyes for a moment. But he only saw Shelby's hand reaching up from her barrel tomb. Only heard the risky promise he'd made to Trish. To find the bastard who'd done it and make him pay.

"Still can't believe you didn't out Bauer to the Chief." JB rang the bell for the second time.

"Why? Because I'm a *snitch?*" Will hated that word. But then again, sometimes he hated himself.

"C'mon, City Boy, you know me better than that." JB frowned at him. "Because he's an incompetent ass. An ass who dated your doctor."

Will shrugged, hating himself even more. Because even with all JB's razzing, he had never used Will's past against him. And yet Will had repaid his loyalty by throwing it in his face. "Well, she's not *my* doctor. She'll probably never speak to me again. And with enough rope, Graham will hang himself."

"With enough rope, Graham will have us all strung up like fish."

Will nodded, feeling antsy. Drea hadn't answered their calls either. "Looks like she's avoiding us." He paced to the edge of the porch, peering around the side of the house at a small shed, grown up with weeds. "Wanna poke around a little? Talk to the neighbors?"

"Nah. This old man needs to save his energy."

"Another tennis date with Tammy?"

"We're going five sets." JB raised one scraggly eyebrow and mashed the bell once more. "And I don't mean on the tennis court."

While JB waited on the porch, Will wandered to the side of the house. Though the weeds had grown thick with neglect, a well-worn path led him to a dilapidated shed on the edge of the property.

Will opened it with effort, dragging the door through the thick grass. The sunlight streamed in, spotlighting the dirt floor and the table at its center. On it, a heap of clay, half-formed into a wilting rose. Several shelves had been affixed to the dusty walls, where Drea's disturbing clay creations had been displayed. Misshapen bodies, skulls with bullet holes, snakes with fangs protruding. Drea had found a way to give life to the brokenness inside her.

Will leaned his head inside, searching for something more. As if Drea herself might be there, a wisp of the girl she'd been, hidden in the shadows.

"You lookin' for the gal that lives here?"

Will started at the voice over his shoulder. He peered at the old man in the neighboring yard through a hole in the fence wide enough for a body to squeeze through.

"Do you know her?" Will turned himself to the side, shimmied between the planks and flashed his badge.

The old man nodded. "She's a loner. But then, so am I. I heard she's got herself a fella up at the prison. So did the last one that lived here. I suppose it shouldn't surprise me. Young ladies today like the bad boys, don't they?"

Will chuckled.

"You know, for a hot minute I thought you might be that reporter who's been snoopin' around here."

Before Will could spit out a follow-up, JB cried out.

"Hey, stop!"

Unholstering his Glock, Will hurried back through the fence and around to the porch. Empty. The front door still closed and locked.

"JB?"

"Back here."

Will rounded the side of the house and dashed across the yard, where he found his partner struggling to climb the back fence, red-faced and out of breath.

JB pointed toward the river, huffing. "Went… that… way."

"Drea?"

"Probably. I didn't get a clear look."

Will scanned the wood planks until he located the hinges of the back gate, hidden behind a small rusted-out fishing boat which had been leaned up against the fence. He pushed through it to the weeds on the other side, jogging a bit until he'd reached the clearing by the river. Looked to his left and right and across the roiling water.

The only sign of life, a gull riding the wind on its way to the sea.

By the time Will returned, JB had taken a seat on Drea's front porch step, dabbing sweat from his brow and nursing his bruised ego. "I told you, City Boy. I don't do fences."

"How 'bout gates? Do you do those?"

JB extended his middle finger.

"Male or female?"

"Can't say for certain. The person had a ball cap on, dark sunglasses."

"Heather Hoffman? The neighbor said she'd been snooping around."

JB shrugged. "Might've been. Might've not."

Will's phone buzzed in his pocket. *What now?* His eyes fixed on the number, tempted to let it go to voicemail. Because a conversation with his ex-fiancée, Amy, struck him as a bad idea. Especially now, when he had the emotional bandwidth of a petulant teenager. Still, duty called.

"How can I help you, Inspector Bishop?"

With laser precision, Amy's laugh jabbed him right in the heart. The broken part he'd patched together with duct tape and time and good old-fashioned avoidance. "'Inspector Bishop'? Must be a rough day if Will Decker is busting out formalities."

It rankled how well she could read him. "Did you need something?"

"Okay. A really rough day then."

He fought back with the only weapon he knew would bring her to her knees. Silence.

"I'm calling about one of your suspects. I figured you'd want to know. But, if it's a bad time—"

"Just spare me the bullshit and spit it out already."

"Chuck Winters' parole agent called. He skipped town." Will barely had time to register his surprise. "And one more thing. Get over yourself, *Detective*."

CHAPTER FORTY-THREE

Olivia left her work clothes in a heap at the foot of the bed and slipped on her sneakers, intent on running this day into the ground. Fueled by worry and regret and half a turkey sandwich, she set a blistering pace, following the trail behind the house down to the Earl River, every step a reckoning. Every breath a repentance.

By the time she'd reached the water, she'd hit her stride. She didn't dare slow down; her demons would catch her. Didn't make her usual turn to the west that would've ended her up at the beach near Little Gull after a couple of miles. Instead, she headed east, following the gentle tug of her heart.

The river narrowed, darkened. The grove of redwoods shaded its banks.

She sprinted up the last hill, relishing the burn of her muscles, before she stopped. Put her hands behind her head and sucked in the spring air that had turned cool in the twilight.

Olivia walked a few steps, peering through the dense tree cover toward the rustic cabins that lined Wolver Hollow Road. She counted them off as she went, pausing at the back gate of 248. The dense forest closed in around the house, nearly blocking it from view. A shiver ran through her, imagining sixteen-year-old Shelby in the bedroom, the Mary Jane doll clasped to her chest as she slept. How lonely she must've felt. How afraid.

A sudden wind kicked up, sweeping the sweaty tendrils of her hair from her neck. The redwood branches, too, surrendered to its mercy, stirring and rustling, while it moved among them like a ghost. Suddenly cold and on edge, she rubbed her bare arms and listened.

A dog barked somewhere in the distance.

Closer, in the brush, a twig snapped, and she commenced running. Full speed ahead, up the path toward the cabin next door. As silly as it was, she didn't dare look behind her. Here, the thistle weeds had been cut back, leaving the dirt trail clear. The grass, neatly trimmed. As she rounded the side of the house, she spotted a light from beneath the half-opened garage, heard the thwack of gloved fists on leather.

Leaning down to look inside, she saw Deck, shirtless and out of breath. Then, and only then, did she feel safe.

CHAPTER FORTY-FOUR

Spent, Will stripped off his gloves and leaned against the truck. He wiped his face on the T-shirt he'd discarded five three-minute rounds ago and tossed it on the tailgate, watching the heavy bag sway with the impact of the last relentless flurry of punches that had finally quieted the chatter in his head.

Usually, when he pummeled the bag, he pictured somebody's face—Drake Devere, Ben, even his father. But today, he'd had no need for faces other than his own sorry mug. He'd let Simpkins get under his skin, then made a fool of himself at the prison. And worst of all, he'd come no closer to getting the answers Trish Mayfield deserved. After searching the woods behind Drea's house with patrol for over an hour, he and JB had called it a day.

Will contemplated throwing one last bare-knuckled bunch, but Cy drew his attention instead. The cat's good eye trained on the garage door he'd left partway open to let in the breeze. Sky-blue running shorts and a pair of toned legs dead-ended into Nikes, the soles covered in trail dust and freshly cut grass.

Against his better judgment, his heart leapt at the sight.

"Olivia?"

She poked her head beneath the door, looking sheepish and windswept. Cy stretched and meandered toward her, weaving between her feet. "Did you out me?" she asked him, scratching behind his ears.

Cy gazed up at her, purring in response. *Traitor.*

"Yeah. He's a real guard cat. No psychologist or rodent gets past him."

He hoisted the door the rest of the way, bringing her fully into view. Her ponytail. Her flushed cheeks. A wry smile and the dimple he hadn't seen in a while. He searched for the right thing to say. *I'm sorry* would've been a good start, but he couldn't bring himself to do it. Not after she'd lied by omission.

Olivia shifted from one foot to the other, staring back at him. Finally, he realized, grabbed for his shirt, and she laughed. "You really need to cover those abs, Detective. No one likes a show-off."

CHAPTER FORTY-FIVE

Tongue-tied, Olivia found a seat on the tailgate while Deck grabbed a clean shirt from inside. When he returned to join her there, he smelled suspiciously good. Even if he still looked pissed at her. She scooted further away, trying to wriggle clear of the danger zone. That two-foot radius within which she felt tempted to put her lips on his.

"So…" He sighed. "Do you want to glove up first?"

She frowned at him, puzzling.

"I figured you came here to hit something. Namely me." He leaned his chin in her direction, offering his stubbled jaw. "Go on. Take your best shot."

"Tempting." She gave his shoulder a teasing push, just to touch him. Ignored the lights and sirens in her head, the vortex pull of him. "But I'm the one who should apologize. I was wrong for talking to Ben without telling you. Talking to him at all, really."

"Yeah. You were. It's dangerous enough for a cop on the inside. You know that. He doesn't need you putting a target on his back."

Olivia hopped off the tailgate, her blood instantly simmering again at Deck and his monumental hypocrisy. She considered the gloves he'd tossed on the floor nearby. Maybe she should've taken him up on his offer. "But it's okay to bust into my office like you own the place?"

"I didn't mean—"

"It's okay to put a target on my dad's back? He protected Ben because I asked him to. And look what happened."

"That's not what—"

"Also, for the record, I defended you to your brother. I told him he was way out of line to blame you for his mistakes."

"Timeout." He reached for the gloves he'd discarded, offering them up with a hangdog look. "Please, just put these on and beat the hell out of me for three minutes. That would be preferable. That, I could take."

She relented and laughed a little, all breath. "Is that your version of an apology?"

"You know, for a therapist, you sure do argue a lot."

Emily had told her the same too many times to count. "No, I don't." She gave him a wry smile.

"You really defended me?"

"For some stupid reason."

"Uh, thanks, I think." His frown didn't hide his amusement. "Did he say anything helpful about your dad?"

"In a roundabout sort of way."

"That sounds like Ben."

Olivia returned to the tailgate, half-smiling. But she avoided Deck's eyes—the gateway to the danger zone—looking down at her lap instead. "By the way, what's a Radovsky?"

A sudden crack reverberated through the cabin, cruel as a whip, and Olivia clutched her chest. As Cy darted beneath the pick-up, cowering behind the wheel, she envied him his hiding place.

"What was that?" she asked, fearing the answer.

CHAPTER FORTY-SIX

Will recognized the unmistakable sound of gunfire. Two shots in quick succession. Then, several more. "It sounded like gunshots."

He headed for the door, intent on retrieving his Glock and a flashlight. Glanced back over his shoulder to Olivia. "Come inside and call 911."

Pale-faced, she nodded, following him through the entryway and into the kitchen. She plucked the old-school phone from the receiver and started to dial.

Another shot sounded from outside, clear and sharp and undeniable.

Will left Olivia there, securing his weapon as he darted out the front door into the darkness. His heart drummed in time with his feet. Fast but steady. His mind singularly focused on the gunfire that had come from the cabin next door.

With only the thin beam of his flashlight to show the way, he slunk into the forest, grateful for the tree cover, and crept with purpose toward the light in the window.

When he neared the break in the woods, his stomach churned. The bedroom windowpane had been splintered. The door left open. Parked alongside the house, a familiar red Corvette.

A blood trail led up the front steps, beneath the crime scene tape, and through the front door. Quiet and careful, Will entered the living room. Lit by the soft glow of the overhead fixture, shadows flickered and flitted in the dark corners, disappearing when he trained his gun on them.

The air felt heavy. Violence lingered there, seeping into the floorboards as tangible as Shelby's blood and making its indelible mark. The smell, too, Will knew. Metallic and sharp, it grew stronger as he worked his way through the cabin, room by room, clearing the kitchen, the bathroom. The entryway.

The silence unnerved him; it didn't last long. The cabin gave up its secrets all at once.

A gurgle. A gasp. A soft, mechanical whirring.

Will followed the trail of blood toward the sounds and positioned himself outside the bedroom, his Glock ready to fire. He peered in, trying to make sense of the scene, methodically cataloguing the evidence as he moved. He shut off the other part of himself. The part that desperately wanted to look away.

The night air rushed in through a smattering of bullet-sized holes in the window. The red eye of a video camera looked back at him, mirroring his own brand of practiced neutrality.

Will skirted the periphery, checking the closet. *Empty.* Kept his eyes on the door, his finger on the trigger, as he finally approached ground zero. The two vacant folding chairs at the center of the room, where blood had pooled beneath the body. Seeped from the mouth and ran down the neck.

He dropped to a knee, pressed his fingers to the woman's carotid, searching for a pulse. He waited. Felt nothing. His fingers came back warm and wet and red.

The creak of footsteps brought Will to his feet in a hurry. He sprang up, aiming his gun at the shadowy figure in the doorway.

CHAPTER FORTY-SEVEN

Olivia stared down the barrel of Deck's gun, its unfeeling eye trained on her. She'd been too afraid to call out to him. Even now, her hands shook as she raised them at her sides. In the last few months, she'd come to realize that shattering her father's beer bottle targets as a kid meant nothing in the real world. Where aiming a gun meant you had to be prepared to fire it, to accept the devastation it would cause, justified or not. Somehow she hadn't understood it until this past December when she'd nearly been shot herself.

"It's me," she said. "It's me."

"I told you to stay at the house."

Olivia noticed his fingers then, blood red.

"You didn't come back. I got worried." She stepped closer, across the threshold and into the room, gasping at the body slumped on the floor. Though she'd only seen the woman once before, she recognized the face from the diner. From the case file, too. Shelby's old friend, Drea.

"Oh my God. What happened?"

Deck pointed to the splintered window. "Shot through the window, it looks like."

"Is she…?"

The approaching sirens came as a comfort. A salve against his words. "No signs of life."

Olivia forced herself to look away from the blood. From the limp body, the pale face. It took her right back to the Double Rock, to Apartment E, to a time and place she never wanted to revisit. "Was there someone else here? I saw a car out front."

"Heather Hoffman." Deck pushed past her, pointing to the floor, where the drops led out the door like breadcrumbs. "I think that's her blood. I'm going after her."

CHAPTER FORTY-EIGHT

Will bounded out the front door, his heart still racing at the thought of Olivia's raised hands, her startled eyes. The job came down to a razor-thin line. A split-second firing of neurons. One quick decision between a moment of relief and a lifetime of regret. Between himself and Ben. A cop and a criminal.

The first in a line of patrol cars sped up the dirt road, wailing, and into the driveway. Its headlamps spotlighted Will, as Graham flung open the door and rushed toward him, with Jessie two steps behind.

"What's going on?" Graham demanded, his eyes darting to the Corvette.

"Multiple shots fired. One female victim inside. No pulse. And we've got a blood trail heading toward the road. A possible second victim."

Graham gaped over Will's shoulder toward the cabin, his face whitening.

"It's not Heather in there."

"Who then?"

Will took a breath, the woman's face—ashen and slack-jawed—fresh in his mind. He'd seen it before on the mug shot he'd printed out and given to JB before their trip to Alder Street. Petty theft the most serious of her offenses. "Drea Marsh. She's connected to the girl we found in the barrel."

"Shit. Where's Heather?" Graham ran a frantic hand through his hair, finally disheveling it. The gelled pieces remained askew. "I told her not to come back here."

"Well, she obviously didn't listen."

Graham looked to the ground, where Will had shined his flashlight on a bright red droplet. "You said there's a second—"

Will let the flashlight's beam fall to his feet. "Not a good idea, man. Go inside. Help Olivia. Your partner and I will find Heather."

"Olivia? What's she doing here?"

But Will had already left him, jogging along the pavement to catch up to Jessie. She'd gone on ahead, following the trail that led into the ditch by Wolver Hollow Road. A few patrol officers tailed her with their flashlights, flagging down the ambulance as it barreled toward them.

Will had nearly reached her when he spotted a small object glinting in the roadway.

"Got a shell casing." He pulled up short and crouched to examine it, its distance from the cabin explaining the lapse in time before the last gunshot. "Looks like it's from a .45 caliber."

"Hey, over here!" Jessie high-stepped through the tall grass, pointing into the trees, already on the radio calling for a second ambulance. Squinting, Will could make out a shape, an unmoving lump on the ground.

Just then, from behind them, "I found something." Will turned to the patrol officer, who'd raised his find into the night air like a fisherman displaying his prize catch. In his gloved hand, a high-heeled shoe.

CHAPTER FORTY-NINE

Olivia hadn't moved. She waited in the doorway of the bedroom where Deck had left her, staring at the red-eyed video camera perched like a bird of prey atop the tripod. Positioned alongside the folding chairs, its lens pointed away from the window. She shuddered at the thought that it had continued to roll, capturing the moment the first bullet had penetrated Drea's chest. Her gray Led Zeppelin T-shirt—the same one she'd been wearing at the café—had turned the color of burgundy wine.

Drea lay splayed on the floor where she'd fallen. Her black hair spilled around her wildly, forming a macabre frame around her pale face. Olivia struggled to imagine her dead. She seemed almost peaceful but for the blood that trickled down her neck, bisecting her spiderweb tattoo.

But Olivia had viewed enough crime scene photos to know the two small perforations in the material above her breast didn't tell the full story. A bullet devastated from the inside, tumbling around and tearing through flesh and bone and muscle. Vital organs too. Before it made its way out or lodged itself in. Like the other bullets that had struck the wall.

Steeling herself, Olivia stepped inside to examine the holes the bullets had left in the redwood paneling. One shot had nearly pierced the ceiling, but most had dead-ended near the heating vent, one of the bullets striking the screw and knocking the cover half off.

Olivia crouched down, peering into the dusty space where the vent had been affixed. In a thick layer of dust, she spotted a strip of corded blue fabric.

"Liv?" Graham burst in with the paramedics, looking like a man possessed. She'd never seen him so disheveled. Even the morning after that one regrettable night they'd spent together. "What the hell? You shouldn't be in here. It's not safe."

"Is she breathing?" The female EMT began cutting away the blood-soaked shirt to affix the AED.

"No," Olivia answered. "She wasn't breathing when we got here. No heartbeat either."

Graham lorded over her. "Olivia. Out. Now."

She nodded, even stood up and pretended to move toward the door. As soon as he'd been sufficiently distracted by the emergency personnel tending to Drea, her curiosity compelled her back to the vent. She reached inside and tugged on the strip, bringing something heavier into view. A quick glance over her shoulder, and she leaned toward the opening, puzzling at what she saw.

A blue duffel, *Bayview Broncos* printed on the side. The team logo cracked with age.

"I thought I told you to—" Graham knelt next to her. "What is it?"

Lightheaded, Olivia sat back against the wall. When she didn't answer, he pulled the bag from the vent, coughing from the dust cloud.

It sat between them. A time capsule, soiled with dirt and all-knowing. On the side of the canvas, a name had been printed in black marker, probably by a mother who knew kids had a tendency to lose things. KRIS MAYFIELD, it read.

CHAPTER FIFTY

Heather Hoffman lay face down in the dirt, bleeding from a gunshot wound to the upper back. Her arm, too, had been grazed, her blouse torn by the bullet. Strands of her hair had tangled in the underbrush; her face scratched by brambles. Jessie discovered her other shoe nearby, the heel broken. Her cell phone, half-buried in a pile of leaves.

"Heather!" Will knelt beside her. He ripped the shredded arm of her blouse and held the cloth against the wound to stop the bleeding. "Can you hear me?"

She groaned against the ground, drifting in and out of consciousness. Her hand curled in the weeds, then went limp again. Will had to talk to her. It might be his last chance.

"Who did this to you?"

He shook her shoulder and asked again, more urgent this time.

Heather turned her head and opened her mouth, her eyes wide and darting. No sound came out. The answer—if she had one—trapped within her.

Will watched as the paramedics carted Heather away on a stretcher, the ambulance blaring up the road toward the highway and taking the turn toward Fog Harbor General. In the sudden silence that followed, Will tried to get his bearings. Tried to make sense of it all. But he came up empty, too stunned to think straight. When they'd unearthed Shelby's body, he'd never imagined it leading here. To another victim. Possibly two.

He trudged back toward the house, pausing at the place where he'd found the shell casing. It had already been flagged with a yellow evidence marker. The whole road blocked now to incoming traffic with Officer "Bulldog" Bullock stationed out front keeping watch. Cops combed the ditch and the woods for the smallest clue.

JB stuck his head out the window of his Camaro as he slow-rolled under the yellow tape Bullock held up for him. "What'd ya get us mixed up in this time?"

Will walked alongside the car, briefing JB on the night's events. He pulled into the yard and parked at periphery.

"Jeez, Louise. Do you think Hoffman was the target? It sounds like the shooter chased her down after she hightailed it outta there."

"I think it was the other way around. I think Heather pursued the shooter. All the shots came from outside the window, and there's no evidence the shooter entered the cabin. You know Heather. She just wanted a better look. Anything for a story."

"Ain't that the truth." JB shook his head, disgusted. "Did she say anything?"

"She tried, but…"

"Then she damn well better live through the night."

CHAPTER FIFTY-ONE

"I think you should wait for Deck… uh, Detective Decker." Olivia looked on while Graham openly violated evidence procedure by hauling the duffel bag into the living room, where he placed it on the raised stone hearth. "At least put your gloves on."

"I'm a detective now too, you know." Thankfully, he complied, slipping on a pair of latex gloves before he started fumbling with the duffel's zipper. "Minor crimes. But I'm working my way up."

Olivia rolled her eyes but kept her mouth shut. She'd go easy on him for now. Since he'd gotten word over his radio about Heather's condition a few minutes ago, Graham had been hellbent on distracting himself, turning his attention to the treasured clue she'd found in the vent.

She couldn't stand to watch Graham rummage through the bag like a hungry bear. But she couldn't walk away either. Not now that he'd opened the duffel and pulled back the canvas.

When Olivia spied Deck and JB at the front door, she let out a breath, relieved to have back-up. The moment she waved them over, Graham started running his mouth, taking credit and trying to explain himself.

"I found it in the heating vent. Naturally, I started to investigate. I had to open it up. It could've been an incendiary device. The kind that would've blown us all sky-high."

Olivia cleared her throat.

"Alright, you got me. *She* found it."

"Incendiary device, my ass." JB let out an exasperated sigh and glared at Graham. "Well, what the hell is it? And why are your filthy paws all over it?"

"It belonged to Shelby," Deck announced. His eyes had gone right to the black marker. "Her mom said her brother's athletic bag was missing."

Graham resumed his single-minded search, his hands hovering over the top of the bag, ready to pluck the Mary Jane doll from the bowels of the duffel where it had been stuffed for the last thirty-five years. Olivia spotted the yarn hair, the yellow button eyes peeking up at them.

"Are you out of your damn mind?" JB's hand shot out, blocking him. "You ever hear of a little thing called chain of custody?"

Olivia fought off a twinge of sympathy when Graham stared at him, dumbstruck.

"How about preservation of evidence? Does that ring any bells?"

As Graham's face finally caught up, turning smug, Olivia's sympathy disappeared. He reached across JB, securing the bag and sliding it toward him. "C'mon, Gramps. Aren't we trying to solve a murder here? I can't be bothered with red tape. Not when we've got two more victims. Heather is counting on me."

"Call me Gramps again, and I'll show you how us old guys handle business."

The two men squared off, both fuming, until Deck put a hand on Graham's shoulder. "You know, you're right. Someone should be there with Heather. The moment she wakes up we'll need to get her statement. Can you handle that?"

Graham shrugged Deck off and huffed out a breath through his nostrils, but he nodded his agreement. He stalked out the front door without another word.

"The moment she wakes up?" JB asked, with raised eyebrows. "And what if she doesn't?"

"At least he's out of our hair." Deck held up a finger and answered his ringing cell phone. He listened for a moment, his face darkening. "Understood. Thanks."

When he turned to face them, Olivia's stomach dropped.

"That was the hospital. They confirmed Drea was dead on arrival."

CHAPTER FIFTY-TWO

Will watched from the porch as crime scene tech Steve Li carefully bagged the duffel and hauled it out to the van for transport to the lab. For the district attorney's sake, he hoped Graham hadn't left his fingerprints all over it. Murder cases were hard enough to prove without an inept cop muddying the waters. Bedside duty at Fog Harbor General seemed a safe spot for Graham. Even so, Will didn't trust him not to screw it up. He'd asked Jessie to tag along to captain the wayward ship. And he fully intended to head over himself when—*if*—Heather opened her eyes.

JB had retreated inside to secure the rest of the evidence, including the video footage, before they headed back to the station to regroup. On the outskirts of the house, the crime scene techs had begun marking the shell casings and dusting surfaces for prints, the same as they'd done inside the bedroom.

From her seat on the front steps, Olivia looked up at Will with worried eyes. "You okay?" she asked. "That was pretty intense."

"Yeah." Will wondered when he'd grown used to the chaos. To the head-spinning adrenaline rush. To the smell of blood and the glazed look of a victim's eyes halfway between life and death. "What about you? I told you to stay at the house."

He joined her on the steps, grateful for the momentary reprieve. For a chance to float a theory. For the opportunity to be next to her, too, if he was being honest.

"You said that once already."

He shrugged, *laissez-faire,* but it irked him the way she took risks. Unnecessary ones. "Here I was thinking that if I repeated myself enough times you'd actually listen."

"Psychologically speaking, the more you repeat yourself, the less I *need* to listen. You're actually just training me to tune you out."

"So, you're saying your stubbornness has a psychological explanation?"

"Not only that." She gave him a teasing smile, bumped his shoulder with her own. "I'm saying you only have yourself to blame."

Will groaned and stood up, planning to head back toward the house to find JB. The guy who still had a flip phone and carried an atlas in his car. With his technological expertise, he'd probably managed to delete the video footage by now.

But Olivia grabbed his arm, pinning him in place. "Your killer is running scared, don't you think?"

"Tough to say. It's still too early to draw any conclusions. We need to review all the evidence."

She huffed out a breath, cocked her head at him. "Is that your official position, Detective? I'm not a reporter, you know. I'm on your team."

"My gut feeling?" Will's gut had been churning from the sound of the first bullet, telling him to keep his eyes and ears open. "Drea knew something. Maybe something she planned to share with Heather. That's what got her killed."

JB strode out the door with a Cheshire cat grin, holding up a small zip drive. "I downloaded the footage. Took a little peek at the playback on the video camera."

"And?"

"That Heather Hoffman deserves a swift kick in the ass. But let me tell you, somebody oughta give her an Emmy or a badge. She did one hell of an interrogation. And bad news for us, the techs said that the video camera was Wi-Fi enabled. I guarantee you the whole viewing public is going to see that interview tomorrow morning."

Will cut his eyes at Olivia. Already, she had that look—eager and determined—and it put him on edge. The disturbing dream he'd had of his own dark basement, of what he'd found there, *who* he'd found, crept back into his mind, slippery as a snake. "C'mon, I'll drop you off at home on the way to the station."

JB cleared his throat with ceremony, no doubt paving the way for a smartass remark. "Did you forget she works with us now, partner? I'd say, the more eyes on this, the better."

"Doctor Rockwell has had quite a night. I thought she might be tired."

"Doctor Rockwell can speak for herself." Olivia stood up and headed straight for JB's Camaro. "I'll ride with Detective Benson," she said, without so much as a glance over her shoulder.

"Good decision. Detective Decker's a horrible driver anyway. He couldn't beat Grammy Benson in a street race. And she's been dead ten years now."

Will felt relieved to see Olivia laughing, but infuriated all the same.

One case. One lousy case. And she fancied herself a real-life Columbo.

Relegated to coffee duty, Will secured three lackluster cups of brew from the break room, filling the Styrofoam half full with cream and sugar to drown the muddy taste. When he returned, he pretended it didn't bother him that Olivia hadn't touched the sweatshirt he'd brought for her—an old relic from his days in the police academy—leaving it slung across the arm of his chair. In running shorts and a tank top, she had to be cold. Cold, and stubborn.

Fine. Let her suffer then.

Will tossed the sweatshirt onto his desk, making a show of it. He rolled his chair to JB's cubicle, positioning himself next to Olivia, the video queued up and ready to play.

"Jeez. This coffee tastes worse than Bev's meatloaf." JB stuck out his tongue in disgust. "That's my third ex-wife," he explained to Olivia, her own cup untouched. "Her cooking was so bad I actually thought she was trying to poison me."

"How do you know she wasn't?" Will teased.

JB took a second glance at his coffee cup.

"Don't worry. I ran out of arsenic."

Olivia laughed at them, then shut them both up. "You two bicker like an old married couple."

JB scrolled through the first ten minutes of video, where Heather roamed the cabin solo with her camera, documenting every inch of the crime scene, including the basement with its creepy bracket and dirt floor.

"You've got to hand it to her," he said, pausing the tape. "She's got cojones."

"And a bullet in her back." Will couldn't believe she'd had the audacity to show up back at the crime scene after she'd been warned. JB had been right. Anything for ratings.

The video picked up in the bedroom, with Heather in full makeup and seated across from Drea.

"Drea Marsh was just sixteen years old the last time she saw her best friend. For thirty-five years, she's blamed herself, wondering if a fateful encounter led to Shelby's death." Heather offered an empathic smile, careful not to overdo it. *"Welcome, Drea. Thank you for joining me for this exclusive interview."*

Drea's eyes, rimmed with mascara as black as her tattoo ink, flitted to the camera and back again, more suspicious than excited. With a boyfriend like Simpkins, life was a battlefield. Sleeping with the enemy, landmines at every turn. No wonder she didn't trust the cops. No wonder she looked older than her fifty-one years.

"Tell us about your friend."

"Shelby was a real sweet girl. A little naive though, especially when it came to guys. She always liked the bad boys. Probably, it had to do with her daddy. He took off right after she was born. I tried to tell her to be careful, but…"

JB harrumphed. "Sounds like the pot and the kettle."

On the screen, Heather nodded sagely. *"How did you find out Shelby was pregnant?"*

"She came over to my house one evening, scared out of her mind because she'd missed her period. We walked to the pharmacy and bought one of those tests. She took it right there in the store bathroom. Two pink lines."

"Did Shelby know who had fathered the baby?"

"Oh yeah, her boyfriend. I figured he wouldn't be too happy about it, since they'd been on the rocks for a while. But she insisted on telling him."

"How did he react?"

"I wasn't there. But right after, Shelby asked me to drive her to the women's clinic in the Mission District. She was upset."

"The clinic?" Heather's voice went up an octave. All show, in Will's opinion. *"And what happened there?"*

"She wanted to get an abortion. But when I came back to pick her up, she hadn't gone through with it. She said she couldn't do it. I took her home, and I never saw her again."

Heather looked at the camera knowingly. *"Did anything out of the ordinary happen at the clinic?"*

Drea nodded, taking a visible breath, and waited for a while. He wondered if she'd been coached to be this coy. *"Shelby talked to a man."*

"Did you recognize him?"

The answer came in a hail of bullets as, off camera, gunshots pierced the glass, rapid-fire. In Heather's scream, as she clutched her arm, the blood already seeping through her fingers. In Drea's sudden slump to the floor.

Will counted seven shots in total, consistent with the number of shell casings found in the grass outside the bedroom window. Which told him just how lucky Heather had been. The eighth and final shot had entered her back after she'd fled the cabin. The shooter, firing to empty. With one more bullet, the night would have certainly ended with two dead women.

They watched as Heather lifted her head from the floor and examined her wound. Then, she turned her eyes to the window. Cursing, she stumbled to her feet, darted out the bedroom door undaunted, leaving a trail of blood droplets behind her.

JB shook his head, as he paused the tape. "Thoughts?"

Will opened his mouth to speak.

"Not you, numbskull. I want to hear the doc's take on the shooter."

"Alright, Doctor, let's hear it. Enlighten us." Will kicked back in his chair, while Olivia gave him a sheepish look. Still, when she began, her voice sounded clear and certain.

"Well, your shooter wasn't very skilled with a firearm."

"*Obviously.*" Will stretched out the word, steeping it in sarcasm. "Two for seven. A total amateur. Must've gotten lucky with Heather."

"Maybe. Or the shooter timed the attack. Hiding behind a tree until Heather passed by him. Then, firing a shot at her back at close range."

He sat up and leaned toward Olivia, while JB looked on with amusement. Her explanation of the bullet to Heather's back made sense, but he hated when she out-detectived him. "I thought you said our perp wasn't skilled. Now he's lying in wait. Are you contradicting yourself, Doctor?"

"No." A flash of fire in those green eyes told him he'd hit his mark. She spun her chair toward him, facing off. Their knees, touching now. "Skilled isn't the same as clever. This was a planned assault with Drea as the intended target."

"The first six shots were fired to the left of the camera where Drea was sitting, so *clearly,* that makes her the intended target."

"Unlike taking an andiron to someone's head, which speaks to a possible personal connection to the victim and a high degree of rage, the use of a firearm suggests psychological distance. In other words—"

Will rolled his eyes, cutting her off. "I know what psychological distance means."

"Possibly the attacker had been following Drea for a while, and might have even been the one who eluded JB at her house. Heather Hoffman doesn't seem like the type to run from police. She's never had a problem blatantly disobeying authority."

"'Eluded' is a strong word. She opened a gate."

Finally, JB piped up. "Hey, I told you. I don't do fences." Olivia paid him no mind, laser-focused on proving her point. Will found her determination maddening. And sexy as hell.

"Assuming it's the same person, the killer escaped both scenes without notice. Which means he's organized and deliberate and smart."

Will shrugged, letting her think she'd won.

"So you don't disagree with my profile?"

"I don't disagree." He matched her victory smirk with one of his own. "But I fail to see how you've told me anything I didn't already know. Hell, I'm pretty sure Graham could've come up with that profile."

JB raised his hand like a schoolboy. "Am I allowed to speak here? Because you two need a referee. I call a foul on City Boy. That's hitting below the—"

The desk phone's ringing interrupted him. While JB spoke into the receiver, Olivia addressed Will.

"If you're so smart, then why'd you show me the case file in the first place?"

He'd never realized he could be told off in a whisper. And why did he feel the urgent need to grab her and kiss her mouth regardless of what came out of it?

With no reasonable answer to her question or his own, Will waited for JB to rescue him. "Steve's about to go through the duffel bag. I told him to wait for us. Unless you two need a little time to make up."

Olivia sat still as a stone while Will snagged his keys and pretended to straighten papers that had been there for weeks. Both of them silent, until Will caved first.

"A badge is required to get into the crime lab, so… I'll get patrol to give you a ride home. If that's okay. I'd take you myself, but—"

"It's fine." She stood up, hand on hip, cocking her head at him. "I'm fine."

"*Fine.*" Will reached for the sweatshirt he'd tossed on the desk. Fog Harbor nights could get chilly in the spring, and he'd only had time to tug on a pair of jeans and a T-shirt. Besides, Olivia clearly didn't want it.

Just as his fingers grazed the arm of the sweatshirt, Olivia snatched it from him.

She grinned unabashedly. "Give it to me. I'm freezing."

CHAPTER FIFTY-THREE

Olivia collapsed onto her sofa, exhausted. Too tired to strip off Deck's gray sweatshirt, she tucked her arms deeper inside the oversized sleeves. The material was soft and stretched out and frayed a little around the cuffs. And it smelled like him. But she didn't have the strength to resist. In fact, she might never give that damn sweatshirt back. Not after witnessing the aftermath of a murder. After going toe to toe with its annoyingly hunky owner.

She stared up at the ceiling, thinking of Drea's face—full of life this morning, drained of it by nightfall—until the tug of sleep dragged her under.

The beep of her phone startled her awake, and she sat upright. Her eyes scanned the room for threats. Found none. But her heart kept pounding against her rib cage. Her amygdala still working overtime.

A text from Emily waited on her screen.

U ok? Just watched the news. Heather Hoffman shot?

I'm ok. It happened at the cabin next to Deck's. The one where they found that girl in the barrel.

Olivia didn't say that she'd been there. That she still felt spooked. No need to worry Em unnecessarily.

That's wild. The cases must be connected, right? Do they know who did it?

They're working on it. How was the drive back to SF? You promised to call from the road, btw.

Uneventful. And I didn't want to be a distracted driver, BTW.

Em always knew how to win an argument with those one-liners and sarcastic capital letters that came standard in the little sister start-up kit.

Fair enough. Talk tomorrow though?

Yes, ma'am. I'll call you after class. *salutes*

Olivia smiled and tossed her phone back on the coffee table next to the Mayfield case file Deck had copied for her. She'd been too tired to give it the second look she'd intended, but Em's questions had prodded her back into action. She wanted to put Deck in his place. To show him solving the Seaside Strangler case hadn't been a lucky break.

She lugged the folder to the kitchen and spread it open on the table, studying the chilling photo she'd clipped to the front, and trying to decipher its secrets.

An impulse struck her then, and she dug through the junk drawer until she'd found her mother's magnifying glass. She placed it above the blurry last photo on Shelby's film, moving it methodically across the image until the sleeve of the jacket grew large beneath its eye.

She still couldn't make out the patch on the shoulder but she couldn't deny its distinctive colors—yellow, red, and black—and its strange shape. She felt certain that patch was the key to unmasking the subject of Shelby's final image.

Newly energized, Olivia scanned the photo into her laptop, then scrolled through the contacts in her cell until she found a name she'd banished to a lock box in her brain, filed under *verboten*.

She composed an email, attached the snapshot, and hit send. Imagined her request hurtling through cyberspace, looping through miles of cable fiber until it pinged the inbox of Supervisory Special Agent Jason Nash at the Federal Bureau of Investigation.

CHAPTER FIFTY-FOUR

Steve ushered Will inside the evidence room of the Del Norte County crime lab, the opened duffel bag already sitting on a metal work table. JB stood nearby, drumming his gloved fingers impatiently.

"'Bout damn time, City Boy. I told you to make it fast. You know, the opposite of the way you drive."

Will had drawn the short straw. So, on the way over, he'd telephoned Drea Marsh's family in San Francisco, delivering the kind of news that brings parents to their knees. The worst part, Drea's mother hadn't cried. Not at first. She'd told Will she'd expected it for years now and asked if they'd thrown that bastard Simpkins back in jail yet. When he'd told her Simpkins had never gotten out, that Drea had been killed by an unknown assailant, only then had she choked out a sob and dropped the phone, leaving Will to eavesdrop on her despair.

"Show a little compassion." Will donned his own latex gloves as he approached. "You sound like you've got ice in your veins."

"Ice in the veins, fire in the loins."

"I doubt anyone says that."

"Tammy does."

Steve raised his eyebrows but kept his mouth shut. He reached into the bag and produced the first item, Shelby's Mary Jane doll. When he laid it on the table, even JB fell quiet as it reminded them all that Shelby was still a girl herself, pregnant or not. Next, came the clothing. A couple of T-shirts, most with hard rock band logos printed across the chest, and a few pairs of denim shorts.

A makeup kit and a hairbrush still tangled with Shelby's blonde locks. Beneath it all, a paperback book Will remembered reading in high school. Artifacts of a life cut short, each item called to mind his promise to Trish. To find out what happened to her daughter.

"That's it?" JB sighed, flashing Steve a sour look. "Where's the smoking gun you promised?"

Steve grinned. "It's not a smoking gun exactly, but I did find something of interest in the outer pocket. It fell out in transport."

He revealed a slip of paper he'd packaged in a plastic bag and placed it on the metal table for inspection. At its center, it was marked GREYHOUND and dated March 3, 1986. Place of Issue: Fog Harbor. Destination: San Francisco.

"Can we get prints?" Will examined the ticket, contemplating what it meant.

"Already on it," Steve said.

"It looks like it hasn't been stamped or marked. I don't think she got the chance to use it."

JB puzzled for a moment. "Are you saying our runaway was running back home?"

Will thought of the bag, stuffed in the heating vent. Hidden, not by the killer, but possibly by Shelby herself. "Or running for her life."

When Will arrived back at the station, his heart sank. Chief Flack's black sedan sat alone in the parking lot, its face scowling. Its headlamps seemed to look down on him with the same kind of judgment and expectation he'd seen from the chief herself.

JB cursed under his breath while they trudged up the sidewalk. "It's nearly midnight. This can't be good."

Will tried to organize his thoughts, to grab them as they flitted past, but they disappeared like smoke in his hands. Fitting, since he was running on fumes and stale coffee. "What do we tell her?"

"Hell if I know. You're the lead detective."

The chief's door stood open. Positioned behind her desk, she glared at the computer screen. Will recognized the news footage. An image of the cabin, cordoned off with crime scene tape. Beneath it, the headline: **Double shooting at cabin, one dead. Reporter in serious condition.**

"Don't engage," JB muttered, darting out of her eyeline.

Will paused, sighed. "Hey, Chief."

"'Hey, Chief'?"

From the relative safety of his cubicle, JB shook his head and mouthed, *I told you so.*

"'*Hey, Chief*'? Are you punking me, Decker?" Chief Flack rose from her chair and stalked toward him. "Because this is not a 'hey, Chief' kind of night."

"Agreed. Bad choice of words."

"I thought I made myself clear. Nobody gets in that cabin but law enforcement. Now, we've got two victims that had no business being there. And a sensationalist reporter, no less. It's an embarrassment to the department."

"You're right."

JB grimaced, sucked in a breath through his teeth.

"*I'm right?* I know I'm damn well right."

"The key was with me all day, Chief. And Graham was just as shocked as anybody. Heather must've found her own way in. She's pretty resourceful."

Eyes wide, JB turned away like he couldn't bear to watch.

"Resourceful, huh? Maybe I ought to give her your job."

Feeling outmatched, Will retreated to his desk.

When the chief disappeared into her office, JB *tsk, tsk*ed. "I tried to warn you, man. That woman is not to be taken lightly."

"I just said 'hey'."

"Would you say 'hey' to a velociraptor? No, you wouldn't. You'd keep walking. No talk. No eye contact. And a pissed off woman? Hell, I'd take my chances with the raptor."

"Get in here, you two." Chief Flack's voice echoed in the quiet stationhouse, compelling them to walk the plank. With a smirk turning up her lip, she watched them until they'd both crossed the threshold and taken their seats. Prepared themselves for the worst. "Detectives, welcome to Jurassic Park."

Neither Will nor JB said a word, while the chief eyed them without blinking. Her gaze faintly predatory.

"Do you know how long I've had this job?"

Will looked at JB, and JB looked back, both hoping the other would answer.

"Ten long years. I've sacrificed friendships. I've lost touch with family. Hell, I've been single for the entire twenty-first century. I worked too damn hard to have the two of you yahoos tarnish my reputation. Because I guarantee you there are plenty of men in this town—in this department—waiting for the first female chief to muck it up."

JB opened his mouth.

"I'm not done yet, Benson. This is a tough case. Believe me, I get it. We're pinning our hopes on decades-old evidence and faded memories. At the end of this, we may or may not get our guy. And as much as that would irk me, I can live with it. All I'm asking… Don't embarrass me. Don't embarrass this department. And for God's sake don't get out-policed by a reporter."

She pointed to the door, and they stood, ready to slink back to their cubicles thoroughly browbeaten.

"And gentlemen, a piece of advice. Next time, don't poke the raptor."

After clearing the police barricade on Wolver Hollow Road, Will pulled into his driveway. Hungry, cranky, and dead tired, he still managed a half-smile when he spotted Cy waiting for him by the front door. That damn cat had worn down his defenses with the kind of scrappy determination you'd expect from a one-eyed feline.

"Come on." He opened the door, conceding. *Just for tonight.* But Cy took his sweet time. "I'm not going to beg you."

After a few ambivalent flicks of his tail, Cy strolled inside like he owned the place.

Will crashed onto the sofa. He'd catch a few hours' sleep and head to the hospital in the morning to check on their only living witness. According to Chief Flack, Heather Hoffman had undergone surgery to remove a .45 caliber bullet from her upper back. Minimal tissue damage, but the bullet had fractured her scapula. *Psychological distance, my ass.*

Will resisted the pull of his eyelids, the heavy tug of sleep. He conjured Olivia here with him, arguing back with her smart mouth. He wished she'd do something else with it.

As Cy settled at his feet, Will forced himself to stay awake. He had one thing left to do. Listen to the voicemails he'd been neglecting all day.

"This is Doctor Paretta calling for Detective Decker. I was able to compare those dental records with the teeth of the decedent, and it is a conclusive match. If you have any questions—"

Will skipped to the next message. He tried not to think of tomorrow when he'd have to pay Trish a visit and tell her what she already knew. When he'd have to face the fact that he hadn't kept his promise.

"Hello. This is Diana Hutchins, assistant to City Councilman Reid Vance. Mr. Vance requested that I return your call on his behalf. He has no comment at this time and requests any future communications be directed to his family attorney, Gerald Waverly, of Waverly and McKenzie in San Francisco. Thank you and have a pleasant day."

Well, screw you too, Reid Vance.

Script: *Good Morning, San Francisco*

Cue Pamela

Good morning, San Francisco. It's 5 a.m. on Wednesday, March eleventh. My name is Pamela Evans, and I'm filling in for Heather today.

Roll intro music

As you may have heard, our esteemed colleague, Heather Hoffman, was the victim of a shooting yesterday evening in Fog Harbor, where she was reporting on the murder of Shelby Mayfield. Local resident, Drea Marsh, was also shot and succumbed to her injuries after being rushed to the hospital.

Cue Drea Marsh photo

At the time of the shooting, Heather was interviewing Ms. Marsh about the Mayfield case. I spoke with Heather this morning by telephone, and she wanted me to tell all her loyal viewers she is recovering and plans to resume reporting on the case as soon as the doctors allow it. In the meantime, in a *Good Morning, San Francisco* exclusive, we have shocking footage from Heather's last interview.

Roll Marsh video

Just after Heather posed that fateful question, a gunman opened fire, fatally wounding Ms. Marsh. What happened at the cabin in Fog Harbor? Is this sudden act of violence related to the death of Shelby Mayfield? Stay tuned to *Good Morning, San Francisco* for the latest updates in the case.

When we return, stylist Heidi Zee will show us the latest looks gracing the runways this spring, and help us plan the perfect outfits for those spring soirées and backyard barbecues.

Cut to commercial

CHAPTER FIFTY-FIVE

A sharp knocking jolted Olivia awake.

Disoriented, she reached for her cell on the nightstand, knocking over the half-empty glass she'd placed there during the night. It cracked against the hardwood, the water seeping into the rug.

Olivia frowned at the phone, disbelieving. But the ray of light through the slit in the curtains confirmed it was past eight in the morning; she should've been at work by now. She should've been leading the 8 a.m. all-staff MHU meeting.

The knocking came again. Three solid raps, skirting the line between polite and insistent, leaving her no choice but to push off the covers and haul herself out of bed. She pondered her bare feet, her messy hair, Deck's police academy sweatshirt. But by the time she'd reached the front door and peered out through the peephole, the man had raised his hand again, knuckles poised. His partner stared blankly ahead, eyes hidden behind dark sunglasses.

She flung open the door, annoyed by her own irresponsibility. By their impatience. By their mere presence. And afraid, too. Of these men dressed in black suits like pall bearers. Harbingers of bad news.

"Olivia Rockwell?"

She nodded, her stomach twisting at the way her name sounded on his lips. Hollow and disapproving, as if he'd caught her cheating on a math test. Still, when he extended his hand, she took it, matching his strong grip.

"Agent Martello, San Francisco Federal Bureau of Investigation. This is my partner, Agent Bixby. My condolences for the loss of your father."

When he flashed his white teeth and his gold badge, her head started spinning. Surely, Agent Nash hadn't sent them here. Her email had gone out less than twelve hours ago. She hadn't even mentioned her father.

"What's this about?" she asked.

"May we come in?"

Olivia opened the door and watched as they breached the threshold. She listened to the synchronized swish of their trousers, their dress shoes thwacking against the linoleum.

Martello sat at her kitchen table before she'd invited him. Bixby lingered, removing his sunglasses and regarding her with stern eyes before he leaned against the wall. She felt relieved when Martello spoke first.

"We understand you collected your father's property from Valley View State Prison, including a sketchbook. Do you still have that in your possession?"

"The sketchbook? Uh…" Olivia willed her brain to focus, but it had been a long time since she'd shared a table with the suits of the FBI. Since Agent Jason Nash had audited her Criminal Psychology class at Stanford and introduced her to the special agent in charge. Since they'd asked for her help on a few cold cases and deemed her profiling skills worthy of commendation. "Yes. I have it. Why?"

"We'll need to take it with us. The prison should never have released it to you."

She balked at the idea. Em would be furious. But not only that. They had so little left of their father. To give any more felt like being robbed. "I'm sorry. Am I missing something here? What would the FBI want with my father's sketchbook?"

Bixby cleared his throat. The first sound he'd made, small but intimidating. "It's classified."

A hysterical laugh bubbled up inside her but she swallowed it down. "*Classified?* I don't understand."

"You worked on some cold cases for the agency in San Francisco, correct?" It wasn't a question. "So you're familiar with the nature of our work. I wish we could tell you more, but…"

"You can't tell me anything?" Olivia sighed. She should've known better than to start asking questions. Shrinks and cops never met a question they couldn't dodge, and FBI agents were no different.

"Do you have the sketchbook?" Martello asked again. He tried to soften it with a smile but his voice had grown more dogged. Same as his knock.

"I told you I do. Just give me a minute."

Fuming, Olivia made her way back to Emily's bedroom and retrieved the sketchbook from the dresser drawer. Though Olivia insisted she could take it with her back to San Francisco, Em had refused. *You need it more than I do,* she'd said. A truth that had made Olivia's chest ache.

Now, she cursed herself for not forcing Emily to take it, for not scouring the pages herself, looking for clues in the shaded drawings. She'd thought she had all the time in the world to study her father's pencil strokes. That was her problem. She'd always thought she had time.

Olivia flipped through the book, baffled. But if the suits wanted it, there had to be a reason.

She turned to the last sketch of the Double Rock and gingerly ripped the page from the binding, careful not to leave any trace. She couldn't give them *all* she had left of her father. She had to save something, however insignificant, for herself. She slipped the drawing beneath Emily's pillow and returned to the kitchen.

Martello held out an expectant hand.

"Will I get it back?"

"Of course." Helpless, she relented, looking on, as he tucked it beneath his arm. "When we're done with it."

CHAPTER FIFTY-SIX

Overnight, dread had settled into Will's bones, turning everything a shabby gray. The pair of tired eyes that met him in the mirror. The slice of dry toast he'd shoveled in, heading out the door. Even the cloudless March sky that had backdropped the drive downtown to Fog Harbor General Hospital.

That morning, Will had planned to make the trek to Pistol River. To deliver the news to Shelby's mother, Trish, face to face. To tell her the dental records were a match. But Graham had called him before he'd hit the freeway, and he'd had no choice but to turn his truck around. Heather was awake and ready to talk.

Outside the ICU, Will took a breath and tried to hide his excitement. The surest way to blow a murder case was to start counting your chickens. Besides, Graham looked so haggard Will actually felt bad for the guy.

"I could've interviewed her myself. She trusts me more than either of you."

But not that bad, it turned out. Will sighed and went in ahead, JB muttering in frustration behind him. The beeps and whirs and soft groans of the ICU twisted Will's stomach, reminding him just how close they'd been to having two new victims.

"Make it brief. She needs her rest." A nurse directed them behind a hanging curtain where Heather lay with her head propped on a pillow. A large bandage had been secured to her back with medical wrap and a sling, another covered the graze on her arm. An IV snaked its way upward toward the metal stand.

Heather straightened up, smoothed her hair, and offered an ironic smile. Will narrowed his eyes at her. Was she wearing lipstick?

"Go ahead and say it." Not even a croak in her throat. But at least he could still make out the scratches on her face.

"Say what?" Will asked.

"That you told me so. I shouldn't have been sneaking around in there. I was careless, reckless. I crossed the line."

"All true. But you didn't deserve to be shot."

"Hmph." JB obviously disagreed. "How'd you get into the cabin anyway?"

"I won't give away all my secrets, Detective Benson. Just because they're pumping me with enough pain meds to sedate a horse, don't think you can take advantage."

Will frowned at her, wondering if being hit by a metal projectile had taught her anything.

"Alright. You got me." Wincing, she gingerly raised one hand in surrender. Will marveled at the small chip in the red polish on her thumbnail. "I left the bedroom window open the night before. Graham wasn't involved, if that's what you're wondering."

Will withdrew a small notepad from his front pocket. "What we're wondering is what the hell happened yesterday. Did you run from us at Drea's house earlier in the afternoon?"

Heather scowled. "Don't be ridiculous. I'm a reporter, not a criminal. We have a code of ethics too, you know."

"Of course," JB muttered. "Your methods are beyond reproach."

"I think what Detective Benson means is we would very much appreciate you telling us what you remember about last night, since you are the best lead we have right now."

That prompted another scornful grunt from JB's throat but at least he quieted down.

"We were just getting to the juicy part of the interview. The part where Drea—God, I can't believe she's dead—talks about taking Shelby to the clinic. Seeing her with that man. I remember a flicker of movement at the window. For a second, I thought it might be you. I was already thinking how I'd probably have to spend the night in jail for trespassing. But then the gunfire started. I saw Drea go down and I hit the floor. I didn't even realize I'd been grazed until I saw the blood dripping."

"Then what?" Will asked, jotting a few notes.

"Then, I did what any self-respecting journalist would do. I ran after the asshole."

"Did you get a look at the shooter?" As he'd suspected, Heather had left the blood trail he'd seen in the cabin.

Heather shook her head. "I lost him in the trees. I thought he'd gotten away, but he must've ducked behind a tree trunk. I heard the snap of a twig behind me and then the shot to the back. I went down hard and passed out for a minute. The next thing I remember was waking up in the hospital."

As much as Will hated to admit it, she knew the case almost as well as he did. Even if she'd come by her information in the least ethical way possible. "So, what's your theory?"

"Someone wanted to silence Drea. Maybe even me. When Drea got to the house, she told me she thought someone had been following her. I figured she was paranoid, but—"

The nurse poked her head around the curtain. "Hurry it up in here. Doctor's orders."

Will nodded and asked the only question that really mattered. "Did Drea tell you anything else that wasn't on the tape? Anything about the man Shelby met outside the clinic?"

A sly grin tugged at the corners of Heather's mouth. "If I tell you, I want an exclusive when you catch the perp."

JB groaned. "You are relentless, woman."

"I'll take that as a compliment."

"Done," Will told her, knowing he'd probably regret it. But right now, a piece of his soul seemed a small price to pay for justice.

Heather grimaced a little as she sat up and adjusted her pillow. She leaned forward, dramatic, as if she still had a mic in her hand. "Drea told me she'd never seen him before but Shelby went right up to him. Like she knew him."

Trish stood in the grass in front of the trailer waiting for Will, wearing the same tattered housedress and world-weary expression. "You didn't have to make the long trip, Detective. You could've just told me on the phone."

Will skirted around three of her cats sprawled in a patch of sunlight and shook her hand. He gave it a gentle pat before taking a seat on an upside-down metal washtub. "It gave me a chance to ditch my partner, so I'm not complaining."

He'd sent JB to pick up lunch. His from the Hickory Pit, and JB's from Saucy Salads, the new health food café downtown. They'd made plans to meet up at Knotted Pines in an hour to follow up on their interview with Donald Eggerton. Hopefully, Grimaldi would shed some light about why he hadn't mentioned Reid Vance helping him find Brenda.

"It's her, then?"

Will nodded. "The dentist says it's definitive, so…"

The news settled onto her face, darkening it gray as ash. He imagined her heart the same color.

"Have you heard about Drea Marsh?"

"Don't have a TV. It only ever brought me bad news. But I picked it up on the radio this morning. Damn shame. Even if I didn't like the girl. No parent should have to go through this. Do you think it's connected to Shelby?"

"It's possible. Drea was at the cabin filming an interview about the case for a show called *Good Morning, San Francisco.*"

"Sounds like her. Trying to capitalize on a bad situation. Her and Simpkins were made for each other."

Will produced a folder from beneath his arm and passed it to Trish. "Do you recognize any of these people?"

Trish made her way to a leaf-covered lawn chair, where she sat, flipping through the movie stills Will had captured on his phone. Victoria Ratcliffe, Brenda Samson, Donald Eggerton. "Don't think so. Is this from a movie set?"

"A movie called *Chained.* It was filmed up at the cabin where we found Shelby but never released."

She closed the folder, dashing Will's hopes. He had to tell her, had to prepare her for the inevitable. That he might break his promise. That Shelby's murder might go unsolved.

"I did housework for a guy with his own movie studio."

Will's heartbeat quickened. "You don't happen to remember his name, do you?"

"Grimaldi. *Grimmy.* That was his nickname. I always thought he was an odd duck. Shelby called him Grimy behind his back because he gave her the creeps."

"Shelby *knew* him?"

Trish shrugged, oblivious to Will's sudden excitement. The sky had turned blue again. A perfect robin's egg shade. "She came with me to the house a few times and helped out. Mostly just did her homework in the kitchen. Why?"

More eager now than ever to face the old man again, Will jumped to his feet the moment Trish realized.

"Is he a suspect?" she asked.

CHAPTER FIFTY-SEVEN

Olivia dressed in a fog. The feeling she'd done something wrong clung to her like sea smoke. After no-showing to her own meeting, phoning in to the MHU had only made it worse. Because Dr. Carrie Stanley had taken the call. The same Dr. Stanley who'd been gunning for the Chief Psychologist job long before Olivia returned to Fog Harbor. *I'd be happy to cover for you, Doctor Rockwell.* And she did sound happy. Delighted at Olivia's misery.

Olivia contemplated staying home wrapped in Deck's sweatshirt, benching herself on the sofa with bad TV and microwave pizza. But she couldn't resist the urge to comb through her father's C-file again. Surely she'd missed something that would explain why the FBI had shown up on her doorstep and deemed her father's sketchbook worthy of seizure.

While she downed the last of her orange juice and watched the morning news replay the events she'd lived through last night, she took another look at the drawing of the Double Rock she'd ripped from her father's sketchbook. Turned it over, held it up to the light, searched for a hidden code in the margin. Nothing there but pencil strokes and bad memories. She felt silly, paranoid even, but she hid it anyway, slipping it in a kitchen drawer, pressed between two placemats.

But then, she reconsidered. Returning to the cabinet, she retrieved the drawing, folded it, and tucked it into her purse where she could keep a permanent eye on it.

Before she fired up her mother's station wagon, Olivia typed a text to Deck.

Weird morning. I overslept. I blame you and your stupid sweatshirt. Which she had no intention of giving back.

When he didn't respond right away, she added: *Anything good in the duffel?* Then, she tossed her phone in her purse like she didn't care in the least if he ever responded at all.

And yet, there she was fishing it out of her bag at the first stop sign. Checking it out of the corner of her eye. Halfway to the prison, she heard it buzz and pulled into the ditch like her life depended on it. She needed to know she could still do some good. That she could solve someone's case even if it wasn't her father's.

Olivia enlarged the photo Deck had sent her. The unused bus ticket came with a dose of mystery and melancholy. Offering more questions than answers, it struck her as a cruel twist of fate. She sat there for a moment, troubled and annoyed with herself. Deck had written exactly nothing, which disappointed her more than she cared to admit.

As she unlocked the door to the MHU, Olivia suppressed a groan at her own bad timing. A smug Dr. Stanley waved to her from the officers' station, while the rest of the staff filed out of the conference room.

"So glad you're feeling better, Chief. Hangovers are the worst."

"I didn't—" Olivia bit her tongue. She didn't have the energy to argue. Instead, she busied herself checking out an alarm and clipping it to her waist. Better than making eye contact with the enemy. "Thanks for filling in for me."

Olivia retreated to her office and shut the door. She wasted no time logging in and typing in her father's inmate number, as familiar to her now as his birthdate. Ever since Martello and Bixby had glided away in their unmarked sedan, she'd been turning a question over and over in her mind like a lucky coin in her pocket.

Could Dad have been informing for the FBI?

By the time she'd navigated to the Visiting tab in Martin Reilly's C-file, she'd all but talked herself out of it. It seemed wild. Far-fetched. Like a plot twist in an overwrought thriller.

Still, she wondered.

It didn't take long to scroll through her father's visiting log, her heart aching when she saw her mother's name listed, and then, no longer. Since her mother's death, he'd only had a handful of visits, nearly all from Carmen Sanchez, his state-appointed attorney. But she noticed a strange pattern within the last six months. Additional visits, at least once a month, sometimes more.

Olivia clicked on the most recent date in February and her mouth went dry.

Visitor: Theodore Reilly
Relationship: Brother

To anyone else it wouldn't have raised an eyebrow but to Olivia it confirmed her suspicions. Something didn't add up. Because Uncle Teddy couldn't have visited her father. Twenty years ago and three sheets to the wind, he'd run his motorcycle straight into the grille of a big rig. He'd made his permanent home in Golden Gate Cemetery ever since.

"Doctor Rockwell?" Olivia startled at the sound of Sergeant Weber's voice outside her office door. Brandon Simpkins stood next to her, a broken man.

She quickly exited her father's file and motioned them inside, taking a few quiet breaths to calm herself.

"Simpkins got a death notification this morning. He wants to talk to a psych. Anybody available?"

Without hesitation, Olivia pointed to the chair opposite her desk. "I am."

Brandon dropped into the seat, his fists clenched on his lap. His jaw muscles, tight as barbed wire. She half expected him to sweep his arm across her desk. To body-slam her computer. To punch a hole in the wall. Instead, he sat there, silent and seething.

"I'm sorry about your loss, Mr. Simpkins. I'm here to listen."

"Yesterday the cops show up here asking me questions about this gal I dated like a million years ago. She got pregnant with my kid and disappeared. Next thing I know, some pretty boy detective tells me they found her dead in a barrel. He got his panties all in a wad like I had something to do with it. Then this morning the COs pulled me out of the chow hall, took me down to the chaplain's office. Ain't nothing good comes from that. They told me my old lady got shot dead last night. All of a sudden my heart starts racing and I can't stop thinking it's my fault. All of this is my goddamn fault."

Olivia nodded and waited for him to continue.

"Drea wouldn't have been here in this shithole town if it wasn't for me. Did she call the cops on me? *Yeah.* Did she blow the whole thing out of proportion? *Yeah.* I barely hit her. But she didn't deserve to die like a dog. You know, I'm the one who told her to go to that reporter in the first place. To earn herself a little spendin' money."

With Olivia's head spinning like a hamster wheel, she decided on a well-timed "Hmm…"

"I know, right? Fuck my life, excuse my French. Do you ever wish you could just start over?"

Olivia traveled back to the Double Rock in an instant. Back to the day she'd tipped the first in a line of dominoes by opening the door to Tina Solomon's murder. If she had a do-over, that's exactly where she would start. Trouble was, no matter how she'd played it, she had a sinking feeling it would've ended the same.

With her father six feet under. "Everyone has regrets. And when we lose someone close to us, it's only natural to feel we let them down. That we're responsible for the harm that came to them. But that's a cognitive distortion. It's not reality."

"It sure as hell feels real when you've got two cops up in your face, pointing the finger at you for a murder. They'll probably try to pin this shit on me, too."

"So what would you have done differently, if you could?" A dangerous question—she was fishing now—but she couldn't help herself. "Where would you start?"

"With Shelby. I didn't help her when she asked. Back then, I didn't have two dimes to rub together, much less the money for a bus ticket home. Besides, I figured she was playing me for a fool. She'd already up and left with our kid. How was I supposed to know what she got herself mixed up in?"

Olivia thought of her cell phone, tucked in the glove box of her Buick. The picture Deck had sent via text. "So Shelby wanted to get back together?"

"Hell if I know. She was crying so hard I could barely understand her. She said there was some guy she was afraid of. I couldn't make heads or tails of it."

"Did you tell the police about this? It might be important."

Brandon's incredulous look gave her the answer. "Until today, the only person I ever told was Drea. And look where that got her."

The images flooded in. Drea's slack face and the blood pooling beneath her. The bullet holes in the wall, in Drea's shirt.

"Last time I talked to Drea…" His voice trailed off and disappeared entirely, even as Olivia leaned forward to hear him better. "Hold up. This is confidential, right?" His urgency startled her.

Before she could give her standard reply—*as long as the information doesn't pose a threat to the safety and security of the institution or the public*—he pressed on. "You're not gonna tell that asshole detective, are you? He's a real wise guy. You know the type."

Olivia *did* know the type. Infuriating. Stubborn as an ox. And yet, undeniably kissable. "No. Of course not."

"She told me she thought she was being followed."

"By who?"

He shrugged, then chuckled to himself. But it had no mirth beneath it. "This is going to sound real stupid. To tell you the truth, I laughed at her when she told me. I even asked if she'd started getting high again. But now…"

Olivia stayed as still and quiet as she could, afraid even the slightest movement would spook him from his confession.

"She found a plastic wrapper on the grass outside her bedroom window. Like someone had been out there long enough to need a snack."

"What sort of plastic wrapper?"

He shook his head, as if he could still hardly believe it. "Gummy fish."

CHAPTER FIFTY-EIGHT

Will checked his phone as he rushed up the cobblestone path toward Knotted Pines Retirement Home, ready to go toe to toe with old man Grimaldi, who'd conveniently forgotten to tell them he'd employed Shelby's mother as his housekeeper.

Will's text to Olivia, marked *read,* still had no reply. He wondered what she'd meant about his stupid sweatshirt. And how much of a creep it made him that he liked the thought of her sleeping in it. That when she gave it back, he hoped it would smell like her.

JB waved to him from the porch, where he sat finishing the last of a barbecue sandwich. As Will approached, he caught the distinct odor of cigarette smoke. A quick scan of the porch revealed a paper bag from the Hickory Pit and the yellow butt end of a Marlboro stuck into the soil of a potted geranium.

"What happened to Saucy Salads? I thought you were on a diet."

JB licked a drip of sauce from his thumb, then gestured to the seat beneath him. "Calories consumed in a rocking chair don't count."

"What about Marlboros?"

JB opened his mouth, thought better of it. Closed it again.

"I am a detective, remember? And you smell like an ashtray. Did you really think I wouldn't notice?"

"A detective, not a bloodhound. I sprayed myself with this." JB produced a pocket-sized bottle of Zero Smoke.

"Have you told Tammy you've fallen off the wagon?"

"Are you out of your damn mind? Of course I haven't told her. It's a lapse, not a relapse." JB hoisted himself from the rocking chair and tossed the empty paper bag in the trash.

"What about my sandwich? A number three on a sourdough roll with a side of coleslaw. Remember?"

Gritting his teeth, JB hurried inside.

"You ate my sandwich too? I hate to break it to you, but that's a full-on relapse, man."

"I can't help it, City Boy. We've got a girl in a barrel. Another one shot dead. My nerves are fried. I'm not sleeping well. If you want me to solve this case, I've got to be sharp. And believe it or not, this brain runs on carbs and nicotine."

"Oh, I believe it."

Nurse Thornton waved to them from the desk. "Here to see Grimmy?"

Will nodded. "But first, do you mind if we ask you a few questions?"

She motioned them over, whispering conspiratorially. "He's cheating at cards in the dining hall. He won't hear a thing."

"Does Mr. Grimaldi ever leave the facility?"

"Not that I've seen. We lock the place down at night. Some of our residents have a tendency to wander. And we have the occasional field trip, but like I told you the other day, Grimmy isn't so keen on the other residents. Unless he's winning at poker, he prefers to stay to himself."

"What about last night?"

"Last night? We can check the security footage." Nurse Thornton pointed to a nearby computer screen. After selecting the day and time, the black and white image of the outer doors appeared. She fast-forwarded through six hours of uneventful footage before Will told her to stop. If Grimaldi had left, he hadn't come through the front or side exits.

"Alright. We'll talk with Mr. Grimaldi now."

"Should I tell him you'll wait for him in his room?"

JB and Will locked eyes. "Absolutely."

They hoofed it down the hall, hoping to have a few moments alone before Grimaldi returned. To spot something useful in plain view. No warrant required.

Grimaldi's bed had been neatly made. The curtains pulled wide, letting in the sun. JB perused the old man's sparse closet, while Will beelined straight for the nightstand, where he'd spotted a row of greeting cards propped during their last visit.

Will peered down at the signatures inside. Every last one— Thanksgiving, Christmas, Valentine's, Easter—signed exactly the same. *Your loving daughter, Caroline.* He felt a pang, thinking of his own father, who'd preferred to display the bullet he'd removed from his vest after he'd been shot at by a bank robber high on cocaine. Cops couldn't afford to be sentimental.

Will examined the other items on the nightstand. An old man's starter kit complete with a pair of reading glasses, a tube of arthritis cream, and a copy of the Fog Harbor *Gazette,* folded to the crossword puzzle.

"So, how do you want to play this?" he asked JB.

"Classic pimple approach."

Will snorted. "Funny, I don't remember hearing about that one in the academy."

"They can't teach that kind of wisdom, partner. You learn it on the streets. It means we give him a little squeeze and see what pops out." JB stepped inside Grimaldi's bathroom and opened the small cabinet above his sink. He grimaced at a pair of dentures on the top shelf.

"I'm gonna pretend you didn't say that out loud."

"Pretend away, grasshopper."

While JB took his position on the sofa, Will's phone buzzed— unknown number—startling him as if he'd just been caught with his hand in the cookie jar. "Will Decker, Homicide."

"Hey, Deck. It's Olivia. Are you busy?"

"Uh, kind of. We're about to reinterview Grimaldi. What's up?"

"Oh. Sorry. It's probably nothing. It can wait." She took a breath. "I'm not even sure I should be telling you."

Will signaled to JB before he retreated to Grimaldi's bathroom and closed the door. "I'm listening."

In the hallway, Will heard Grimaldi approach with Nurse Thornton, pleading his case about his card game winnings—a bag of Swedish fish. He locked eyes with JB, marveling at their luck.

"You're pre-diabetic, Grimmy. You can't eat those."

"I'm eighty goddamn years old. That's old enough to make my own decisions."

Grimaldi burst through the door with a red fish poised above his mouth. He dropped it in, smacked his lips.

Nurse Thornton sighed. "At least put your teeth in first."

He grinned, his gums on full display. If Grimaldi was at all surprised to see a familiar pair of detectives waiting in his room, he didn't show it.

"You two bring my movie back? I've been itchin' to see the end of it." Grimaldi popped in his dentures and promptly put them to use, beheading a green fish.

"Don't you remember how it ends?" Will would never forget it. Voyeur-like, the camera had panned to the kitchen window. To the Unfaithful Husband digging a hole in the backyard at the Vengeful Wife's direction, while the Tortured Lover wailed on in the background. In the final shot, the sharp end of the shovel stabbed into the soft earth.

With Nurse Thornton's help, Grimaldi lowered himself into bed and shimmied beneath the covers. "Brilliant, wasn't it? That last scene really gets my juices going."

JB raised his eyebrows, twisted his mouth. "I'll bet it does."

Will couldn't bring himself to make small talk. After his meeting with Shelby's mother, the questions burned inside him like hot coals. "Did you make any more movies with Victoria Ratcliffe?"

"Hmm. Can't say I did. She didn't last long in the movie business. She found her true calling."

"And what was that?"

"Motherhood, I suppose."

"She told us you liked trashy women."

Grimaldi threw back his head, his jaw opening wide with laughter. The remnants of the green fish stuck to his dentures. "Who doesn't?"

JB shrugged. "The man's not wrong."

"Why didn't you tell us her husband worked for you?"

"You didn't ask. And besides, Reid was one of those artsy-fartsy stoners who thought he could be the next Scorsese. No one took him seriously. Frankly, I still don't know what Victoria saw in him."

"Did he help you recruit Brenda for the film?"

"Not that I recall." Grimaldi's eyes wandered to the window, where a bluebird had landed on the sill. "Come to think of it, he might've been in the car when we drove up to Fog Harbor to film. I think I asked him along, just in case Brenda got feisty. Didn't trust her one bit. My daddy always told me streetwalkers are known to keep shivs in their garters."

"And guns in their bras," JB quipped, with a sage nod at Grimaldi.

"You know, after you left last time, I saw the whole thing on that morning show. Heather Hoffman is a real looker. She's got a face for the movies." Grimaldi selected another candy fish and spoke while he chomped. "The girl's name was Shelby, right? Shelby Mayfield."

Will reached into his pants pocket and produced the photo Trish had given him two days ago. He'd been carrying it with him ever since, paper-thin but weighty as an albatross. "Did you know her?"

Grimaldi glanced at Shelby's picture, then away. "I was just gettin' to that. It hit me halfway through my scrambled eggs the next morning. Patricia Mayfield used to clean my house. She had a daughter, looked just like that." He placed a gnarled finger on the picture, and Will resisted the urge to yank it away. "The girl came with her a few times."

"And?"

"And that's it. I certainly didn't kill her if that's what you're getting at, Detective."

The condescension in his voice got under Will's skin. "You admit you knew her. And she turned up in *your* barrel on *your* property. So that's exactly what I'm getting at."

Grimaldi seemed unbothered, gulping down another fish. It seemed like the perfect time to pose the question that had been lingering at the back of his brain since Olivia called.

"What about Drea Marsh? Did you ever follow her?"

"Who?"

"Shelby's childhood friend was killed last night. Someone had been following her. Someone who liked Swedish fish. Remind you of anybody?"

Grimaldi scrunched his wrinkled face in indignation. "That's rich. You think I left Knotted Pines and committed a murder? Why don't you check the log? I haven't left this place in years. Now, unless you're going to arrest me, I don't have anything else to say to you and I'd like to get back to my crossword."

Frustrated, Will huffed out a breath and nodded at JB. They couldn't prove a damn thing. A candy wrapper was no smoking gun. And Grimaldi was right. It seemed damn near impossible to imagine him chasing Heather down in the woods outside the cabin.

Grimaldi gave them a stiff wave and reached over to the nightstand, the bag of gummy fish balancing precariously on his midsection. When he grabbed the newspaper, an ink pen slipped from its fold and clattered to the floor.

"I need an eight-letter word for 'a scoundrel's specialty' that starts with a 'v'."

Will picked up the pen and examined it, disbelieving his eyes. On its barrel, the Ratcliffe Chemicals logo. He placed it in Grimaldi's outstretched hand, as JB spouted the answer.

"Villainy."

Now that Will had seen it, he spotted it everywhere. That same logo, a swirling atom, on the nurses' station paperweight. Another RATCLIFFE CHEMICALS pen tucked into the pocket of a doctor in the hallway.

"Do you still have the Knotted Pines brochure?" he asked JB. "The one Nurse Thornton gave you."

"Hold up. Not even a comment on my crossword skills? I never told you my first wife was a crossword whiz. Too bad she—"

Will stopped and held up the pen he'd swiped from the front desk. He watched JB's jaw drop as he realized.

"What the—"

"Exactly." Walking faster now, Will called over his shoulder. "Brochure?"

"In the glove box."

JB unlocked his Camaro, retrieved the fancy brochure from beneath an unopened Twinkies package, and passed it to Will. Leaning against the car, Will flipped through the photos of the manicured grounds and the breathtaking sea view, past the smiling faces of models dressed as nurses and the assurances that every patient was treated like family. To the back, where they stuck the stuff nobody cared to read.

"Holy shit." He squinted at the fine print, read it aloud. "Knotted Pines, a Ratcliffe Chemicals property."

JB gave a woeful shake of his head. "This case just keeps getting weirder."

"Tell me about it."

"You thinkin' what I'm thinkin'?" JB's eyes narrowed, serious as a heart attack.

"That Grimaldi killed Shelby? *Maybe.* Him or Winters. But no way a man as old and feeble as Grimaldi chased Heather down. And I have no clue what this means." He tossed the brochure back onto the seat. "I think we need to talk to Victoria's husband, Reid. He's been holding out on us for way too long. Maybe I'll put in a call to Victoria and see if she can nudge him in the right direction. She's been cooperative so far."

JB reached around Will, snatched the Twinkies, and ripped into the plastic, the processed cake poised on his lips. "C'mon, City Boy. You know me better than that. I'm thinkin' if this is a relapse I might as well do it big."

CHAPTER FIFTY-NINE

Olivia waited until Sergeant Weber had unlocked the door and ushered Brandon Simpkins back onto the mainline, where he'd have to put on his tough guy mask and pretend he didn't care his girlfriend had taken two bullets to the chest. These domestic violence perps were all the same; they were stone-hearted until you scratched the surface, dug down to the brittle insides where the ego was as fragile as an eggshell. How many times had he backhanded Drea and choked her till her face turned red? Told her if he couldn't have her no one would? But in a world without her, he didn't make sense. He was a straw man.

When Brandon had disappeared from view, she returned to her computer with renewed focus, mulling over what he'd confided. She opened a blank document and typed the same questions she'd asked herself that first day when she'd sorted through Shelby's photographs. The same questions she always asked, knowing that victims could speak if you knew how to listen. Shelby, her father. Even Tina Solomon.

Who are you? How did you end up dead?

She understood Shelby now. A pregnant teen, overwhelmed and alone, she'd considered getting rid of the baby but changed her mind. Drea had seen Shelby talking to someone she knew at the clinic. Maybe he'd encouraged her to keep the baby or shamed her into running away. Even with all she'd been through, the pictures she'd taken spoke of a resilient girl who could find the daisy among the weeds. But something unexpected had happened in Fog Harbor. Something bad. Shelby had been afraid. She'd wanted to come home. So desperately that she'd reached out to slimeball Simpkins for help. But she'd never made it to the bus station. The ticket had gathered dust in the duffel bag for the last thirty-five years.

While Olivia racked her brain, she gave her hands something to do, typing the names of the whole sordid cast of characters—Max Grimaldi, Reid Vance and Victoria Ratcliffe, Donald Eggerton, Chuck Winters, Brandon Simpkins, Trish Mayfield, Drea Marsh, and Brenda Samson—and placing an X beside everyone Deck and JB had talked to so far. She stared at the name she'd left unmarked until her eyes glazed over and the screensaver kicked in. Until the clock's predictable ticking had faded into the background. Until she knew exactly what she had to do next. For Shelby, for her father. For herself.

Olivia dialed the number on the list she'd printed from her online search and listened to the shrill ringing. She'd all but given up—he hadn't returned any of Will or JB's messages—her office phone poised above the receiver, when a man's voice interrupted, taking a hammer to her ear.

"Who's calling me at this hour?"

Olivia winced, holding the phone a few inches away. She checked the clock, wondering if she'd stumbled into a wormhole. But no, still nearly two in the afternoon. "Is this Earl Samson?"

"Who's asking? That newfangled caller ID says unknown number."

"My name is…" She hadn't thought this far ahead. Rookie mistake. Searching her desk, her eyes landed on a package of file labels. "Avery."

"Avery what?"

Then, her computer. "Avery Dell."

"Well, Avery Dell, you don't sound like a cop. At least, not the two bulldogs who've been hounding me."

"That's because I'm not."

"Then what the hell do you want to sell me?"

She laughed a little. "Absolutely nothing. But I'd like to ask you a question."

"If it's something to do with who I'm voting for or whether I've found Jesus, save it for the next guy."

"Jesus is not involved. And I don't care who you vote for."

He sighed. "Alrighty, then. Shoot. But make it snappy. *The Price is Right* comes on in ten minutes."

"Do you know a girl named Brenda? Brenda Samson."

The sharp intake of breath told her he did, and she matched it with a steady exhale, trying to sound the exact opposite of how she felt. *Excited.* "Please don't hang up."

"Are you with that reporter chick? I swear that lady left about ten messages on my machine. Nobody leaves messages anymore, ya know? Unless they want something real bad. She's got her nose in everybody's business, showing that disgraceful film on her TV show. I'm not surprised she got herself shot."

"I'm not a reporter. Or a cop. I'd just like to talk to Brenda, if you know how to reach her. I'm an old friend of hers."

"Good luck with that. You ain't gonna find her. Nobody's heard from my kid sister since the spring of '86."

"She disappeared?" Olivia's heartbeat pounded in her ears like footsteps approaching from behind her.

"Ran away is more like it. At least that's what she said in that cockamamie letter she sent."

"Letter?"

"It arrived about a year after she'd gone. But I didn't believe a word of it. Something about traveling the world with a nice boy.

Hell, Brenda wouldn't have known a nice boy if one bit her in the ass. I thought once she had the baby she'd get her life together. Maybe stop sticking a needle in her arm and spreading her legs for money. But no dice. Some folks just ain't meant for this world. They spend their whole lives trying to escape. It's a pity, though. Wherever she went, she took Jamie with her. I wish she'd have left that little girl with me. She was such a pretty thing, with her mama's green eyes. But hell, what would I have done with a one-year-old?"

"Brenda had a baby?"

A pause. A click. Olivia cursed herself. She'd pushed too hard, too fast. Her words hung in the air, unanswered.

"If you'd like to make a call, please hang up and try again."

And that's exactly what she did, dialing another number this time. One she'd known by heart as a kid and dialed anytime things in Apartment E went to hell. Which was a regular occurrence. Right now, Olivia desperately needed a listening ear and a soft place to fall. Miss Pearl answered on the first ring.

Ten minutes later and already Olivia felt better. Miss Pearl's soothing tone had a way of ironing out the wrinkles in her soul.

"Oh dear. Those poor young women, both just starting out on the adventure of a lifetime. Motherhood. What had they ever done to anyone?"

Olivia let Miss Pearl's words resonate. Brenda had disappeared around the same time Shelby had been murdered. It seemed more and more likely that they'd met the same terrible fate.

Miss Pearl cleared her throat softly, preparing the way for something unpleasant. "Have you heard from Termite?"

"Not since he showed up at Dad's funeral uninvited."

"I tried to tell him not to go. But you know Termite. He always did march to the beat of his own drum. I thought you might've run into him since he's been holed up there at Rocky's."

Olivia heard the hitch in her breath. "Rocky's Salvage Yard?"

"That's right."

She'd never imagined Termite had stayed close. That the answers she needed about her father's death were only a few miles away.

Miss Pearl seemed to sense her intentions. *Be careful, dear,* she'd said. *Something's up with him. He told me he might need to go away for a while.*

Olivia returned her alarm to the desk, ignoring the judgmental look Dr. Stanley cast from her own open doorway, where she stood watching Olivia.

"I'm taking a late lunch," Olivia told Sergeant Weber, speaking louder than was necessary. "I'll be back for my three o'clock client." Never mind that her three o'clock had been transferred to another prison two weeks ago.

Without an ounce of guilt, Olivia booked it down the long hallway back toward the control booth. As she neared the warden's office, she spotted a familiar pair of broad shoulders, clad in the standard white SNY jumpsuit. His escort busy chatting up a female officer, Ben waited alone outside the administrative office.

When she got close enough to whisper, she joined him at the door. "Thanks for the intel."

"Don't know what you're talking about, Doc." He looked straight ahead, grinning. "How's my little brother?"

"What's a Radovsky?"

"You heard that, huh?" He snickered. "Did you ask Deck?"

"He wouldn't tell me."

"Can't say I blame him. Phil Radovsky was—"

The door swung open, Warden Blevins on the other side. "Mr. Decker, you're right on time. I would expect nothing less on your first day on the job."

Confused, Olivia's eyes darted between them. The warden ushered Ben inside, pointing to his office at the end of the hall. After Ben had slunk past him, Blevins turned back to Olivia.

"Job?" she asked.

"Yes. I've hired Ben to work as a clerk in my office. You'll have to thank Detective Decker for me. It was his idea."

CHAPTER SIXTY

With one hand, Will shoveled in a slice of cold pizza he'd scrounged from the wasteland otherwise known as the break room refrigerator. The other pecked REID VANCE into the Fog Harbor PD database. Across the divider, he'd put Jessie to work mining the Internet for Reid's buried secrets and ferreting out the connection between Ratcliffe Chemicals and Knotted Pines Nursing Home. Thankfully, Graham hadn't put up a fight when Will told him to stay at the hospital to keep an eye on Heather.

Will's phone buzzed on the desk. Olivia had finally responded to his text about the Greyhound bus ticket, but not in the way he'd hoped.

> *Ben working for Blevins was your idea? Have you lost your mind?*

He nearly choked on a slice of pepperoni.

"Anything good?" JB asked over his shoulder.

"Maybe." Will took a swig of water, swallowing his anger—Ben and Blevins?—and flipped his phone face down. No time for that now, he gestured to the ancient mug shot on his screen. At age twenty-five, ponytailed Reid bore little resemblance to the kind of too-slick guy who'd get his assistant to call you back. He'd even worn a single hoop in his right ear. "Check out Reid Vance, circa 1984."

"You mean Mr. City Councilman's got a record? That might be why he lawyered up."

Will scanned the rap sheet. It began with a DUI at age twenty-one and ended with a citation for misdemeanor trespassing five years later. "I doubt it. It's pretty minor stuff."

A frown furrowed JB's caterpillar brows. "Disturbing the peace, resisting arrest, DUI, possession of marijuana, trespassing. I'll bet his father-in-law wasn't too happy about all that."

Lieutenant Wheeler rounded the corner, giving them a wave. "I thought I heard you knuckleheads. While you were out, we got a call from the lab about that bus ticket. Turns out those other prints on it are a match for your guy, Winters."

"Perfect," Will said, burying his face in his hands for a moment. "Just perfect. We've got one suspect in the wind. Another in a nursing home. And the third referring us to his lawyer."

"Hey, at least you've got options." The lieutenant patted him on the shoulder.

"Which would be great if we were stockbrokers, LT."

Jessie poked her head up, peering uncertainly into Will's cubicle. "Uh, I found something, I think. It's probably nothing though."

"Well, don't oversell it," JB chuckled, while he and Will made their way to Jessie's desk where Lieutenant Wheeler had already posted up, reading an article on her screen.

San Francisco Post
"City councilman bails out local protestors"
by Angela Nguyen

A small group of protestors received an unexpected surprise yesterday evening when city councilman Reid Vance, husband of Ratcliffe Chemicals public relations manager Victoria Ratcliffe, paid $3,000 to bail them out of jail, following a sit-in demonstration at City Hall in San Francisco. The group of ten young adults, which included nineteen-year-old Amanda Murphy, were protesting for stricter gun laws in the wake of the June 2019 shooting inside the Cherrywood Mall, which left five dead and dozens more injured. Murphy said she was surprised and humbled by Vance's gesture, especially since Vance is widely known for his conservative views on gun control. "He really cares about the issues facing youth. I wish all politicians would follow his example."

Vance, who was elected to his first term on the Board of Supervisors in November 2018, said he was simply doing what was right, no matter the politics. "Believe it or not, I was a young man once, and I got arrested a few times. Even if we're on different sides of the issue, I support the youth of San Francisco getting into the right kind of trouble, speaking out and making their voices heard."

According to a city council source who wished to remain anonymous, Vance left behind his difficult past when he met his wife. After they started a family together, his career

blossomed, and he was eventually appointed vice president of Human Resources. As previously reported by the _Post_, Vance overcame a troubled childhood and a litany of minor arrests on his way to success.

Will turned to his partner, who wore the same skeptical expression as the rest of them. Minimal faith in humanity was a perpetual job hazard. "Sounds like Councilman Vance is a real man of the people."

"Yeah, so was Charles Manson."

Chief Flack craned her head out of her office, silencing their laughter with the subtlety of an axe. "Detectives, if you're not too busy amusing yourselves, there's a telephone call for you. Apparently, Councilman Vance has been trying to reach you regarding your yet-unsolved murder investigation."

Will didn't let his confusion slow him down. Jogging back to his desk, he told Chief Flack to put the call through and clicked the speakerphone.

"Hello, Mr. Vance. Detectives Decker and Benson here. We were actually just talking about you, wondering why it is you preferred that we speak to you through an attorney."

Reid released an exasperated breath. "That's my fault. There was a misunderstanding with my assistant, Ms. Hutchins. It wasn't until my wife told me you'd spoken with her and might be trying to reach me that I realized the error. Needless to say, Ms. Hutchins has been moved to another role in the company. And if you were speaking of me, I hope it wasn't all bad."

"You'll talk to us then?" Will readied his pen above a blank page in his notepad.

"I'm happy to help in any way I can. The loss of a young person is always a tragedy. And then, to hear about the death of her friend yesterday evening. It's just unfathomable."

"So, you heard about the shooting up at the cabin? Drea Marsh? Heather Hoffman?"

"Indeed. I heard the story on the radio on the way home from my city council meeting. Of course, they hadn't released the victims' names yet, but I saw the story this morning on *Good Morning, San Francisco.*"

As Will jotted Reid's alibi for follow-up, JB had already found the city council home page, confirming last night's meeting.

"Does the name Brenda Samson ring any bells?" Will asked.

"If you'd asked me that a week ago, I would've come up empty. But it's difficult not to be reminded with *Good Morning, San Francisco* playing clips of that disgraceful film. I'm sure my wife told you it wasn't one of her finer moments. Mine either. We had stars in our eyes back then."

"What can you tell me about Brenda?"

"Not much, I'm afraid. As best I can recall, Max Grimaldi—I call him Grimmy—asked me to ride with him to Fog Harbor for the movie shoot. When he picked me up, Brenda was already in the car. She looked a little worse for wear, but I didn't ask any questions. We shot the film in one day. At that time in my life, I just wanted to be a famous director. Victoria was much more sensible. She realized we'd have to give it all up once we started a family."

"So, Victoria drove to Fog Harbor separately?"

"That's right. Grimmy wanted it that way. The women kept apart. He thought it would help them get into character. It seems silly now, of course." Reid's half-hearted chuckle clunked down the phone line.

"Donald Eggerton told us you'd helped Grimaldi recruit Brenda for the film. That you knew she was a prostitute."

"Totally false. But I'm not surprised Donald would say such a thing. He was always jealous of my relationship with Grimmy, and his morals were questionable even then. Now I hear he's in the sex toy business. A real shame."

JB shrugged, smirked.

"Have you had any contact with Brenda since then?" Will asked.

"None. A while after the film wrapped, Grimmy told me she'd disappeared, after she'd made some nasty allegations against him. I was relieved for his sake."

"What about Shelby Mayfield? Did you know her?"

Will tapped his pen against the desk, counting the long seconds waiting for an answer.

"I've racked my brain over this one. Because the photograph on the news looked so familiar to me. I think I must have met her at Grimmy's house. He had a housekeeper with a teenage daughter. I don't recall that we ever had a conversation. Looking back, I wish we had. Maybe I could've helped her in some way. She must've been going through a hard time, being pregnant and all. I can't imagine becoming a father at age sixteen."

"Any idea how she ended up dead inside a movie prop at Grimaldi's cabin?"

Another breath, this one lamenting. "It's awful, isn't it? And do you know the worst part?"

Will mirrored JB, leaning toward the phone on his desk as if they could discern the truth better that way.

"I remember that barrel. Grimmy and I went back there with the movers to clean out the place after his film studio went bankrupt. We tried to load the thing up. As I recall, Grimmy thought it might have some resale value. But we couldn't budge it. It was filled with sand."

"How do you know there was sand inside the barrel?"

"Oh. Grimmy told me, I suppose. I'd have had no reason to doubt him."

"What's your relationship with him now?" Will asked, wondering if his faith in Max Grimaldi had wavered.

"Grimmy? He's like family. Our daughter, Jacqueline, looked up to him as a grandfather-type figure. His own daughter lives out of state, so we try to take care of him. A while back we paid to have him moved to Knotted Pines Retirement in Brookings. That's one of our real estate holdings."

JB rolled his eyes and tossed his notes aside. "Let's get right down to brass tacks, Mr. Vance. Do you think Gramps is capable of murder?"

Reid's laugh cut the tension, but neither Will nor JB cracked a smile.

"I trust Grimmy with my life. But I'm also smart enough to know you wouldn't be asking if you didn't think he might be. Besides, don't they say that anyone is capable of anything under the right circumstances?"

CHAPTER SIXTY-ONE

Olivia piloted the station wagon down the dirt road toward Rocky's Salvage Yard. The last time she'd come to the Oaktown Boys' hideout she'd been knee-deep in the Seaside Strangler case. And when she'd spotted Termite there, she'd been terrified. Of him, of the past. All of it. But she wasn't afraid anymore. Deep down, Termite hadn't changed since that day twenty-seven years ago at the Double Rock. Sure, he'd gotten taller, collected a few tattoos. Grown an unruly beard. He'd learned to ride a motorbike and shoot a gun and pretend to be a badass like his father. All of that was just window dressing on scrawny, pimple-faced wannabe Xavier Colvin.

Her half-brother. She still shuddered to think it.

Olivia parked outside the chain-link fence in front of the metal carport at the main entrance. She cracked the door and listened for signs of life beyond the chirping crickets and chattering swallows, but all she could hear was the whine of the rusted WELCOME sign as it swung in the breeze.

She'd been prepared for a fight, hoping for it even. To walk right up to Termite and poke her finger in his chest until he told her what he knew. But now, standing like a tree among the dandelion weeds, she realized she'd been stupid to show up here. The place seemed deserted. But on the telephone, Miss Pearl had assured her Termite had been holed up at the junkyard since the funeral.

The padlock on the gate had been opened, and Olivia slipped in through the seam, careful not to rattle the chains hanging useless against the fence.

As she tromped through the grass, a dragonfly buzzed her ear, zipping beneath the ramshackle carport and settling upon the corner of a detached pick-up bed. She followed its path inside and tried the door to the shop, wincing as a set of small bells announced her entry.

The clock on the wall had given up ticking, and a thin layer of dust coated everything in sight. Cash register included. Behind the counter, she nearly stumbled over a black knapsack and a helmet that she assumed must belong to Termite. As if he'd been packed and ready to go. She wondered where he'd parked his bike. Where he'd gone to. If he was watching her right now.

When she heard the sound of distant voices—*angry* voices—a chill passed through her, and she thought of running. Instead, she searched the room for a weapon, chastising herself for not stopping off at home and retrieving the revolver from her nightstand. But there'd been no time.

In the far corner, behind a hat rack, a tire iron caught her eye. Olivia hoisted it and slunk out the back into the junkyard, where the rust buckets were lined in rows three deep. Termite's Harley sat parked in the dirt, both tires slashed, next to three other bikes that remained untouched. Out past the fence, the redwoods stood watch, disinterested observers of the drama that unfolded beneath them.

"You're way out of line, Termite. And you need to step back in or…"

Olivia crouched behind a stack of crushed cars, watching while the man with a ponytail stepped up to Termite, chest to chest. Two muscled men backed him up, their fists clenched. In one of their hands, a knife glinted, the blade reflecting the sun.

"Or what? You gonna put me back in line, Chance? Fuck you." Termite gave him a push, and Chance pushed back. They were evenly matched, both lean and wiry. "I don't take orders from you. I'm in charge around here, and you best not forget it."

"The General ain't happy with how you handled the Mad Dog situation. You let that snitch go too long." *The General.* Two words that always sent a chill through Olivia.

"He was my goddamned father. What the hell do you want from me?"

"Loyalty, man. Loyalty to the General and to Oaktown. You're only loyal to yourself."

"So that's how it is? The General don't bleed for Oaktown. You punks let an outsider tell you what to do?"

Chance laughed joylessly, an awful soul-scraping sound. "This ain't about the General. It's our decision. You know what happens next. And it's best if you don't fight it." He motioned for the knife, gripping it with reverence. "Hold him down, boys."

Olivia felt like she might be sick. The metal tool in her hand, slick with her own sweat. When Chance moved the tip of the knife toward Termite's bicep, just above his Oaktown tattoo, she realized. *A snip-out,* they called it. She'd never seen it before but she'd heard about it. She'd always thought it was a myth, a legend. Something the older kids at the Double Rock talked about in hushed voices the way other kids told ghost stories. *Once you get that tattoo, you have to do something really bad to get a snip-out.*

While Olivia grappled with what to do, Termite struggled too, fighting against the men. But like a fly caught in a web, his effort only made it worse. They had him pinned to the dirt in seconds, his writhing body kicking up dust around them.

"Hold him still, goddamnit."

One of the men raised his fist and pummeled Termite in the face. His head snapped back, and he went still for a moment, dazed by the impact.

Chance brought the knife down, drawing blood. From her hiding place, Olivia saw the bright red against Termite's freckled skin. His howl of anguish confirmed it. He struggled harder, but they had him now. The two men, bearing all their weight on either side of him.

She'd thought she could watch this. After all, he'd had a hand in their father's death, hadn't he? Didn't he deserve to suffer? But hearing his animal scream was too much to bear.

Olivia skirted to the other side of the stack. With a clear path to Chance, she charged forward, raised the tire iron like a baseball bat and swung, making contact with Chance's ribs. A hideous thwack left him slumped on the ground and rendered the other two speechless and distracted.

As Olivia went for the knife, securing it in her hand, Termite's terrified eyes met hers. He pushed himself up and managed to land a solid punch to the jaw of the man on his left. Then, he reached into his boot and pulled a small gun from a concealed holster.

"Get down, Axel." He waved the gun as he backed away. "You too, Don."

Their muscled hands up, both men lowered themselves to the dirt, which had been spotted with the blood dripping from Termite's arm. He kept the gun's eye trained on all three of them while backpedaling to his bike.

"Shit." Termite kicked the back tire, toppling the whole bike onto its side. Then, and only then, did he address Olivia. "What the hell are you doing here?"

Olivia tossed the tire iron into the grass, her hands shaking. Reluctantly, she returned the knife to Termite, who stuck it in an empty sheath on his belt. A snip-out with his own knife; the ultimate humiliation. "I'll give you a ride somewhere, but you have to tell me everything you know about Dad. Deal?"

Don struggled to his feet, his nose already swelling from Termite's punch, and staggered forward.

Termite fired a shot at the first motorcycle, flattening its back tire. Then another, piercing the middle bike's gas tank. And a third, rendering the last of the bikes inoperable.

Next to Don, Chance groaned and rolled onto his side, reaching beneath his jacket for his waistband. For the butt end of his own gun.

Termite fired one last shot that buzzed the air by Chance's hand. Then he risked a glance at his bloody bicep—"Deal"—before he took off running for the shop and beyond it, to Olivia's station wagon.

Termite's blood darkened the rag Olivia had found in the glove box. He winced as he pressed it against his wound. "Are you sure you want to know everything? Because there's no going back."

The smell of his blood nauseated her. Somehow, it had gotten on her shirt, smearing it bright red. Though she wasn't sure at all, she nodded. "*Everything.* Starting with what happened that day at the Double Rock. Did you kill Tina Solomon?"

"You want me tellin' my own tales? Hell, naw. That wasn't part of the deal. I ain't sayin' shit about that day."

Olivia braked hard, right there in the middle of the road, sending Termite into the dash. "Get out, then. You can get a ride with your friend, Chance. I'm sure he'll be thrilled to see you." She paused for a beat. "I'm surprised you didn't shoot him. Or the other two."

"Like I don't already have a target on my back. Besides, me getting away is better than shooting them. It was a three on one. That's straight up humiliation."

"Three on two," she reminded him. "And start talking."

"Alright, alright. I'll tell you this and this only. Our dad didn't kill Tina. Next question."

Reluctantly, Olivia raised her foot from the brake, and the car began to roll forward. "Why is he dead?"

The silence between them stretched out as long and empty as the highway in front of them.

"Mad Dog was an informant."

"I already know about SFPD."

"Not for those assholes. That was back in the old days. When they were done with him, they hung him out to dry. They just let him rot in prison, knowing he was innocent."

"For who then?" Olivia barely breathed the words. Not knowing if she could handle the answer.

Termite paused, and she wondered if she'd have to make him get out of the car after all. "For the FBI."

"Where the hell are you taking me?" Termite asked.

Olivia parked the Buick at the edge of the Shells-by-the-Sea lot and dialed Leah's number. While she listened to the phone's plaintive ringing, she surveyed the damage. The nasty wound to Termite's arm, his busted lip. The blood on the passenger seat. The unshakeable feeling she hadn't known her father at all.

"I can't afford this place."

"It's my friend's B&B."

"B and *what?*"

Olivia shot Termite a look as Leah answered.

"Hey, Liv. What's—"

"Can you do stitches?"

"Like sewing, you mean?"

"Sewing…" Olivia watched Termite's eyes widen and let herself enjoy the discomfort on his face. "Sort of."

CHAPTER SIXTY-TWO

Will drove home in a daze, his thoughts jumping like live wires. From Vance to Winters to Grimaldi and back again with no resolution in sight. He'd been convinced of Winters' guilt before he disappeared. But now, with Grimaldi hiding the fact that he'd known Shelby's mother and sucking down gummy fish—the same sort of candy wrapper Drea had spotted outside her house—he wasn't so sure. And Councilman Vance hadn't exactly helped plead Grimaldi's case.

Then, there were the things he couldn't let himself think about. Like Ben working for Blevins. And Olivia avoiding him all afternoon. He'd cut himself off after three unanswered calls, trying to preserve the last shred of his dignity. But then he'd texted anyway. Pathetic.

When his phone buzzed on the passenger seat, he considered pulling over right there in the ditch or stretching his seatbelt in a desperate reach. But with his luck, he'd careen off the road, hit somebody's mailbox, get arrested by a cowboy cop like Graham Bauer, and spend the night in jail. So, he white-knuckled it all the way home.

Can you meet me at the beach in front of Shells-by-the-Sea?

Olivia's friend, Leah, owned that little B&B on the outskirts of town, overlooking Shell Beach. Will had been there once, a month ago, investigating a domestic assault.

When?

Now.

He ran inside his house, topping off Cy's food and water and contemplating a quick change before deciding against it. She'd said now—and only that—which left him worrying and still wearing his slacks and button-down.

Coming, he texted back, before he headed the way he'd come, more on edge than ever. This is why you don't get involved. You keep it simple. You keep it professional. Friendly. Just like she wanted.

He repeated those words like a solemn oath, even as he jogged down the steps to the beach, his heart in his throat. Even as he saw her, sitting barefoot on a driftwood log, her hair whipping in the wind like the first day they'd met. But the moment she stood and raised her eyes to his, he forgot any promise he'd ever made to himself.

The jacket she wore fell open. Her shirt was covered in blood.

CHAPTER SIXTY-THREE

Like the waves at high tide, relief pushed Olivia forward and into Deck's arms.

"It took you forever." She grumbled the words against his chest, inhaling the familiar scent of him. She only half listened to his reply, preferring the steady brag of his heart in her ear.

When he let go first, she shivered, despite the warmth of the day. Hugging Leah's jacket against her, she sat back on the log. Deck joined her there, his dress shoes covered with sand. She'd shed hers by the stairs and carried them in her hand down the beach while she tried to make sense of the afternoon.

"Are you okay?"

She'd been prepared for the question, of course. Still, the words felt jumbled, hurtling like pinballs through her brain, so she just nodded.

"Is that your blood?" Deck winced.

"Termite's."

"Termite? As in your half-brother, Termite? Of the Oaktown Boys?"

"Do you know any others?" The tinny sound of her laughter got lost in the wind. Deck didn't laugh. Didn't even crack a smile.

"Olivia, why is his blood on your shirt?" He turned to her, imploring her with those brown eyes. "On second thought, don't answer that. Do I need to call you an attorney?"

She laughed again, wilder this time. The tension of the afternoon unspooling from her mouth in hysterical half-gasps. "I—didn't—I didn't—he's…" She pointed over her shoulder at Shells-by-the-Sea, where she'd checked Termite in two hours ago. She and Leah had stitched up his wound with a needle and fishing line.

Deck's hands went to her arm, stilling her. Instantly, she sobered. "Tell me what happened."

"Can we walk?" She felt restless, like she couldn't sit still. She kept replaying what Termite had told her, disbelieving, though she recognized it as the truth.

"Okay." He kicked off his shoes and balled his socks inside them. Rolled up the legs of his pants. "Let's walk."

As she spoke, they trudged through the softer drifts toward the packed sand at the water's edge. By the time they'd reached the rocks that bordered Shell Beach, she'd gotten through the hard part.

Deck stopped, ran a hand through his hair, and sighed.

"Don't say it."

"Say what? That you were out of your mind to try to break up a gang fight? That would be stating the obvious."

"So what then?"

"I just… I'm just glad you're okay." He kept walking, and she watched him for a moment, certain he'd meant to say something else. Something more. "So I'm guessing that asshole shirked on his promise to tell you everything?"

Olivia didn't want to lie. Not to Deck. But Termite had sworn her to secrecy, reminding her that whoever knew the truth about her father had a target on their back. "How'd you guess? Anyway, he won't be sticking around Fog Harbor much longer. I told him he has to be out of here by morning. And that I don't want to see his face again."

"I should probably send a few patrol units up to the junkyard. Make sure everything's okay."

He slipped his phone from his pocket and started to dial. With a mind of its own, her hand wrapped itself around his wrist. His skin, warmer than she'd expected. Or maybe it was just the point of connection between them that radiated heat.

"You won't leave, though? Not yet."

He shook his head, pressing the phone to his ear. Asked, "Why?"

The real answer had little to do with the words that came out of her mouth. "Because I have a lot more to tell you."

CHAPTER SIXTY-FOUR

Will stood in the soft, wet sand and let the water glide over his feet. As the setting sun lit the sky on fire, he listened to Olivia tell him the rest. Her call with Brenda's brother. Her run-in with the warden. And he filled her in on what they'd learned about Max Grimaldi and Reid Vance. Will had no intention of leaving. Not until she told him to, and even then he'd drive away under protest.

"By the way, I never told Blevins he should hire my brother. I may have insinuated that having a cop on his side could be useful, but only so he'd approve the transfer. I didn't think he'd take it literally."

"What do you think he's up to?" she asked.

"Probably what Blevins does best. Covering his own ass."

"You still owe him a visit, you know?"

"Blevins?"

"Ben. It's clear that he misses you."

Will scoffed. "Clear to who?"

Olivia's dimple made a sudden reappearance. She reached toward the water, laughing, and splashed him. "Phil Radovsky."

"He told you?"

She nodded gravely. "He told me *everything.*"

The spray of the ocean didn't help cool his flaming cheeks. Not one bit. They'd probably turned the color of the sunset by now. "I'm going to kill him."

But then, he realized. If she really knew about Radovsky, she'd have been just as embarrassed. He darted toward her, trying to splash her back, but she'd jogged just out of his reach. Her green eyes twinkled in the light off the water, while she backpedaled in the sand. When she stopped, he'd never wanted to kiss her more.

"Just kidding," she said. Until right then, when she gave him that little smirk.

Will stalked toward her, anticipating that she'd bolt down the beach. But Olivia didn't run as he'd expected. She waited for him to reach her.

He could already conjure the taste of her lips, the way her hair would feel tangled in his hands. But the sliver of space between their bodies felt like a mile. A mile he wouldn't cross. Couldn't cross. Not unless he'd been invited.

"Deck—"

Later, he'd lie awake and analyze the single syllable she'd spoken. He'd try to parse the meaning in her voice.

But now, the ringing of his phone stopped him cold. She stepped away, the spell broken.

"Answer it. It might be important."

When he saw the number, the San Francisco area code, he nearly laughed. Or hurled the phone into the ocean. Before he'd left the office, he'd put in a call to Amy to get an update on their parolee-at-large, Chuck Winters.

"Will Decker, Homicide."

"I've got good news and bad news." Amy never did bother with pleasantries. "I assume you want the good first."

"You know me, ever the optimist."

"We found Winters."

Will's gaze met Olivia's, and the whole day caught up with him—Trish's sad eyes, Grimaldi's denials, the bloodstains on Olivia's shirt. The realization he couldn't protect her the way he wanted.

"And the bad?"

"He's got a bullet in his head."

CHAPTER SIXTY-FIVE

Olivia kept her hand raised in a wave as Deck's taillights grew smaller and disappeared. Shaken to her core, she stood there for a moment in the twilight, processing it all. Termite's revelation. Chuck Winters' death.

Surely Amy's call had been a sign from the universe. A sign that she'd been about to repeat a colossal mistake. Still, she wouldn't have been disappointed if the universe had held off until after Deck had kissed her senseless.

Leah joined her on the hotel's wraparound front porch. "Liam's napping, and Jake's repairing a creaky floorboard in the Sand Dollar Suite. Want a cup of tea before you go?"

"Tea sounds great." Though it was the company she needed most.

Leah delivered two steaming cups to the table.

"Thanks." Olivia wrapped her hands around hers, savoring its warmth. "Not just for the tea, but…" She jerked her head in the direction of the guest rooms, leaving the nitty-gritty unsaid. The stitches, the guest room. The blood Leah had helped her clean from her car. "You really went above and beyond. Jake too."

"Are you sure he's going to be okay? He should really see a doctor. He'll end up with a nasty scar."

Olivia gave Leah an incredulous look, remembering the raised skin on her father's midsection, where a rival gang member had stuck a knife. "To guys like that—guys like my father—scars come with the territory."

"Well, what about you? Can I worry about you?"

"I told you—"

"I know. You took a tire iron to a psychopath. Got blood all over you. But you're *fine*." Leah disguised the twist of her mouth with a sip from her teacup. "Detective Decker sure left in a hurry."

Olivia ignored the obvious hint in her voice. Once Leah got started, it was hard to slow her down. "He got a call about the case. One of his suspects turned up dead."

"Wow. This case sure heated up fast." She wiggled her eyebrows. "Kind of like the two of you, if you know what I mean."

"Were you spying on us?"

"Me, spying? Never. But I may have been cleaning the windows in the Bridal Suite when the curtains just happened to open a tad. I can't be held responsible for what I saw."

"And *what* did you see, exactly?"

Leah smirked at her. "You tell me."

The clunk of footsteps interrupted their conversation. Termite posted up in the doorway, holding his arm to his chest like a broken wing. Something about the set of his jaw, the way the light hit his face, made her think of her father and the resemblance between them she'd never noticed before. "My ride will be here in twenty."

With his gang ties all but severed—literally—Olivia wondered who he'd called. An Uber for criminals? But she didn't dare ask.

"Can I pack you any food for the road?" Leah asked. "I made a few loaves of banana bread for the morning."

Termite shrugged. "Sure."

After Leah vanished into the pantry, Termite got right down to business. Two long strides and he stood over Olivia, glaring down at her teacup. "Remember what I told you."

"I remember."

"*Do you?* Because I saw you with that cop again."

Had everyone been watching her? "I didn't tell him anything."

"Better not. Unless you want him to end up like—"

Leah's eyes widened at the sight of them, at the hard edge in Termite's voice. She thrust a paper bag in his direction, not meeting his eyes. "I threw in a loaf of the day-old pumpernickel, too. It was just going to get stale in there anyway."

Termite reached inside and pulled out one of the Saran-wrapped loaves. He tore into the plastic and ripped off a hunk with his teeth, chewing noisily as he spoke. "Your hospitality is much appreciated."

Driving home from Shells-by-the-Sea, Olivia could barely focus on the road. The afternoon's events looped on a technicolor reel in her mind. Blue for the perfect spring sky pierced by gunfire. Red for the blood spilled from Termite's arm. Gray for the ocean rolling in, kissing the sand with white foam before it retreated again. She felt unmoored, adrift. Uncertain what to do next. Worried for herself and for Emily, who she wished wasn't so far away so she could lay eyes on her just to reassure herself.

A flash of blinding light in the rearview caught her attention. Motorcycle headlights. Two of them. And not Termite, who'd ridden away in the passenger seat of an old pick-up truck over an hour ago.

She moved to the shoulder, rumbling to a stop to let them pass. When they stopped too, revving their engines at her menacingly, she felt the vibrations in her skin and straight down her spine.

She floored it then, trying to lose them downtown, zipping down the side street adjacent to the courthouse, but as soon as she hit Pine Grove Road, they popped up behind her, as ominous as a shark's fin.

Her heart at a full-blown gallop, she sped up. Slowed down. Sped up again. Slammed on the brakes, sending her purse to the floorboard. No matter how she maneuvered, the headlights matched her pace.

Desperate now, she struggled to reach her phone but it stayed just out of her grasp, mocking her from the spot where it had tumbled.

She flew past a speed limit sign and the turnoff for Route 187, the decommissioned highway that dead-ended after a few miles.

No way in hell could she go home, but the farther out she drove the more afraid she felt. Out here, no one would see her car fly off the highway and dive head first into a redwood. No one would hear her scream.

With a death grip on the wheel, she turned it suddenly and sharply to the left, as far as it would go. The old station wagon squealed into the hairpin U-turn, its back end fishtailing across the center line. She jammed the accelerator and held the wheel steady until she regained control, leaving the two motorcycles in her wake.

While they pivoted their bikes in her direction, Olivia made up her mind to go to the one place they couldn't. She booked it back down Pine Grove in the direction she'd come, driving even faster now. Her breath came in stops and starts and little gasps every time the bikes closed the gap.

By the time she reached Crescent Bay State Prison, the motorcycles flanked her tail end, their engines a pair of mad dogs growling on either side of her.

A quick right turn after the welcome sign, and she floored it, screeching up to the entrance. The correctional officer on duty jumped out of the way, gaping at her once she'd brought the car to a stop. He moved toward her cautiously, as she rolled down her window.

"Jesus, lady!" He frowned in confusion. "Doctor Rockwell? I—I didn't recognize you. Are you alright?"

Terror squeezed her stomach, but she raised her eyes to the rearview mirror anyway. The asphalt glimmered, awash with the light from the floodlamps that surrounded the prison. Behind her, the road was undeniably empty.

"I forgot something." She swallowed hard. "Something important."

He waved her through with a shake of his head.

Olivia parked in her spot and cut the engine, double-checked the locks. Ironic, that she felt safe here of all places. Even with the creepy redwoods keeping their silent watch across the half-empty lot. Beyond the tree line, she'd never seen such darkness.

After an hour had passed, Olivia forced herself to start the car and head for home. White-knuckling it the whole way, she pulled into her drive a little after nine and hightailed it inside. She collapsed against the door, bolting it immediately, and turned on the light.

Dropping her purse on the kitchen table, she went straight for the bedroom, securing the snub-nosed revolver from her nightstand. Keeping it close, she checked every room for signs of intruders.

Satisfied, she dropped to the sofa and clicked on the TV to take her mind elsewhere. But her eyes wouldn't rest. She still felt uneasy. Like she'd stumbled into a dream where nothing seemed quite right.

When she finally realized, panic rose up in her throat. The books that usually sat on the left side of the credenza had been stacked on the right instead, next to the picture of her and Emily. She ran to the bedroom, where she immediately spotted another anomaly. Deck's sweatshirt lay on her rocking chair beneath yesterday's work clothes, not on top as she'd left it.

A shiver whipped through her like a cold wind. Someone had been here, rifling through her possessions. It could only mean Termite had been telling the truth. Her father had information. Information important enough that someone—the FBI? The Oaktown Boys?—had come here looking for it.

Moving with urgency, Olivia double-checked her purse, ensuring the drawing was still tucked safely inside. Relieved, she headed to the bedroom, where she packed a bag and emailed Dr. Stanley, who'd no doubt be more than happy to cover for her tomorrow. If she left now, she could be in San Francisco by early morning, with enough time to catch a few hours' sleep before planting herself outside the door of FBI headquarters, ready to demand some damned answers.

CHAPTER SIXTY-SIX

When Will pulled into the parking lot of Crescent Bay Regional Airport, he spotted Chief Flack lingering outside the hangar. JB had already arrived. Chuck Winters' dead body awaited them in San Francisco.

"They don't pay me enough for this shit." JB's relapse still in full effect, he took a final drag from his cigarette and tossed it onto the tarmac, stamping it out with the toe of his dress shoe. Then, he lugged his small suitcase from the back seat of the Camaro, groaning. "Dragging me and Tammy out of bed at nine o'clock."

"Since when do you go to sleep at nine?"

"Who said anything about sleeping?"

Will had walked right into that one. He laughed, giving JB his due. Slinging his own duffel bag over his shoulder, he waved at the chief.

"Brown-noser," JB muttered. "I don't understand why the chief is in such a goddamned rush. The guy will still be dead tomorrow."

Will didn't dare say the trip had been his idea; that he couldn't stand the thought of leaving their investigation in Amy's hands. Not that JB was wrong, per se. According to San Francisco's chief medical examiner, Chuck Winters had been dead for at least forty-eight hours from a single bullet to the back of his head. A .45 caliber bullet Will would've bet good money was a match for the one they'd pulled from Heather's back. Same kind as the one that had stopped Drea's heart beating.

"You sure this isn't about something else?" Will asked.

"Such as?"

"Your fear of flying." Smirking, Will dropped his bag on the tarmac. "Oh, excuse me. Your fear of—"

"Don't say it." JB grimaced, put his hands to his ears.

"*Crashing.*"

"Jeez, Louise. You don't say 'crash' in an airport. Just like you don't say 'bomb' on a plane. C'mon. You're just asking for trouble."

Chief Flack approached, looking as tired as Will felt. He didn't envy her job. She'd been taking shit from all sides since the Drake Devere debacle. "Thanks for coming on such short notice. I don't like it any more than you do. But I'm getting sick of the media dragging us through the mud, showing us up on our own turf. We need to get to the bottom of this case. And we need to do it now."

JB saluted her. "Right to the bottom of the proverbial barrel, Chief. That's where we'll be."

"Uh…" Will shook his head. "I think what Detective Benson means to say is that we have some solid leads. And we're not coming back until we know who killed Shelby and Drea."

"Good. I'll hold you to that."

JB held his lengthy sigh until Chief Flack had walked out of earshot. "If you're making promises like that, City Boy, I hope you got a damn good cat sitter."

As the Cessna rattled down the runway and picked up speed, JB cinched his seatbelt and maintained an iron grip on the armrest. The nose tilted upward; JB sucked in a breath. When the front wheels lifted, and the plane left the ground, he squeezed his eyes shut. By the time they'd reached cruising altitude, the single bead of sweat that had appeared on his forehead had multiplied. He leaned away from the small window as if the portal to hell lay on the other side.

"You okay?" Will asked from his seat across the aisle.

JB pulled a tissue from his pocket and wiped his brow. "Do I look okay?"

"I'm gonna plead the fifth on that one, partner. But on the bright side, it's a short flight. Just a little over an hour."

"Great." JB grimaced at his watch. "Fifty-nine more minutes in this steel coffin."

Opening the Mayfield case file, Will passed him the autopsy photos and the stack of pictures Shelby had taken on the Nikon FA. "Here. Take a look at these again. See if you spot anything new."

"Thanks, brother."

Will wondered what it said about the both of them. That pictures of a dead girl would be a welcome distraction.

JB began to flip through the stack, while Will studied his notes from the Winters' interview. With the ex-con's prints turning up on Shelby's get-out-of-town ticket, it seemed likely he'd been the one to buy it for her. When Simpkins had turned her down, she'd sought help from good ole Chuck. Shelby liked the bad boys. That's what Drea had said. And it was true. But even worse, the bad boys liked her. Probably, Winters had pawned something belonging to Margaret Rollins, hoping to tag along on the trip, earn his brownie points, and get lucky after she'd had the baby.

"Hmph."

Will turned to his partner. "You got something?"

Just then, the plane wobbled, and JB tensed, gritting his teeth. "Hopefully a parachute."

"It's mild turbulence. Nothing to worry about." Will leaned across the aisle to study the autopsy photo on JB's lap. In it, Chet had captured Shelby's swollen abdomen, his ruler laid adjacent to the laceration he'd found there.

"Easy for you to say. You're the kind of Bear Grylls type who survives a plane *you know what* in the wilderness and whittles his own canoe to row himself to safety. I'm the guy who gets impaled by a nail file in his wife's carry-on bag."

Will chuckled, then sobered fast when he pointed to the cut on Shelby's stomach. "What do you make of that? Wounded in the struggle with our perp?"

"Maybe. Or…" Another bump, and JB suddenly found religion, making the sign of the cross.

"Or?" Will tried to keep him focused.

"Olivia told you she thought the baby was the key to the whole shebang, right?"

Her name came with a pang. Seeing her standing there, hand raised, in his rearview, Will had wanted nothing more than to turn around. *The baby is what brought her here.* That's what Olivia said that night at the Hickory Pit. "More or less."

"And Chet said it was a cutting wound."

Will nodded, already knowing where JB was headed. But he didn't want to think it. Certainly didn't want to say it out loud.

"What if our perp wasn't after Shelby at all? What if our perp was—"

When a sudden jerk of the plane dropped the photo from his lap, JB stopped pontificating and unleashed a stream of curse words.

Will stared at the small incision, finishing JB's thought. "After something else."

"My whole goddamned life just flashed before my eyes." Still shaky, JB gripped the railing with one hand as he lowered himself down the wobbly airstairs and onto the tarmac, where Will waited for him. "And it really got me thinking. I realized a few things."

"This I've gotta hear."

"Come closer, City Boy. Let me impart some wisdom."

Cupping his hand to his ear and grinning, Will leaned in JB's direction. But JB said nothing. Just smacked Will's shoulder with the case file instead. "I didn't learn shit. Except that you're driving my ass back to Fog Harbor. There's a reason people don't have wings."

"Fine. We solve this case, I'll drive you anywhere you want to go." Will walked on ahead, stopping alongside the rental Inspector Amy Bishop had arranged for them.

"Shake on it?" JB extended his hand, and Will took it, already eating his words. "I know just the place."

Will popped the trunk and tossed his duffel inside. "Don't get ahead of yourself, partner. Because the only place I'm driving tonight is to the Embarcadero police substation."

But when Will looked up, JB had already planted himself in the driver's seat, leaving his suitcase behind for Will to manage.

"I thought I was driving."

"We need to get there tonight, don't we?"

CHAPTER SIXTY-SEVEN

Homicide Inspector Amy Bishop glanced up at Will and JB from her desk inside the Robbery/Homicide Division at Embarcadero substation in San Francisco, still bustling well past midnight. "Well, look what the cat dragged in."

JB marched ahead, introducing himself to Amy. Judging by their whispers and conspiratorial laughter, Will figured they'd become fast friends, probably bonding over their shared joy in needling him unnecessarily.

But Will hung back, took his time. The place looked familiar, of course—his desk had been right *there* less than a year ago—but he'd forgotten what it felt like. The energy that coursed through the building, igniting a fire in his veins. Even as a boy, visiting his dad here, he'd felt it. The pure rush that came with catching the bad guys.

"You owe me one, Deck." Amy nudged him out of his reverie. "Do you know what torture I had to agree to in order to convince Agent Merriweather to wait for you? Dinner at the Top of the Mark. Gag me." She stuck a finger in her mouth.

"The horror," Will replied, knowing full well Amy hated schmaltzy restaurants. "White tablecloths. Silverware. Leather-bound menus. How will you ever survive?"

She rolled her eyes at him. "I swear that man Merriweather has eight hands. And every time I turn around, one of them is grabbing my ass."

"I appreciate the sacrifice. It means a lot. Do you want me to talk to him?"

"I can handle myself."

Her eyes cut to the hulking figure who had just appeared in the doorway. "You certainly can," the man told her, winking at her lasciviously. Octopus Arms himself, Will figured, judging by Amy's thinly veiled disgust.

Will's fists clenched at his sides. This guy was even smarmier than he'd expected. And he planned to give him an earful just as soon as he got the info he needed.

"Detectives Decker and Benson, this is Brian Merriweather, Winters' parole agent. He'll fill you in on what he found."

"So this is the infamous Will Decker?" Merriweather slapped him on the back, and Will prepared himself for the worst. The look of disdain he usually got from law enforcement because he'd crossed the blue wall of silence. To report his own brother, no less. "Rumor is you and Amy were engaged once. You'll have to give me some pointers, man. Because that little filly keeps freezing me out."

Will couldn't stand to see Amy shrink down in her chair. "Lesson number one, take a hint."

JB guffawed, then covered it with a cough. "I think what my partner means to say is we're working a hell of a case, so let's stick to business. Tell us what happened with Winters."

Merriweather leaned back against Amy's desk, leering at her. "There's not much to tell. Winters was a lifer. Easiest guy on my caseload. After you two rolled into town, he started acting squirrely. Talking crazy. I thought he might be using again, so I gave him a piss test on Monday. But it came back clean. Right after that, he left Second Chance without permission and didn't show up for our meeting on Wednesday morning. I talked with the house manager and retraced his steps down to the pier. Found the poor sucker by the rocks, bobbing up and down in the water like a buoy."

"Acting squirrely, how?" Will asked, putting a pin in his revulsion.

"Well, he was real jittery when I saw him. He told me he thought he was being followed. Like maybe you guys were tailing him."

"So, how'd you know to go down to the pier?" JB asked.

"Winters told Guthrie he had a job interview down there on Monday. Some kind of construction company." Merriweather chuckled. "Guess he didn't get the job."

Sickened, Will turned to Amy. "Did you find his phone?"

"No. But we requested the records. It'll take a day or two at least."

"Can we take a look at the photos of the pier?"

With a few clicks, Amy pulled up a series of images on her computer, scrolling through them at a slow and steady pace. The conclusion, foregone, like a march to the guillotine. Pier 28 had seen better days. So had Chuck. He lay half in the water, half out, his belt buckle caught on a piece of fishing net discarded at the end of the boardwalk.

Amy narrated the sad scene. "We feel pretty confident he was killed there and rolled into the water. The perp didn't count on him getting tangled in the net. There's a camera in the area, installed by the city, but apparently it hasn't been turned on for years. No word yet on the ballistics."

Will forced himself to lay eyes on Agent Merriweather. He'd maneuvered himself behind Amy, one tentacle suctioned to the chairback near her shoulder.

"What do you think happened to him?" Will asked.

"No telling. Pier 28 gets a lot of action. Druggies, hookers. Plus, Guthrie said a few of his housemates caught wind of his sex offense, started giving him a hard time. If you ask me, it seems like his past might've caught up with him."

"You're probably right." That Will could agree on. But as he watched Merriweather's hands find Amy's shoulders and give her an unsolicited squeeze, he'd had about enough.

"Hey, Merriweather. Can I have a word?"

With a clueless grin, Merriweather joined him in the hallway. "What's up?"

"You wanted some advice, right? Some pointers? Man to man."

He nodded eagerly. "She likes to play hard to get, doesn't she? But I'll bet she's a real tiger in the sack."

Will stepped into Merriweather's personal space. *Let's see how he likes it.* "If you know what's good for you, you'll show Inspector Bishop some goddamned respect. She's trying to do her job, and she doesn't need you tripping over your tongue and getting in the way."

Merriweather raised his hands and backed away. "C'mon. It's all in good fun. She deserves a night on the town."

Will stared back at him. "Yes, she does. Lucky for her, she can buy her own overpriced dinner."

"What're you thinking?" Amy asked Will as she walked them to their rental in the parking lot.

"Nothing."

"BS. I know you better than that. You're being too quiet."

Will's sigh turned to a groan when JB nodded his agreement. "She's right, City Boy. Spit it out."

"I'm just working through the details. If we assume the same perp killed Winters on Monday and Drea on Tuesday night…"

"Yep. Plenty of time to make it from San Francisco to Fog Harbor. Even for an aerophobe like me." JB gave Amy a wave and climbed in the driver's seat, shutting the door behind him. But Will caught him watching through the side mirror.

"So what're you really thinking, Deck? Just between us."

Amy sized him up with her stormy blue eyes. He'd forgotten what that felt like, too. Her look came straight out of June, three years back, when he'd dropped to one knee on Baker Beach and listened to her enthusiastic *yes* as he'd proposed forever. Turned out he hadn't read the fine print.

"*Just between us,* I feel guilty. I got Winters involved in this thing. Now he's dead. I know we had to talk to him—I liked him for a suspect. Still, I can't help but wonder if—"

She stopped him talking with a hand to his chest. "And that right there is why we just weren't meant to be, Detective. First, you stand up to Merriweather for me. Now you're apologizing for doing your job. You're too good of a guy. It makes me look bad."

So, she'd heard him pull Octopus Arms aside and give him a piece of his mind.

From the rolled-down window of the rental, JB's head craned out toward them. "How do you think I feel?"

Laughing, Amy brushed the back of Will's hand with her fingertips. "But I'm okay being bad."

One thing he hadn't forgotten. How good Amy had felt in his arms. Too good, like the fourth shot of tequila. It goes down smooth but you always regret it the next morning.

He took a step back from her, putting a safe distance between them, and opened the passenger door. "I'll call you after we check out the scene in the morning."

JB fired up the rental car and sped toward downtown. At the first stoplight, he side-eyed Will. "Damn, City Boy. How'd you let that one get away?"

Not in the mood, Will stared out the window, until JB prodded him with an elbow. "So?"

"What makes you think I'm the one who ended it?"

A wry smile stretched the corners of JB's mouth. "I've been your partner for at least six months."

"And?"

When the light turned, JB screeched ahead, maneuvering around the car in front of them. "And I rest my case."

Will lamented the inevitable lack of a heavy bag and gloves in the sad hotel room that awaited him. He'd have to go old school, hammering his fist into his pillow instead.

"Besides, Amy told me." JB accelerated through the next yellow, still grinning.

"What?"

He shrugged smugly. "She called a couple times to check in on the barrel case. We got to talking. I'm a good listener, you know. I've had four wives."

"*Ex*-wives."

JB took a quick right turn, narrowly missing a pedestrian. Will looked back apologetically, while the man offered them his middle finger. "At least I made the trip to the altar."

"It's an aisle. Not a conveyor belt."

JB drove the rest of the way in silence, screeching into the parking lot of the Cozy Bear Inn. The hole-in-the-wall motel on Mission Street had earned a full one and a half stars online. Only the best for Chief Flack's homicide detectives.

JB jerked the car into park and turned to Will. He'd had six blocks to prepare a comeback. "You know your problem, Decker. You're a chickenshit when it comes to women. When I was a little kid, I used to beg my dad to take me down to the five-and-dime and let me ride Bucky, the mechanical pony. But once I'd get down there, I'd start to cry, thinking I'd fall off the damn thing. Finally, Dad shook me by the shoulders and said, 'Jimmy, if you want to ride, you've got to get on the goddamned horse.'"

Script: *Good Morning, San Francisco*

Cue Heather

Good morning, San Francisco. I'm Heather Hoffman. It's 5 a.m. on Thursday, March twelfth, and I'm thrilled to be back to tell you it's time to rise and shine.

Roll intro music

I'm joining the show today from my hospital room here at Fog Harbor General. As you all know, I was the victim of a shooting on Tuesday evening that claimed the life of Fog Harbor resident, Drea Marsh. I would like to extend my gratitude to all the doctors and nurses here at Fog Harbor General and to the officers of Fog Harbor PD who responded so quickly to the scene. A special thanks goes out to Graham Bauer of Fog Harbor PD, who has guarded my bedside like a true hero for over twenty-four hours. Detective Bauer, I salute you!

Cue Graham Bauer photo

Sources close to SFPD believe the shooting on Tuesday may have been related to the Mayfield murder. Overnight, there have been even more shocking developments in the case. As reported exclusively here at *Good Morning, San Francisco,* the body of person of interest, Charles "Chuck" Winters, was found floating near Pier 28 in San Francisco, prompting the Port of San Francisco to renew their focus on addressing crime and homelessness at the waterfront. Pier 28 has been identified by the city council as one of the areas most in need of extensive repair and revitalization. Police have ruled Winters' death a homicide.

Roll Pier 28 crime scene video

Like Ms. Marsh, did Mr. Winters know too much? I'm no detective, but it certainly seems someone is intent on making sure the secrets in that barrel remain buried forever. Stay tuned to *Good Morning, San Francisco* as we bring you the latest developments in the case.

Next up, Pamela is back in the studio with celebrity astrologer Marie Orion, to find out if the fault really is in our stars.

Cut to commercial

CHAPTER SIXTY-EIGHT

"Cozy Bear Inn, my ass." JB rolled his head from one side to the other, massaging his right shoulder, while they stood outside Second Chance Halfway House, waiting for the house manager, Mr. Guthrie, to start his eight-to-five shift. "I've got enough kinks in my neck to make a stripper blush. You think Chief Flack would spring for a massage?"

Will had to agree with JB's assessment of their lodging, because even a bear would've passed on the rock-hard bed, pancake-flat pillows, and walls so thin he could hear his partner snoring. Since he hadn't slept a wink, Will had plenty of time to mull over the events of the past week and stare at his phone, thinking of texting Olivia. Thinking, but not doing. Maybe JB was right. *Chickenshit.*

"You fellas are early." Closing the door of his sedan, Guthrie waved at them. "Running a halfway house, I'm not used to early birds."

"Well, we're hoping to catch ourselves a mighty big worm," JB said. "We've got three unsolved murders and a lot of loose ends."

Guthrie shook his head, suddenly morose. He opened the door, and they followed him inside the house. "The guys are having a hard time with it. Chuck had his enemies, being a sex offender and all, but most of the residents here didn't have a problem with him. Lifers are pretty mellow. Been there, done that. Bought the blue jumpsuit."

"How about you?" Will asked, remembering how Winters had been convinced Guthrie detested him and his perverted kind. "Did you like him?"

Guthrie didn't answer, distracted by the handful of men gathered in the living room lobby, all of them waiting patiently with the Narcotics Anonymous Big Books in their hands or on their laps. Guthrie greeted each of the men by name. "We've got a daily NA meeting at eight fifteen," he explained, as he led them to his office.

Guthrie sat with a sigh, gesturing to the chairs across from his own. Where men came to be sized up or dressed down for violating curfew or breaking house rules. Really, the place wasn't much different than a prison, with Guthrie as the warden of the day shift. "Chuck always figured I didn't like him. Probably 'cause I told him I had a niece who was raped. He thought I had it in for him. But to be honest, the guy was clean as a whistle. Seemed like he was trying to get it right this time."

"When was the last time you saw him?"

"Monday afternoon. He was at the two o'clock NA meeting."

"And he told you he had a job interview?"

"'Told' would be an understatement. He was proud as a peacock. With his history, he'd had a pretty rough go of it. Most employers see a sex offense on your record, they'd just as soon hire a third grader. He said that he'd gotten a call from a construction company doing revitalization work down at the pier. He had an appointment there with some lady at six o'clock that evening."

"A lady?" JB gave Will a pointed look. "Did he say anything else? A name, maybe?"

Guthrie squinted past them, as if the name itself was written in tiny print on the wall. If only he could see it. "Well, he did say she was highfalutin. He asked to borrow a button-down shirt."

"Any idea what made him say that?" Will asked.

Guthrie piped out a laugh, so loud and sudden it startled Will like a shot of cold water. "She told him to show up with his *curriculum vitae.* He told me he had to look it up online 'cause he didn't know what the hell that meant."

CHAPTER SIXTY-NINE

Olivia watched the sun rise from outside the FBI headquarters on Golden Gate Avenue in San Francisco. When the clock on her dash read seven thirty, she gathered her thoughts. At seven forty-five, she eagle-eyed the front doors, preparing for her mission. Predictably, by seven fifty, a familiar lanky frame approached on the sidewalk. His shoulders, back. His walk, determined. Behind his wire-rimmed glasses, a pair of dangerous blue eyes.

Agent Nash—*Jason*—never showed up late a day in his life. Once upon a time, she'd liked that about him. Liked it enough to share his bed, to call herself his girlfriend for six months. To meet his stuck-up mother for brunch in Marin. Until a disagreement on their last case had blown it all to bits. Seeing him now reminded her why she couldn't take the same chance with Deck. Her heart still bore the scars, the pieces of shrapnel lodged in deep.

Before she opened the door of the station wagon, Olivia straightened her hair in the mirror. Thankfully, she looked better than she felt. Which was somewhere south of hell.

"Jason!"

Puzzled, he stopped and looked over his shoulder. "Olivia?"

"I need to speak to you. Do you have a minute?"

"Nice to see you too."

She hadn't expected him to be so cold. Like he had the right. He'd been the agent in charge of the FBI cold case investigations unit. The one who'd recruited her to help with the unsolved murder and dismemberment of ten-year-old Jenny Whitaker. The one who'd ordered the police to arrest the wrong guy. Who'd ended her and the cops up on the wrong side of a lawsuit. "Is this about your email, because—"

"No. Well, *partly.* I have some questions about my dad first."

He checked his watch, kept walking toward the entrance. "Your dad? I thought that topic was off limits."

"Can we grab a coffee?"

"It's five till eight. I don't want to be late." Still, he paused before the glass double doors. Behind them, armed guards and a metal detector awaited.

"I drove all night to talk to you."

He studied her face, looked right into her eyes. The way he'd size up a suspect. "Are you out of your mind?"

She shrugged and offered a hopeful smile. "Maybe."

CHAPTER SEVENTY

"Are you sure this is the place?" JB asked, frowning at the abandoned warehouse. Alongside it, the remnants of Pier 28 stretched out toward the ocean. "There's no construction here."

Will consulted his phone, comparing the crime scene photos he'd downloaded from Amy's computer. The dilapidated boardwalk, the rebar, the empty oil drums. It all matched up. "This is it."

They took cautious steps down the pier, careful to avoid the rotted planks. To sidestep the holes that went straight through to the water below.

JB kicked a broken board out of his path. It skittered down the planks and came to rest in the refuse near the warehouse's outer wall. "Revitalization? This place needs goddamned CPR. Better yet, an electric shock to the heart."

"You think the interview with the woman was bogus?"

"Sure looks like a set-up. That, or our perp was already on his tail and saw a good opportunity."

When they'd reached the end of the pier, Will pointed to the spot on the rocks where Winters' body had been discovered. "The warehouse obscures the view from the road. The killer could've dumped him here unseen, thinking he'd float out to sea."

"So, killed inside, then? No reports of anybody hearing a gunshot."

Will scanned the area, looking for signs of life. A homeless woman, her white hair wrapped in a scarf, pushed an overflowing shopping cart up the adjacent Pier 27. Otherwise, the only eyes belonged to the gulls soaring overhead, the sea lions popping up above the water for a peek. "Probably. But the place isn't exactly crawling with witnesses."

The wind picked up off the ocean, swirling around Will's feet. He thought of Winters, waiting here patiently, not knowing those minutes were his last. How excited Guthrie had said he'd been. How you never knew when the solid ground would drop out beneath you, ending you up on a metal table in the morgue.

"Hot damn." JB studied the screen of his flip phone. "I just got a message from your ex-fiancée."

"Why'd she text *you?*"

"'Cause she likes me better, City Boy. Face facts. But that's not the point. Ballistics came back. We were right. Drea Marsh and Chuck Winters were killed with the same gun."

Will nodded, distracted by the sign he'd spotted partially obscured behind a soggy cardboard box. When he revealed it in its entirety, he held it up to JB.

NOTICE: CHEMICAL STORAGE AREA.

CHAPTER SEVENTY-ONE

"I wish I could help you." Jason hid behind his latte, taking a long sip. The din of the morning crowd droned on around them in the corner coffee shop, buzzing in Olivia's tired brain. "But what did you expect?"

"A little honesty. I'm not some bum off the street."

"Even if I did know that your dad was an informant—which I don't, for the record—do you really think I'd tell you? That's straight-up unauthorized disclosure and grounds for dismissal."

"You owe me."

Jason sighed. And Olivia knew why. They were about to do it again. The argument they'd had no fewer than ten times before the final big one that had sent her packing. But it felt inevitable. She had to say it.

"I covered for you on the Whitaker case. I kept your name out of the papers. But we both know—"

Jason's eyes darted to the door. A block from the federal building, the place was crawling with agents. "Keep your voice down."

Not a single octave lower, Olivia continued. "We both know you're the one who ordered the cops to show up at that man's house. To harass him. You let everyone else take the fall for your mistake."

And they were in it now, Jason's face darkening. "*You* said he fit the profile. And I never told them to beat the guy up, to tase him. To break his ribs. None of that."

"I said he was a *possible* suspect. And the *guy,* as you call him, had a heart attack. He almost died. Do you remember that?"

"Do you really think I don't?"

Olivia had all but forgotten why she'd come here. Anger burned clear through her reasons, razing her logic to ash and accusation. But beneath it all, one undeniable truth. He'd used her. "Well, it certainly didn't seem like you cared too much. It was just a speedbump on your way to middle management, Mr. Supervisory Special Agent. "

"If that's really what you think, why'd you show up here? Why'd you send me that email?"

Olivia stood up, flustered. "I don't know. Obviously, I made a mistake thinking you could help me with anything. Thinking you'd want to. You know, my dad died and you haven't even offered your condolences."

She tossed a few dollars in his direction, regretting that she'd let him pay for her coffee. Still steaming, she pushed her way through the crowded entrance and out into the street. She'd made it halfway to her car when he caught up to her, spinning her around by her arm.

"What?" she asked.

"I thought you'd want to know what Photo Ops thought about that picture you sent me of the blurry shoulder patch."

CHAPTER SEVENTY-TWO

"Let's park a few blocks down." Will directed JB to an open spot on Lake Street in the upscale Sea Cliff neighborhood, where the trees were symmetrically planted alongside manicured sidewalks and the cheapest real estate went for a cool four mil.

"You sure about this, partner? Everything we've got is circumstantial."

Will couldn't argue with that. But the fact that Ratcliffe Chemicals had previously owned the warehouse at Pier 28—a fact he'd uncovered with a quick search on the Internet—seemed like the kind of circumstance that made a homicide detective's mouth water. Especially coupled with Ratcliffe's ownership of Knotted Pines and the speculation Reid Vance had helped to bring Brenda to the movie set against her will. "I'm sure. We start with Victoria. Press her a little. Hopefully, get her talking. Who knows what information she might give up?"

"Classic. The pimple approach then. Should we let Inspector Bishop know?" JB grinned like he already knew the answer.

"Have you told Tammy about the Twinkies or the cigarettes?"

"Hell no."

"Exactly. Amy will just put the kibosh on it. Besides, this is *our* case."

"Now you're talking."

JB trailed behind Will, admiring the houses as they passed. The Vance-Ratcliffe property—a pale yellow Mediterranean-style villa—had been built right into the cliffside, with a front row seat to San Francisco Bay and the Golden Gate Bridge. "I'm tellin' ya. I'm in the wrong line of work. I couldn't afford a dog house in this neighborhood."

Will laughed nervously as he stared into the doorbell camera and pressed the small white button. The bell's summoning ring pricked the hairs on the back of his neck.

A woman opened the door, a thirty-something brunette clad in a color-coordinated tank top and leggings that Will guessed had never seen a drop of sweat. Behind her mask of heavy makeup, she seemed familiar somehow. "May I help you?"

"Detective Will Decker, Fog Harbor PD. Is Ms. Vance home?"

"You must mean my mother, Victoria. She's due back from yoga any minute now." The woman smiled, revealing a white picket fence of teeth, and extended her manicured hand. "I'm Jacqueline. Mom and Dad and I meet here for lunch every Thursday."

"So, your father is home?"

She gestured behind her to a grand and winding staircase. "He's in his office meeting with someone from the Veterans Memorial Commission. They might be a while."

"May we come in?"

"I assume this is about that poor innocent girl in the barrel?"

Will nodded but Jacqueline had already turned, leaving the door open behind her. She beckoned them inside.

Just before he breached the threshold, Will checked his phone. A few missed calls and one new voice message, left forty-five minutes ago.

Returning it to his pocket, he reluctantly followed JB into the foyer. Olivia would have to wait.

"Nice place." JB examined a statue stanchioned in the entryway. He extended his hand toward the smooth marble, stopping short when Will frowned at him. He shrugged, touched it anyway. "It's like a museum."

Jacqueline laughed. "I always say I won the parent lottery. I mean, who gets adopted into this?"

"I didn't realize you were adopted," Will said.

She nodded, leading them into the expansive living room. Elegant, but a little cold for Will's tastes. Two dove-white sofas bordered the stone fireplace. The walls hung with original art. At the center of it all, a massive art deco chandelier, the glass twinkling in the sunlight, casting rainbows around the window. As Jacqueline found a seat in a leather armchair, JB glanced around, dumbfounded, before he took a seat next to Will.

"It's kind of a crazy story."

JB raised his eyebrows, charming her already. "Well, my partner knows I love crazy stories. Let's hear it."

"My mother had ovarian cancer as a teenager. It's a pretty rare diagnosis for someone of that age. She knew she'd never be able to have a baby. And they'd been turned down by quite a few adoption agencies. You'd never know it now, but Dad was a small-time rebel in his youth. He had a few arrests, enough to get them crossed off the list. Don't tell him I told you that. He'd kill me."

JB pretended to zip his lips.

"Anyway, they were big into the pro-life movement back then, and my birth mom met them at a rally outside a clinic. She decided not to go through with the abortion, and the rest is history."

"Wow. That is some story. It's like a movie. Huh, Decker?"

"Have you been in contact with your birth mom?"

Jacqueline looked away, the muscles in her neck tensing. "No. She wanted it that way. She told my parents it would be too hard. But one time when my mom got a little drunk, she told me that I looked like her."

Will watched Jacqueline's green eyes fill. His heart tightened into a fist when it came to him why she'd looked familiar.

CHAPTER SEVENTY-THREE

Olivia felt the weight of the gun in her hand. As she studied its scratched barrel, its well-worn grip, she pretended to be impressed. The way she suspected Avery Dell of the Veterans Memorial Commission would be, if such a person existed. Really, though, she felt a little disappointed it wasn't a .45 caliber.

"Smith and Wesson Model 10 Revolver. I have the field belt and the holster too." Reid Vance grinned at her from behind his ornate desk. A gold-plated lion rested at its edge, weighting a sheaf of papers with its giant paw.

"Amazing. The Commission will be so pleased. These are relics." Olivia sized up her customer and played to his wants. His head swelled, his eyes brightening. "You said your father was Navy, correct?"

Olivia already knew the answer. After she'd spotted his name on the list Agent Nash had forwarded to her from the Department of Defense, she'd confirmed it herself on the Internet. In Bernard Vance's June 2001 obituary.

A proud member of the United States Navy, Bernard served during World War II between 1943 and 1945 and was a decorated pilot. For thirty-seven years, Bernard owned and operated Bernie's Auto Garage in Hayward, California. He was preceded in death by his wife, Amelia. He leaves behind a son, Reid, a daughter-in-law, Victoria, and his precious granddaughter, Jacqueline.

"That's right. He was awarded the Silver Star."

"A true hero." Olivia gave a pointed glance around the room. "Do you have any of his clothing? Perhaps a jacket or helmet? We want the exhibit to be as authentic as possible. Since you are a city councilman, we would be thrilled to have you say a few words."

While Reid beamed, Olivia studied him, the way she studied her patients at Crescent Bay. He didn't look like a murderer. But then, most of them didn't. His sportscoat couldn't hide the potbelly that spilled over his khaki pants. His hands fiddled nervously with the fancy pen on his desk. In Olivia's mind, she pictured them thirty-five years ago. Not the sun-spotted hands of an old man, but the strong hands of a killer, gripping tight to the andiron before he'd hammered it against Shelby's skull.

Reid jumped up from his desk, suddenly spry. "That would be an honor. Give me a moment. Let me see what I can dig up in the closet."

When he left, her lungs felt a little less tight. She breathed deep, surveying the rest of his desk, where he displayed his commendations from the city and a series of photographs of his wife and daughter. All professionally done, of course, and framed in Tiffany silver. Not a trace of spontaneity in those smiles. She plucked the most recent photo from the desk and examined it. A close-up of his daughter in a wedding dress, a hopeful young man at her side. Olivia marveled at those glinting green eyes that reminded her of her own, but also—

"I found it!" Reid bounded in like a boy on a scavenger hunt, holding his find up high.

Olivia forced herself to stay calm. But underneath skin and bone, the muscle of her heart had begun to pump wildly.

"This was my father's Navy jacket." The emblem on the shoulder appeared just as Jason had described. An eagle perched atop a Flying Fortress aircraft.

"The patch is quite unique." Only a few hundred names had been entered onto the squadron list.

"It's the symbol of the 228th Bombardment Squadron." Reid slipped the jacket on, craning his neck to see the marking on the shoulder. "Cool, right? I used to wear this thing all the time. It was a real hit with the ladies."

"We'll have to take a photo of you wearing it at the exhibition for the newspaper."

Reid paused, frowned. Olivia felt her whole world freeze on its axis. She'd gone too far, said too much.

"As long as you get me from my good side."

CHAPTER SEVENTY-FOUR

"Oh, good. There's my mother now." Jacqueline pointed out the large picture window on to the street, as a Range Rover glided past like a black swan. "Was she expecting you?"

Will shook his head, trying to think, to plot the right angle. Suddenly, it all felt precarious. Like a tightrope walk above a canyon. "Does your mother work?"

"Her official title is Public Relations Manager for Ratcliffe. But between you and me, she has a lot of lunches at The Rotunda."

Will had never dined there himself but he knew the place. When he still worked patrol in San Francisco, he'd responded to a snatch-and-grab there once. The airy restaurant—a place to see and be seen—inside Neiman Marcus, where a salad cost the same as three large pizzas from Sal's downtown.

"What about travel?"

Jacqueline hesitated. "Um, should I be telling you all this? Is she a suspect?"

"Is *who* a suspect in *what?*" Reid Vance bore little resemblance to the scrawny, long-haired stoner in his mug shot. And his booming voice sounded nothing like the placating city councilman they'd spoken to on the phone.

But Will barely registered his presence. Because the *someone from the Veterans Memorial Commission* Jacqueline had mentioned looked a hell of a lot like Olivia. In her hand, a gun belt. Draped across her arm, a jacket. She looked at it, then back at him.

"It's okay, Dad. They're here to talk to Mom about that girl they found in a barrel."

"Oh, really." Reid shifted his steely gaze to the two detectives. "Have you two been out here interrogating my daughter? Victoria and I have been more than cooperative with your investigation, but coming into my home and nosing around? That's crossing the line. If you have any other questions, I'm afraid I will have to refer you to our attorney."

JB stood up and took a step toward the staircase. "Well, why don't we wait and see what your wife has to say for herself? If she's like any of my exes, you don't speak for her."

"I'll just be going then." Olivia tried to sneak down the staircase past Reid, but he turned toward her, blocking her exit route. If she panicked, she didn't show it. "It was a pleasure meeting you. Thank you for donating these items to the exhibit, especially this jacket."

Olivia raised her eyes to Will's. "It's truly *photo*-worthy."

Will fumbled with his phone, quickly scrolling through until he'd found the image he'd saved there. That blurry spot in Shelby's last photograph, a match for the sleeve which rested on her forearm.

CHAPTER SEVENTY-FIVE

With Reid blocking the narrow staircase, Olivia felt trapped. Especially now that she saw the fire in Deck's eyes.

"May I take a look at that jacket?" Deck walked across the plush carpet, each quiet step reverberating through her like the banging of a gong.

Reid held out his arms now, so she couldn't get past, and answered the question for her. "No. You may not. I allowed Ms. Dell to take the jacket for a Veterans Memorial. Not to be examined by your grubby hands."

Reid reached for the jacket, grabbing onto the sleeve. But Olivia stepped back. She wrestled it free from him and held it close to her chest. She glanced behind her, wondering where she'd run. Where she'd hide. By the time she looked back, Victoria had appeared at the bottom of the staircase, alongside her husband and daughter.

"Oh my goodness. Jacqueline, honey, what is going—? *Reid?*" Victoria's face didn't move, per se. But Olivia could read the unadulterated shock in her voice. "Who are all these people?"

JB gestured toward the dueling sofas. "I think we should all take a seat and get acquainted, unless you'd rather take a ride down to the station. Except for you, Miss—uh—*Dell.* You're free to go."

But Olivia couldn't bring herself to move past the top step. Not with Reid standing there, fuming.

"And I'm not?" Jacqueline asked.

"Detective Decker and I need to talk to your parents. You're welcome to stay if you'd like."

Jacqueline looked to her mother, who gave a small shake of her head. "Go on. It's okay. We'll be fine."

"Should I call Mr. Waverly?"

"Yes, right away." Reid's face reddened as he barked his orders. "Tell him we're being harassed by these two-bit cops and will be filing a formal complaint with the department."

As Jacqueline shuffled toward the front door, with her cell already pressed to her ear, Victoria raised her hands to settle her husband. "Relax, Reid. We're not criminals. We don't have anything to hide. You're on the city council, for crying out loud."

With JB waiting at the landing, Deck started up the steps, keeping one hand on his service weapon. "You were wearing that jacket when you bludgeoned Shelby Mayfield to death. She took your picture, even though you didn't want her to. Is that why you killed her? Because she was running away to tell on you? Because she changed her mind about giving you her baby?"

"*Her baby?* What are they talking about, Reid?" Each word more strident than the last, Victoria's neck strained as she spoke. The tension between them felt as threatening as a lit fuse. The kind of couple who dig in their heels, both accustomed to getting their way. Olivia wondered how many breakable objects had met their end against these white walls.

"Does Grimaldi know?" Deck kept prodding, intent on cracking Reid like an egg. "Is that why you put him up in that fancy nursing home? To buy his silence?"

JB took a different tack, moving Victoria aside and beckoning to Reid the way you'd coax a frightened animal. "C'mon down, Reid. I'll handle my partner. Then we can figure this out together. I'm sure there's an explanation for the jacket, right? Just let us take it to the lab for analysis. Clear your name."

"Or I can leave Detective Benson here and come back with a search warrant. Either way, we know you're guilty. And we're going to prove it."

The logical choice would've been to call Deck's bluff. But Olivia could sense Reid's panic.

"I didn't even know that girl!"

His denial exploded down the staircase and thrummed through the living room, leaving everyone stunned in its wake. Everyone except Reid himself.

He reached into his sportscoat and lunged for Olivia, ripping the jacket from her arms and pinning her face down against the banister. Something hard and vicious pressed into the soft spot at the base of her skull, and she understood now why he'd hung back, letting her go ahead when they'd heard the voices downstairs.

She opened her mouth to scream, but Deck's urgent voice eclipsed her panic.

"Gun!"

CHAPTER SEVENTY-SIX

Instinct took over.

Will grabbed for his Glock. Raised it, aimed. Then froze. Reid's murderous eyes and the barrel of a handgun were trained on Olivia.

"I'll blow her head off." Reid had her flush against the railing, folded over the wooden banister. The jacket had fallen to the ground in the struggle, pooling around their feet. Down a step, the gun belt hung halfway off the staircase. "I swear to God I'll do it."

"Reid! No!" Behind Will, Victoria wailed, her breathing frantic. Without turning his focus from the stairs, Will slipped a pair of cuffs from his back pocket. He'd been unprepared once before and paid for it with a fist to his face. He'd never make that mistake again.

"Detain her," Will said, tossing the cuffs behind him to JB.

"I love a good old-fashioned standoff." JB's laugh clunked out, hollow, as he secured Victoria to a spindle on the staircase and pointed his own weapon at Reid. "Especially when the guns on my side outnumber the guns on yours. What do you think is going to happen here, buddy?"

"I'm not going to the station."

"You don't have to." Will tried to walk it back, realizing he'd grossly overestimated Reid's self-control. Which was the only thing keeping Olivia alive right now. "We can talk down here. We'll wait for your lawyer, if you'd like. Just put down the gun."

Will couldn't look at Olivia's terrified face. It made him think of the horrible dream he'd had. Of his childhood basement. Of her eyes, lifeless but still somehow looking back at him with blame.

"I'm not talking to you here either. I'm not talking at all."

"Okay. Fair enough. That's your right."

"I didn't kill anybody. And I'd never take a baby from a loving mother. My own daughter is adopted, for Christ's sake."

Will watched as Olivia's mouth moved, whispering to Reid. His finger still poised to end her. He leaned in closer to catch every word, his face pale as a ghost.

CHAPTER SEVENTY-SEVEN

"And her mother's name was Brenda Samson." With her life at stake, Olivia made a bluff of her own. She couldn't be certain, of course, but Jacqueline had Brenda's face and those haunting green eyes.

As soon as she felt Reid tense behind her at the revelation, she spun around and stepped under his arm, grabbing for the muzzle of the gun. His strength surprised her. Muscling the gun from her grip, he regained control of the weapon and latched his forearm beneath her chin, dragging her backward. Her body, his shield.

She clawed at him, tried to kick herself free, but he kept moving, even as Will and JB advanced up the stairs toward her. When he'd reached the landing, he stopped, positioning the gun at the side of her head. "Don't come any further."

"Reid, put the gun down." Deck's measured voice came as a comfort, even if she heard the fear beneath it. "You don't have to do this. It's not too late to do the right thing."

With a sudden push, Reid launched Olivia toward them. She stumbled against Deck. He fell back, steadying himself against the wall and held her upright. "Are you okay?" he asked.

She nodded. "I'll call for help."

But Deck had already bounded up the staircase, with JB huffing behind him. They headed into the hallway, where Reid had disappeared.

As Olivia dialed the police, Victoria stared at her handcuffed wrist. Her gaze, blank. "What did you say to my husband?"

"That Jacqueline's mother was Brenda Samson. She and her one-year-old daughter disappeared in the spring of 1986."

"He told me it was an accidental overdose."

Olivia struggled to make sense of it all. "Shelby, you mean?"

Victoria breathed a single word. *No.*

A hail of bullets weakened Olivia's knees. Though it came from upstairs, she dropped to a crouch anyway and scurried to duck behind the sofa. Her heartbeat drummed in her ears, until the operator finally picked up.

"9-1-1. What is your emergency?"

CHAPTER SEVENTY-EIGHT

A bullet pierced the wall over Will's shoulder, and he returned fire. Two quick shots. Retreat and repeat. Until the smell of the guns' propellant bit at his nose.

Reid had sought cover at the end of the L-shaped hallway, firing at them in a flurry. Another bullet zipped past and ricocheted, striking the chandelier that hung above the living room. Pieces of the ornate glass shattered and rained to the carpet below.

Will counted the shots, noted the aim. Reid was no amateur.

When it had been quiet for too long, Will waved JB forward. He crept down the hallway at JB's six, making his footsteps as soft as he could manage against the hardwood. Every intake of breath, every creak of the floorboards, made him curse himself and the entire goddamned day.

He should've called Amy. Then, the entire Vance-Ratcliffe compound would be crawling with cops, instead of just him and JB sneaking around like rebellious teenagers through a sprawling maze of rooms. He felt like a contestant in a twisted game show. A cold-blooded killer lurking behind any one of the cherrywood doors.

At the L, they stopped, waited. His gun at the ready, JB peered around the corner and gave the all-clear.

Will approached the first door. Sliding his back against the wall, he twisted the knob and thrust it open. JB swept his gun across the guest bedroom.

They moved in tandem toward the closet, where Will nudged the sliding door with his foot. A few winter coats swayed, disembodied in the darkness, until JB pushed them to the side, revealing nothing. After they checked beneath the bed, they inched back into the exposed hallway.

Two rooms to go.

In Reid's office, they searched another closet and the crawl space under his desk and came up empty. That left door number three.

Careful to stay out of the line of fire, Will tried the knob. Locked. He felt certain now. Certain and desperate.

"Cover me."

JB nodded, and Will drove his heel into the weakest part of the door, near the keyhole. The impact juddered his teeth. But after three solid kicks, the wood began to splinter, and the lock gave way.

Finally, it bent to his will, revealing a floor-to-ceiling library. Two oversized reading chairs stood guard in each corner. He found the gun discarded on the shelf of a bookcase. And beyond it, a single, opened window.

CHAPTER SEVENTY-NINE

By the time Olivia heard the wood splinter from the floor above, she'd already begun to run. She'd spotted Reid Vance clinging to the drainpipe, working his way down until he'd dropped onto the lawn. She'd watched it all from her position behind the sofa, where she'd had a clear view of the yard through the picture window.

Victoria whimpered as Olivia hurried past, dodging the shards of glass that littered the floor. "Don't let them hurt him. He's not a bad person, I swear."

In Olivia's ear, the operator droned on. "Are you still there, ma'am? Please stay on the line." She tucked the phone into her pocket and burst out the front door, leaving Victoria alone in the house.

Sirens keened in the distance, yet the picturesque street remained quiet and deserted. Not one neighbor peeked out from behind a curtain. Not a single cloud marred the sky. The bent grass beneath the drainpipe the only tangible sign of trouble. Unnerved by it all, Olivia stood on the sidewalk, watching Deck crane his head out the window.

"Did you see where he went?"

"He was right *there.*" Olivia pointed to the spot in the manicured lawn, alongside the spiral-shaped topiaries.

Behind her, the sirens grew louder, more insistent. Deck hoisted himself onto the window ledge and shimmied partway down the pipe, before jumping to the ground below.

JB looked out after him, shaking his head. "Hell no. I don't do fences. And I definitely don't do drainpipes."

"Go check on Victoria. Make sure she's secure. I'll meet you around back."

Olivia flagged down the first cop car as it sped down Lake Street. A second followed close behind. Then, a third. The officers spread out, combing the property with their weapons drawn.

From behind the blue lights, Jacqueline ran toward the yard. A stocky, mustached man tailed behind her, barely keeping up.

Between heavy breaths, he wrangled the attention of the nearest officer. "I'm Gerald Waverly, the attorney for Ratcliffe Chemicals. I represent Mr. Vance, and I demand to talk to the sergeant."

Just then, Deck yelled from the back of the house. "Reid! Stop!"

CHAPTER EIGHTY

Reid Vance stood on the edge of the cliffside. Beneath him, a sheer drop down the bluffs to the bay. He balanced precariously, while he sidled out farther onto the rock face, sending a small stone skittering. It tumbled through the shrubs and down to the rocky shore hundreds of feet below.

Will stopped on the landing, beneath the massive balcony, and returned his gun to his side holster. He didn't fear much but he sure as hell didn't like high places. *Acrophobia.* That's what Olivia would've called it. Will just called it common sense. "Reid, let's talk. You don't want to do that."

But Reid inched forward, putting out his hands to steady himself. Patrolling in the Tenderloin, Will had seen his share of suicide attempts. Overdoses, mostly. An occasional blade to the wrist. But once, he'd been called to a jumper. A woman who'd planted herself on the razor-thin ledge of a twenty-story condo building after her husband had filed for divorce. The acidic burn of fear in his throat felt the same as it had then.

A group of cops rounded the side of the house, ready for a gunfight. Will held up his hands, easing them back.

"C'mon, Reid. Whatever it is, we can work it out."

Like the scream of a gull, Reid's laugh caught on the wind and disappeared. "You don't understand. A man like me won't last a day in prison."

Standing in the shadow of his multimillion-dollar mansion, Will couldn't disagree. "And nobody is saying you'll end up there.

We haven't even arrested you yet. And if we do, you're innocent until proven guilty, right? You've got a damn good lawyer."

"He's right, Reid. Don't say anything. Just come on down from there. We both know they've got no evidence." Will recognized the face of Chief Counsel Gerald Waverly from the Ratcliffe Chemicals website. "But even if they do, the judge will set bail, and you'll pay it. Let's take it one step at a time."

Reid's face crumpled, and he began to cry. His loafered feet dangerously close to the brink. His daughter's voice brought him back.

"What're you doing out there, Dad?" Jacqueline pushed through the crowd of cops, JB clearing the way.

"Jackie, honey, I want you to leave. You shouldn't be here right now."

Jacqueline slipped out of JB's grasp and joined Will on the deck, pacing to the edge and back. "I'm not leaving until you come down from there. Until you tell me what's going on. You said you didn't have anything to do with any of it. You and Mom both."

Reid turned, slipping a little, and Will heard Jacqueline gasp, his own breath caught in his throat. "That girl, Shelby, she wanted to get rid of her baby. I saw her outside the clinic and told her she didn't have to go through with it. That me and your mother were desperate for a child and couldn't have one. I told her I'd put her up at Grimmy's cabin in Fog Harbor and nobody had to know. But then, it all went wrong. She would've doomed that poor baby to a life of struggle and suffering."

Waverly groaned. "Reid, think about what you're saying. Do not incriminate yourself."

"It's too late for that, Gerry." A sob racked his body, and he took another shaky step. Beyond him, the world was a magnificent shade of blue. All sky and ocean. "I didn't mean to kill her, Detective. It was an accident."

"Of course." Will swallowed his disbelief. "How did she die?"

"She wanted to leave, but I wouldn't let her. I had to keep her there. I only wanted what was best for her and the baby, but she couldn't see that. She told me if I didn't let her go, she'd send my picture to the paper and tell them what I'd done. It sounds silly, I know. But I panicked and smacked the camera from her hand. We struggled, and she hit her head on the andiron. After I... well, once she was gone, I tried to—I thought I could get the baby out of her. I thought I could save it, but..." His shoulders hunched limply, the weight of it all too much to bear. "But it was too late. I couldn't go through with it. I put her in the barrel "

Like most confessions, Will figured it contained a kernel of truth and a whole lot of bullshit. Blunt objects don't wield themselves.

"And what about *my* mother?" Jacqueline cried out. "That story you always told?"

"*A lie.*"

Waverly threw up his hands. "Reid, please. For the love of God, stop talking."

"Your birth mother's name was Brenda Samson. She couldn't take care of you. Your mom and I found her overdosed on heroin. What were we supposed to do? The state would've taken you. Placed you in foster care or worse—with her good-for-nothing family. We saved you, Jackie. We saved you."

"What happened to her? Where is she?"

Again, Reid turned to look at her, tears streaming. "Buried in Fog Harbor."

"You killed all these people to cover up your lies? How could you?"

"No, no, no. When Shelby's friend was shot in the cabin, I was in the middle of a city council meeting. I swear it." Reid offered his vow to the sea, to the wind. Will thought of the jumper in the Tenderloin. That split second, when she'd launched herself into the air. Will couldn't be certain but he suspected she'd regretted it. Because her arms had flailed wildly as she'd hurtled to the sidewalk below. "After what I'd done all those years ago, I made a vow to myself. I knew I had to do better, be better. *For you.*"

"Dad?" Suddenly, Jacqueline rushed forward, her hand outstretched and reaching. Her plaintive wail sent Will running. A step behind, he tried to hold her back.

"I'm sorry." Reid took the final step into thin air. In a blink, he'd disappeared from view.

Jacqueline stumbled and fell forward in desperation. Fear be damned, Will flung himself after her.

CHAPTER EIGHTY-ONE

Olivia stared in horror. She willed her legs to move but her feet stayed rooted. A scream had lodged itself in the back of her throat, demanding release.

At the cliff's edge, Deck lay on his stomach, straining. Though Olivia couldn't see down below, she could hear Jacqueline's shrieking and Deck's breathing, labored with the effort of holding her. Pieces of the soil gave way, crumbling into the ocean below.

"A little help here," Deck said, through gritted teeth.

As JB hurried across the landing with a few officers behind him, Olivia finally found the courage to move. But the cop nearest her grabbed her, held her back.

One quick glance down, and she felt sick. Like she'd stepped from a spinning merry-go-round.

Jacqueline clasped Deck's arm, her fingers slipping. Her feet struggled to get ahold of the rock face. But each time she dug in, her toes scrabbled against the loose dirt, and she slid further down, pulling Deck with her. "Don't let go. Please don't let go."

Olivia's mind played tricks with her. Reid's broken body lay on the rocks. The shallow water pooled around him. But when she looked again, it wasn't Reid. It was Deck she saw.

CHAPTER EIGHTY-TWO

Will marveled at how fast it could happen. One minute he'd been sure-footed on solid ground. The next, precariously positioned above the craggy shoreline, ready to meet his end.

Before he'd made it right with Ben. With his father.

Before he'd seen Olivia first thing in the morning, sleepy-eyed and wearing his T-shirt.

Before he'd found Drake Devere again and finally watched him fry.

But most of all, before he'd solved the one case that stuck to him like his own shadow. His mother's disappearance.

The burning in his forearm felt unbearable, but he couldn't let go. His muscles, stretched like cord to the breaking point. Every time he tried to reach for Jacqueline with his free hand, she panicked, kicking her legs against the rock and soil below her and dooming them both.

He tried not to look at the body below them. The neck, turned at an unnatural angle, the head bobbing and lilting in the water, mocking him. Reid had taken most of his secrets to the grave.

Will felt the cliffside shift beneath him, giving way. Bits of loose soil and rocks tumbled down, sending Jacqueline into a panic. His grip loosened, and for the first time, he considered letting go. He imagined her face, the dark cave of her mouth, getting smaller and smaller as she fell until—

"I got you, partner."

Overcome by fatigue and relief, Will let out a hysterical laugh, as JB grabbed onto Jacqueline. He didn't do fences. Or drainpipes. But apparently, he did cliffs.

CHAPTER EIGHTY-THREE

Olivia's knees weakened with the shock of it all. She released a grateful sigh.

JB had lowered himself to his belly, joining Deck at the cliff's edge. The other officers formed a chain behind them, securing them both to the ground. After a few solid efforts, Jacqueline's head appeared. Two more pulls, and she collapsed onto the ground, sobbing.

Deck sat on his haunches, unmoving. His eyes, a million miles away. After he stood, finally, Olivia ran to him, to reassure herself more than anything. But when she reached him, he collapsed into her arms, knocking them both breathless. She wished they were alone.

"Did JB just save my life?" he whispered against her ear.

Jacqueline lifted her head, interrupting Olivia's relieved laughter. She wiped her face, searched the crowd. "Where's my mother?"

"Hey, you. Torres, was it?" JB pointed to an officer in the back, talking with his buddies. His mirrored sunglasses and slicked-back hair, his frat boy high fives and devil-may-care attitude made Olivia sick with worry again. "I told you to stay with the lady in the house, remember?"

"Easy, Pops. She's cuffed to the staircase. And I heard a big commotion out here, so…"

JB's face paled, and he took off running. Olivia followed.

CHAPTER EIGHTY-FOUR

Another surge of adrenaline pushed Will to his feet and drove him forward. He caught up to JB and Olivia at the front door.

It stood wide open. As inviting as a vampire's smile.

JB cursed under his breath and breached the threshold.

Will trailed him, his weapon drawn.

The wooden spindle had been splintered, more than likely cracked by a solid kick. Its pieces, scattered on the steps.

In the absolute quiet, chandelier glass crunched beneath their feet. The jacket had fallen from the staircase in the commotion to the floor below. An innocent witness, it lay there, spotlighted in the sun that streamed through the window.

They'd need to search the house, the garage. The whole damn compound. But Will already knew the outcome.

They wouldn't find her. Victoria was gone.

"You two sure do know how to make a scene." Amy gave them that look. The look of a woman accustomed to wearing a badge and barking orders at very bad men. To moving them with her bare hands if the situation required it.

"We're also pretty good at finding murderers." Will passed her the Colt 1911—registered to Victoria Ratcliffe—they'd uncovered hidden in a hatbox in her closet. Though they'd have to wait for the ballistics, Will felt certain it would be a match for the gun that killed Drea and Chuck.

"And losing them."

Will looked around for JB, but his partner had ducked off to talk to Olivia. He caught her eye and flashed a tired smile. "I think we can both agree your guy, Torres, is to blame for that."

"Torres *is* an idiot, that's true. But who cuffs a suspect to a staircase?"

Will shrugged hopelessly. "We were in the middle of a gun battle."

"Sure, you were."

"And she wasn't a suspect… *then.*"

An SFPD officer approached from the house, interrupting them. "Hey, Inspector Bishop, check this out. We downloaded video from the doorbell cam."

He displayed a few still images that he'd captured from the screen with his cell phone. The black and white view from the exterior camera.

The first showed Victoria exiting the house, a bag slung over her shoulder. In the next shot, she'd advanced past the empty police cars, leaving the chaos behind her. Cool as a cucumber.

"It confirmed what the attorney told us." The officer pointed to the last still, Victoria climbing inside a Mercedes sedan parked behind the blockade, where Waverly claimed he'd left his keys behind in the excitement. "She stole his car."

CHAPTER EIGHTY-FIVE

Olivia only half listened while JB recounted his heroic rescue of his partner, and not for the first time. Her gaze drifted to the periphery. To Jacqueline. She sat on the back of the ambulance, an oxygen mask affixed to her nose and mouth. Shortly after they'd discovered Victoria missing and sent a team down to the shore to retrieve Reid's body, Jacqueline had fainted, dropping to the ground like a felled tree, overcome with shock. Olivia could relate. A father is a father, no matter how flawed.

"It's a damn good thing for you Tammy's got me on a strict regimen." JB flexed his biceps at Will. "This body is a finely tuned machine."

"Yeah." Deck rolled his eyes. "Like a carburetor. *Obsolete.*"

"Throw your insults, City Boy. But we both know who just pulled ahead in the race for Detective of the Year."

"If you wanted to win *that* race, you should've let me fall."

JB snorted, prompting a laugh from Inspector Amy Bishop.

Purely in the name of scientific research, Olivia studied Amy—the infamous engagement ring thrower. A petite brunette. Undeniably pretty, with a low tolerance for BS. Olivia had no doubt that ring had gone flying. The only surprise, she hadn't chucked it right at Deck's head.

Deck gestured to Olivia with a mischievous glint in his eyes that made her blush. "To be fair, I think we may have a dark horse here."

"Technically, I'm not a detective."

"Oh. Finally, you admit it. Can I get that in writing?"

Olivia shifted awkwardly from one foot to the other, acutely aware of the flirtatious tone of Deck's voice and her own stupid need to encourage him. Blame it on the adrenaline. Thankfully, his cell phone interrupted, drawing his attention.

"It's Chief Flack calling." Deck walked away with JB, leaving her alone with Amy.

Amy cleared her throat with purpose, examining Olivia with curious amusement. Like she'd stumbled across a clue that didn't quite fit. "Frankly, I'm surprised Deck let you anywhere near his case. He doesn't trust shrinks. As a general rule."

"Well, I don't trust cops, so…"

Amy smirked. "Okay. I get it now."

Confused, Olivia waited for an explanation. But Amy kept her cards close, daring Olivia to ask. "What do you mean?"

"He's got a thing for you."

"No. I don't think so. It's not like that at all. Our relationship is completely professional." Olivia stopped herself, already knowing she'd protested too much.

Amy's smile widened. Like she could read the truth on Olivia's face. "I hate to break it to you, girl. You have a thing for him too."

Script: *Good Morning, San Francisco*

Cue Heather

Good morning, San Francisco. I'm Heather Hoffman. It's 5 a.m. on Monday, March sixteenth. Time to rise and shine.

Roll intro music

Today, we have a very special episode for you. Our segment, *Murder in the Bay,* has been expanded to a full hour to bring you the latest coverage on the shocking case that began with the discovery of the body of a young pregnant girl in a barrel. As you can see behind me, the Fog Harbor Police Department has been working diligently for the last twenty-four hours, excavating the wooded area surrounding the cabin on Wolver Hollow Road, where, just eleven days ago, a man accidentally uncovered the mummified remains of Shelby Mayfield and her unborn child. Speaking exclusively to *Good Morning, San Francisco,* Detective Will Decker shared the details of the investigation, confirming suspicion that police and canine units are indeed searching for the remains of a second female victim. According to Decker, early this morning, forensic archaeologists unearthed an intact femur and lower mandible which have been transported to the crime lab for further testing.

Cue Will Decker snippet

This shocking news comes on the heels of the Thursday evening arrest of prominent San Francisco resident, Victoria Ratcliffe. Ratcliffe was apprehended at the Buchanan Field Airport, attempting to board a Ratcliffe Chemicals private jet. She is believed to have shot and killed victims Drea Marsh and Chuck Winters, in an effort to conceal her husband's involvement in the 1986 deaths of Mayfield and the yet unnamed woman. A weapon registered to Ratcliffe was recovered from the family home, and sources close to the investigation confirmed that cell phone data put Ratcliffe in the areas where Marsh and Winters were fatally shot. Ratcliffe's husband, City Councilman Reid Vance, committed suicide on Thursday, after providing police with information implicating himself and his wife in the crimes. Vance jumped to his death from the cliffs surrounding the family's extravagant home in Sea Cliff.

Roll Sea Cliff video

Detectives believe that the couple acted out of their desperation for a child, after they had been turned down by several adoption agencies due to Vance's criminal record. Sources close to the investigation have suggested that Mayfield may have initially agreed to give up her child to Vance and then changed her mind, prompting Vance to hold her captive in the cabin's basement, where she was found dead thirty-five years later.

In the wake of the murders, the Ratcliffe Chemicals stock price plummeted with investors questioning the stability of the company's future. Rumors have begun to circulate that long-time rival, Zenigenic Corporation, may initiate a hostile takeover of the failing company. As Reid Vance himself said in a speech to the Board of Supervisors last year, during which he criticized corruption in the government at the highest levels: The higher you climb, the harder you fall.

Cut to commercial

CHAPTER EIGHTY-SIX

Will plucked a stray cat hair from his button-down. *Damn, Cy.* But he only had himself to blame. When he'd lugged the overpriced cat bed from the garage to the living room, he'd made the surly one-eyed tabby his unofficial roommate. This morning, he'd found Cy curled in the corner of his closet, atop his dress shoes. The cat even had the nerve to hiss at him when he shooed him out.

Pink box in hand, Will pushed through the station doors and headed for JB's cubicle.

"About damn time, City Boy. We've still got a few loose ends to tie up."

"For saving my ass." He offered the box to his partner with a grin, the sweet smell of Myrtle's blueberry scones wafting even with the lid closed. "But don't tell Tammy. I can't have her thinking I'm corrupting you."

JB peeked inside and released a frustrated sigh. "I can't do it, man. I'm back on the wagon. I pinkie-promised."

"Oh, well. In that case—" Will opened the box and reached for the biggest scone. JB snapped the lid shut, held it tight to his chest.

"It's got blueberries, right? Tammy says they're a superfood. How bad could it be?"

While JB stuffed his face, Will checked his email, starting with the one titled URGENT—DNA RESULTS. "Hey, the DNA from the envelope seal on that letter to Shelby's mom came back."

"And?"

He scanned the letter, looking for the name. Held it out and watched JB's eyes widen. "Bingo."

Orange was definitely not Victoria's color. Blame the jumpsuit or the drab jail interview room for washing out her skin. Either way, she looked like a woman who didn't take kindly to being told what to do and when to do it.

"You wanted to speak with us?" Will dampened the surprise in his voice. Truth be told, he'd been shocked as hell when an officer from Del Norte County had telephoned that morning, telling them she'd changed her mind. That she didn't want her attorney, Gerald Waverly, present after all.

"Not particularly." She raised one thin eyebrow. "But Jacqueline told me I had to if I wanted to ever see her or my grandkids again. Apparently, the evidence against me is…"

"Overwhelming. That's how I'd put it," JB said, pulling up the seat next to Will. "Especially since we found your DNA on the seal of an envelope addressed to Trish Mayfield."

Victoria heaved a sigh of resignation that drooped her shoulders.

"So, what can you tell us about Shelby's murder?" Will asked.

"Only what Reid shared with me after the fact. I had no idea what he was planning. Back then, he was something of a loose cannon and desperate to prove himself to my father. It came as a real blow when we couldn't adopt. I'll admit I lapsed into a depression, and my father blamed him for that."

"When did you find out what he'd done?"

"A couple of months after we rescued Jacqueline, he broke down and told me. Reid was never good under pressure. He'd packed the barrel with the sand, intending to sink it in the ocean, but he'd filled it too full. It was too heavy to move. That's when I had the idea to send the letter to her mother. To Jacqueline's family, too. It worked like a charm."

JB gave a rueful shake of his head. "Until Sam Weatherby opened the barrel."

"I told Reid a hundred times we should go back there. Truth be told, we did once, before Grimmy lost the place. But we still couldn't budge the thing, so we left it. It had been there so long. Over time, you learn to forget. You move on. You think it was all a terrible dream."

Will knew what she meant. As a cop, he'd learned some memories were best left buried. The only problem, the worst ones didn't stay that way. "Why Drea?"

"She could identify Reid. Her and Winters. Reid suspected Winters and Shelby had a thing going. That she'd told him everything. I didn't want to hurt anyone, but what choice did I have? I couldn't let Jacqueline find out. We'd have lost her forever. Those poor souls were just collateral damage."

Will let that settle into his bones. As proper as she seemed, Victoria had the heart of a gangster. No different than Termite. "How'd you know she'd be at the cabin that night?"

"It wasn't hard to find her. Foolish girl with her doomed romance. I didn't plan to hurt her. Not at first. I wanted to pay her off."

"You followed her?"

"I watched her a few times from the woods outside her house. I needed to know what she knew. What she was capable of. I went through a whole bag of those damn Swedish fish Grimmy sent me, just waiting for her to reveal herself. She spent most of her time in that dusty shed making these disturbing little clay creations. I'd almost decided she was harmless before I saw that reporter, Heather Hoffman, approach her door. A day later, she met with Hoffman again at the café. I tried to track her back to her house, but she was on to me by then. She didn't come home. Instead, the two of you showed up. In the end, she left me no choice."

"And Brenda?"

"What about her?"

"An overdose? *Really?*"

"I can't pass judgment on her since she gave me Jacqueline." Victoria shrugged, straightening up her spine again. Feeling superior, no doubt. "But that woman was in no position to be a mother to anyone. Can you imagine how Jacqueline might've turned out? I shudder at the thought."

CHAPTER EIGHTY-SEVEN

Olivia pulled into the parking lot of Crescent Bay State Prison, bringing the old Buick to a rest. She composed a quick text to Emily, letting her know she'd completed the long and winding drive back to Fog Harbor. After everything that had happened in Sea Cliff, she'd decided to spend the weekend at Em's, eating pizza and watching chick flicks to forget the gun to her head and Jacqueline's choked sobs and Reid's battered body floating in the shallows.

That morning, she'd left under the cover of darkness to be back in time for her ten thirty meeting with the interns. Only because she couldn't stomach the thought of Carrie Stanley smugly informing them she'd be out again today.

Olivia let herself in to the MHU and waved to Sergeant Weber at the desk before unlocking her office.

When she pushed open the door, a small scrap of paper, much like the one Ben had left for her days ago, fluttered across the room and came to rest in a dusty corner. She picked it up and read two words that sent her reeling.

Olivia watched the clock all day, nodding and smiling through her meeting with the interns, while the second hand seemed to slog through mud. At five o'clock, she tore out of the parking lot on a mission and headed for Big Ed's Hardware on the town square.

With her purchase in hand, she locked herself inside her bathroom, setting her father's pencil drawing on the floor before turning off the lights.

Black light, the note in her office had said. Her hands shook as she held the portable device, turned it on, and pointed it at the thick paper. At the images of the Double Rock brought to life by his hand.

Her father's writing glowed in the margin. The message brought her to her knees.

> *Mac Boon involved in drug smuggling. I'm getting close to IDing the General.*
> *Need more time.*

CHAPTER EIGHTY-EIGHT

Nurse Thornton roused Max Grimaldi from his post-breakfast slumber. "You've got visitors, Grimmy."

He opened his one eye, then the other, and groaned, wiping a bit of drool from his chin. "You two again? Can't you leave an old man to die in peace?"

Will dragged the folding chair over to the bedside. Today, he wanted to be close. "That depends on you. You tell us the truth, we leave you here to live out the rest of your days eating gummy fish and solving crosswords. In the nursing home owned by Ratcliffe Chemicals."

"*Retirement* home," Grimaldi retorted.

JB approached him from the other side of his bed. "A retirement home which just happens to belong to our two prime suspects in a slew of murders."

"C'mon, Detectives. What do you want from me? We both know the truth is subjective."

"Not when it comes to dead girls." Will spoke through gritted teeth. "If you don't cooperate, we'll haul your arthritic ass down to Del Norte County Jail and charge you with obstruction."

"Or worse." JB jangled his handcuffs in Grimaldi's face. "You think your little film was dark. Wait till you see the inside of Crescent Bay, and those guys aren't acting."

He heaved out an exasperated breath. "Sheesh. What do you want to know?"

"What really happened to Brenda Samson, for starters? We know she's buried at the cabin." Will flashed his phone at Grimaldi, displaying an image of the smooth white bone the cadaver dogs had unearthed in the backyard. The old man's face twisted in disgust. "We found this."

"I had nothing to do with that. Reid told me he and Victoria had gone to talk to her, to see if she'd drop the charges against me. When he found her at her apartment, she'd overdosed. Not surprising, if you ask me. Her kid had been there—God knows how long—starving, in a dirty diaper, and staring at Mommy's dead body. Naturally, Reid felt the little girl would be better off with him and Victoria. He told me only what I needed to know. No more, no less."

"And Shelby? Did you know about her murder?"

Grimaldi smacked the bed in protest. "Of course not. Do you really think I'm so dense that I'd leave behind a barrel with a body inside it? I'd have pushed that thing into the ocean years ago."

"I'm not buying it," Will told JB. "Are you?"

"Nope. You're selling a lemon, Grimaldi. It's not gonna pass muster with the DA." He pulled out the handcuffs again and lowered the bed's side railing. "Go on. Get up. Or should I get Nurse Thornton to help me put these cuffs on you?"

"Alright. I saw her up at the cabin one time. I'd given Reid the key, told him to check in on the place for me. One day, he called me in a panic, asking if I'd help him. He didn't say with what. I showed up there, and he had the poor thing chained in the basement. He wanted to know if I could find a doctor to help deliver the baby. I said 'hell no' and didn't look back."

"And you didn't ask any questions? You didn't wonder what happened?"

Grimaldi shrugged, fixing his steely blue eyes on Will. "I've lived long enough to know there are some questions best left unanswered."

In the silence, JB's gaze drifted to Grimaldi's nightstand. "Are those photos new?"

"Sure are. After I dug *Chained* out of that box in my closet, I ran across a couple of these snapshots from some of my movie sets. Figured I might as well put them on display and enjoy them while I still can." He reached for the first photo, stuck inside a cheap wooden frame, and displayed it proudly to JB. "Me in my glory days."

Will couldn't ignore the goosebumps that appeared on his arms, as JB passed him the photograph. "That's a hell of a lot of sand. What movie was that?"

"*Demon in the Desert,* I called it. Filmed in 1979." Grimaldi let out a raspy laugh. "I bought the stuff in bulk. Took me years to get rid of it."

Thirty minutes later, Will steered the Crown Vic into the ditch on County Road 37, where Trish Mayfield had been waiting for thirty-five years for her daughter to come home.

"You want me to go with you?" JB asked.

He shook his head. "If it's all the same to you, I'd like to make this trip alone."

"As long as you know where you're driving me next, partner."

"The Earl River." Will gestured to the back seat, where JB had loaded two fishing poles and a tackle box. "How could I forget? My sensei is teaching me to meditate."

With a wave to JB, Will turned toward the redwood grove. He walked with purpose through the underbrush, marveling at the tiniest of miracles. The honeysuckle vine had begun to blossom, the pink flowers brightening the gloom. At the end of the overgrown path, the trailer door stood open. Trish waited for him there, bracing herself against the door frame. A calico cat weaved between her legs.

Will caught his breath, suddenly overcome by a memory of his mother, and he realized then that Trish reminded him of her. The day before his mother disappeared forever, Will had caught her crying in the bedroom, searching the drawers. Talking to herself. He'd snuck into the bathroom and counted her pills. She'd been skipping doses again.

"Detective Decker, I knew you'd be back."

He nodded, taking Trish's hand. It felt as fragile as a bird's wing in his grip, but there was strength there too. "I promised I would."

He guided her outside to her lawn chair and took his own seat on the washtub. "We found Shelby's killer. I want to tell you what we know about how she died and why."

Tears filled Trish's eyes but she didn't stop them. "I never had any doubt. You look like the sort of young man who keeps his promises."

EPILOGUE

March 1986

Shelby forced her swollen legs to move. Only five steps up to the kitchen, but each one felt like a small mountain, testing her resolve. Her bruised wrists ached, her back too. She'd lost track of how long she'd been chained in the basement—Four days? Five?—and she'd started to lose her mind, scratching at the bricks like a caged animal.

Though she couldn't tell day from night down there, she knew it was nearly time. Her belly strained against her T-shirt. The baby as big as a head of lettuce now. When she'd arrived, it had only been the size of a plum. She'd read that fact for herself nine months ago in a book in the school library. She'd torn out the page, stuffing it into the pocket of her jean shorts, red-faced, like it was one of Kris's dirty magazines. Back then, it had helped to think of the baby like that. But now, she preferred to try on names instead. Joshua for a boy. Jessica for a girl.

Reid would be back soon. He'd told her as much. She'd done her best to act the part of a woman in labor, writhing and crying and moaning until he'd unlocked the shackles around her wrists that had rubbed her skin raw and brought her a pillow and a mound of blankets from the back bedroom that he'd once let her call her own.

Her dramatics persuasive enough to convince Reid he needn't worry about her escape, Shelby pushed open the basement door.

Blinded by the light streaming through the kitchen window, she stumbled and bumped her hip against the table. She felt alien and lost. Like a subterranean creature that had accidentally surfaced too fast, withering in the bright sun.

Shielding her eyes, she headed for the bedroom, praying Reid hadn't found the bus ticket Chuck had bought for her. When she'd told Reid she was taking the bus back to San Francisco, he had torn up the whole room looking for it. Then, he'd slapped her so hard she saw stars and dragged her to the basement where *Grimy* kept his creepy movie props—those chains, she'd found out, were all too real.

Chuck would be worried sick about her. She'd heard him pounding on the door that first day, and her heart had cracked in two. The crack widened and fissured, as she turned the ruby ring on her finger. A promise ring, he'd called it. A promise to save up the money to come to San Francisco with her. To take care of her and the baby. To give Brandon a piece of his mind and a knuckle sandwich too. She wished she'd told Chuck everything, but then again she didn't. Because Reid would have locked him up down there with her, destroying her last hope of escape.

Shelby stuffed the duffel as fast as she could, her breath coming in little gasps. She clumsily dropped to her knees before the heating vent, the ticket in sight. Hands trembling, she worked the screws off and tucked the slip of paper inside the outer pouch.

Already tasting the salty air of freedom, she struggled to her feet, when a noise at the door startled her. She tossed the bag deep inside the vent, hurrying to conceal it.

When the front door yawned open, she tried to scream but her throat closed up the way it did in the worst of her nightmares. No sound came.

Reid glared at her in that awful jacket she'd once thought was cool. He dropped the plastic bag he carried to the hardwood. She stared at its contents, sickened—towels, sterile gloves, a clamp—

and cursed herself for how stupid she'd been. She'd followed all of his rules—no visitors, no wandering, no communication with anyone back home. Well, most of them. He'd told her this was her choice. That she could back out at any time. But now, she understood. Reid intended to take her baby whether she gave him permission or not.

She searched for a weapon. But the only things in the bedroom were hers, and she'd packed most of them away in the duffel.

"I told you to stay in the basement." He advanced toward her with no effort, slithering like a snake, while her every breath pinched her lungs. Her every step required focus.

"I have to leave. I'm sorry. I thought I could go through with it, but I can't. Please. Just let me go or…"

"Or what?"

Then, she saw it, resting on the floor beside her bed, beneath a half-propped magazine. "I'll tell everyone about you. About what you did. Your wife won't want anything to do with you. You'll be all alone."

Shelby reached for the Nikon, and Reid retreated from her, from the camera's all-seeing eye, just as she'd hoped. Clutching it to her, she followed him. The need to protect her baby as strong as the need to save herself.

For a moment, she felt powerful. She raised the camera like a gun.

As Reid extended his hand, pale and desperate, the release of the shutter beneath her finger was the only sound.

A LETTER FROM ELLERY

Want to keep up to date with my latest releases? Sign up here!

www.bookouture.com/ellery-kane

We promise never to share your email with anyone else, we'll only contact you when there's a new book available, and you can unsubscribe at any time.

Thank you for reading *Her Perfect Bones*! With so many amazing books to choose from, I truly appreciate you taking the time to read the second installment in the Rockwell and Decker series. Many more thrilling cases await Olivia and Will, and I hope you'll continue on this journey with them. Shelby's story is loosely based on the murder of Reyna Marroquín, a Salvadoran woman who was killed by businessman Howard Elkins in 1969. Her body remained undiscovered in a barrel in the crawl space of a home in New York until 1999, when a homeowner uncovered her mummified remains. Police were able to follow the clues left behind in the barrel to unmask her killer, but Elkins ended his life before he could be punished.

One of my favorite parts about being an author is connecting with readers like you. You can get in touch with me through any of the social media outlets below, including my website and Goodreads page. Also, if you wouldn't mind leaving a review or recommending the Rockwell and Decker series to your favorite readers, I would really appreciate it! Reviews and word-of-mouth recommendations are essential, because they help readers like you discover my books.

Thank you again for your support! I look forward to hearing from you, and I hope to see you around Fog Harbor again soon!

TheLegacyBooks/

@ellerykane

ellerykane.com

ACKNOWLEDGMENTS

Though writing is a solitary pursuit, so many hands go into making a book successful. But an author is nothing without a reader. So above all, I owe a tremendous debt of gratitude to you, my avid readers. Knowing my writing has affected you, inspired you, and even scared you just a little, makes every word worth it! I am having a blast getting to know Olivia, Will, JB, Emily, and the rest of the Fog Harbor crew, and I hope you will stay tuned for more of their adventures.

Words don't always come easy for an author, but I've been so lucky to have a fabulous team of family, friends, and work colleagues who have always been there to support me! Your encouragement keeps me going when the words come slow. Though my mom is no longer with me, she taught me her love for writing, and I know she's cheering me on even though I can't see her. Thanks, too, to my dad, who's never been a reader but thinks I'm brilliant anyway. And to all my favorite English teachers, who gifted me with a passion for reading and creating my own stories and who inspired me to share those stories with others.

To Gar, my special someone and the unofficial president of the Ellery Kane fan club, for the countless hours of plot discussion; for the kick in the butt to keep writing; for the occasional bad review pep talk; and, above all else, for guarding my heart like a dragon and believing in my dreams as fiercely as if they were his own. I couldn't have done any of this without you and I wouldn't want to!

Last but not least, I have been fortunate to find an amazing editor, Jessie Botterill, and a fantastic publisher, Bookouture, who truly value their authors. Jessie's spot-on instincts, creativity and sharp editorial lens have helped shape this book into something fantastic, and I continue to grow as a writer with her support. Like Rockwell and Decker, I think we make a great team, and I feel so lucky to be working with Jessie and the entire Bookouture family!

I have always drawn inspiration for my writing from my day job as a forensic psychologist. We all have a space inside us that we keep hidden from the world, a space we protect at all costs. So many people have allowed me a glimpse inside theirs—dark deeds, memories best unrecalled, pain that cracks from the inside out—without expectation of anything in return. I couldn't have written a single word without them.

Made in the USA
Las Vegas, NV
05 March 2021

19006316R00203